a
wedding on
bluebird
way

Read more by Lori Wilde in *Happy Is the Bride*

Also by Allyson Charles

Putting Out Old Flames

The Christmas Tree

Why Did It Have to Be You?

The Christmas Wedding Swap

Forever Home

Also by Stacey Keith

Dream On

Sweet Dreams

Dream Lover

Also by Janet Dailey

Sunrise Canyon

Refuge Cove

Texas Fierce

Texas Tall

Texas Tough

Texas True

a
wedding on
bluebird
way

LORI WILDE

JANET DAILEY

ALLYSON CHARLES
STACEY KEITH

ZEBRA BOOKS
KENSINGTON PUBLISHING CORP.
http://www.kensingtonbooks.com

ZEBRA BOOKS are published by

Kensington Publishing Corp.
119 West 40th Street
New York, NY 10018

All Kensington titles, imprints, and distributed lines are available at special quantity discounts for bulk purchases for sales promotion, premiums, fund-raising, educational, or institutional use.

Special book excerpts or customized printings can also be created to fit specific needs. For details, write or phone the office of the Kensington Sales Manager: Attn.: Sales Department. Kensington Publishing Corp., 119 West 40th Street, New York, NY 10018. Phone: 1-800-221-2647.

Zebra and the Z logo Reg. U.S. Pat. & TM Off.

First Printing: June 2018
ISBN-13: 978-1-4201-4677-6
ISBN-10: 1-4201-4677-7

eISBN-13: 978-1-4201-4678-3
eISBN-10: 1-4201-4678-5

10 9 8 7 6 5 4 3 2 1

Printed in the United States of America

Contents

The Wedding That Wasn't

Lori Wilde

Prologue

The Lore

At the moment of the baby girl's birth, a bluebird, attracted by the shiny prism hanging in the bedroom window, hit the glass pane and broke its beautiful azure neck. The superstitious midwife clucked her tongue at the dark omen, and told the laboring mother that, alas, her baby would never know true happiness.

To counter the nay-saying nurse's dire prediction, the determined mother purposefully named her child Felicity, meaning happiness, refused to tell her daughter about the midwife's bleak forecast, and did everything in her power to make sure Felicity grew up feeling safe, healthy, and loved.

The child's mother encouraged her gifted girl to sing with a voice as clear and unwavering as a bluebird's buoyant warble, and they lived blissfully together in a small cottage on the outskirts of Serendipity, Texas—planting gardens, nurturing animals, humming tunes of thanksgiving for their bountiful blessings.

That was, until the mother died in a freak farming accident on her daughter's eighteenth birthday.

And, from that moment on, Felicity's life went right to hell in a wicker handbasket.

Chapter One

At forty, Felicity Patterson knew how to take a licking and keep on ticking. Life had kicked her in the gut, the teeth, the kneecaps . . . oh, just about anywhere it was possible to get kicked and survive . . . and, against all odds, she'd managed to stay perky, plucky, and optimistic.

Her resilient ability to rebound, no matter what, was why most everyone in Serendipity loved her. In fact, she was so bouncy, people said her middle name should have been Super Ball.

Until the day Aunt Molly spilled the beans.

When it happened, Felicity and her aunt were standing amidst the metal folding chairs sectioned into rows and aisles underneath the newly installed pergola in the middle of the Bluebird Inn's backyard garden. On the morning Felicity's long-held dream of turning her struggling bed-and-breakfast into a wedding venue was about to come true.

It was late March, and spring flowers bloomed in wild profusion—yellow daffodils, grape hyacinth, pink petunias. The air smelled of honey, hope, and happiness. It was seven-thirty in the morning, barely light, but Felicity had already been up for three hours, prepping for the eleven a.m. society wedding. Her first at the Bluebird. The breeze was cool at sixty-four degrees, and the forecast promised clear skies and a high of seventy-five. Perfect weather for an outdoor wedding.

The only things missing from the garden were the bluebirds that had once been so plentiful on the grounds. Several years ago urban sprawl, and the common house sparrows that came with it, had driven the migrating birds from their natural nesting grounds.

A dozen contract workers buzzed around, setting up the altar, arranging flowers, putting the finishing touches on the reception tables in the ivy-draped pavilion.

It had taken Felicity months to convince the wealthiest family in town to hold their only daughter's wedding at the Bluebird Inn. But now that she'd persuaded the Lovings (yes, they were descendants of the famed cattle baron Oliver Loving) that she was up for the task, the Bluebird was booked solid with weddings every weekend all the way through September.

What a blessing!

With more bookings and deposits coming in every day, for the first time since she and her husband, Steve, had opened the Bluebird Inn, it was running in the black. Steve would have been so proud.

At the thought of her late husband, Felicity's eyes misted. Steve had been gone two years, and, for the most part, she'd come to terms with losing him far too young, but there were times like this when grief still ambushed her.

She bit down on the inside of her cheek to stay the tears.

By all rights, Steve should have been here with her. The dream of running a B&B had initially been his. He was the extrovert who thrived on being around people. And while Felicity enjoyed people too, she was an empathetic introvert who needed to go off by herself from time to time in order to recharge her batteries. But she did love running the grand old Victorian and creating a hospitable environment for her guests.

"Sweetheart," Aunt Molly said, peering at her from behind gray, round-framed Oakleys that softened the rectangular shape of her face. "Please, don't expect too much to come of this wedding."

"What?" Felicity glanced up from where she was tweaking a large bow anchoring the aqua slipcover to a cushioned folding chair.

"I don't mean to be a downer." Her aunt's face was kind. "I just don't want to see you get hurt."

"Why would I get hurt?" Felicity cocked her head, confused. "Things have never been better. My business is booming. I've got more bookings than I can handle. Friends and family I love. I'm healthy as a horse. Life is pretty darn good."

Well, except there was no man in her world, but she wasn't sure she was ready to date anyway. Maybe she never would be, and Felicity was okay with that. She'd had her one great love. She wasn't greedy.

"Which is precisely why I'm worried." A frown knitted Aunt Molly's brow, and one side of her mouth kicked up in uncertainty. "Every time things are going good for you, *bam!* That old midwife's curse comes true."

"What midwife? What curse?"

"Oh." Aunt Molly exhaled sharply, shook her head, and the silver feather earrings nestled in her lobes trembled with movement. "Never mind."

Huh? Felicity straightened, squinted against the sun, scratched her head. "What are you talking about?"

"It's nothing." Aunt Molly pushed a hand through her coifed pageboy. "Do you need me to check on the caterers?"

"The wedding planner takes care of that." Felicity touched her aunt's elbow. "What did you mean by the midwife's curse?"

Aunt Molly shifted uncomfortably. "I'm being a silly old woman. Don't pay me any mind."

"You're only sixty. Far from old. What curse?"

"It's not a curse." Aunt Molly fidgeted, tugging at the collar of her blouse. "Not really. More like a prophecy."

Something niggled at the back of Felicity's mind. A memory of a disturbing encounter between her mother and an older woman who'd shown up at Felicity's high school graduation with a gift.

"You'll not poison the well, crone," Mom had hissed at the woman. Her mother was never rude, and her behavior had alarmed Felicity. "Your jinx didn't work. She's happy as a bluebird. Stay away from my daughter."

Then Mom had tossed the gift in the trash.

"Who was that?" Felicity had asked, looking longingly over her shoulder at the brightly wrapped package in the garbage can.

"A superstitious old fool," Mom had said. "Never mind her. Let's go celebrate your diploma."

Three weeks later her mother had been killed when the tractor she was riding on turned over in the pasture.

A light breeze stirred the hairs on Felicity's arms, and she shivered and met her aunt's Plymouth-blue eyes, a shade lighter than her own. "Just tell me."

"Your mother made me promise never to tell you. It was a slip of the tongue. It means nothing."

"If it doesn't mean anything, then why not tell me? All this mystery is making me itchy."

"Well, you *are* forty," Aunt Molly said. "Halfway through a tough life. I don't see any reason to keep it a secret any longer."

Felicity folded her arms over her chest, suddenly chilled to the bone. She wanted to go get a thicker sweater, but her aunt had perched on the edge of one of the folding chairs, blocking her way. She took a seat beside her aunt and waited.

Aunt Molly rubbed her thumb across her chin and related the tale about the superstitious midwife and the circumstances of Felicity's birth. "Your mother didn't tell you because she didn't want you to believe you were jinxed and doomed to be unhappy. She didn't believe in the curse. Not for a second."

Felicity absorbed the information, felt it hit her like the bumping updraft of air turbulence. Dozens of images tumbled through her head, starting from the day she'd heard her mother was dead.

Mom's funeral. Discovering the dark secret that her biological father was serving a life sentence for murder. The visit to the prison, finding out her father was on dialysis and needed a kidney. Donating one of her kidneys. Only to have him die on the operating table.

More events piling up, one after the other.

Complications from donating the kidney. An infection that damaged her ovaries. Her first real boyfriend joining the military right after September 11, 2001, and dying in combat training from friendly fire. A year of therapy to help her deal with all that loss. Meeting Steve, the love of her life. Things finally looking hopeful. Trying to have babies. Several rounds of IVF until they were wiped out financially. Getting pregnant during that last ditch effort, only to lose the baby in her second trimester. Steve's parents killed in a car crash and leaving him the Victorian on Bluebird Way. Struggling to make a go of turning the house into a B&B. Feeling disheartened when the bluebirds disappeared. Steve contracting cancer. Watching him fade away . . .

All this by the time she was thirty-eight. One of her favorite sayings was, *what doesn't kill you makes you stronger.* She'd picked up the pieces and carried on as best she could. Titanium had nothing on her.

People kept telling her she should write a book about her life because she'd been through so much, and she hadn't let it dampen her fighting spirit.

That was only because her mother had instilled in her faith, hope, and love. But now, to find out she'd been jinxed from birth? If she let herself look for a pattern, it was certainly there.

It was a silly old wives' tale. Logically, she knew that, but a part of her couldn't help thinking that now there was an explanation for all the crappy stuff that had happened to her.

She shook herself, slapped her palms to her knees. She didn't have time to indulge in self-pity. Her future was riding on the success of this wedding.

"Thank you for telling me. I appreciate your honesty." Felicity brushed her hands together, put on her best get-'er-done smile. "Duty calls."

"Oh good." Aunt Molly exhaled. "I was afraid you'd believe you really were jinxed."

"My mother didn't believe it. Why should I?"

"You've had so much tragedy in your life." Aunt Molly lowered her voice, touched Felicity's shoulder. "Far more than your share."

"Maybe that's true," Felicity said, putting an efficient tone in her voice. "But not because a bluebird broke its neck against the window at the moment I was born. Now . . ." She firmed up her chin. "Let's get back to work."

From the moment newly retired Army Major Tom Loving laid eyes on the sexy blond innkeeper, he was smitten.

She had a bright sparkle in her eyes and a winsome bounce to her step that immediately drew his attention and his interest.

And that voice!

She stood behind a reception desk in the small front room of the Victorian house turned B&B, rearranging a lush bouquet of white lilies and singing "All of Me" in an angelic voice that could have drawn tears of joy from John Legend himself.

Tom's forty-two-year-old heart skipped a beat, and he forgot to exhale.

When she looked up and spied him standing in the doorway, clutching his backpack in one hand, her full lips melted into the most genuine smile he'd ever seen. A wide tent of a smile, big and sheltering.

One look and she made him feel like he was the only person on the face of the earth. It was compelling, and more than a little intoxicating. Strangely, Tom felt as if he'd finally come home after an interminable journey.

Truth was, he wasn't from anywhere in particular. As the son of the black sheep, Carl Loving, Tom had been raised a military brat, and he'd easily followed in his father's wandering footsteps. His older half-brother, Joe, had gone in the opposite direction, making peace with their dad's family, taking up the Loving mantle, fitting right in with kith and kin.

Tom held no grudges. The feud between his father and his uncles had never been his battle. He preferred staying clear of emotional shrapnel. He and Joe had not ever been close. They were five years apart in age, had different mothers and vastly different personalities. Joe had a shoot-from-the-hip-take-no-prisoners style, whereas Tom was a strategic team player, who listened more than he spoke. In all honesty, he'd been pretty surprised to receive an invitation to his niece's wedding.

He'd almost not come, but in the end sentimentality won out. Maybe it was time to start building bridges, reconnecting with family after a lifetime of being on the move.

The Army had taught him how to pack up, pick up, never look back, and just keep on going forward. But it had not taught him how to linger or develop deeper relationships. The ability to skim the surface was the reason he'd shaken off his divorce without too much drama. Of course, Heidi claimed that detachment was the reason *for* the divorce. As if sleeping with his best friend hadn't had anything to do with it.

Heidi was right about one thing. Staying in one place was hard for Tom, and two weeks into retirement, he was already at loose ends. Even though his Loving ancestral roots were sunk deep in Texas soil, and he'd been born in Wichita Falls, just south of the Oklahoma border, he'd never considered the Lone Star State home.

Until now.

Serendipity, he thought as he peered in the gorgeous blonde's big blue eyes, and laughed. It was crazy really, but he couldn't help what he felt.

"Hello," she said in her soft Texas drawl, and he could

hear her heritage in the way she drew out the long *O*. "And who might you be?"

"Running late," he said.

"Now that's an odd name, Mr. Late," she teased. "Welcome to the Bluebird Inn. Are you with the wedding party?"

He deposited his backpack on the ground, grinned like a fool at her corny joke, and strode forward, hand outstretched. "Tom Loving. I should have been here last night, but my flight out of LaGuardia got canceled. I'm sorry to have missed the rehearsal dinner. But, hey, I'm just the uncle. Hopefully, my absence was easily overlooked."

"I seriously doubt you've ever been overlooked, Mr. Loving," she said, and shook his hand with a firm, yet delicate grip.

"Flattery will get you everywhere, Miss . . ."

"Mrs. Patterson," she said. "Felicity."

Fantasies that he didn't even know he was having dropped and shattered against the hardwood floor. She wasn't wearing a wedding ring, and he'd just assumed she was single.

"Your husband," he blurted, "is a very lucky man."

"I'm a widow," she said, and for a fraction of a second her dazzling smile slipped, but she quickly hoisted it up again.

Widow. A sad word, especially for a woman so young and full of life. Was it wrong that his dreams hopped right off that floor and jumped back into his chest?

"Do you have a car that needs to be valeted?"

"Motorcycle."

"Oh," she said in a tone that he couldn't decipher. Did she disapprove? Or was she impressed? "Harley?"

"Ducati."

"Ahh."

Another tone that told him nothing. She was good at hiding her opinions. Cagey, this one. "I parked under the carport next to a green Prius. Yours?"

"It is."

"Ahh," he said, serving cagey right back to her.

She smiled, a slight, but definitely amused smile. "The other members of the wedding party are already here. Some of them are in the meditation room. Others are walking the gardens. Your niece, her mother, and the bridesmaids are upstairs in the bridal suite getting ready."

"And my brother?"

"I'm not sure where Joe is at the moment. Let me show you to your room, Mr. Loving, so you can get settled before things kick into high gear. It's already nine-thirty," she said in an efficient voice, and reached for his backpack.

"No, ma'am. I'm not letting a lady carry my baggage." He grabbed for the backpack at the same time she did.

Their fingers touched.

Snap!

Electricity arced between them. The old AC/DC song "Thunderstruck" bulleted through his head with the power of raw lightning, hot and powerful and stark. His heart pounded; his knees quivered; he broke out in a cold sweat.

Mind blown.

Her eyes widened, and she jerked her hand back, tucked it into her armpit as if she'd received a jolting shock and didn't know how to shake it off. "Yes, well, okay," she mumbled, and backed up. Stuck her hands in the pockets of her blue dress with its wide, swingy skirt. "This way."

Like a cowboy taking one last deep breath before pulling up his bandana as he moved a high-plains herd, Tom inhaled from the base of his belly all the way up to his throat and followed those lovely, swaying hips.

Cowboy metaphors? Lord help him, he had been back in Texas for all of two hours, and already he was falling into the old family ways.

And for the life of him, Tom couldn't figure out if he was happy about that or not.

Chapter Two

The Saturday morning edition of the *Serendipity Gazette*—yes, there was still a charmingly antiquated town newspaper sporting a surprisingly robust subscriber rate of two thousand in a town triple that population—declared it the wedding of the decade and cleared its front page to describe the setting for the union of Serendipity's hottest bachelor, Dr. Chance Worthington, to Savannah Loving, daughter of the famed ranching family.

"Lookie!" Aunt Molly waved the paper under Felicity's nose. "You made the front page!"

Indeed, two days ago a reporter had come out to photograph the grounds. The interview complimented the renovations that Felicity had undertaken in order to restore the inn to its Victorian grandeur. At the end of the article, the reporter declared the Bluebird fit for royalty and Lovings alike.

What the piece did not say was that Felicity had sunk every last penny of a hundred-thousand-dollar loan into the improvements. If the gamble didn't pay off, she could lose everything.

It's going to be fine, she told herself. She had all those bookings, and it was such a glowing article. She could relax. She'd finally made it.

Normally, that would have been enough to reassure Felicity. But today, the day she'd learned she'd been jinxed at birth, a strange sense of foreboding lifted the hairs on the back of her neck.

Silly. Oh gosh, she knew it was silly and superstitious, but if for some reason things did fall apart, she could lose Steve's family home and the last shreds of the dream they'd dreamed together.

"This is so exciting," Aunt Molly said. "I'm so happy for you. Fingers crossed the jinx is broken."

"Put the paper down. The wedding guests are starting to arrive. Grab the programs and man the garden gate," Felicity told her aunt, tired of this jinx nonsense.

"Okay, okay." Aunt Molly put down the paper and picked up the stack of wedding programs. "But I just have to say your mother would be so proud of you."

Felicity gave her a quick one-armed hug. "Thank you. That means a lot."

The wedding planner buzzed through the room and gave them a thumbs up as she spoke into a headset nestled at her chin, barking out instructions to the underling in charge of the ushers.

Felicity took her place, waiting on a hilly area, slightly to the right and behind the altar, at the ready if the wedding planner should need her. From this vantage point, she had a perfect view of the proceedings.

The guests filtered in through the garden gate. Aunt Molly passed out the programs. The ushers escorted wedding goers to their seats. The wedding singer belted out "Marry Me" from a raised stone dais to the left side of the gathering. The videographer captured the event on his state-of-the-art, high-def video camera. The gardens were beautiful. The visitors well-heeled. Everything was moving along as scheduled.

Felicity nodded. It was going to be okay. Not a single glitch.

The patio door leading from the Bluebird Inn into the gardens opened, and Tom Loving, dressed in a sharp tuxedo with a white rosebud at his lapel, stepped into view. He was tugging at his wrists as if testing the cufflinks on the French cuffs, in a gesture so accomplished and regal it took her breath away.

She didn't know if his majestic bearing came from military service or from being part of the imperial Loving clan, or both, but he moved with a rare carriage and grace. His salt-and-pepper—for now more pepper than salt—short-clipped hair glistened in the sun. He wore shades, but slipped them off, tucked them in his front jacket pocket, raised his head, and looked straight at her.

His gaze was a kick, spicy as Sriracha, and she was a good fifty yards away. She had no idea how his eyes had zeroed in on her past the guests and the altar and the flowers, but she felt them land on her as firm as a grip.

He knew she was watching him.

The corners of his mouth turned up into a smug smile. He gave a slight shake to his head and winked.

Felicity jerked her gaze away. Good grief, but he was handsome and far too out of her league. She had a job to do. He was just traveling through. But it had been a very long time since she'd felt the touch of a man's hand on her skin. Tasted a man on her lips.

She gulped and swallowed, alarmed. She'd thought all her sexual desire had died along with Steve; to feel herself come roaring, quite wildly, back to life, was a surprise.

Eyes on the prize. Head in the game. High profile wedding under way. A wedding that was going to leave the Bluebird Inn with a lasting legacy, or so said the reporter from the *Serendipity Gazette*.

Dr. Chance Worthington took his place at the altar, with Savannah's brother at his side as his best man.

Chance's back was to Felicity. He held his shoulders straight. Head up. No fidgeting. Here was a man ready to settle down. He had his pediatric practice established. He was thirty-three years old. Yes, his bride was a bit younger at twenty-five, but merging the Worthington name with that of the Lovings . . . Well, Chance and Savannah were building an empire.

It was romantic and compelling, and Felicity's eyes misted as she remembered her own wedding day and just how over-the-moon happy she'd been.

Of course, if she'd known she was jinxed, she might not have been so optimistic.

Knock it off. She was not jinxed. Gee thanks, Aunt Molly, for picking today of all days to tell her about that nutty story.

Whatever. Forget it. She waved the thought away. Smiled big. But she couldn't help glancing over to where Tom had taken a seat on the Loving side of the aisle. He was still looking at her.

All right. Serious business. It was eleven o'clock. The wedding march was starting. No more jinx nonsense. No more Tom Loving nonsense either.

The patio door opened again. Joe Loving, Savannah's father, emerged from the house with his daughter on his arm.

Everyone turned in his or her seat to watch the bride. The crowd murmured in awe at her youthful beauty. Everyone, that is, except for Tom Loving, whose eyes were fixed firmly on Felicity.

She frowned, pursed her lips, shook her head.

His grin split wider.

She stuck out her tongue.

His eyes rounded, and he slapped a palm over his mouth to hold back laughter. She pointed her finger at his niece, who had stopped at the top of the carpet leading to the aisle.

Finally, thank the Lord, Tom turned to look at his brother and his niece.

Savannah ducked her head, her face obscured by the lace veil she'd ordered from Neiman Marcus. Her father nudged her forward.

The bride stumbled.

Felicity automatically reached out as if to catch her, realized what she'd done, and stuffed her hands into her pockets.

The father strong-armed his daughter, pulling her up against his side. Felicity cocked her head. Joe seemed to be forcing Savannah down the aisle.

A portentous wriggling began in the pit of Felicity's stomach, and she heard Aunt Molly's words in her head.

At the moment of your birth, a bluebird, attracted by the shiny prism hanging in the bedroom window, hit the glass pane and broke its beautiful azure neck.

Savannah dug in her heels, shook her head.

Joe literally dragged her forward.

Chance moved toward his reluctant bride.

"Maybe," Felicity whispered to herself. "Maybe the poor girl is just having a wardrobe malfunction." She crossed her fingers, held her breath.

Joe glowered, bent his head to Savannah's, said something to her.

Half the guests were on their feet, craning their necks to see what was going on. Savannah looked at her uncle, and her mouth pressed into a grim line. Tom was facing toward his niece, so Felicity couldn't see his face.

The next thing Felicity knew, Savannah was kicking off her high heels, yanking her arm from her father's hand, gathering her frothy white train in her arms, and sprinting away through the garden gate.

And, with the runaway bride, went Felicity's future.

The congregation sprang to its feet, and half a dozen people, the groom included, went running after the bride.

Tom heard his Ducati start. Gulped. Oh shit. He should have seen this coming when he'd jokingly given Savannah the keys and told her she could always run away. Never in a million years had he thought she'd take him up on it.

He closed his eyes, blew out his breath, wondered how she'd managed to straddle that motorcycle in her wedding gown, and prayed like hell the dress didn't get caught in the spokes.

Tom stayed welded to the chair, feeling guilty as sin, but also strangely exhilarated by his niece's bold escape. What was wrong with him? Was he that soured on marriage?

People milled around him, chattering excitedly.

What happened?

What's going on?

Is she coming back?

Did Savannah just ditch the most eligible bachelor in Serendipity?

Honestly, I'm not surprised. The Lovings shouldn't have held the wedding at the Bluebird Inn. It's jinxed.

What was that last part? Tom cocked his head, listening for more gossip. Felicity Patterson jinxed?

What did that mean? Tom searched for Felicity in the crowd, but she'd left her post on the hilly rise behind the altar, and he couldn't find her in the throng.

Suddenly, the guests gasped, and Tom turned to see what had drawn their attention.

The groom, Dr. Chance Worthington, was coming back through the garden gate, clutching Savannah's wedding gown to his chest. He looked stunned, but at the same time, oddly relieved.

The way Tom imagined he'd looked on the day his divorce became final.

"She stripped off her wedding dress," Chance mumbled. "She had on leggings and a T-shirt underneath. Took her dress right off and left it trampled on the front lawn. Jumped on someone's motorcycle and took off. She was *planning* this. . . ." His voice hitched; he staggered.

Had Tom's niece been planning it? Or had the idea first taken root when Tom had gone upstairs to see Savannah in her suite and wish her well—and had joked about her escaping on his Ducati. Had he caused this?

Aww, the ego on you, buddy. Yeah, sure, the world revolved around his sage advice.

Women immediately surrounded the bewildered groom. Patting him on the shoulder, clucking their tongues, telling him everything would be all right.

Tom wanted to get the hell out of there, but Savannah had taken his motorcycle, and the aisle was clogged with people. No way out.

"Brother—" Joe's voice slammed into his ear like a sledgehammer, hard and loud. "What the hell kind of ideas did you plant in my daughter's head?"

Tom got to his feet and faced his older brother, who was standing there in his tux, skin flushed, veins throbbing at his temples, hands knotted into fists at his sides. Joe was furious and looking for someone to take the brunt of his anger.

"Did you give Savannah the keys to your Ducati?" Joe ground out.

"Yes," Tom admitted.

"Why the hell did you do that?"

"It was supposed to be a joke."

Joe's eyes narrowed to slits. "You see anybody around here laughing, *little* brother?"

Tom swallowed his pride, which tasted bitter and prickly. He wasn't accustomed to apologizing. "I never thought—"

"That's just it, you *never* stop to think about how your actions and words affect other people."

It was a sweeping statement, and not really accurate. Joe was upset, and Tom was a handy target, but there was a tiny slice of truth in his older brother's accusations. Tom cared about people, yes, he did, but he was military born and raised and trained. Leaders had to make hard decisions sometimes, and a good commander didn't let messy emotions cloud objective thinking. Joe was a civilian. He didn't get it.

Tom was a civilian now too. It was time to start living . . . and thinking . . . like everyone else.

"Do you know how much this damn wedding cost me?" Joe growled. "Sixty thousand dollars down the drain in the blink of an eye, just because you decided to be a smart guy and shoot off your mouth. I know your marriage was crappy, and you have no idea what a happy relationship is supposed to feel like, but did you have to poison my daughter with your piss-poor attitude?"

Tom winced. Joe's words peppered him like buckshot. This was a mistake. He shouldn't have come to the wedding. He raised a hand. "Look, I'm sorry that I gave Savannah the keys, but if she was truly ready to marry Chance, she wouldn't have used them."

"Were you trying to sully my good name?" Joe said. "Are you that jealous of me?"

"Joe, I'm not jealous of you. I'm happy for you."

"Your words say one thing, but your actions say something else entirely." Joe snorted.

Tom chuffed out a heavy breath. If he could go back in time, he would have ticked the *Will Not Be Attending* box on the wedding invitation.

"You know," Joe said, "when we got your RSVP, Marion was so excited, and I was hopeful that maybe we could finally let go of the past and become a real family." Joe grunted. "Should have known better. A leopard can't change his spots."

Tom was vaguely aware that people were ringed around them, watching the two Loving brothers toe off. Ha! *Loving.* Their surname was a cosmic tease. There was no love lost between the two of them.

Joe's eyes drilled into him, but underneath the cold hardness Tom saw a vulnerability he'd not noticed before. There was a tremor in his brother's hands and a crack in his voice.

Joe was visibly upset, and it had nothing to do with Tom, money, or the hit to Joe's reputation. Joe was hurting for his baby girl.

"Hey." Tom reached out, touched his brother's upper arm.

Joe raised both arms in a get-off-of-me gesture and backed away. His wife, Marion, rushed over, took Joe by the elbow.

"Let Tom alone," Marion said, picking up the wedding dress that the groom had left draped across a chair before he'd disappeared. "He's not ever going to be the brother you need him to be. Let's focus on finding Savannah. Our daughter is what's important."

Joe turned his back on Tom and walked arm in arm with his wife into the B&B, the guests falling in behind them and filing away. Many of them planning on heading to the reception, despite the lack of a wedding. Several people shot Tom dirty looks and murmured unpleasant things under their breath, making it clear he was persona non grata.

Leaving Tom standing by himself in the sunlight, feeling lonelier than he'd ever felt in his life.

Then a soft, kind, feminine voice whispered, "Are you okay?"

Chapter Three

Four cancellations.

It was two o'clock in the afternoon, three hours after the wedding that wasn't, and four couples had already called to say they would not be holding their weddings at the Bluebird Inn after all, and, oh, by the way, could they have their deposits back?

"When I made the reservation, I pictured a wedding just like Savannah Loving's, but now, of course, I don't want that," the last bride-to-be had said.

"You could still hold your wedding here at the Bluebird Inn," Felicity had said, trying not to sound desperate. "In the peach orchard instead of the gardens. Or in the house. Or . . ." Oh God, she sounded desperate.

"No, that's okay," the bride-to-be had muttered, and hung up.

Felicity shook her head, tried hard not to think *jinx*. But the minute she'd seen Savannah rip off those high heels and go sprinting out the garden gate, Felicity had known her business was in trouble.

By the end of the afternoon, the Lovings and their guests had packed up and taken their leave. They'd gotten a text from Savannah saying she was safe with a friend, but she needed to be alone and get her thoughts together. The wedding planner and her crew had dismantled the wedding setup astonishingly quickly and were busy loading up.

Leaving Felicity at loose ends, feeling hit by an unexpected tornado that had dipped down from the sky and laid waste to her life.

It wasn't as if she couldn't bounce back. She was a Super Ball, after all; she'd bounced back numerous times.

Rather, in light of what Aunt Molly had told her this morning, Felicity couldn't help wondering if bouncing back was even worth the effort. Could she possibly be fated for unhappiness? Was it her lot in life not to have what everyone else got? Family. Children. A job that satisfied and sustained her.

Lasting love.

"Stop it," she told herself. "Stop having a pity party."

She had a roof over her head—for now at least. An aunt who loved her. Friends galore. Maybe the B&B had been Steve's dream, but it had become hers too. She wanted this. Had chosen not to sell the house, and she'd sunk her reputation and savings into fixing the place up. She was dug in.

Her cell phone rang. She snagged it off the counter of the reception desk. "Bluebird Inn," she said in her cheeriest voice.

"Um, yes, my name is Carly Brown. I need to cancel my wedding reservation. . . ."

Felicity closed her eyes, took a deep, steadying breath. "I'm very sorry to hear that. Is it a personal situation or is there a problem with the venue?"

"Well—" The young woman's voice rose. "Word around town is that the Bluebird Inn is jinxed. If you hold your wedding at the Bluebird, your marriage is destined to fail."

"Seriously?" Felicity said, feeling a waspish tone fly into her voice. "Do you really believe saying 'I do' at the Bluebird is an accurate predictor of how likely you are to get divorced?"

"Mmm, not really," Carly Brown admitted. "But I figure better safe than sorry, right? So if you could just PayPal my deposit back to me, that'd be great."

"The deposit is nonrefundable," Felicity said, wishing

she'd been stricter with the other four brides-to-be that she'd allowed to talk her into a refund. "It's in the contract you signed."

"Hmph! I know you gave a refund to Diamond Causby. You'll be hearing from my lawyer." Carly Brown hung up.

Felicity sighed. She wasn't worried about the lawyer threat, but it was only fair to give Carly her money back since Felicity had caved on the other refunds.

Sap.

Footsteps squeaked. A pair of Nike sneakers appeared on the steps in her line of vision, followed by a pair of muscular, masculine calves, cute knees, lean thighs, then the whole package.

Tom Loving.

Wearing navy-blue running shorts and a white T-shirt, looking like a shipshape athlete straight off a Wheaties box. He had a smooth way of moving, easy and unrushed, a man comfortable in his own skin.

He cleared the last step, turned toward her, raked a casual hand over his close-clipped hair.

Their eyes met.

"Hi," she said, and raised a hand.

"Hey," he answered back.

She arched an eyebrow at his clothing. "Going for a run?"

"That's the general idea." His grin was soft and sexy.

Her heart thumped. "You're staying?"

His shoulders went up, an unhurried shrug. "I'm paid up through Monday."

"I thought . . ." She bit down on her bottom lip. Maybe he didn't want to talk about the wedding snafu. His brother, Joe, had raked him over the coals pretty harshly in front of everyone.

Tom came closer.

She could smell his scent, a compelling fresh-laundry and sage aroma.

"Yes?" he said.

It was her turn to shrug, but her gesture was terse and quick. Tread lightly here. "I didn't think you would want to stick around."

"Couldn't leave if I wanted to." His grin was a rueful apology. "I gave Savannah the keys to my Ducati."

"It wasn't your fault," Felicity murmured.

"Feels like it was."

"It wasn't. Your niece already had running on her mind. You just gave her the means of escape."

"That's what my brother is holding against me."

"Joe will come around." She didn't want to get in the middle of his family argument, although she was suffering the backlash. "He's blustery, but a reasonable fellow."

"Yeah, well, I'm not banking on that."

"You two aren't close." She said it as a statement. She might not know the Lovings well, but Serendipity wasn't a big town. If Joe and his brother had been close, surely she would have come across Tom at one time or another over the years.

"We're half-brothers. When our dad got divorced from Joe's mom, she took Joe away with her."

"You weren't raised together at all?"

Tom shook his head. "I only saw Joe on holidays and in the summers. He's five years older, and we didn't have a lot in common. Plus, I just retired from the Army after twenty years of service. I've lived all over the world. It's hard staying in touch when you're always on the move."

"I'm surprised you came to the wedding," Felicity said.

"I'm surprised I was invited."

"You're not married?" she asked, and immediately regretted it. The question made it sound like she was interested. Okay, yes, she *was* interested, but only out of curiosity. She wasn't in the market for a man.

He came closer, rested his elbows on the desk. Because the floor behind the reception desk was raised, they were eye-to-eye. Her pulse took off, zipping through her veins.

"Divorced," he said, his smooth voice thick as clotted cream.

"What happened?"

"Old story. Heidi cheated on me with my best friend while I was deployed in the Middle East. Yes, I am a walking cliché."

"Ouch." Felicity winced. "How long were you married?"

"Seven years."

"How long since the divorce?" *Was he on the rebound?*

"Five years."

"You ever think about remarrying?" *Shut up!* She should stop asking him personal questions.

"Do you?" He spun it back on her.

"Steve was the love of my life," she said. "Lightning doesn't strike twice."

"Sometimes it does. When we lived in Germany there was this tall old tree in our backyard that took a lightning strike twice."

"It happens very rarely."

"Given enough time, it's actually inevitable that lightning will strike again."

"So you're a weather expert?"

He stepped closer, and Felicity forgot to breathe. "You're lucky," he said, his mouth pulled up in a wistful pinch. It looked funny because he wasn't the wistful type. "Some people never get hit by that kind of glorious lightning."

"I know," she said softly.

"I've never been hit."

"No lightning with your wife?"

He shook his head.

"Why did you marry her?"

"She was gorgeous, and I used to be a sucker for damsels in distress." He got a faraway look in his eyes. "Maybe that's why I gave Savannah the keys. I could sense she hadn't felt the lightning either. Everyone deserves lightning."

"Lightning hits quick and hard and hot." Her gaze locked

with Tom's, and she couldn't seem to wrench it away. "It's fierce and beautiful, but a lightning strike leaves you split wide-open. Raw and vulnerable and . . . when it's all over . . . ruined."

"Still, it's better to have loved and lost than never to have loved at all," Tom quoted.

She nodded, put a hand to her belly, looked away to study the bluebird sculpture on the top of the filing cabinet.

"No children?"

Felicity shook her head and bit her bottom lip. The topic was too tender to discuss with strangers.

"Me either," he murmured.

She heard a note in his voice that pulled her gaze back to his face. His eyes were solemn; his mouth sad. As if he'd missed out on something monumental.

"Heidi didn't want kids," he explained.

"And you?"

He gave her a faded ghost of a smile. "I'm like you. I wasn't blessed." A quick wince, the smile again. "But I've made peace with it."

"You're a guy; you could still have children if you met the right woman," she pointed out. He deserved to have children.

"And you're still young enough to have kids if you met the right man."

If only it were that easy! He had no idea what it was like to pine for the thing you wanted most deeply, knowing you could never have it. Buying baby clothes and furniture only to have to sell it all when the dream died.

"It's not that simple."

"Oh." He blinked, catching on. "I'm sorry. You and your husband never considered adoption?"

"It's really none of your concern." She and Steve had been looking into adoption when he'd gotten the cancer diagnosis.

"You're right." Tom pressed his lips together in a thin line.

His eyes were so kind and full of sympathy that it hurt her chest. "I shouldn't have pried."

She fiddled with the edge of the appointment book. She kept a calendar of the bookings on her computer, but she liked to keep a hard copy too, just in case something happened. She hadn't cut her teeth on technology, and her computer had crashed too many times for her to trust it completely.

The corner of a piece of paper slipped from the pages of the appointment book. The sonogram of the baby she'd lost. She'd slipped it into the appointment book when she found it while she'd been clearing out the desk drawer during the renovations, still too attached to discard the last shred of the dream.

"My runaway niece is hurting your business," Tom said, staring at her hand on the appointment book. "You've already had numerous cancellations since Savannah escaped, haven't you?"

She shoved the sonogram image back inside the book and snapped it closed. Hoped he hadn't seen it. "Weren't you going for a run?"

"I've upset you?" His expression was contrite. "Forgive me, it was never my intention to upset you."

"It's not you." She met his dark eyes again. "It's just that, well . . . it's been a rough day all the way around."

"That it has," he agreed. "But don't worry, I have a good feeling that everything is going to turn out perfect for you in the end."

A grand statement, but an empty one. She couldn't help feeling he was simply trying to placate her, but it was nice of him to try.

He turned and jogged out the door, giving her a splendid view of his taut butt. A myriad of unwanted sexual fantasies spilled into her brain. Thank God, he'd be gone by Monday.

Because Tom Loving was an irresistible temptation she could ill afford.

* * *

Tom jogged for over an hour, covering seven miles that took him past the Loving Ranch. He hadn't been there since he was twelve, when Joe's mom had taken the two of them to visit their cousins one summer. Later, Tom learned from his father that Joe's mom had actually gone to hit their grandfather up for money, and to park Joe there for the summer while she took off with some guy.

It occurred to Tom that Joe hadn't been as lucky as he. Joe's mother, like Heidi, had hated the roving nature of military life, and she'd bailed out of the marriage to their father not long after Joe was born.

Tom's mother had been a military brat herself, and she and Dad fit hand in glove. They still traveled around the world together, for the most part living on cruise ships or in their RV. Right now, they were on a cruise around Cape Horn, and they had not been invited to the wedding.

Tom paused outside the majestic iron gates of the Loving Ranch, and thought about how disconnected he was from his only sibling. He considered climbing over that gate and jogging right up to the house.

But he didn't.

Joe was angry with him. Savannah was on the loose with Tom's Ducati. Tom wouldn't be welcomed. Besides, he was sweaty and in jogging shorts. Reasons enough to keep going.

On the way back to the Bluebird Inn, he noticed bluebird houses and nesting boxes in yards, gardens, and fields up and down Bluebird Way, but no sign of a single bluebird. In a town that had named a street after the happy little birds, he expected to see a whole sky full of the creatures.

A shame, because this part of Texas was one of the few places in the country, parts of Colorado being the other, where all three species nested—eastern, mountain, and western bluebirds.

Tom stripped off his T-shirt and used it to mop his brow as

he climbed the steps of the Bluebird Inn. There were no cars in the driveway, parking area, or carport, other than Felicity's Prius. Was he the only guest left at the B&B?

Inside, there was no one at the reception desk. The guest book was open, and he couldn't resist taking a detour to peer at it and see how much damage his niece had done to Felicity's business.

Lines had been drawn through name after name on the booking calendar. Reservations canceled. Not just for upcoming weddings, but for stays at the inn itself as well. There were still names scattered here and there, but nothing for the upcoming two weeks, and Tom could see she'd lost more than half her bookings.

His gut nosedived. Felicity had gotten caught up in the downside of catering to the wealthy and well-known. When you fell out of favor with them, you fell out of favor with their followers. He ran his hand over his head. Damn, he felt bad for her.

The clock struck five, chiming loudly and startling him. He jumped and hit the reservation book with his elbow, knocking it to the floor. A piece of paper fluttered from the pages as the book fell.

Tom bent to scoop it up. It was a baby's sonogram. He studied the grainy image. Saw it was dated over four years ago, and written across the bottom was Felicity's name.

She'd told him she didn't have any children.

But there'd been a sonogram.

At one point, she'd had a baby. He could only assume she'd lost it.

Gently, Tom tucked the picture into the back of the book and returned the book to the desk, a heavy feeling settling in the pit of his stomach.

He glanced around the inn for Felicity, but didn't see her. Felt a sudden urge to find her. Maybe she was outside in the gardens. His instinct was to go to her and tell her how sorry he was for her loss, but he realized how inappropriate that would be.

Besides, he was rumpled and sweaty and bare-chested. First, he needed a shower.

And then what?

He had nothing to offer her but a weak apology. He was leaving on Monday. That was, unless he could think of a good reason to stay.

Tom *wanted* to stay. To get to know her better. What excuse could he give her for lingering?

He had no ride? Easily solvable.

To make amends with his brother? But that would mean he'd actually have to do something about his relationship with Joe. Tom wasn't sure he was prepared to do that.

His gaze landed on the bluebird sculpture perched atop the filing cabinet, and Tom came up with the best excuse of all.

Chapter Four

On Sunday morning Felicity came up the back steps with a basketful of laundry in her arms. She liked to hang the sheets on the clotheslines to dry. Sure it was old-fashioned and extra work, but the healthy smell of fresh, sun-dried linens couldn't be beat, and guests complimented her on it often.

Besides, there was something Zen about hanging out clothes that calmed the mind.

Granted, it was a dumb time to be hanging out laundry when her future was in shambles, but she'd needed something to do beside sit around, field reservation cancellations, and feel sorry for herself. She washed sheets and towels, hung them on the line, mixed a batch of cookies, and put them in the oven for her only guest. She retrieved the dry laundry and came into the house just in time to hear Tom Loving go upstairs.

Suddenly, it felt weird being alone with him in the big rambling Victorian. She'd never felt this way before with a guest, and she had no idea why she was feeling it now.

Really, Felicity? No idea at all? How about the fact that the man turned her on, and it had been over two long years since anyone did that for her?

Okay. So she was attracted to him. Big deal. Yes, he was

very easy on the eyes, but that probably just meant he had tons of women chasing after him.

She went to the kitchen, took out the batch of cookies from the oven, and set them on the sideboard to cool before popping in a second pan. She didn't know why she was making so many cookies when she only had one guest to eat them. She'd freeze the rest of the dough.

Ruefully shaking her head, she took the laundry upstairs to make up the empty guest rooms. She passed by Tom's door, heard the shower come on. He'd gone for another run.

Immediately, the image of a starkly naked Tom Loving popped into her head. She stopped in the middle of the hallway, frozen stiff by the visions she could not shake.

"Stop it," she hissed under her breath, but oh, her treacherous mind was in full-on revolt, picturing all manner of sexy things. It bewildered her, this instant attraction. Even with Steve, she hadn't felt such intense physical longing.

That's what bothered her. Right there. Disloyalty to her husband.

But Steve was gone. He would want her to be happy. He'd told her to marry again.

Marry? Good grief. Where was that coming from?

Determined to snap out of her odd mood, Felicity marched into her bedroom, which was next door to the room Tom Loving was staying in. She'd make the beds tomorrow. She dropped the laundry basket at the foot of her bed.

Heard him singing in the shower: "Bluebird." He didn't sound the least bit like Paul McCartney, but he was belting it out as if he were the superstar ex-Beatle.

She swayed in time to his music, swept up, dancing along with the song and the sound of the shower, waltzing around her room like a middle-aged Cinderella. The stress and strain of the previous morning drifted away.

His voice rose and fell, sometimes in tune, sometimes not, and her crazy heart swooned. Downstairs, she heard the kitchen oven timer ding, startling her out of her dreaminess.

The shower went off abruptly, and so did his song.

A fresh batch of naked Tom imagery tempted her. In her mind's eye, she saw him stepping from the shower, toweling off those sexy muscles. . . .

Stop it!

She raced down the stairs, not really knowing why she was running; her heart was an out-of-control pump, shooting spurts of blood through her veins. Once she reached the kitchen, she had to stop and take a deep breath.

Her hands trembled, and her knees were none too steady. She turned off the oven and searched for a potholder. What had she done with the thing?

She searched high and low, her head cocked, ears attuned for footsteps on the stairs. Finally, she spotted the oven mitt dangling from the magnet she used to fix it to the refrigerator.

Good gravy!

She jammed her hand into the oven mitt, opened the door to a blast of heat, and wondered if maybe she was losing her mind.

Tom strolled into the kitchen, hair damp from his shower, and found Felicity bent over the oven. Not the least bit ashamed of himself, he took a moment to admire the sight of her lovely fanny.

Finally, he cleared his throat. "How long have the bluebirds been gone?"

"What?" She jumped, blinked and straightened upright. A tray of chocolate chip cookies in her hand.

"There are no bluebirds on Bluebird Way. How long have they been gone?"

"Umm." Her eyes were wide and dazed; her pink mouth formed a pretty *O*. "Several years now. No one has seen bluebirds in Serendipity for quite some time."

"What's being done about it?"

She shrugged. "Nothing, I suppose."

"No county extension agent has gotten involved?"

"We only have one agent for the entire county. I doubt she's got the time."

"It's called Bluebird Way. This is the Bluebird Inn. I'm assuming at one time there were lots of bluebirds." He came closer.

She set the cookies on the counter, took off the oven mitt, looked flustered. By his questions? Or him? "Well, yes."

"It's a shame," he said.

"I agree." She pressed her lips together, reached for a spatula, and tackled a second pan of chocolate chip cookies that had already been cooling on the sideboard. "We had an influx of house sparrows, and new housing developments went up in the fields where the bluebirds used to mate, but what am I supposed to do?"

"Bring them back."

"You make it sound like that's within my control."

"It is," he said.

"How? I'm not a birdologist."

He laughed, delighted. He loved teaching people about birds. "Ornithologist."

"What?"

"Ornithologist is what a birdologist is officially called."

"Oh, I didn't know. Cookie?" She held out the plate of cookies. "We could have lunch on the patio. Sandwiches, and potato salad. Cookies for dessert."

"I didn't know that the B&B service included lunch."

"It doesn't." She shook her head, sending her golden-blond hair, which was pulled back into a low ponytail and clipped in place by a brown barrette, swaying. She looked both efficient and effervescent. An appealing mix of zeal and decorum. "But since it's just you and me, I thought why not? Unless you have other plans."

No, no other plans. "I can't think of anything I'd enjoy more," he said, and held her gaze.

Her cheeks turned pink, and she dropped her head. "It's settled. I'll make the sandwiches. Turkey okay?"

"May I help?" he asked, having visions of working beside her at the butcher block island, their hips touching as they stood side by side.

"I've got it." Her eyes twinkled. "I'm pretty proprietary about my kitchen. You can just relax. Have a seat." She pointed the spatula at one of the stools at the bar.

He swung the bar stool around so he could watch her work and sat down. He expected her to open a package of luncheon meat from the fridge, which was what he would have done, but instead, she took out a roasted turkey breast and sliced it up on a wooden cutting board with an electric knife.

Her movements were graceful, adept. She'd done this many times before. Constructing sandwiches. Carving turkey. Slathering made-from-scratch mayo onto thick slices of fresh-baked rustic bread. Washing delicate garden lettuce in the sink, arranging the frilly green edges on the bread just so. Topping it with ripe red tomato slices and razor-thin shavings of baby Swiss cheese. She added crisp kosher dill pickles, three large, green Cerignola olives stuffed with pimentos, and a generous scoop of potato salad to each plate.

Felicity straightened, dusted her fingers on the utilitarian cornflower-print apron tied at her waist, and eyed her handiwork with pride.

Tom eyed her with lusty interest. She fascinated him for about nine different reasons—that she was gorgeous, sexy, and big-hearted to name a few. And there was a self-contained peacefulness about her that called to his world-weary soul.

She started putting away the sandwich-making ingredients and nodded at the laden plates. "Could you take those out to the patio? I'm right behind you with cookies and lemonade."

"Absolutely." He carried the plates outside, bumping open

the lever handle of the back door with his knee, and left the door hanging ajar so she could come through behind him.

The afternoon sun was shaded by the treetops and cast soft shadows. A gentle breeze blew over the garden patio. Yesterday the place had been set up for a wedding. How quickly life had changed and rearranged.

A fresh pang of guilt plucked at Tom's heart like a pucker pulled tight in the center of his chest. Rationally, he knew he wasn't the cause of his niece's cold feet, but he still regretted giving Savannah the keys to his Ducati.

Lighten up, bucko. He had managed to strand himself at a quaint inn with a beautiful woman. He should enjoy it while it lasted.

Good advice. He decided to take it. He set down the plates, turned to intercept the pitcher of lemonade and cookies as Felicity came up behind him. She smiled during the handoff, then headed back to the house for napkins, silverware, and glasses.

They sat under the sheltering branches of a stately old oak tree, near the gurgling garden fountain. The smell of flowers tinged the air.

"This turkey sandwich is so good," he said. "Perfect. The best I've ever had."

"You exaggerate." Her laugh was light as the breeze.

He set his sandwich back on the plate, wiped his hands on a pretty linen napkin, angled her a sidelong glance. "I can't believe you're in such a cheerful mood after all those cancellations."

She smiled, but he caught a glimpse of sadness in the way her mouth tugged to one side. "I'll bounce back," she said, "I always do. What worries me is your niece."

"Why are you worried about Savannah after she caused you so much grief?"

"Small towns can sometimes be cruel. Don't get me wrong. I love Serendipity, but there's no anonymity here. Everyone knows everyone else's business. Savannah is accustomed to being treated like a princess, and it's going to be a shock when she comes back to face the music." A far-away look entered Felicity's blue eyes, as if she was speaking from experience.

Tom felt a quick swell of empathy. He wanted to ask her a million questions, but he didn't want to pry.

Her smile bounced back to normal, and she took a sip of lemonade. A squirrel chattered at them from the branch of the oak tree, and a pair of redbirds chased each other through the fountain.

"I love redbirds." She sighed. "Wouldn't it be awesome to see the bluebirds in here with them again?"

"If you've got a healthy garden full of different varieties of plants," he said, working the conversation around to the idea that gave him a reasonable excuse to prolong his stay in Serendipity, "you could bring the bluebirds back to Bluebird Way. It would just take a little care and hard work."

"Really?"

"Absolutely."

"How do you know so much about birds?" she asked, cutting her sandwich in half.

"I got my undergraduate degree in wildlife biology with a specialty in ornithology from Colorado State at Fort Collins."

Felicity crinkled her nose in a completely adorable way, and took a bite of her sandwich, chewed thoughtfully for a moment, and said, "That doesn't seem like a degree that would translate well into the Army."

"It wasn't. I had big plans for being a game warden, but ultimately I was unable to refuse the call of the military. What can I say? The Army is in my blood." He shrugged. "I signed up for ROTC during my junior year."

"ROTC?"

"Reserve Officers' Training Corps," he explained. "It's a path to military service you can begin while you're in college. They teach leadership skills and offer scholarships that help pay for school."

"What was your job in the Army?" She dabbed at her mouth with a napkin. A dainty movement that captivated him. Hell, everything about her captivated him.

"Civil affairs officer," he said.

"What's that?"

"Civil affairs specialists deal with things related to civil-military operations."

"That sounds vague and very military-ish," she commented. "Does it mean you help the civilians in countries we're at war with?"

"Among other duties," he said. "There's a lot of researching, coordinating, and planning. I spend . . . spent . . ." he corrected. His retirement was still so new he hadn't yet gotten used to thinking of his career in the past tense. "More time at a desk than I would have cared for, but I loved being in the field during a crisis. And it felt good to know I was making a difference in difficult situations."

She leaned over to pour him another glass of lemonade. "How did you get into civil affairs since your education was in wildlife biology?"

"The Army gave me an aptitude test, and it's what I scored the highest in. I loved the job because I was good at it, but my heart"—he tapped his chest—"was always in wildlife biology. Particularly birds."

"Interesting." She propped her elbows on the table, her chin in her upturned palms, and leaned in closer. In that cute pose she looked all of sixteen, and in that moment he could see exactly what she'd been like as a teenager—coltish, observant, curious. "What fascinates you most about birds?"

"They're free," Tom said. "Truly free. There's something primal and powerful about their ability to fly."

"Is it their ability to escape?" Her tone carried weight and meaning, and her gaze was trained on him. She wasn't talking about birds.

It was odd, how well she seemed to understand him when she knew nothing about him beyond what he'd just told her, and the fact that he was a Loving. Though not really a Loving in the Texas sense of the word, because he'd never identified with the cattle-baron history of his larger-than-life family.

He polished off the delicious turkey sandwich and ate a pickle. The sun glinted off her golden hair. She crossed her legs, and he caught a glimpse of her thigh as her skirt moved.

The redbirds sang. The perfume of roses decorated the air. It was a perfect moment. Tom felt as if he'd stepped into some quaint painting, or a time machine that had jettisoned him back to a kinder, gentler era.

"You're different," she said.

"Different?"

"From the Serendipity Lovings."

"Is that good or bad?"

"Neither." That enigmatic smile of hers again. "Just different."

"I wear that as a badge of honor."

"Bad blood?"

"Not on my end," he said. "Just a disconnect. Ancient history. A conflict between my father and the . . ." He paused, used her words. "Serendipity Lovings."

"It's left you something of a loner." A statement of fact, not a question. She was right. "The Army became your family, your community."

Her voice was soft, alluring, drawing him in, almost as if she were using it to cast a spell. Tom scooted his chair closer to her.

She raised an eyebrow.

"Sun was in my eyes," he lied.

Her sly smile outdid the Mona Lisa. She knew the sun wasn't in his eyes.

"How long have you been retired?" She pushed away her empty plate, sat back in her chair, and lowered her lashes.

"Two weeks."

"You haven't had time to settle into civilian life."

"No." He watched her watching him.

Felicity studied him as if he were an interesting, but totally foreign insect that had crept into her gardens overnight, and she was trying to figure out if he was useful or a pest.

"Do you know what you want to do with the rest of your life?"

Ah, there was the rub. "Quite honestly? Not yet."

"What are the options?"

"That's the thing—they are endless. I could go anywhere, do almost anything. I don't know which path to choose."

"Something to do with wildlife biology perhaps?"

He shook his head. "That degree was so long ago and far away—"

"But you just said wildlife biology was in your heart."

"Following one's heart isn't very practical."

"All the more reason you should follow it. Nothing truly rewarding ever happens by taking the practical route. Stretch, grow," she challenged, passion flowing from her like lava waves. "Open your heart to possibilities as yet undreamed."

"Poetic," he said. "Do you really believe that?"

She nodded, swept her hand at the lush gardens. "That's how I ended up here."

"With an empty B&B," he said, and immediately regretted it.

"Temporarily." Her smile was warm, but her eyes cooled.

Tom pulled a palm down his face. "Forgive me for saying that. I don't know—"

"It's okay." She tilted her head at him like a wise sage showing compassion for a clueless novice. "I get that you're scared."

"Scared?" That blindsided him. "What are you talking about?"

"You're at loose ends. The job that was your identity is over. You're disconnected from your family. And you're worried about your niece."

"You're right." He nodded, scraped up his courage to broach the topic he'd been working around the entire meal. "About all that. And I feel bad that you have no guests."

Her spine stiffened. "I don't need your pity."

"It's not pity," he insisted. "It's my guilt."

"I don't need that either."

"Okay, truth?" Tom held up a palm.

"Why would I want you to lie?"

Well, well, she was feisty. He liked that. Liked it a lot. "I don't have anywhere else to be right now. I am waiting to hear back on the resumes I have out, but until then . . ." He gave a rueful shrug. "I've got nothing to do, and I'm not a do-nothing kind of man. I hate that the bluebirds have gone away, and I'd like to see them make a comeback in Serendipity."

Felicity studied him for so long without saying anything that his skin started to itch. "What are you saying?"

"Since you don't have any guests, and I wouldn't be taking up prime real estate, can we strike some kind of deal? Discounted room and board in exchange for helping you lure the bluebirds back to Bluebird Way? You could consider it my way of making up for causing so much chaos at the wedding. If the bluebirds come back home, how in the world could anyone consider this place jinxed?"

"It's not the place that's jinxed," she said, her expression deadly serious. "It's me."

Chapter Five

What alarmed Felicity the most was how badly she wanted Tom to stay, and not just because she yearned for the bluebirds to return to the inn.

She yearned for other things too. Like the touch of a man's hand on her body, and the feel of his lips on her skin.

But they were strangers, and she'd never in her life done anything as bold as have a casual fling with someone she didn't know.

Then again, why not? There was a first time for everything, right?

Why not? Because she was jinxed. It could only end badly.

Stuff and nonsense. That was illogical. And yet the notion had burrowed into the back of Felicity's brain and sat there like a virus.

"There's no such thing as a jinx," Tom said, his tone not poking fun or judging, just a simple statement of fact. "The jinx lies only in the interpretation of unfortunate events."

Felicity considered telling him about the lore surrounding her birth and the series of sorrows that had dogged her life. But confiding in him was unprofessional. She was an innkeeper, and he was nothing but her guest.

A stranger. He did not want to hear her tortured story.

Telling it made her more vulnerable, and she was already susceptible enough where Tom Loving was concerned.

"I need to get the dishes done." Felicity stood, started gathering their plates.

"I'll help." Tom pushed back his chair, rose.

"No," she said, her tone much sharper than she intended. She took a deep breath and gentled her voice. "That's okay. I've got this."

"Your kitchen, your kingdom." His tone was mild, but his eyes flared with interest.

"Something like that." She stacked the lemonade pitcher, half-empty now, onto the plates. Realized they'd never gotten around to the chocolate chip cookies. She balanced the plate of cookies on top of the pitcher and headed for the house.

"At least let me get the door," Tom said, running ahead of her to push open the French doors leading into the B&B.

"Thank you," she mumbled, and hurried past him.

"Felicity," he called to her from the doorway.

She stopped, blew out her breath, turned back to him. "Yes?"

His face was earnest in the shadows, dark and handsome. "You never did answer my question."

She blinked, her mind so wrapped up in the turmoil of her attraction, she'd forgotten what he was talking about.

"About my staying for a while, helping you bring back the bluebirds . . ."

"Oh yes, that."

"I can take no for an answer," he said. "Just say the word. I can stay, or I leave. The choice is yours."

Her pulse throbbed at her wrists, bounding, bounding, bounding. Her fingers clutched the dishes tightly, knuckles aching from the pressure. Her chest tightened, and her tongue felt thick and heavy in her mouth.

Tell him thanks, but no thanks.

She met his eyes, absorbed the brunt of his gaze, felt something cosmic afoot. "It would be very nice. . . ." Felicity paused, ensnared in a maelstrom of radiant awareness, caught on the twin prongs of fear and desire. *Leave. Go.* She should tell him to pack his bags and hit the road before he dismantled her.

His smile never faltered.

Finally, she finished, with her truth winning out over her doubt. "I would love to see bluebirds in the gardens again."

His exuberant grin was her reward. He was as thrilled about helping her bring the bluebirds back as she would be to have them.

"Well," she said, "since you're going to be staying a while, I guess you'll be needing your own key to the front door."

"First order of business," Tom said the next morning after they'd had a breakfast of scrambled eggs and toast at the kitchen table. "We relocate the bluebird houses."

They were both dressed for a day of yard work. Tom, in faded jeans and a long-sleeved red T-shirt. Felicity in workout clothes, black and purple Lycra jogging pants with a matching top. The outfit adhered to her youthful figure, showing off her curves. She had her hair pulled back off her face with a purple stretch headband, and her face was scrubbed free of makeup.

She looked gorgeous in the morning light, healthy and glowing.

"What's wrong with where the birdhouses are now?" She shaded her eyes against the sun, studied the birdhouses erected between the flower beds, fountains, and stone walking paths of the gardens.

"You're not going to attract anything but house wrens keeping them this near dense vegetation." He motioned at the lush foliage of flowers and plant life. "Bluebirds prefer semi-open grasslands. For instance, expanses of mowed lawns or meadow grass or orchards or roadsides. They especially like dirt roads. Places where the trees are scattered and the ground cover is short. We also want to avoid ponds or open water so tree swallows don't take over."

"Oh!" Felicity's eyes—as blue as the birds they were discussing—lit up, and Tom felt a happy stirring in the pit of his stomach. "The dirt road that runs down the back of the peach orchards would be the perfect spot."

"Good choice." He nodded. "I'll mow the grass around it first, and then we can put up the houses."

"What can I do while you're mowing?" she asked, looking as excited as a kid on the first day of summer camp.

"Clean any old nests from the bluebird houses and wash them down with a water hose, then put them to dry in the sun."

She gave him a cheery salute, clicked heels shod in purple Keds. "On it, Major Tom."

A tug of lust pulled the stirring in his stomach down to a lower level, and his throat went dry.

She pranced off, fanny bouncing provocatively in those butt-enhancing pants.

"Hey," he called.

She spun around to face him again. "What do you want?"

You.

The word formed inside his brain clear and bright as a neon sign. "Um," he said. "Where do you keep the lawn mower?"

"That's right, you wouldn't know, would you? C'mon." She motioned for him to follow her.

It was not an invitation he was going to pass up. He took off after her, joining her at the garden shed on the left side of the house. It was hidden away behind trellised vines. She spun the combination lock, clicked it open, and stepped aside so he could have at the mower shed.

He mowed while she washed the birdhouses and set them out to dry. They took a break for lunch—turkey salad this time—eating in the gardens once more.

"The birdhouses look great," he said. "Good job."

"I've got them in the direct sun. They should be dry soon."

"By the way," Tom said, "I forgot to ask. Do you have paper wasps?"

"I don't know. Sometimes they're around, but I haven't really noticed any this year yet." She bit her bottom lip, and he couldn't help staring at her sweet, pink mouth. "Are they a problem?"

"They could sting the nestlings to death. It wouldn't be a bad idea to soap the roofs of the bluebird houses to prevent paper wasps from building nests, just in case you do have them."

"How does that work?"

"Do you have any Ivory bar soap? We'll need a mild soap that will keep away wasps, but not harm the birds."

"I do have some. I'll go get it." She disappeared into the house, returned a few minutes later with the bar of Ivory soap in her hand, and came over to where he was filling the lawn mower with gas from the can he'd found in the shed.

"What now?"

"We melt it in a saucepan." He put down the gas can. "Let's go."

"You don't have to help. I can handle it. Just give me the deets."

"Wouldn't it be more fun to do it together?"

She grinned, a big bear hug of a grin, hearty and enthusiastic. "C'mon then."

They walked into the kitchen together, and it felt as natural as if they'd been hanging out all their lives. He liked the feeling. Wanted more of it.

She unwrapped the soap.

Tom moved closer, eager to be near her, caught a whiff of her fragrance. She smelled like flowers and fresh baked bread and morning dew. Something in his chest expanded, as if his lungs and his heart were growing, pushing firm against his ribs.

Felicity shifted, making room for him at the stove.

"Cut up the soap and put the pieces in a little water to

heat. When it cools we'll apply it to the inside ceiling of the birdhouses with small paintbrushes."

"How does that keep away wasps?"

"The soap makes a coating that prevents the pulpy wasp's nest from sticking to the wood," he explained. "We'll need to be careful to keep the soap on just the ceilings and not the walls because it could prevent the baby birds from climbing the sides of the wood to reach the hole when it's time for them to leave the nesting box. We don't want them to get trapped inside."

"I'll be very careful." Felicity set a saucepan on the stove, added a bit of water. Tom took out his pocketknife to shave off soap slivers into the saucepan.

Once the soap was melted, she found some old paint-brushes, and they took the mixture outside to paint it on the tops of the bluebird houses. There were twenty houses, and, even with both of them working on the task, it took almost an hour to carefully coat the small ceilings.

When they finished, Tom stretched out his arms, limbering up his shoulders, which had tightened up from hunching forward over his work. "That was fun. I've had a blast."

"There's such joy on your face. Honestly, you should get back into ornithology."

He felt it too, the joy she saw in him, but the feeling had as much to do with working beside Felicity as it did with the birds.

He waved a hand. "I'd have to go back to school and get a master's degree. Technology has changed things so much since I graduated."

"So go back to school." Her grin enticed him like a bowl of homemade vanilla ice cream. "You're in your early forties. No reason why not. Plenty of life left in you."

Tom found himself hoping that none of the jobs he applied for would pan out so he could stay here and paint soap on birdhouses with her.

"Do you own a house?" she asked.

"No. Gave it to Heidi in the divorce. Life is easier when you rent."

"Have you considered making Serendipity your home?" she asked, her tone light, as if she didn't care, but she was leaning in toward him, head cocked at an inquisitive angle. "Fort Worth is only forty miles away. Not a ridiculous distance to commute to school. You could take night classes once or twice a week."

"Living in Serendipity never crossed my mind." *Until now.*

"Why not? Joe's here. . . ." She smoothed down her hair and seemed to be actively avoiding looking him in the eyes.

"That's not a big selling point."

She met his gaze head-on. This woman didn't miss a trick. "What is the deal between you two? The way he yelled at you at the wedding, as if he considered it your fault that Savannah ran. He was looking for someone to blame, and you were the lightning rod."

"Joe feels like he got the short end of the stick. I remind him of that daddy-done-me-wrong chip he's been waggling around on his shoulder since I was born."

"Given your history," she asked, "why do you suppose Joe invited you to the wedding?"

Tom raised his left shoulder and tilted his head to the right. His "zigzag" pose as Heidi had called it. "It's a tic you have when you're conflicted," his ex-wife had pointed out. "But you didn't do it the day I asked for a divorce. You weren't conflicted then. Admit it, you want out of the marriage as much as I do."

Maybe he had.

"I figure Joe invited me as proxy for my dad. He didn't invite him because Joe hates my mother. She always made him follow the house rules, and he didn't like that. Joe's mom had a freer parenting style."

"Do you think part of it could be that as he's getting older, Joe is realizing the importance of having strong family ties?"

"I don't think that's it. He's gnarled up with the Loving

family like hundred-year-old tree roots. My dad and I are the ones who've kept our distance."

"Then perhaps Joe is reaching out because he wants you to know how good it feels to have family you can count on."

Ha. Not likely.

"What about you?" he asked, changing the subject. "Any brothers or sisters?"

"I was an only child," she said, pressing her lips together, folding her arms over her chest, closing off, shutting down. He could see the rich ore of backstory running through her veins. But it didn't appear she was willing to share it with him.

At least not yet.

Compelled by the sadness shining in her eyes, he moved closer.

They were standing in the warmth of the afternoon sun, in the middle of the gardens, birds singing and flitting around them. It felt like something out of a Disney flick. He half-expected a cartoon mouse to appear.

Her sweet pink mouth was a whisper away.

If he dipped his head just a little bit . . .

She stared up at him, eyes wide, lips pursed, but she didn't stop him, didn't turn away. He could see the pulse at her throat throb with each heartbeat. His pulse was throbbing too.

Tom cupped the back of her head in his palm, his splayed fingers sliding up into her hair, felt her ponytail trail over his wrist.

She stiffened under his touch. Was this a mistake? Should he back off?

Tom stilled.

Her eyes searched his face. She didn't pull away. Didn't speak.

Lightly, he brushed his lips against her hot cheek.

When she didn't resist or protest, he slid his mouth down to capture hers. She closed her eyes. He knew because he kept his open, studying the dreamy softness of her features, savoring the moment of their first kiss.

He cradled her face in his hands, his calloused thumbs hooking on either side of her jaw, his fingers tilting her head so he could deepen the kiss.

Kissing her was the best thing he'd done in ages. His mouth claimed her, his tongue asking for entry.

Felicity parted her teeth, let him in. She softened against him, muscles relaxing. He teased her with his tongue, inviting her to play. *Let's run and frolic.*

She was so damned hot.

And she made *him* hot. Inside, he was on fire. Blazing from his mouth straight down to the stiffest part of his body. He could barely breathe, all common sense going up in flames.

Felicity kissed him back, running her hands up his arms to his shoulders, encircling his neck, pulled his head down farther. She felt so good, so soft and down-to-earth. Warm and welcoming.

His shoulders sagged, and his hopes soared—he was giddy with desire, dizzy from lack of air, thrilled with relief that she'd kissed him back. It had been so long since he'd felt this way. Too long.

Had he ever really felt this way?

He cast his mind back, couldn't recall a single time a woman had stirred him to such heights with just a simple kiss.

She pressed closer, flattening her breasts against his chest, making him forget where he was, hell, who he was. All that mattered was her mouth and how she was using it to twist him inside out and upside down.

His hands went to her waist. When she didn't draw back, he slipped them underneath the hem of her shirt, caressed her smooth, creamy skin, marveled at the contrast to his rough palms. He was acutely aware of her small fingers kneading the nape of his neck. She clutched him as if she were drowning, rocking her pelvis against his erection.

Rocking his world.

He groaned low in his throat, tugged her closer until there wasn't a millimeter of space between them.

Yes.

The word smashed through his brain, a wrecking ball destroying all argument and resistance. He was an old building, getting torn down at the hands of an expert demolition crew. He came completely untethered. Blasted. Blown away by the strength of his desire.

Her fingers contained lightning. Everywhere she touched he felt tiny jolts of electricity burning up his nerve endings, sending one insistent imperative—*yes, yes, yes.*

He'd been hit. Lightning struck. Agog with the mystery of his overwhelming desire for this beautiful creature.

Then Felicity placed a firm palm against his chest, pushed herself away from him.

"Stop," she said helplessly. "Please, stop."

Immediately, Tom let go of her, dragged in desperate breath over a ragged tongue. God, it felt so lonely without her in his arms.

Her face was pale, taut, and she was just as breathless as he was, sucking in air in tight, shallow pants.

"I . . ." he said. "I . . ." What was there to say? He couldn't apologize. He wasn't sorry for kissing her. "You . . . we . . ."

"Please," she whimpered again. She was shaking her head, but that word dropping from her lips sounded like an entreaty, not an edict.

He locked eyes with her, felt a powerful shift inside him, like sidewalks buckling and cracking. An earthquake. "What is it?"

"I like you, Tom. I truly do."

"I like you too," he murmured. "A lot."

"Yes, we're attracted to each other. But that doesn't mean anything. We've just met. We're both in a transitional phase. You with the retirement. Me with . . ." She brushed a lock of hair from her forehead. "Well, my business is caving in. To start something now . . . It wouldn't be smart, would it?"

"Foolish."

"You understand." She looked so relieved, her knees actually sagged, and she grasped the back of a nearby lawn chair.

"You're right," he said, fully meaning it, but unable to stop opposing feelings from rushing through him. He wanted to argue, deny . . . kiss her again.

What was going on here? He was not an impulsive guy by nature. Why now? Why Felicity? *Because she is freaking awesome.*

"If you're going to stay here and help me bring the bluebirds back, this can't happen again." Her voice was soft, but firm. Setting boundaries. He respected her all the more for it. "Is that understood?"

"Yes, ma'am."

"Otherwise, you have to go."

"I understand."

Her forgiving smile held a note of wistfulness, or maybe he was projecting. She extended her hand. "Friends?"

"Friends," Tom agreed, even though shaking her hand left him feeling that he was nothing but a guest who'd already overstayed his welcome.

Chapter Six

The kiss left Felicity completely off balance.

She was proud of herself for setting up ground rules, but disturbed that she'd ever let Tom kiss her in the first place.

Why had he kissed her?

Okay, she had a decent figure and blond hair. For some guys that was attraction enough. But she was selling them both short. What had her wincing—and regretting—was the unbridled way she'd responded to him. She should have set the boundaries immediately, instead of kissing him back.

Ugh! She had to stop replaying it. The kiss was over and done with. It wasn't going to happen again. Tom had promised to keep his mitts off her, and she certainly wasn't going to initiate another kiss, so problem solved.

She tackled garden weeds while Tom situated the bluebird houses on the outskirts of the peach orchard, and they kept their distance for the remainder of the day. At five o'clock, Felicity took off her gardening gloves and dusted her hands, preparing to head into the house to start dinner when Tom sauntered over.

"May I take you out to dinner?" he asked.

"As friends?" She felt a muscle in her eye twitch.

"Of course. What else would it be?" He sounded so surprised by her question that she started to wonder if she'd imagined how intense that kiss had been. If he was able to dismiss it so easily, maybe it hadn't been as world-rocking for him as it had been for her.

"In that case," she said, "I accept."

They had dinner at Bubba Red's, a popular barbecue joint on the town square. Heads turned the minute they walked in. Uh oh. This was a bad idea.

And when Tom put a hand to the small of her back to guide her through the door, Felicity should have pulled the plug on the whole thing, but his powerful hand touching her tenderly felt so good that she sensed her boundaries melting away.

She'd missed this so much. The gentle touch of a commanding man's hand.

Damn her. This wasn't good. She purposely stepped away from him, and Tom dropped his hand. People in the restaurant exchanged knowing glances, and she could almost hear the buzz of the grapevine.

"Sorry," he apologized. "I didn't think. I just wanted to make sure you didn't trip over the threshold."

"Boundaries," she murmured lightly, praying she'd be able to keep to her own rules.

The waitress seated them. Felicity studied her menu, purposely not meeting any of the curious stares coming their way.

The front door opened. She heard a familiar laugh and cringed. It was Aunt Molly with a group of her friends. Felicity pulled the menu up high, trying to hide her face.

Did trying to hide make her look guilty? Why was she feeling guilty? She had a right to go out to dinner with a handsome man. No matter what it might look like to the Nosy Rosies in Serendipity, they were not on a date. This was innocent. Two friends out to dinner. No one else knew about the kiss.

"Excuse me," Tom said. "I forgot to wash my hands after the yard work."

"Surely," she mumbled.

The second Tom left, Aunt Molly abandoned her friends and made a beeline to Felicity's table.

"What are you up to, missy?" Aunt Molly asked, plunking down in the seat Tom had vacated.

"Having dinner with Tom Loving."

"I can see that. . . . But why?" Her aunt's voice and eyes were full of curiosity and innuendo.

Felicity shrugged. "Why not? I'm entitled to have dinner as much as the next person."

"Why are you with *him*?"

"Because he asked. What's wrong with that?"

Aunt Molly tapped her chin with two fingers. "There's nothing wrong with him. In fact, he's quite yummy. It's just that, well, he's not going to stick around for long, and I hate to see you get hurt."

"Steve stuck around, and I still got hurt."

"That's not the kind of hurt I'm talking about."

"You've already told me I'm jinxed either way—"

"That was a mistake. I should have kept my mouth shut. Your mother would be so mad if she knew I told you. It's a silly myth."

"So what's the problem?"

"You deserve all the happiness in the world, but I'm not sure Tom Loving can give you what you need."

"Auntie, I appreciate your looking out for me, but it's just dinner." And a dynamite kiss.

"Ada Millstone saw Tom mowing your lawn." The way Aunt Molly said *mowing your lawn* made it sound like a euphemism for sex.

"Tom feels responsible for Savannah's running away from the wedding, and he's trying to make it up to me."

"You're a grown woman," Aunt Molly said. "You can do whatever you want. Just be careful." She patted Felicity's shoulder, hopped up as Tom appeared across the restaurant, leaned down, and whispered, "And use protection. I know you can't get pregnant, but he's a military man, and you don't know where he's been."

"Auntie!"

Tom strolled up to the table. Aunt Molly sent him a look over the top of her glasses and said to him, "Behave," before she zoomed back to her friends.

"What was that all about?" Tom asked, an amused expression cutting a deep dimple into his right cheek. He had the best smile. "Did you tell her I kissed you?"

"Heavens no! I'd never hear the end of it. You've been in town for three days, and they're already making up stories."

"About us?" His eyes twinkled.

"Don't let it go to your head. The gossips have nothing better to do than speculate about people's love lives."

"That bothers you?"

"No," she said. "Well, okay, yes, I'm a people-pleaser by nature, but I've decided I'm over it."

"Good for you." He settled back in his seat just as the waitress returned to take their order.

The meal was delicious, the conversation light and fun. They talked about books, art, music, sports, casual interests. Nothing serious or weighted with any kind of significance. Certainly no mention of The Kiss.

Thank God.

She learned that Tom loved Banksy, silent movies, and kayaking. He was a fan of John Grisham novels, preferred waffles to pancakes, enjoyed ghost stories told around a campfire and college baseball. He wasn't enthusiastic about white chocolate, reality TV, people who wore their caps backward, or cookie-cutter housing developments. His idol was his father, which she thought was very sweet. He was a Libra to her Aquarius, and, when she commented that two air signs could stir up a storm, he laughed like it was the most amusing thing he'd ever heard.

It was one of the nicest dinners she'd had in ages, and it was something of a surprise when the waitress announced, "We close at nine."

"What time is it?" Felicity asked.

"Eight forty-five."

Wow. She couldn't believe how they'd lost track of time.

"Forgive us," Tom said. "We got carried away."

"We are air signs after all." Felicity giggled.

The waitress looked at her strangely. Tom paid the bill, left a large tip, and they walked out of the restaurant laughing.

"You're a great conversationalist," Tom said, opening the driver's side door of her Prius so she could get in. "It's been a long time since I've had this much fun."

"I feel the same way." She hesitated before sliding behind the wheel. He was standing close, and, for a moment, she was absolutely certain he was going to kiss her again.

She held her breath. Waited. Thrilled and equally terrified. Dammit, she wanted him to kiss her again. But not here. Not in public.

Their eyes locked, held.

How could they be feeling so connected when they barely knew each other? Felicity had been through enough sorrow in her life to be skeptical of feelings that burned hot and fast, but there was something undeniable passing between them. Something much stronger than simple physical attraction. If she were being fanciful, she might say their souls were calling to each other. But if she were being honest? Maybe it was just loneliness.

His mouth was so tempting.

She leaned in, closed her eyes, parted her lips, thought, *kiss me*. Oh yes, she did. What was wrong with her? How could she want something so badly when she knew it was not right for her? Boundaries. She'd set boundaries, and she wanted him to honor them, but when he did, she was disappointed.

A cell phone dinged.

Not hers.

She opened her eyes. Tom sheepishly pulled his cell phone from his pocket, glanced at the screen.

"It's from Savannah," he said. "She's brought my Ducati back. It's at your place."

"Where is she? *How* is she?"

"I'll ask." Tom texted his niece.

Felicity hugged herself against the evening breeze and gazed up at the stars. Breathed deeply, tried to resolve the emotional conflict churning inside her with regard to Tom Loving. It wasn't fair to keep sending him mixed messages. Telling him to back off and then closing her eyes and leaning in when she sensed he wanted to kiss her.

His phone pinged again. "She's fine. She's back at her condo now."

"Did she contact her parents?"

Tom winced. "Yes."

"How do you feel about that?"

"I still feel guilty that she took off on my bike, but I figure she must have had a good reason. I'm staying out of it."

"I hope she's doing okay emotionally," Felicity fretted. "Running away couldn't have been easy on her."

"I'm guessing it wasn't so easy on Chance either," Tom said.

"Or her parents." Felicity paused. "Or you."

"Or you," Tom added.

"I'll be fine."

"She ruined your business."

"I'll bounce back. She took your most prized possession," Felicity pointed out.

"Gotta admit, it might be shallow of me, but I was worried about the Ducati." He chuckled. "I've had the bike for twenty years."

"But still, you cared enough about your niece's happiness to put your beloved motorcycle at her disposal."

"I'm glad to have it back."

"Now you're free again. You can ride away any time you want." She was appalled to hear a wistfulness in her voice. "You're no longer stuck here in Serendipity." *With me,* she added silently.

"I don't want to ride away," he said, his voice low and deep. His eyes dark and enigmatic in the shadows from the restaurant's neon light. "I'm committed to bringing those bluebirds back. That is unless you *want* me to ride away."

"No," she said, inhaling when she should have been exhaling, her chest growing tight beneath the added pressure. "I don't want that at all."

Once they were back at the Bluebird Inn, Tom couldn't resist going over every inch of the Ducati, on a search for dents and dings. He knew he was inordinately attached to the machine, but he'd bought it with the first money he'd earned in the military. Heidi had accused him of loving the motorcycle more than he'd loved her.

Maybe he had.

Didn't say much for their relationship.

"How is the bike?" Felicity snuggled deeper into the folds of her thick knitted sweater as she stood underneath the carport watching him examine the Ducati.

"Looks good." He bobbed his head.

"Where did Savannah leave the keys?" Felicity asked.

"Good question." Tom searched the saddlebags, found the ignition key tucked inside.

"Luckily, Serendipity has a low crime rate."

Tom straightened, stuck the keys into his pocket, caught Felicity studying him intently. "What?"

"Just now, in this light, you looked all of eighteen." She smiled. "I wish I could have known you when you were eighteen."

"Good thing you didn't," he said devilishly. "I would have gotten you into so much trouble."

"Bad boy, were you?" She took a step closer, laughter in her eyes.

"Not bad so much as mischievous." His gaze hung on her lips, and he remembered exactly what they tasted like. He wanted to kiss her again, but he'd promised to keep his hands to himself. When he'd made that promise he hadn't realized how hard it was going to be.

He ran a hand over the motorcycle's handlebars, thought about the open road and freedom. Maybe he *should* go. Bringing bluebirds back to Bluebird Way was just an excuse to be near her, and they both knew it.

Clearly, Felicity wasn't ready for a relationship. She was still mourning her dead husband. How could he ever hope to compete with a dead guy?

"I'm calling it a night." Felicity suppressed a yawn. "Are you coming in?"

"In a bit," he said, needing to be alone with his thoughts.

"All right." She turned toward the door that led from the carport into the house.

"Felicity," he called.

She stopped, turned back. "Yes?"

"Are you happy?"

Her eyes widened, fringed by those lush lashes. "What do you mean?"

"Does this"—he waved a hand at the house—"fulfill you?"

The corner of her mouth twitched. "I like what I do. I enjoy running the inn and looking after people and the gardens. I'm a nurturer. It's in my blood. I—"

"It's okay," he said. "You don't owe me any excuses."

She pulled her spine up straight, frowned a little, and her voice sharpened. "I'm not making excuses."

They'd had such a nice night together, why was he pushing her?

"Sometimes people end up on a path not of their own choosing. Are you one of them?" he asked, hoping she'd tell him she was a secret vagabond and wanted nothing more than to go riding on the back of his Ducati with him into the sunset.

She smiled a lost Madonna sort of smile, and he couldn't help thinking of that sonogram picture that had fallen out of the reservation book. It was a smile that said she'd suffered much, but was still quite content with her lot in life.

"Good night," she murmured, and went inside.

He watched her walk away, jealous of her bravery and resilience. Humbled and ashamed that he could not measure up to her example. She was a fine human being. Bold in a quiet way. Continuing to live a productive life even though she'd lost so much. Shining her lovely light out into the world.

Tom went back to his motorcycle. Straddled it. Wondered if he should just pull up stakes and go. His cell phone dinged in his pocket.

A text from Joe. **Savannah brought your bike back?**

Yes, Tom texted.

Joe: **She came to see us.**

Tom: **What did she say?**

Joe: **It's complicated.**

Tom: **How did you know about the bike?**

Joe: **Felicity texted me.**

Tom raised his head, looked toward the door. Felicity couldn't leave well enough alone. She knew Joe and Marion had to have been worried sick about Savannah. She must have felt compelled to pass along what she knew. He didn't blame her. He should have been the one to do it.

Joe: **She likes U.**

Tom: **Savannah?**

Joe: **Felicity.**

Tom: How do U know?

Joe: She told me.

Tom: Just now? In a text?

Joe: No. Last night. She called to see how Marion and I were doing. She told me UR staying to help her bring the bluebirds back.

Tom: Why did she tell U that?

Joe: Because U won't. I have to find out from someone else you're staying in Serendipity.

Tom: What's the deal with everyone in this town? People can't wait to crawl up in your business.

Joe: Get used 2 it. That's how it is when people care about U. But you're getting itchy to leave now, huh?

Tom sucked in his breath, felt the old anger creep in. Then Joe surprised the hell out of him by texting: I love you, little brother.

Chapter Seven

Two weeks flew by without a single other guest checking in, and there were no new bookings either.

But Felicity wasn't too upset. She was having a grand time just hanging out with Tom. No kisses involved.

They ate every meal together. Worked side by side in the gardens. Went to the movies a couple of times. Took long rides on his Ducati. Swam in the pool most evenings. They sat outside and listened to the tree frogs and the crickets and the chuck-will's-widow calling in the night. They talked and talked and talked underneath the stars. Shared their innermost dreams and fears, doubts, and plans.

They even got invited to the Loving mansion for dinner with Tom's brother, Joe, and his wife, Marion, and their son, Joshua.

Joshua was studying to be a veterinarian, and he and Tom bonded over the idea of bringing the bluebirds back to Serendipity.

Savannah's name was never mentioned, and it turned out to be a surprisingly pleasant evening. At the end of the night, Marion drew Felicity aside and apologized for how the failed wedding had ruined Felicity's business and promised to do her best to squash the rampant rumors that the Bluebird Inn was jinxed.

But Felicity knew it was going to take a brave soul from the Serendipity social registry to book a wedding at the Bluebird to banish those rumors. She didn't see that happening anytime soon.

Tom and Joe had some private time together too, and Tom came away from the evening with a renewed spring in his step. The Loving brothers, it seemed, were starting to make peace.

Her time with Tom was a glorious vacation from her daily life, and she cherished every minute they spent together, because Felicity knew it could not last.

Which worried her a bit, because she should have been more concerned about the future of the inn. If the lack of bookings kept up, she wouldn't be able to make the payments on the loan she'd taken out to renovate the B&B.

Maybe you could just sell the house, whispered a voice at the back of her mind. She'd never traveled. Never lived anywhere but Serendipity, except for when she was in college. Those questions Tom had asked her that night Savannah arranged to have the Ducati brought back had stirred up things.

Immediately, Felicity felt disloyal to Steve, his family, her community, for such thoughts. She loved her hometown and the Bluebird Inn. Aunt Molly was here. All her friends. Where would she go? What would she do if she left?

The truth of it was, she'd been having silly romantic fantasies of taking off with Tom Loving. Foolish. Yes, she knew that, but she'd been having them nonetheless.

He was just a Band-Aid. He was fun and handsome and paying her attention, and he distracted her from the fact that her business was going down the tubes at lightning speed. Her daydreams wouldn't withstand the harsh light of reality.

Nothing wrong with enjoying the moment. It wouldn't last, but that was okay. Nothing ever did.

Several times she thought Tom might kiss her again, but he never crossed that line. He wanted her, she could see it in his eyes, just as much as she wanted him, but he didn't make a move. He'd promised her that he would respect her boundaries, although she couldn't help thinking there was more to his hesitation than that.

Maybe he was afraid of starting something he couldn't stick around for. He'd made it clear he was a wanderer by nature, and she accepted that. Respected him for his honesty. He was not a man who toyed with a woman's affections. He could control himself.

It felt like an old-fashioned courtship, but she couldn't afford to let herself think along those lines. He was *not* courting her. He'd be leaving when the bluebirds came back or when he got the job offer he was holding out for. Hopefully, they could remain friends.

Long-distance friendship would be enough.

Or so she told herself.

On Monday, sixteen days after Savannah Loving ran away from her wedding, Felicity and Tom fell into step as they headed to the back of the peach orchard where they'd set up the bluebird houses. In that short time, it had become a comfortable routine. The two of them walking together in the silence of the early morning. Dew gathering on their shoes as the morning birds sang.

Tom kept the grass clipped short here, mowing it every three days. As they had every day since they'd started this project, they put mealworms and bright red berries into the small, blue plastic open containers they'd tacked onto the top of the birdhouses. The blue flags they'd staked out in hopes of attracting the bluebirds' attention fluttered in the breeze, sending the message: *Free meal! Stop here!*

The mealworms were pricey, especially since, so far, other birds had been dining on them, but Tom had assured her they were worth the investment. Mealworms were filet mignon to bluebirds. Tom promised as soon as the bluebirds found the mealworms, they would be hooked.

Unfortunately, that had not yet happened.

"What are the odds we can bring the bluebirds back this spring?" Felicity asked, wondering how much longer she could go without wedding bookings.

"Truth?"

"I wouldn't have it any other way."

"Less than fifty-fifty."

"Is it worse than that? I mean if it were easy to lure the bluebirds back to Bluebird Way, you'd think someone around here would have already done it."

"Probably." He gave her a keep-your-chin-up-Champ grin. "But you've got a secret weapon the others don't have."

"What's that?"

"Me."

"There is that." She laughed. "If nothing else, you've kept me from dwelling on my problems."

"I have a feeling you're not the kind of person who dwells. You strike me as a bootstrapper from way back."

She was. Felicity tucked a strand of loose hair behind her ear, smiled, and cast a sidelong glance at him.

He one-upped her smile with a bigger one that lit his entire face. "We're doing everything we can do to court those bluebirds. We've worked to reduce the house sparrow population on the property by putting fishing line and sparrow spookers on the boxes." He ticked off the measures on his fingers. "We've bought predator guards to put over the bird-house entrance holes after the first bluebird lays an egg. It's the best we can do short of trapping and killing the sparrows."

The house sparrows loved to harass bluebirds and would often peck bluebird eggs, and kill both nestlings and adults. Even so, neither Felicity nor Tom wanted to actively exterminate the sparrows unless there was no other option. Fortunately, a large number of the house sparrows that had initially chased off the bluebirds had recently migrated over to the big-box home improvement store that had just opened down the road. The house sparrows loved to fly into the garden section, peck open the bags of birdseed, and scrounge for discarded crumbs left by shoppers in the parking lots.

"Thank heavens for Lowe's," Tom said. "They're going to give your bluebirds a fighting chance."

Her bluebirds. Not *our* bluebirds. But of course. Why would he say "our" bluebirds?

"We've put out the right kind of birdbaths." Another tick of his fingers as he waved at the three shallow birdbaths with gently sloping sides and a rough surface to provide good footing. He changed the water in the birdbaths every time he mowed, and they'd positioned the baths at least fifteen feet away from any of the peach trees where cats could hide.

"And," he finished, flaring out his thumb to join his raised fingers. "We've planted blackberry bushes because bluebirds love 'em."

"But we won't see any blackberries before late May," she pointed out. What she didn't say was, *will you still be around then?*

He extended the index finger of his other hand, marking off the sixth measure that he and Savannah's brother had brainstormed over dinner. "We've faced the entrance holes to the east because bluebirds prefer the morning sun more than some species, and it shelters them from prevailing winds."

Felicity cocked her head, admiring how his eyes sparkled when he talked about the bluebirds. She moved closer to Tom. She couldn't seem to stay away. The thought that he would eventually leave kept stabbing at her heart with sharp little knife cuts. After the past two weeks, she'd gotten used to having him beside her, gotten used to working as a team to lure the bluebirds back to Bluebird Way.

It had been fun and exciting, and she'd come to depend on him.

She should have known better, had known better, but she'd allowed herself to fall for him anyway.

"We added a longer roof to the houses and a longer lip

under it so the birds have to go up and under to get to the hole. That will discourage tree swallows because they prefer a straight shot." He had seven digits in the air, her amateur ornithologist.

"And, we painted bluebirds on the boxes." Felicity giggled. "I know that probably doesn't matter, but seeing the bluebirds on the birdhouses makes me happy."

"A form of positive thinking." Tom nodded and held up eight fingers. "We stenciled a dark faux entrance hole on the roof as an attraction spot to indicate to passing birds it's a nesting cavity." Nine fingers now.

"Plus we painted the front a lighter blue to make the actual dark entrance more visible." Felicity bent to trace a finger around the opening of a nearby birdhouse.

"We've done all we can do," Tom concluded, holding up both hands, all fingers splayed wide. "Nothing left to do but sit back, cross our fingers, and wait."

"*We're* going to sit and wait? As in you and me?"

He looked uncomfortable. "I didn't . . . I . . ."

"I was just wondering how long you're planning to stay," she said lightly, as if she didn't care. "You said it could be years before the bluebirds come back. Are you planning on hanging around in Serendipity for that long?"

Oh gosh, why had she asked that?

Tom stepped nearer, dipped his head, pressed his mouth to her ear, murmured, "This place is special. Just like you. The bluebirds will show up whether I'm here or not."

His knuckles lightly grazed her breasts. So lightly she couldn't decide if it was accidental or on purpose. His touch felt so good, she had to bite down on her lip to keep from groaning.

"Don't say sweet things like that." She shifted away from him.

"Why not?" He sounded perplexed.

"We've been building birdhouses, but . . ." Felicity trailed off.

"What?"

She shrugged, couldn't meet the heat of his stare. "When you say things like that it makes me believe we're building something more."

He let go of her waist, and the absence of his arm stirred a fierce loneliness inside her.

Her feelings took her breath away. She could hardly stand the pain of it. "Tell me more about bluebirds," she said, to distract herself.

He looked relieved that she'd changed the topic. "Bluebirds are recognized everywhere as symbols of happiness. Almost all birds have some negative legend or myth attached to them, but not bluebirds. Bluebirds are family-oriented, and they are only found in North America. . . ."

He went on, but Felicity didn't hear what he was saying; she was too caught up in watching the utter joy on his face when he talked about the birds. In that moment, she knew exactly what he must have been like as an enthusiastic little boy looking up birds in the bird book he'd told her that he used to carry around with him everywhere he went. She could almost see him, binoculars around his neck, tramping through the woods, on the hunt for some rare species in whatever country he found himself living at the time.

A strange sensation tugged at the bottom of her stomach, and she felt an overwhelming sense of sadness. The baby she'd lost had been a boy. She would never have a chance to teach a child about the joys of watching bluebirds, never have a baby of her own.

She *was* jinxed, and that was the truth of it.

"You're crying," Tom said, sounding alarmed.

She shook her head because she couldn't speak, her throat clogged with tears. Damn it. Why was she so overcome?

"Felicity?" He came toward her. "Are you hurt?"

How could she explain to him all that she'd lost? All the things she'd never had. Could not have. Yes, she'd told him about her past, her unlucky history, her inability to have children. But she'd glossed over it, had spoken quietly and straightforwardly about her life as if it had happened to someone else, as if she was well and truly over it.

But she was not. She still had that ghost of a sonogram in the back of her reservation book. Haunting her with all the things she could not have.

He reached out a hand to touch her, but in that moment, she could not bear his sympathy. The pity in his eyes.

Pulse pounding, an unnamed fear coursing through her blood, she turned and fled to the house.

But Tom wasn't going to let her get away with running off. She heard him come after her. Not quickly, but steadily. He was following her. His footsteps breaking fallen peach twigs with a sound like snapping bones in the quiet morning air.

She ran into the house, stood in the dining nook, suddenly frozen, legs wobbly, heart pounding.

He came up the back steps and opened the door.

Her gaze seared into his, hot as a branding iron. Her heart bubbled like champagne, sparkly and delicate.

The sun was to Tom's back, casting his face in shadow. His broad shoulders filled the door frame; his tanned hands, roughened by callous and nicked with scars from years of hard work, dangled loosely at his sides.

Her breath caught at the beauty of his rugged masculinity. Short black hair sprinkled with gray, a beard stubble salting his angular jaw because he hadn't shaved that morning. His beguiling smile, those astute dark eyes.

Handsomer than Steve. Taller too. Heartier.

She'd never found Steve lacking, but her late husband paled in comparison to the bundle of testosterone standing in the doorway. Immediately, she felt disloyal and guilty and any number of uncomfortable things, primarily among them, an irresistible attraction to Tom Loving.

The Army had honed and shaped him into a warrior, but there was a natural gentleness to him that he'd managed to hang onto. She admired how he could turn tough or tender depending on the situation.

His eyes pierced her, sharp as laser beams. It was as if he knew everything about her, all her flaws, mistakes, and misdeeds, and liked her anyway.

It was too much. His understanding.

Felicity let out a cry of pain and dropped down into the kitchen chair. How could he understand the depths of her sorrow, when she herself did not?

Why was she doing this? Breaking down for no discernible reason. Yes, there were things she would never be able to have, but she had been so very lucky. She'd been loved. Deeply, fully.

It hit her then. The root of her sorrow.

She missed being loved like that. With so much devotion and intensity. In Tom, she saw the potential to have such love again, but she dared not hope for it.

Lightning had indeed struck twice, and she wasn't the least bit prepared for it.

She sank her hands into her upturned palms, did not want to sob. Tried to hold it back, but the tears were rain, pouring down her face.

He came and stood next to her, but did not touch her. Just his presence. Standing there. Holding space for her grief. Breathing audibly, long and slow and deep. A sweet soothing rhythm of breath. A mountain of man, steady, immovable, rock solid.

Her body quivered, wracked with grief.

Tom squatted beside her, patted his shoulders with crisscrossed arms. "I've got some pretty big shoulders if you need to cry on them."

The next thing she knew she was in his arms, sitting on his strong thigh, head on his shoulder, sobbing uncontrollably. She cried and cried and cried as all her sorrows washed over her. Dampening his white T-shirt with tears.

And finally, she could cry no more, her body limp and wrung out.

He just held her. Calmly. Quietly. Powerfully.

In his arms, she felt safe in a way she hadn't felt since her mother died. He was a comfort. A strength she hadn't known she needed.

He cradled her head in his palm, held her as if he could wait here all day if she needed, crouching, her arms around his neck, her fanny resting on his thigh. Hungry for more, eager to have the man she'd been dreaming of for sixteen long days, Felicity raised her face to his.

"Make love to me, Tom," she begged. "Please, make love to me now."

Chapter Eight

No matter how much he wanted to, Tom knew that he could not make love to Felicity. She was vulnerable. Hurting. He didn't know why, but he didn't need the answers to understand she was in pain. Did it really matter what was the cause?

She was seeking comfort, not sex. Even if she might think otherwise, he knew better. Her request to make love stemmed from a place of loss and lack, and he didn't want to take advantage. Didn't want it for either of them. When he finally made love to her, he wanted pure, unbridled electricity. He wanted them both strong and powerful and knowing exactly what they were getting into, eyes wide open.

Slowly, he shook his head, eased her off his lap, and set her gently aside. Managed to stand from a crouching position without losing his balance. "Now is not the time."

Felicity stared up at him, her blue eyes wet and baffled, so lost in her world of sorrow he wasn't sure she heard him.

How easy it would be to scoop her into his arms and take her to bed. He wanted her as much as she wanted him. Probably more. He'd wanted her from the moment he first saw her, smiling at him from behind the reception desk as if just by walking through the door he'd made her day. From the very beginning, whenever he was around her, he felt manly, desirable.

Heady stuff.

Her mouth dropped open, a perfect circle of surprise. "Oh," she said, then again, "Oh." Her tone flattening out, deepening, shifting from confused to hurt.

Tom could tell from that one word spoken twice that she took his refusal to mean that he did not want her.

Her cheeks reddened as if she'd been scalded, and she slammed her lips together.

"Felicity," he murmured, keeping his voice soft, even. He reached out a hand to reassure her, but she spun from his touch.

She was embarrassed. From her point of view, she'd put herself out there, and he'd rejected her. Tom fought the urge to gather her in his arms again, knew it would only make things worse. He hated so much that he'd caused her to doubt herself, feel foolish and ashamed. She might be perky and bouncy and full of pep and heart, but she was a sensitive soul. Empathetic and attuned to the needs of others. Sweet and kind and just plain nice.

And he'd hurt her.

Christ, he'd made a mess of things.

Not a mess, he corrected. This could be fixed. He'd do whatever it took to fix it.

"I get it," she said. "No need to explain. You're just not that into me."

"No," he said, his tone coming out harsher than he intended. "That's not it at all."

"If you say, 'it's not you, it's me,' I'm going to slug you," she warned, fire igniting her flame-blue eyes.

"You've never slugged anyone in your entire life," he said confidently.

She sank her hands on her hips and scowled at him. "Yes, well, there's a first time for everything."

He wanted to smile at her fierceness, but knew that now was not the time. "I should find somewhere else to stay."

"You're leaving?" Her face paled, eyes clouded, shoulders slumped. She looked both bruised and defeated. "Why?"

His heart hammered. Because if he didn't get out of here, he was going to sweep her into his arms, take her to the bedroom, and make love to her, whether it was smart or not.

He tried to think of a way to say it so that she wouldn't take it personally. "Because we're finished"—*not* finished, *don't* say finished—"there's nothing more we can do to lure the bluebirds back. It's just a waiting game now."

She slanted her head, studied him with somber, sad, serious eyes. "I see."

It was as if she could see right through him. Past the excuses and lies he'd been telling himself. His throat tightened, and he started to sweat.

"Do I get to weigh in on this?" she asked.

"Nothing to weigh in on. It's time for me to go."

His words brought a fresh round of red to her cheeks. Her chin firmed, and her spine straightened. "You don't have to run away. I promise you won't have to worry about my throwing myself at you again."

"It's not that—"

Her blush darkened, but being Felicity, she plunged ahead courageously. "Is it because I started crying? You don't want to deal with a weeping woman, is that it? I'm too much trouble?"

"Huh? No. It's not that. You're good." *Good?* Christ, he was mangling this. Why couldn't he handle this with grace and style? She deserved grace and style. How about, *you are the most fascinating, amazing, awesome woman I have ever met, and I don't deserve you?*

The thought of making love to her drove him insane. Didn't she get that? Didn't she understand how hard it was for him to hold on to his last shreds of control?

"Felicity, I consider your tears a gift." He touched his

shirt, still damp from where she'd wept on him. "I'm not scared of them."

She looked bewildered. Yeah, no wonder. He was pretty damn bewildered himself.

"You trusted me enough to fully let go. That's big. Huge."

"So what's the problem?"

He clenched his fingers into fists to keep from touching her, let his arms dangle at his sides. No way around it. He was going to have to face the truth.

"I can't make love to you," he said. "Not because *I can't*; I can. . . . Rather, I *won't*. You deserve someone for a lifetime, and I can't offer that."

"Good grief." She snorted, her hands back on her hips, looked offended. "I'm not asking for anything beyond a great time in bed."

Tom pressed the heel of his palm against his forehead. He was messing this up, big time. "It's not just about sex. You're a widow who was married to the love of your life. I'm the guy who couldn't make marriage work. You deserve someone who can put down roots with you . . . and I'm . . . well, I'm not the kind who sticks around."

"That's what my aunt Molly said about you."

Tom winced, surprised by how much this hurt, but he was making the right choice . . . trying to make the right choice . . . for both of them. Felicity was wedded to this place, this town. Any man who wanted to be with her needed to understand that if he stayed with her, he was committing to Serendipity, and to a life running a B&B, living in a fishbowl.

She's worth it, whispered a voice in his head. *She's your salvation.* Yes, but was he hers?

"Your aunt makes a good point," Tom said. "The thing is, Felicity, I can't make a commitment to you, to anyone right now. I don't even have a job. I have nothing to offer you but sex, and, even though you say that's all you want, I know it's not true." He paused. "And so do you."

Her eyes turned steely, and her chin hardened. She crossed her arms over her chest. "Okay then."

"I'm going to go pack."

"You do that." She turned away from him, but not before he saw fresh tears shimmering in her eyes.

They were a knife to his gut, those tears, but he couldn't back down now. He'd convinced her that it was best for her to let him go. Now, the hard part.

Convincing himself.

It was only after Tom packed up his meager duffel bag, told her one last good-bye, and walked out of the house that Felicity understood why she'd broken down in helpless tears.

It was April 9th.

Her baby's due date.

Stephen Michael Patterson would have been four years old today if he'd been born on schedule, and she hadn't lost him.

The realization caught her low in the belly, and Felicity had to sit down in the rolling leather chair behind the reception desk, or risk falling over. She'd wanted to have sex with Tom as a way to salve the old, open wound that still hadn't fully scabbed over.

Thank God, he'd had the presence of mind to turn her down. He was right. Sex today would have been a disaster.

Why then did his rejection and departure hurt so damn much?

The light on the voice mail machine blinked at her. Two messages. How long had the messages been there? She and Tom had been having so much fun together; it had been days since she'd checked.

All the more reason to be grateful that he'd gone. He'd

been a huge distraction, and her business was struggling enough as it was.

She punched the message button, heard the first message spin out into the room. "Hello, my name is Jane Cowden. I need to cancel the reservation for my December wedding. . . ."

Felicity stabbed the "erase" button. Listened to the next message.

"Felicity, this is Mary at Dr. Honeywell's office. He's concerned about your mammogram results. Could you please call the office so we can schedule a biopsy within the next couple of weeks? No reason for alarm. This happens a lot. Eighty percent of the time, the lump is benign."

Lump.

Felicity slapped both hands to her breasts.

Eighty percent of the time, benign.

She closed her eyes, exhaled. Heard another statistic. *Less than twenty percent of miscarriages happen after the first trimester.*

Yes, she'd been on the wrong side of the statistics then. What made her think these odds would be any different.

Feeling as if she'd driven headlong off a cliff, Felicity sat in the chair, her entire body shaking. A one-word mantra circled around and around inside her head—*jinxed, jinxed, jinxed.*

This was it. Her past was gone. Her future was crumbling, and her present? Well, it was pretty damned miserable.

"No more of self-pity," she scolded, picked up the reservation book, and flipped to December to cross off Jane Cowden's reservation.

And there she found the baby's sonogram stuck to the calendar.

The tears rushed back, fresh and cathartic.

Felicity rested her head on the desk and listened to the sound of the wall clock ticking. A big old-fashioned clock with a second hand that jumped in stiff jerks as it marked off each passing second.

The noise filled her head until all she could hear was *tick, tick, tick.*

Time passing. Flying by her. Leaving her with nothing.

Gone. All the things she'd once held on to were gone, but she'd been unable to let them go. That's why she was stuck. She couldn't embrace the future as long as she had both hands grasping the past.

Tom was right. She knew the rambling man thing was just an excuse, an easy out. The real reason he was keeping her at arms' length was that he knew he couldn't compete with those memories she wouldn't release.

Until she could accept what had happened to her and let go of her grief, she never would find happiness.

That was the real jinx.

Living in the past.

Felicity picked up the sonogram. Studied it for a long moment, traced a finger over it. Shed a few more tears.

"Good-bye, sweetheart," she whispered. "Mommy will always love you, but it's time to let you go. It's not fair to either of us for me to keep holding on. Fly, my little angel. Fly high with the bluebirds."

Then summoning every ounce of courage that she had in her, Felicity spun in the chair and slowly fed the sonogram into the paper shredder.

Tom went to see Joe. He had no one else to turn to.

Oh, sure, he had friends he could call. People he usually met for beers or ball games. He could have gotten a motel room. Or left Serendipity entirely. But he couldn't bring himself to go when he'd left things in such a mess with Felicity.

The problem was, he had no idea how to fix things.

And he needed someone to talk to about it.

Joe had taken one look at Tom standing on the front porch of the Loving mansion, his duffel bag thrown over his shoulder, the Ducati parked in the driveway, and waved him inside, then hollered up the stairs, "Marion, make up the guest room."

Tom stayed for two weeks with his brother. At loose ends about what to do with his life, he hid out on the ranch. Helping Joe. Bonding with his brother. Avoiding going into Serendipity in case he came across Felicity.

Thinking about her turned him inside out as he vacillated between coulda, woulda, shoulda. What would have happened if he'd stayed? If he'd made love to her? Was it that he was afraid of hurting her? Or was the truth something much more selfish? Was it that Tom was terrified that making love to her would change him in ways he wasn't ready to be changed?

He heard back on one of the four resumes he'd sent out. A position working for a military contractor on the West Coast. He turned it down.

Joe raised an eyebrow when Tom told him about it, but didn't say anything else. Just kept shoveling out the horse stall he was working on.

When Tom turned down the second offer, Joe grunted.

After the third offer, Joe finally said, while they were watching baseball in the den, "I love having you around, little brother. Stay as long as you want, but what the hell are you holding out for?"

"Dream job," Tom mumbled, cracking open a pistachio.

"And that is?"

"Something where I'm never stationary. I'm holding my breath for that crisis response position working for the UN."

Joe grunted. "Ironic."

"What is?"

"You're holding out for a job where you jump into the middle of other people's crises, but you can't even manage your own."

"I'm not having a crisis," Tom disagreed.

Joe shook his head. "You sure?"

"I'm perfectly fine."

Joe threw a couch cushion at him. "Not from where I'm sitting."

Tom caught the pillow with one hand before Joe knocked over his beer bottle. "So tell me, big brother, since you know everything. What's my crisis?"

Joe's smile was doofus big, and he affected a pronounced redneck drawl. "Why you're scared shitless because you've done gone and fallen in love with Felicity Patterson."

The following morning, a bouquet of Felicity's favorite wildflowers—bluebonnets and Indian paintbrushes and black-eyed Susans—clutched in his hand, Tom mounted the steps of the B&B, mentally rehearsing his apology. *I'm sorry; please forgive me; I love you.*

Should he just blurt it out like that? Should there be more of a lead-up? A longer apology? More of an explanation?

Before he had a chance to figure it out, the front door opened, and Felicity's Aunt Molly emerged, a worried frown on her face.

"Oh!" Aunt Molly started, house keys in her hand, and pressed her free palm over her heart. "You about scared me out of my skin."

"I didn't mean to frighten you."

"Sorry, my mind is somewhere else." Aunt Molly turned and locked the front door.

"What's going on?" Tom asked, tightening his grip on the bouquet.

"Felicity sent me over to check to see if she left the stove on, but I think it was just a ploy to get me out of the hospital waiting room. She knows how much I hate hospitals. And she's never in her life done something so careless as to leave the stove on. She's a cautious one, that Felicity. But this morning was so hectic, I thought maybe . . ."

"Wait, what?" Tom's heart slammed against his rib cage. "Felicity is in the hospital?"

"She's having a breast biopsy. I'm on my way back over there—"

"I'll go," Tom said. "You stay here and look after the Bluebird."

"Really?" Aunt Molly looked utterly relieved. "That would be amazing. Did I mention I hate hospitals? Ever since my sister . . ." She waved a hand, shooing off the past. "Never mind that. Go. Felicity is in outpatient surgery. I'll turn down her bed so it will be all comfy for her when you bring our girl home."

Our girl. As if she belonged to them both.

It felt good. Right. That belonging.

And Tom couldn't get to the hospital fast enough.

Chapter Nine

"Morning, Sunshine," greeted the smiling nurse as she pulled aside the privacy curtain. "Are you a little more awake now?"

Felicity nodded, trying to shake off the effects of the anesthesia. She couldn't wait to get out of here and back home.

"You came through with flying colors," the nurse went on, leaning over to press the button on the monitor that caused the blood pressure cuff on Felicity's arm to inflate. "The procedure went smooth as silk, but we won't have the results of the biopsy until tomorrow at the earliest, but it could take longer than that depending on how backed up the lab is."

Felicity touched the small bandage on her right breast at the biopsy site.

"Try not to worry." The nurse's smile was compassionate, encouraging. "Eighty percent of the time, these lumps are benign."

"Thanks," Felicity mumbled, not the least bit comforted.

"By the way, you have a visitor." The nurse recorded the blood pressure reading on the computer keyboard attached to the screen mounted to the wall above the gurney. "Are you ready?"

It must be Aunt Molly. Felicity nodded again, sat up higher in bed.

The nurse left, pulling the curtain closed behind her. In a few minutes, the curtain moved again, and Felicity put on her brightest smile for her aunt.

Except it wasn't Aunt Molly.

Tom stood there in starched jeans and white, button-down shirt with the sleeves rolled up, dark eyes solemn, looking uncertain, as if he were searching for an uncomplicated mercy in a world filled with obstacles, as he held up his little wild bouquet.

She lost her breath.

"Hello," he said.

"Hi," she whispered.

"You look beautiful."

His grin reeled her in. She laughed, ran a hand through her hair. She had on no makeup and was in a notoriously un-flattering hospital gown.

"I brought wildflowers." He thrust them toward her.

"I can see that."

"I'll just . . ." He cast around the small space, looked at a loss. "Um . . ." He approached the bedside table. "Put them here."

"Thank you." She smiled again, amused by his awkward-ness.

He set the flowers on the table, clasped his hands behind his back, shifted from foot to foot. "How are you doing?"

She gave him a tight smile, shook her head. "I'll bounce back."

"My little Super Ball."

My little Super Ball? Felicity's heart flipped over in her chest. Twice. *Don't read anything into it. He didn't mean anything by it.*

"How are you?" she asked.

"I'm not the one in a hospital bed."

"They'll be letting me go within the hour," she said. "So I won't be here for long."

"Why didn't you tell me you were having a biopsy?"

"We haven't spoken in two weeks."

"You could have called," he said.

"You're the one who said you were moving on."

He ran a hand over his jaw. "I handled that poorly. I was running scared."

"I know."

"I've never . . . since my divorce . . . You're the first woman that I've wanted."

"Wait a minute. Are you saying you haven't been with a woman in the seven years you've been divorced?"

He nodded.

"Seven years without sex?"

"What can I say? It was easier to avoid all that drama and focus on my career. Until I retired." He inhaled deeply, eased down on the side of the gurney. His butt was touching her thigh. It felt intimate and sweet all at the same time. "Until you."

Their eyes met.

"Suddenly, the world was filled with all these possibilities I never considered before, and dammit, you scared me because I was feeling things again. Things I'd been afraid to feel because I didn't want to get hurt again."

"And you think I did?"

"No, no, it's just that you feel so deeply, and care so much for people. I wasn't sure I could give you the kind of love you needed."

Love?

Felicity inhaled sharply. What was he saying?

His eyes searched her face, his expression raw and vulnerable. "I want a do-over. Please give me a second chance."

"What's changed?"

He reached over and took her palm in his warm, strong hand. "Me."

"How did you change?"

"You're not going to make this easy, are you?"

"No way." She graced him with a small, but encouraging grin. "Like you said, I deserve the best."

"Yes," he said. "I just pray I can live up to your expectations."

"Tom," she said. "It's not my expectations you have to live up to. It's your own. I accept you completely for who you are."

"You are such a wonderful person," he said. "Because of you, I've had an epiphany. I realized I've been spending my life hiding from complications. From family drama. From messy emotions. Even when I was married, I wasn't fully invested, which was why my ex-wife cheated on me. She tried to explain it, but I put all the blame on her. That wasn't fair. I had a hand in it too. If I'd loved her the way she deserved to be loved, she wouldn't have had to go looking for love somewhere else."

"And now?"

"This is not a romantic place to tell you, but I can't wait any longer. It happened quick and I fell hard, but I love you, Felicity Patterson, and I want to be with you for the rest of my life. What do you have to say about that?"

Her pulse hammered in her throat. Her palm went sweaty between his hands gripping hers. It was everything she wanted to hear from him and more, so much more. But she couldn't accept his proclamation of love.

"I'm sorry, Tom," she said. "But I just can't afford to let myself love you."

Her words were a sword, running him straight through. He'd gone out on a limb, told her exactly how he felt about her, and she'd sawed the branch right out from under him.

"What are you saying? That you don't love me?"

"I'm saying let's just enjoy each other right now, Tom. Be in the moment. I'm not in a position to ask for or accept anything more than that. Please just take me home and make love to me and let it be enough. That's all I ever wanted from you."

"What if that's not enough for me?" His voice cracked like brittle ice, startling them both. "What if I want forever?"

"There's no such thing," she said, her own voice soft and dull.

It dawned on him then, what was going on. She was as terrified of this relationship as he was, but for a different reason. "It's because of the biopsy, isn't it? You're worried you have cancer."

She swallowed so hard her throat quivered visibly, nodded. "I . . . can't invest in anything permanent."

"That doesn't make any sense," he said, feeling his own throat tighten as he scrambled for ways to convince her of the wrongness of her thinking. "What if it's benign? Odds are it's benign."

"What if it's not?"

"Okay, let's look at that. Odds are they caught it early, you'll get treatment and live to be a very old woman."

"I can't begin to tell you how many times I've been on the wrong side of the odds," she said, and retold him the story of her birth. "I'm jinxed."

Jinxed.

He hadn't taken her seriously when she'd told him that the first time. He'd assumed in her heart of hearts she truly didn't believe it, but apparently she did.

Then one by one, she listed all the awful things that had happened to her. The deaths, the losses, the disappointments. Too many for someone so young.

"All right." He squeezed her hand tightly. "Worse-case scenario. It *is* cancer, it's bad, and you're going to die. Wouldn't you rather spend those last days with someone you love?"

"No!" Her vehement tone turned him inside out. "I watched my husband die of cancer, in pain, fading away bit by bit, and I'll be damned if I'll do that to you." She pulled her hand from his, tears in her eyes. "I love you too much for that."

Wow. Tom dropped his hands at his sides, pulled in a deep breath.

"Here's the deal, Loving," she said. "If you want to be with me, you can take me home and make love to me and don't speak another word about the future, or you can hit the road."

"I don't get a say in this?"

"You do not."

The curtain drew back, and a bubbly nurse appeared with a wheelchair. "You ready to go home?"

Felicity's eyes met Tom's. "What is it, Loving? Are you ready to go with me?"

Tom didn't flinch. This was a tough time for her, and he had to respect what she was going through. He'd take what he could get, and maybe somewhere along the way he could convince her to change her mind.

"Sweetheart," he said. "I'm all in."

When they pulled into the driveway of the Bluebird Inn, Felicity could have sworn she saw a flash of blue zip by. Her heart fluttered in her chest at the possibility.

"Was that a bluebird?" she asked Tom.

"I don't know," he said. "Was it?"

"Let's go see." She hopped out of the car.

"Slow down," he said, following her. "You just had surgery."

"Biopsy. Minor. I'm fine." She plunged ahead, plowing through the garden gate, Tom on her heels.

He caught up to her by the time she reached the edge of the peach orchard. Felicity stopped in her tracks.

For there, flitting among the birdhouses, were dozens of bluebirds.

A shiver of joy passed over her. The moment was so miraculous that she dug her fingernails into her palms to see if she was dreaming.

"Look," she whispered. "Just look at all the bluebirds!"

"Wow," he breathed, slipping an arm around her waist. "We did it," he whispered. "We brought the bluebirds home."

Home.

Such a lovely word, warm and hopeful and full of promise.

This place was her home . . . but not his. Maybe it could be if she stopped pushing him away. Stopped erecting those boundaries to protect her heart. He said he'd had an epiphany, and she believed him.

"This is amazing," he said. "Absolutely amazing."

"They're here. You brought them back. You did this."

"*We* did this."

"So much happiness," she whispered. "It's magic." Did she dare hope that with the coming of the bluebirds, her jinx had been broken?

For a long time, they stood in the orchard, hugging each other, watching the bluebirds flit in and out of the peach trees. There were things they did not say. He was a solitary, independent man, and she had to admire that. She wished she could be so self-contained, but she needed people. Always had, always would.

"They are such a good omen." Tom tightened his grip around her waist, pulled her closer. "I take this as a sign everything is going to be fine."

He didn't say the word *biopsy*, but she knew what he meant.

"The best omen," she whispered, locking eyes with the man who'd brought her back to life. She wanted him to kiss her, make love to her so badly she couldn't stand it.

Feeling air-starved and dizzy, Felicity realized she'd been holding her breath. She exhaled deeply. Her skin felt cool, but, inside her, blood pumped wild and hot.

In soft sunlight he smiled at her, and she could see that he was feeling it too.

He held out his hand, and her heart thudded crazily. His lashes lowered to half-mast over bedroom eyes.

Shakily, she reached out and took that warm, welcoming palm.

Tom interlaced their fingers, pointed at the bluebird perched in the doorway of one of the nesting boxes. "Just look at what we did. You and me. We can build anything together."

Suddenly shy, she briefly dropped her head to his shoulder.

"And here I was skeptical that you could really bring the bluebirds home."

"Oh ye of little faith," he said softly, and led her up the steps to the back door. "Together we can do anything."

She hesitated on the threshold.

"What is it?" he whispered, his eyes shining bright with desire.

"I'm glad you gave Savannah the keys to your Ducati. I know you feel bad about it. I know it was rough on Chance—"

"And you." He squeezed her hand gently.

"But if you hadn't given her the keys, she might not have had the courage to go through with it, and, if she hadn't run away, Savannah would be miserable and Chance would be miserable and you wouldn't have had anything to feel guilty about and you never would have stayed and we never would have had . . ." Felicity swallowed, met his eyes, squeezed his hand right back. "This."

"Felicity," he whispered, and her name on his tongue filled her with longing so thick and hard she couldn't speak. "I want to kiss you more than I want to breathe. May I kiss you?"

"Please," she said. "Oh, please do."

He swept her into his arms, their bodies in full contact. He buried his nose in her hair, took a deep breath. Laughed. "You smell so good. Like flowers and sunshine."

"So do you." She giggled and looked deeply into his friendly eyes that offered so much love. She opened her mouth, waited.

He dipped his head.

Her heart was hammering, knocking and knocking and knocking.

His kiss was light, exploring, as if memorizing every part of her—lips, tongue, teeth. As if wanting this to last a lifetime. His chest rose and fell against her breasts with every breath he took.

Her body melted into his. She felt boneless. Liquid. Like stardust and rainbows.

Tom swayed with her in his arms, rocking her, his mouth still on a great getting-to-know-you-better adventure. He tasted of peppermint and salt, cool and earthy.

Salt of the earth, she thought dizzily, and went up on tiptoes, telegraphing that it was okay to take the kiss deeper.

But instead, he stepped back, bent down, and scooped her into his arms.

"Oops, whoa!" She giggled. "What are you doing?"

"Sweeping you off your feet."

He carried her to the front porch and only set her down because she kept insisting. They were still high on bluebird magic.

"Are we all alone?" he asked.

"No guests," she said. "But Aunt Molly might be here."

"Her car wasn't in the drive."

"She lives three doors down. She usually walks."

"Her car was in the drive when I came by earlier."

Felicity opened the back door, stuck her head in. "Aunt Molly?"

No answer.

"Aunt Molly?" she called again, louder this time.

Silence.

"I think the coast is clear." She turned back to Tom, touched his back, felt his warmth through his cotton shirt. "So where is that kiss you promised me?"

He dipped his head, and she leaned in to kiss him softly.

Tom kissed her back, and, when they came up for air, he whispered, "That's the second best kiss I ever got."

"What was the first?"

"The first time I kissed you."

"Really? Second best? I can't top the first time? At this rate, the hundredth kiss will be one hundredth best."

"Nah, just means we'll have to work harder to make each kiss more special than the last."

"Oh, game on, buddy." She kissed him again, throwing in every ounce of passion she had inside her. She wanted forever, but she wouldn't ask for it. Couldn't ask for it until she knew for sure the lump wasn't cancerous. In the meantime, there was nothing wrong with celebrating the return of the bluebirds by loving each other's bodies fully and completely.

Leisurely, as if the world were their oyster and time, that abstract concept, had ceased to exist, he braced her against the door frame, and they kissed on the back stoop.

"Hey," he whispered. "Look up."

Felicity raised her head. Perched on the roof gutter above them were two bluebirds. He slipped his arm around her waist again, and they stood holding each other and admiring the bluebirds, until finally the birds flitted back to the peach orchard.

"If there was only one thing in the world that could make you happy," she whispered, "what would it be?"

His smile was tender, soft-edged. "Being with you. No, not just being with you, but really being together. A couple. Man and wife. Because, sweetheart, I will never love anyone the way I love you."

"Even if I have cancer?"

"No matter what, Felicity. There's a reason they say in sickness and in health. I mean it, no matter what, I'm all in."

"Oh, Tom," she said, and kissed him again, the way she'd been aching to kiss him from the minute he'd walked into the inn. "Why are we standing outside talking, when we could be inside making love?"

"Sweetheart," he whispered, "I thought you'd never ask."

Chapter Ten

Tom and Felicity celebrated the return of the bluebirds in the best way possible.

In her bed.

Tom undressed her tenderly, filled with concern for her health. She assured him she was fine and that she wanted this more than she wanted to breathe. She stood naked before him, feeling completely comfortable and at ease, knowing this was the right thing.

He smiled down at her with such love in his eyes she could scarcely believe how lucky she was. In the tree outside her window, she could hear the sweet warble of a bluebird, and she matched Tom's smile.

"I can't believe how beautiful you are." He tugged her into his arms. "I love to feel your heart beating against mine."

"Oh, Tom."

He bestowed on her a hundred kisses, each more passionate than the last. "Making up for lost time," he gasped, then dove in again for more.

Tom delivered a merry-go-round of kisses until they were both giddy and dizzy with it. He dropped down on one knee.

"Are you okay," she asked, grasping his shoulders, her head spinning, her lips swollen and tingly.

"Marry me, Felicity."

"What are you doing?" A bit of panic set in. "You promised we'd be in the moment."

"I am in the moment. This glorious, rare moment when I'm asking you to marry me. I don't have a ring, and I'll do it up proper later, but I don't want to make love to you until I know you're in this as much as I am."

"Ask me again after we find out the biopsy is benign."

"No," he said. "I've been thinking about this. I want you to be my wife. Just as you are. I love you and I need you and I want you and there's no sense in holding back. We've already spent two weeks apart, and that's far too long. Say you'll marry me, Felicity. Make me the happiest man on earth."

"Tom—"

"I want to wake up to you every morning, go to bed with you every night. I want to stop rambling and settle down with you. You're my anchor, Felicity, my lifeline."

"And if I'm sick?"

"We'll deal with it and live every moment as if it's our last. That's what we'll do no matter what."

"What if I'm not sick and somewhere along the line you decide you want children?"

"I already do want children. We'll adopt."

Adopt! Her heart leapt at the thought of having her deepest dreams come true. A man who loved her and children to call her own? It was almost too good to be true. Did she dare hope she could have it all?

"What if you want *biological* children?"

"Stop stalling with the *what ifs*." His tone was firm, but his smile was gentle. "Nothing is guaranteed. All we know is that we love each other right here, right now. That's enough for me. Is it enough for you?"

Tears misted her eyes. He stood up and she wrapped her arms around him and kissed him until neither one of them could catch his or her breath. She was madly in love with this sweet, wonderful man.

"Say it," he gasped.

"Yes, Tom," she said because she could resist him no longer. Didn't want to resist. Wanted to fall headlong into the dizzy whirlpool of his love. "Yes, I'll marry you."

He took her hand and led her over to the bed. She undressed him, slowly, filled with delight at everything she discovered. Once he was naked, they tumbled onto the bed together, smiling at the happiness they'd found and giggling with excitement.

Felicity felt as if she'd been a wilted flower, dehydrated and thirsty, and Tom the life-giving water that roused her. He touched her everywhere, kissing her all over her body, in warm secret places that sent shivers through her, loving her the way she'd dreamed of.

They weren't kids anymore. They were mature adults who'd weathered life's slings and arrows, but that was what made this beautiful second chance so much richer than anything they'd ever experienced before.

Truly, they were in the moment. No thoughts of a future or past. Absorbed in the timelessness of each other. Wrapped up in the physical, mental, and emotional expression of their newfound love.

Bluebirds sang outside the window serenaded their joining, and, when it was over, they lay in each other's arms, spent and spooning close. He curled himself around her, moved her hair aside to kiss the back of her neck.

"How are you doing?" he asked, his hand carefully touching the small bandage over the biopsy site.

"Wonderful, perfect. No pain at all."

"That's awesome," he said. "You want to do it again?"

"You're up for that?" She giggled. "At forty-two?"

He pressed his hips against her, and she discovered, that oh, my yes, he was definitely up for another round. "When I'm with you, I feel twenty-two."

Tom turned her in his arms, kissed her hard and long, lit a toasty hot fire inside her again, and they were off once more on the magic of their love. This time was slow and tender as they explored the map of each other's bodies, learning, revering, cherishing the beautiful, abiding present.

The third time, near midnight, was a blaze of unending passion, the culmination of everything that had gone before. The crescendo to the opus of their love story. Their bodies intertwined, their hearts beating together, souls connected in an irrevocable way.

Just before she fell into a deep, untroubled slumber, Tom kissed her forehead and said, "You are the best thing that has ever happened to me, Felicity Patterson, and I will love you to the end of my days."

They woke the next morning to the smell of coffee, bacon, and eggs. They sat up at the same time, looking at each other, wide-eyed and ravenous.

"Who's in the house?" Tom asked.

Felicity threw on a bathrobe, just as a knock sounded on the door. Tom pulled the sheet up to his neck.

She opened the door, peeked out.

There was Aunt Molly with a tray of food. Two plates and a small vase with a red rosebud cut from the garden.

"Breakfast in bed is in order," Aunt Molly said efficiently.

"Mmm, why is that?" Felicity stood so that she blocked her aunt's view of the room.

"Well, for one thing, you finally have a man in your bed again. Hi, Tom."

"Hi, Molly," Tom called out from behind Felicity.

Aunt Molly smiled slyly. "I'm happy for you both."

"You warned me off Tom, remember?"

"That's before I knew he had staying power."

"How do you know he has staying power?" Felicity accepted the tray her aunt passed to her.

"He didn't tell you he registered to get his master's degree at TCU?"

"Thanks for spoiling the surprise," Tom hollered.

"Oops, sorry. Remember, you're living in a small town now. The grapevine is very efficient. Everyone has already heard about the bluebirds, which is why I made blueberry pancakes."

"That was so sweet of you." Felicity stood in the doorway, holding the tray, grateful for the food, but wishing her aunt would scoot.

"There's some more good news," Aunt Molly said.

"What's that?"

"One, Savannah called to reserve the Bluebird Inn for a wedding. She's getting married after all."

"What? She and Chance got back together?"

"Nope."

"Who is she getting married to?"

"You'll have to get out of bed if you want that bit of gossip." Aunt Molly's eyes twinkled.

"Not right now," Tom called.

Aunt Molly's grin was huge. "I saved the best news for last."

The tray was getting heavy, and Felicity couldn't wait to dive back into bed with Tom and celebrate the news that Savannah was willing to take another chance on the Bluebird Inn. "What's that?"

"The doctor's office called. The lump is benign."

Oh, happy day! Joy shot straight to Felicity's heart.

"Now, go have breakfast with your man," Aunt Molly said, then turned and went back downstairs.

As soon as Felicity closed the door with her foot, Tom was out of bed, naked as the day he was born. He took the tray from her, set it on the dresser, and pulled her into his arms. "Did you hear that? No cancer."

She bobbed her head, flooded with bliss. "And you're going back to school!"

"I decided this county needed another extension agent."

"It does!" she said, her heart overflowing.

"And," he said, "I've decided a cold breakfast isn't so bad."

"What do you have in mind?" she asked, leaning in and kissing him lightly on the lips.

"Showing you all over again just how much I love you." He led her back to bed.

Tears misted the corners of her eyes. Felicity could hardly believe her good fortune. She had found a man who loved her; she had a clean bill of health and a new booking for a wedding.

And outside her window, bluebirds sang in the trees, a beautiful symbol of all the happiness that lay in store.

There Goes the Bride

Allyson Charles

Chapter One

The wind whipped her hair into a frenzy around her head. The late morning sun kissed her bare arms. And her eyes watered as she rocketed down the back highway at seventy miles per hour.

Savannah Loving was finally free. And crazy screwed, but she was going to ignore that last bit for as long as she could. The Ducati hummed between her legs, and she opened the throttle further, let the vibrations speed her from the disaster she'd escaped back at the Bluebird Inn. Or was it a disaster she'd created?

A mess of hair blew across her mouth, and she shook her head, knocking the hair free. The rushing wind tore the air from her throat, and she was only able to suck down short, fast breaths. A wave of panic threatened to crash over her, and Savannah pushed all thoughts of the look on her dad's face from her mind. Of Chance shouting after her as she'd sped off. She was finally making her own choices, damn it, and she was going to enjoy every second of her motorcycle ride as she fled from Serendipity, Texas.

Her newfound freedom didn't last long. A siren echoed in her ears, the wails growing louder, and blue and red lights flashed in her side mirror. For one crazy moment, she thought about testing the Ducati, seeing just how fast her uncle's bike could go, before sanity set in. Well, her version of it anyway.

Pulling to the side of the road, she stopped beneath the shadow of an old billboard. It advertised a gas station three miles down the road that had shut its pumps over twenty years ago. Strips of paint had peeled from the billboard, and other patches of the advertisement had blanched almost white from the sun. Frayed, worn, and colorless. Savannah knew just how the billboard felt.

The Ducati hummed softly as she watched the cop step from his truck, adjust the wide brim on his black cowboy hat, and make his way toward her. His short-sleeved black shirt stretched across a wide chest and showcased a pair of strong, bronze arms. Large, mirrored sunglasses hid half of his face, but a niggle of recognition slid beneath her breastbone, and she squeezed the grips.

"Ma'am, turn off the motorcycle, please."

Savannah looked down the empty road ahead of her, an enticing serpentine path through grassy fields dotted with wildflowers. She'd only made it ten miles out of town, and the thought of turning back closed her throat.

"Hank Evans, is that you?" She scraped her teeth against her top lip. "I heard you'd moved back from Dallas."

He took off his sunglasses and slid them in his breast pocket, right below the silver badge pinned to his shirt. Deep, whiskey eyes examined her, looking her up and down, and pausing on her bare feet.

She curled her toes into the dirt on the shoulder of the road. When she'd first started planning her great escape, she'd thought to wear the tank top and leggings under her wedding dress, but she'd forgotten to set aside a pair of sneakers. She should have kept her heels on.

"Savannah Loving?" He shook his head. "I hardly would have recognized you all grown up. Now, please turn off your motorcycle and show me your license and registration."

"You know who I am. My ID won't tell you anything

different." Glancing over her shoulder, she saw a dust trail from someone cutting across a dirt road rising into the sky. Her heart pounded. But no one would be coming for her from that direction. It was just someone going about his daily business. She let out a shaky breath. But someone could be coming, and soon. She didn't have time for a ticket. "I'm sorry I was speeding."

She looked up at Hank. He'd been eighteen the last time she'd seen him. On that birthday, he'd hightailed it out of Serendipity, and she hadn't thought he'd ever come back to the small town. He looked taller than she remembered, but maybe that was only because he'd filled out, added muscle to his rangy frame. Ten years in the military would do that to a man.

A sinister thought crossed her mind, and she narrowed her eyes. "Did my parents send you after me? I'm not going back. You'll have to drag me, kicking and screaming." The crazy idea to bolt, to open the bike's throttle to the max and dare anyone to catch her, shot through her head again.

Hank's lips flattened, and he leaned over and flipped the engine cut-off switch. The Ducati grumbled before cutting out. The sudden silence rang in her ears.

"I stopped you because you were going seventy in a fifty zone. I haven't spoken to your parents in years. Now, license and registration. Please." He rested his hands on his duty belt and shifted his weight. The leather of his boots creaked.

"Oh, all right." Pulling the neck of her tank top from her body, she dug into her bra and pulled out the driver's license she'd stashed away along with her credit card and a small bundle of cash. Hank raised an eyebrow, but took the license silently. "I don't know why you need it. You know who I am," she repeated.

"But I don't know if you're licensed to operate this vehicle."

"You taught me how to ride!"

He sighed, as if the memory of that day was one best forgotten. "Registration?"

She looked at the bike, but there weren't any saddlebags,

no storage that she saw. "I don't know where the registration is. It's my uncle's bike."

"Fine. Stay here." He strode back to his truck and leaned in the front door.

Her phone rang, for probably the tenth time in as many miles, vibrating against her belly. She ignored it. Swinging her leg over the bike, Savannah paced around it, kicking up dirt. Her new pedicure, her toenails painted a delicate Pink Lace that her mom had said was perfect for a bride and that Savannah had hated on sight, would be ruined. She kicked up more dirt.

Disgust twisted her stomach. When had she started letting her mom pick her nail polish color? She was twenty-five years old, and she still let her parents make her decisions. It hadn't always been that way. She glanced at Hank. He was talking into a radio, but his gaze was focused on her. Like he thought she was a flight risk.

He was right. She eyed the Ducati and sighed. She wanted to take her life back, but becoming a fugitive probably wasn't the way to go.

She used to be independent. Strong-willed. Heck, when she'd been twelve and determined to learn how to ride a motorcycle, she hadn't let her dad's refusal to teach her get in her way. Nope, she'd hunted down the biggest, baddest, roughest twelve-year-old in her class who she knew had a motorcycle at home, and demanded that he teach her.

Much to her disappointment, Seth Evans hadn't known how to handle a motorcycle. But he, Savannah, and his friends hadn't given up. They'd revved the engine to his dad's Honda and fallen off the back end until they were covered in scrapes and bruises. Until the biggest, baddest, roughest twelve-year-old's older brother, Hank, had stepped in and taught them all how to ride so they wouldn't kill themselves. Or permanently damage the Honda.

Her mother had been appalled when she'd gotten her

motorcycle license right along with her driver's license on her sixteenth birthday. Her father had bought her a moped.

It was that moped, she realized, that had been the beginning of the end for strong-willed, independent Savannah. It had been generous of her dad to buy it, even though she would have preferred the oldest, most rusted-out bike to that pristine, powder-blue scooter. But her parents had been so much happier seeing her on the girly-mobile that she'd swallowed down her disappointment. The moped had been next to useless on her parents' ranch, so she'd ridden it a couple of times through town and then let it sit in the garage.

The Cadillac Coupe her parents had bought her for her eighteenth birthday had been much more practical than a bike. And they'd been so pleased that they could provide for her, and so bighearted, that she'd ignored the fact that it made her feel like an old lady to drive it.

When she'd come back from college with her bachelor's degree and teacher's certification, she'd known she wouldn't be able to afford much. But she'd eagerly hunted for apartments in her price range, because the place would be hers, a home of her own that she had earned.

Her parents bought her a condo.

How can you be anything other than grateful and humbled when your parents buy you a frickin' condo?

All those gifts, all those times Savannah had done the polite thing, thanked her parents and accepted instead of forging her own way, and it had all come down to this. Pink Lace on her toenails and a jilted fiancé back at the Bluebird Inn.

Hank came back and handed her the license. "Here you are, Miss Loving. Since you have no prior tickets or warrants—"

She threw her hands out wide. "Of course I don't have any tickets. I'm Savannah Loving. Prom queen and class valedictorian. President of Alpha Phi." All those wasted years being what everyone else wanted her to be. She circled the motorcycle, kicking at loose stones and ignoring the sting. "I'm the obedient daughter. The soon-to-be-mother to the great

Loving-Worthington dynasty. Women like me don't have records." She laughed, the sound bordering on the hysterical. "I was supposed to be married by now. Did you know that? At this very moment I should have been saying 'I do' and becoming Mrs. Chance Worthington. Everyone told me I was the luckiest girl in the world."

Her phone rang, the lyrics to "Oops! . . . I Did It Again" filling the air. Tears burned the backs of her eyes. Whatever "It" was, she'd never even done it the first time.

A pucker appeared between Hank's eyebrows, and he glanced down to where the sound was coming from at her stomach. "Uh, do you want to get that?"

"No." The music stopped, then started again as a new call came in. Growling, Savannah hiked up her tank top and pulled the phone from the waistband of her leggings. Hank's eyes flared wide when he caught an expanse of skin, before going hooded again. Without checking the caller ID, Savannah turned off the phone and stuck it back in her pants.

She tugged her top down and glared at Hank. "I'm not going back."

"I didn't say you had to." He rocked back on his boots. "Uh, are you telling me you ran away from your wedding?"

"Yes!" she shrieked. The enormity of what she'd done hit her anew, and her legs wobbled. "Oh my God. My parents are going to kill me. All the money they spent on that wedding . . ." That, and the fact that she wasn't going to become a Worthington. Was no longer the golden child. She swallowed and tasted bile.

Hank raised his hands, palms out. "Calm down. It can't be that bad."

"Have you ever stood someone up at the altar? Kicked off your heels as your father tried to lead you down the aisle and hopped on the back of a motorcycle, leaving all your friends and family behind in the dust?"

His lips twitched. "Can't say that I have."

"Don't you dare laugh at me, Hank Evans." She poked

him in the stomach and then shook out the hurt in her finger. Damn, his abs were rock-hard. "I am a woman on the edge."

"Of that I have no doubt. You always were a bit crazy."

She'd been thirteen the last time he'd seen her, a child, but his statement still sent relief pounding through her. She flung her arms around his neck and squeezed him tight. "Thank you," she whispered.

"Uh . . . okay." He patted her back.

She held on for several moments. Held on to the memory of herself that a virtual stranger had brought back to life. The woodsy scent of his soap filled her nose, and she inhaled deeply. His hand was large, comforting, and he pressed it into the small of her back, pulling her snug. Her chest pressed against his, and she started to tingle in places that hadn't tingled in years. Dropping her arms, she stepped back.

He shifted. "I'm going to let you off with a warning this time. Let's get the bike in the back of my truck, and I can take you back to Serendipity."

She fell back a step. "I told you I'm not going back."

"Well, I can't let you ride barefoot." He pressed his lips into a pale slash. "And why aren't you wearing that helmet?" He jerked his chin at the yellow brain bucket that was strapped down behind the seat.

"It's locked." She shrugged. "I didn't have time to ask my uncle for the key."

Hank huffed out a breath and pulled the Ducati keys from the ignition. He held up a small key on the ring. "I think this one will do the trick."

"Oh." Savannah tested it, and the cable lock that wound through the straps at the ear of the helmet popped open. "Well, there you go."

"You still aren't wearing shoes."

"I can't go back." She shook her head, her pulse kicking up again. "Not yet."

Hank stared at her. Assessing. Unspeaking.

She curled her toes. He had handcuffs and the authority to

arrest her, but if he tried to put her in his truck, she was going to fight.

Clapping a palm on the back of his neck, he sighed. "Hold on a sec."

Striding to the truck, he pulled open the door to the back seat and pulled out a duffel. He dug through it, coming up with a worn pair of white sneakers and a thick pair of socks. He walked back to her. "You can take my workout shoes."

"They're huge. It will be like wearing clown shoes."

"They're better than nothing." He handed them to her and walked back to the truck.

Sitting in the dirt, she pulled on the socks and sneakers, and tried to knot the shoelaces as tightly as possible. She raised one foot. The heel of the sneaker swung several inches from her own heel. Were they better than nothing?

Hank dropped into a squat in front of her and grabbed her ankle. Holding a roll of duct tape to his mouth, he bit down on the end and ripped the roll down, exposing a long stretch of tape. He wound it around his shoe and up to the hem of her leggings.

"Hey!" She tried pulling her leg back.

Hank flicked his gaze to her. "Are you worried about your fashion statement? Now?"

Savannah grumbled, but let him finish taping the shoes to her pants. When he was done, he tossed the roll aside, gripped her under her arms, and lifted her to her feet. "Let's see if you can walk without falling on your face."

It was awkward. She had to take large, unwieldy steps, but it worked.

"Now get on the bike," he told her.

She did and played with the gearshift lever and rear brake pedal while those absurdly long shoes lay on the footrests. If she kept her toes pressed up in the front of the shoe, it all worked fine.

"I'm good to go," she said brightly, and gave him a wide

smile. She might have been temporarily delayed, but her escape was still a go.

"Where are you heading?" He handed her the helmet and stuck the key back in the ignition.

With her feet planted on the ground, she rocked the bike back and forth, making sure it was in neutral. She shrugged. "I don't know. I'll figure it out on the way."

"Any friends you can go stay with?"

She shook her head. They were all back in Serendipity. And would all think she was a fool for leaving Chance Worthington. Or call her parents. Or both.

"Family?"

She shook her head again. Ducking her chin, she slipped the helmet on, avoiding eye contact.

He blew out a big breath and stared at the sky. "I'm going to regret this," he muttered.

"Regret what?"

Instead of answering, he walked back to his truck. He leaned in, grabbed something, and came back to stand beside her. He unwound a key from his key ring. "Here. I haven't sold my place in Dallas yet. You can stay there for a bit. It's pretty empty," he warned. "Just furniture that the stagers set up. But it's safe. In a decent part of town."

She closed her fingers around the key, squeezed it tight. "Thank you. That's . . ." She cleared her throat. "That's very kind of you." And before he could change his mind, she slipped the key into her bra, next to her license and cash.

A flicker of interest danced across his face, before his expression returned to its stern set. "Do not speed. Stop at the first store you see to buy yourself some shoes that fit. Is that understood?"

She saluted him. "Aye, aye, sir."

Tipping his cowboy hat up, Hank pinched his forehead between his thumb and middle finger. "Already regretting it."

"What's the address?" She pulled her phone out and typed it in.

"Don't look at the directions while you're driving," he ordered.

She nodded and bit back her retort. She might have a little bit of crazy left in her, but she wasn't an idiot. But she didn't want to argue with the man; she needed to get back on the road and put miles between her and Serendipity. She started the Ducati, the thrum between her legs making her stomach quiver. She was going to get away. She looked up into his eyes, a startling golden brown, and the quiver turned into a shiver.

"And call your parents, would you? They must be worried."

She nodded. Guilt took a tiny bite at her conscience, but she kicked it aside. Guilt would only make her apologize, and promise to do as they wanted. And then she'd be right back where she'd started this morning. In a wedding dress she hadn't chosen, about to marry a man she didn't love. She'd send them a text when she got to Dallas. Let them know she was safe.

Shifting into gear, she gave Hank one last smile before pulling the detachable muzzle on the helmet across her mouth and nose. Letting out the clutch, she gave the bike some throttle and rolled onto the highway. She raised a hand in farewell and kept the speedometer at a careful forty-seven miles per hour until Hank and his police truck were out of view.

Then she gave in to the itch and revved the engine, blasting down the empty road. Only the racing of her heartbeat could match the Ducati's speed.

Chapter Two

From a half-mile away, Hank heard the Ducati's engines growl, and a reluctant smile tugged at his lips. Savannah hadn't changed much from the fierce and wild girl he'd known. Still pushing her limits. Determined to have her way.

Hank walked back to his truck and climbed in. On the other hand, he hardly recognized the woman she'd become. Physically, leastwise. Gone was the coltish girl who was all legs and sharp elbows. He should have arrested her for her outfit alone. The way those pants and tank top clung to her lush body was criminal. He'd never been jealous of an inanimate object before, but he had to admit to a longing to switch places with her phone, if just for a moment. Seeing it nestled against her stomach, jutting out of her pants, he'd almost drooled.

The *welcome* sign to Serendipity came into view, and the knot of tension that always seemed to sit at the base of his skull eased, as it inevitably did at the sight. He'd been gone from Serendipity too long. Angry for even longer. It had taken him twelve years to come to grips with his childhood issues, to come to appreciate his small hometown. Unfortunately, it had taken his father's death to make Hank see what an ass he'd been and bring him home.

He drove past the Bluebird Inn and saw it was a hive of activity. Wedding guests dressed in their Sunday best gossiped in clusters, no one seeming to want to get in his or her car and drive away from the excitement. Hank waved at the minister and turned at the next street.

Stomach rumbling, he pulled into a spot near Bubba Red's, the barbeque place on the square. Stepping out of his truck, he stretched and enjoyed the mild temperature. Perfect weather for a wedding. Shaking his head, he strolled into the restaurant and found a seat in a booth along the far wall.

What on earth had Savannah been thinking? How could a woman leave the man that she loved standing at the altar? And if she didn't love him, why had she agreed to marry him in the first place? Hank didn't know Chance Worthington well, but he seemed a decent enough guy. And Hank had been told enough times by enough people in Serendipity that Worthington was the perfect man for their darling Savannah Loving. Wealthy, respected, with a good family name.

Hank's stomach turned. Everything his family hadn't been.

Marlene, one of the waitresses, walked up with a big smile and a pot of coffee. "Afternoon, Deputy. What can I get for you?"

"The tri-tip platter. Medium rare." Hank flipped his mug over, and Marlene filled it with coffee.

She put the pot down and wrote his order on her pad. Cocking a hip on the table, she leaned close. "Did you hear the news? Savannah Loving up and left Chance standing at the altar. Some people are saying she must have started doing drugs while she was away at UT, that being the only thing that can explain her ditching such a fine man. Others think a business deal went bad between the fathers." Marlene looked over her shoulder, then dipped her head. "Personally, I think there must be another man," she whispered. "She's a damn fool for listening to her hormones instead of using her head, but what can you say about girls these days. It's all me, me, me."

Hank blinked. He'd missed the easy familiarity of small-town life while he'd been living in Dallas, but he wasn't used to how up in everyone's business everyone was in Serendipity.

Marlene went on. "I can't believe Serendipity has its very own runaway bride! And I heard poor Chance was so riled, he smashed the wedding cake."

A group of customers, obviously having left the wedding that wasn't, entered the restaurant, and Marlene hurried to greet them. Eager for the latest gossip.

On their heels was a familiar face. By the stained jeans he wore and wrinkled T-shirt, one who obviously hadn't been at the town's royal nuptials.

Seth dropped onto the bench seat across from Hank and took off his baseball cap. "Hey, bro. What's up?"

"Not much. Helped old man Gunthrie repair his tractor, which was broken down on the side of the road. Gave a speeder a warning. Same ol', same ol'."

His baby brother snorted. "Only you could call the biggest social scandal in town history just another day. Haven't you heard the news? The phone's been ringing for the last half hour, and Momma's been talking to everyone."

"Yes, I've heard all about the Loving-Worthington split." Hank shrugged. "What's it to us?"

"Nothing." A smirk crossed Seth's face. "Except Savannah Loving is on the market again. I always regretted not getting my chance with her."

Hank snorted. "You think just because she's not marrying the doctor that you now have a shot with her?" He shook his head. "Her father would rather see his ranch burn than his baby girl with an Evans."

"You've been gone for over ten years," Seth said. "Serendipity has changed."

"Not that much." Never that much. Hank had learned to

accept his father's failings. That getting addicted to pain pills made it hard for a man to provide for his family. But he knew the town elders wouldn't have looked on his dad with the same sympathy. Hank planned on building his future in Serendipity, becoming a respected member of the community, but Serendipity's influence makers would never look on him as anything other than the hired help.

And that was all right with him. Hank only wanted the respect of those he cared about. The whole town royalty BS struck him as silly and outdated. He ran his thumb over the rim of his mug. He wondered how Savannah had managed to keep it together until today. By all accounts she was a proper young woman. A credit to Serendipity.

And she'd been panicked out of her mind when she thought he'd take her back home. She must have been suppressing her spirit for a while now.

No, the princess crown didn't sit well on her head. Hank just couldn't believe that it had taken a broken wedding for everyone else to see that.

She should be getting into Dallas about now. Taking refuge in his condo. The near-empty condo with bare cupboards and an unplugged refrigerator. He drummed his fingers on the table. Damn, how much cash did she have shoved down her bra? Would it be enough to get her a decent meal? A toothbrush and some toothpaste?

Crap. Hank's heart sank. She'd be fine, he told himself. Savannah Loving was all grown up, and he was sure she could take care of herself. He was not going to worry about her sitting all alone and hungry at his place. Lying in his bed in those tight leggings and that clingy top. Nope, he wouldn't think of her like that, either.

"Hello?" Seth waved a hand before his face. "Earth to Hank. You're not having a PTSD episode, are you?"

Hank knocked his brother's hand down. "Don't make jokes about shit like that."

Marlene bustled over, carrying two plates in her hands.

She laid a plate heaped with smoked meat, corn on the cob, and macaroni salad in front of Hank and a pulled pork sandwich before Seth.

"Thanks, Marlene." Seth shoved a fry in his mouth. "I didn't even order yet."

"I know what you like, sugar." And with a wink, she was off.

Seth waggled his eyebrows. "She really knows what I like, if you know what I mean."

Hank shook some salt and pepper on his corn. "When did my brother become such a jackass?" he asked no one in particular.

"Twelve years is a long time to be gone." Seth shrugged, his cocky smile fading. "We've all changed."

Truer words were never spoken. Hank sure as hell was a different man. Ten years in the Army would do that to a person. The two as a beat cop in Dallas had changed him even more.

Taking a big bite of his tri-tip, he pushed those thoughts away. That's why he was back in Serendipity. Still in law enforcement, true, but breaking up drunken fights at the local bar and handing out speeding tickets was the extent of his workload. After years of living in a constant state of alert, he could finally relax. Maybe think about his future. A family.

Savannah's sweet smile and endless legs drifted through his thoughts again. If that was how Serendipity grew its women, then Hank had definitely made the right decision to come back home.

He blocked his brother's fork as it moved toward his macaroni salad. Smiled as Seth scowled.

Yep, there was definitely no place like home.

Chapter Three

"Shoot!" Savannah snatched the nail polish remover from where it had toppled onto the comforter and tried to brush away the acetone. It soaked into the cotton, and she hopped off the bed and hobbled for the bathroom and its one roll of toilet paper, trying not to ruin her new pedicure. She ran back on her heels and blotted as much liquid as she could.

It didn't help. A circle of blue, a paler shade than the rest of the comforter, refused to disappear. Savannah didn't know if it was from the damp or if the acetone had damaged the comforter. She rolled her head and sighed. That comforter was the only thing for her to sleep on. The bed was bare beneath it, stripped of any sheets. But there was nothing for it. Peeling it off the bed, she hurried to the bathroom and turned on the tub. She stuck the affected area beneath the stream of water, squirted some hand soap onto it, and tried to scrub away the stain.

She didn't think Hank would appreciate it if she ruined the stager's property. She could only hope it would dry in time for her to sleep.

Someone knocked on the door, and Savannah stopped by the narrow shelf that ran the length of the living room where she'd dumped her cash, cards, and phone. She picked up some money and opened the door. The delivery man held up a plastic bag full of cartons.

"Thanks. How much do I owe you?" she asked, the smells of Chinese food making her stomach rumble. The teenager told her, and she gave him a big tip, and pulled the bag in close. She'd been on a diet since the first day of her engagement. Strictly enforced by her mother and every waitress and store clerk in Serendipity. Sure, Savannah could have gone to the Piggly Wiggly and bought a bag of Snickers, but she would have received a raised eyebrow from the cashier, and a phone call from her mother five minutes later telling her to throw the candy away.

No more dieting. She said good-bye to the delivery man and shut the door with the ball of her foot, careful of her toenails. She was going to eat as much tonight as she could without getting sick and then do it all over again tomorrow.

She had just set everything down on the kitchen counter when the soft click of the front door opening hit her ear. She froze, and the visual of the sweet teenage delivery boy turned into a true crime story of a deviant youth. She must not have closed the door all the way, and now he was coming back to rob her because she hadn't tipped him big enough. Or he'd seen she was a woman alone, and—

A floorboard creaked in the living room, and Savannah's gaze darted around, looking for anything to use as a weapon. But the kitchen was empty except for her food . . . and the chopsticks that came in the bag. There would be something infinitely fitting about a Chinese food delivery man turned rapist skewered by the very tool he had delivered.

Another creak, closer. She didn't have time to unwrap the chopsticks, just fisted the package. Movement in the corner of her eye, and her time to plan was over. Gripping the handles of the plastic bag, she swung with all her might. The sack smacked against the intruder's face, a carton went flying, and the man swore and bent double, covering his face with his hands.

Something niggled in the back of her brain, but her body was in fight mode and ignored it. She kept swinging, bringing the bag down on the back of his head again and again, cartons popping out and flying around the kitchen. When she swung nothing but a torn and empty bag, that's when she turned to the chopsticks in her left hand.

Luckily, her left arm wasn't as strong, her swing not as assured. After the first stab of the sticks to his back, the man roared. That little niggle in her brain went to a full-blown warning alert system, blaring in her mind.

The man's back looked a little too familiar. And the sound of his voice as he cursed sent a shiver of recognition sliding down her spine.

"Are you done?" he bit out. Slowly, he straightened, revealing a broad chest encased in a worn T-shirt, a thick column of a throat, and . . . yep, that was Hank Evans's grim face glaring down at her. Her fingers loosened, and the plastic bag drifted to the floor.

He snatched the chopsticks from her still raised left hand. "What the hell are you doing? Trying to kill the one person who knows where you are?"

"You didn't knock." She licked her lips, refusing to feel guilty. "You should have knocked. I thought it was the delivery man coming back to . . ."

"Get his ass handed to him? Besides, this is my condo. I've never knocked entering my own place." Hank blew out a breath and fisted his hands on his hips. "Woman, you are a menace to society."

Her heart swelled. "That's so sweet."

Muttering to himself, Hank picked up a carton of sweet-and-sour pork. Half of the bright orange meat slid out and plopped on the floor. He swore again.

"Go sit on the sofa." She prodded him from the kitchen. "I'll clean up. It's the least I can do after beating you up."

"You didn't beat me up. I only let you get your whacks in because I didn't want to hurt you."

"Of course you did." She patted his chest, her body taking notice when she felt how firm his pecs were. Her mouth watered. "Now, go sit down, and you can tell me why you're here while I clean up the evidence of your ass-whooping."

He narrowed his eyes, the color of them darkening from a medium-aged whiskey to one that had been sitting in a barrel for twenty years. She'd never seen such beautiful eyes on a man, even when they were squinty with irritation, and she stared back, mesmerized.

He stepped forward, slipped in some sauce, and the connection broke.

Savannah sidled around him. "Don't move. You'll track sweet-and-sour into your living room." She ran for the toilet paper, the only paper in the whole condo, and came back to kneel at his feet. "Okay, lift your foot, and I'll wipe it off."

He didn't move, and Savannah looked up. The corners of his lips twitched, one dark eyebrow arched. She frowned, then realized just what thoughts her position must be putting in his mind. She flushed. "Just lift your foot," she muttered.

He complied, and she wiped off the sauce. She scooted back, not meeting his eyes. "You can go sit down now. I'll clean up the rest of this."

With the small amount of toilet paper she had left, she wiped up the spilled chicken from one carton, the noodles from another, and put it all in the torn plastic bag as best she could. "I'm going to have to go shopping for cleaning supplies. And more toilet paper. You weren't kidding when you said this place was empty."

He leaned against the doorjamb and crossed his arms over his chest. "So you do have some money on you? That's one worry gone."

"Is that why you're here?" She tied the bag up and set it on the counter. She ran her hands under the faucet and dried them on her pants. "You thought I was penniless?"

"I'm sure the princess of Serendipity has a trust fund a mile wide," he said. "I just didn't know if you'd be able to access it. Not without letting your father know where you were. And you're just stubborn enough to starve."

"Is that what you think of me?" She leaned back against the sink and grabbed the counter at her sides. "That I'm a bimbo living off of Daddy's money?" A knot formed in her stomach, and she swallowed down a sick taste. That's probably what everyone thought. That's what Chance had thought. He'd never been mean about it, but he assumed her teaching career was just a hobby she'd give up once they'd married. Same princess, just moving into a different castle.

His mouth softened. "I didn't say that. I just meant that I'm sure you're comfortable. Your family wouldn't let you go without."

"I work," she told him. Why she wanted this man to respect her, she didn't know. But it suddenly felt urgent. "I'm a teacher at Serendipity Elementary. It's a job I care about. I'm not just there killing time until I have kids of my own."

He stepped forward. "Is that what people think? What your fiancé told you?"

She scratched her thumbnail over a line of grout. "Not Chance. My parents." Chance hadn't wanted children, but her mother had assured her that, after he and Savannah were married, Savannah would be able to change his mind. And instead of telling her mom that was a crappy way to start a marriage, Savannah had smiled and agreed with her mother, once again. "They always assumed that if I got a degree it would be in either education or an M.R.S."

"Uh, you did go into education."

She slapped her hand on the tile. "My parents were paying for college. It's what they wanted." She brushed past him and stalked into the living room. "Luckily for me, it turned out I enjoyed it."

"That's good, I guess." He followed her out, rubbing the back of his neck.

"But it can be hard work. I might not be chasing down

criminals, but keeping twenty first-graders safe, entertained, and educated isn't for sissies."

"I feel like we're having an argument, but I don't think we're disagreeing about anything." Resting his hand on her shoulder, he squeezed, the pressure warm and reassuring. "I think being a teacher is a fine job."

She swallowed. "I'm twenty-five, and I've never supported myself. I have no student loans, my parents paid for my college; they've paid for my home, my car." Hanging her head, she stared at her fire-engine-red toenails. "I am a trust-fund bimbo."

"Hey." He cupped her cheek and raised her face up. "That's not true. We haven't seen each other for a long time, so I'm not quite sure what you are. But I know what you aren't. And you aren't a bimbo. Bimbos don't steal their uncle's Ducati and go tearing out of town with a phone shoved down their pants while barefoot." His eyes danced with humor, and she felt her own spirits rise.

She smiled weakly. "Borrowed, not stolen."

Hank brushed his thumb over her skin, and the hair on her nape lifted. He was close. A big, solid man wearing jeans with a small tear at the knee and a shirt that looked like it had gone through the dryer a thousand and one times. Completely unlike the well-groomed Chance Worthington, but something about Hank felt completely right.

She leaned forward and inhaled his musky scent. Hank's eyelids dropped to half-mast. The tip of his boot brushed against her toe as he stepped close. Heart pounding, she flicked her gaze from his hooded eyes to his full lips and back again. Was she crazy? She was supposed to be on her honeymoon right now with another man, but she wanted nothing more than to kiss Hank Evans.

He lowered his head, achingly slowly, and her breath sped up every inch he got closer.

Her stomach growled, the sound loud and echoing in his spartan living room.

The tension broke, and Hank stepped back, chuckling. "Since I ruined your dinner, how 'bout you get your shoes on, and I'll take you out." He glanced down at her feet. "You did buy shoes, right?"

"Yes, the first drugstore I came to." That and pedicure supplies, a King-sized Snickers bar, and the latest thriller to hit the best-seller list. She trotted into the bedroom and slid the flip-flops onto her feet. Slapping back into the living room, she went to the built-in shelf and folded her cash neatly around her driver's license and credit card before slipping them into her bra cup. She tucked the phone back in her pants and looked up at Hank.

He was staring at the ceiling, a muscle twitching in his jaw.

"Problem?" She tilted her head.

"You didn't manage to find a purse while you were at that store?"

"I didn't look." Swiping up her keys, she walked to the door and pulled it open. "Purses don't really work while driving a motorcycle."

"Of course." With a martyred look, he followed her outside and pulled the door shut.

Hank's condo was on the second story, so they climbed down the stairs. At the parking lot, he guided her to a Jeep streaked with mud. He held the passenger door open, and she slid inside, finding the interior as clean as the outside was dirty. The dash was buffed a glossy black, the floors spotless. A plastic crate was nestled behind the driver's seat, a coil of neatly tied black nylon rope, a large flashlight, and a tub of plastic zip-ties stacked within. Not a candy-bar wrapper in sight.

Hank rounded the hood and slid into the driver's seat.

"Interesting tools you keep in back. Preparing for a kidnapping?"

He twisted around and saw what she was looking at. He shrugged. "You never know when you'll have to tie down a load. Or restrain a crazy woman."

"Funny man," she muttered.

"What are you in the mood for? Something other than Chinese, please. After having sweet-and-sour pork pounded into my head, I can't say I'm up for it."

"I don't care. Something I can't get back in Serendipity."

He nodded and started the ignition. He took back roads, avoiding the congested freeways, until he finally pulled into a parking lot near Cotton Bowl Stadium. A side street was closed off to traffic and was filled with food trucks and picnic tables. Strings of white and colored lights circled the trucks, and someone had filled the area with large potted plants.

On the sidewalk in front of the parking lot, a tent had been erected. A tarp stretched from a shopping cart handle to the fence behind the tent, a makeshift shelter for one of the city's homeless. A lump filled Savannah's throat. She'd run from a beautiful home that most people would be lucky to have.

"There." Hank pointed, getting her attention.

"A taco truck? You're taking me to a taco truck?"

"Can't get it in Serendipity." Cutting the engine, he stepped out. Hank walked to the back of the Jeep and opened the rear door. He unzipped a black bag and pulled out a sweatshirt with the emblem of a Dallas PD badge on the back. "And trust me. You haven't tasted anything until you've tasted a Sanchez taco."

He held up the sweatshirt, and she stared at him. He shook it. "Here. Put this on."

"I'm not cold."

"The sun will be setting soon, and the temperature drops quickly. Besides"—he stepped behind her and held it out while she slid one arm in the sleeve—"it's an extra-large. It should keep everyone from staring at your butt in those yoga pants."

She paused, trying to determine if she should be offended. "Are you implying something about the size of my butt? Or that a woman should cover up so men don't behave badly? 'Cause neither one of those suggestions will end well for you."

"I'm not worried about a jackass behaving badly. I can handle that. I just don't *want* every jackass getting a look." Slipping his hands into the front pockets of his jeans, he shrugged. "Anything wrong with that?"

Her heart tripped. "No," she said slowly. Nothing *wrong*. Only a bit unsettling. "I guess I'm just not used to anyone's caring about things like that." She turned for the taco truck, passing one that sold calzones and another selling Indian food. Examining the menu board next to Sanchez's truck, she felt Hank move behind her, his body heat warmer than the sweatshirt.

She ordered tacos al pastor and a diet soda, changed it to a full-sugar soda, and started to dig in her bra for cash.

Hank put his hand over hers, his fingertips grazing the skin right over her breasts. "I've got it."

She nodded, her breath coming quicker, and looked for a spot at a picnic table. She slid onto the bench seat, and Hank dropped down next to her, placing her soda before her.

"What do you mean you're not used to it?" he asked.

Her cheeks burned. She should have kept her mouth shut. Tugging at the drawstring on one side of the hoodie, she shook her head. "Forget it. I didn't mean anything."

He opened his mouth, and their order was called. Pressing a hand to her shoulder, he pushed her back down. "I'll get it." He came back carrying two large paper plates, with two sets of forks and knives rolled up in napkins tucked under one arm.

She helped him set everything down. Scooping some rice that was piled on the side of her plate onto a taco, she rolled it up and took a bite. The adobo marinade of the pork exploded on her tongue, the spicy heat tempered by the sweet juices of the pineapple slice that topped the meat. "Hot damn, this is good." She went in for another bite.

Using his napkin, Hank dabbed at her chin. "You're not

the only one who can be stubborn. What did you mean that you weren't used to my behavior? I can't imagine your fiancé's being happy when other men looked at you." A line creased his forehead at the word "fiancé," as if the reminder made him less than happy.

She took a long sip from her soda, wanting to just enjoy all the sugar and fat she was consuming. But he kept waiting. His dark eyes never left her face.

"This is embarrassing," she muttered, and looked at the couple across from them. They were wrapped up in their own little world, feeding each other bits of food, giving each other sweet little pecks on the lips.

"I think we've moved past embarrassing today." He knocked her shoulder with his. "I almost arrested you. You assaulted me with chopsticks."

Her lips curved up. She couldn't help it.

"Come on now," he coaxed. "Spill."

"Okay, but you have to promise not to tell anyone."

"Now I'm really interested." He shifted closer.

"Promise?"

His eyes went serious. "On my father's grave."

She took another bite and tried to sort her thoughts. This was probably something a man like Hank wouldn't understand. She glanced at him from the corner of her eye. Rugged, sexy, full of testosterone. Nope, he wouldn't understand at all.

"Chance and I had been dating for two years—the last year of that we were engaged." The fact that her sentence came in the past tense didn't escape her notice. In her heart, their relationship was over. Maybe had never truly begun. "Before that, I'd dated a bit, had some fun in college, but nothing too serious."

Hank nodded and kept silent, letting her take her time.

"Chance was very . . . proper when we began dating. Very respectful." Something she'd appreciated, at first. Especially as they'd had very little chemistry. She'd hoped it would develop as they got to know each other better. As their relationship deepened.

She swirled her soda can, feeling the cola slosh about. "Everyone thought we were the perfect couple. The pediatrician and the schoolteacher. A Worthington and a Loving. So we kept dating, even though there wasn't much heat. But we had fun together. He's a good guy. A good friend." She wanted to stress that point. Didn't want anyone to think it had been any failing on Chance's part that had made her run.

"But we never . . ." She bit her lip. "And then everyone thought it was time for us to get engaged. It was expected. We'd been dating a year, were perfect for each other, our parents really wanted the match, so he proposed—in front of my family. And I said yes." Even though the tacos were delicious, she pushed the plate away, her appetite gone. "And then, since we'd already waited so long, we decided to wait until we were married."

"Hold up." Hank raised his hands, palms out. "Are you telling me that you and your fiancé never slept together?"

That earned a curious glance from the couple across from them, and Savannah's body flushed with heat. "Why don't you say that a little louder? I don't think Mr. Sanchez heard you in his truck."

Putting his hand on her knee, he leaned in close. In a low voice, he said, "Savannah, are you trying to tell me that you haven't, I mean that you're a . . ."

She shot him a disgusted look. "I'm twenty-five, and I told you that I'd had fun in college. No, I'm not a virgin."

His cheeks went pink, and his Adam's apple bobbed up and down. "Right. Sorry."

"Anyway, what I'm trying to say is that Chance was never jealous over me. If other men looked, he didn't notice." She blew out a long breath. "I should have realized. I kept trying to convince myself that heat wasn't important in a relationship. That having a stable guy you could depend on was what mattered. And my parents just loved him so much . . ."

"When did you start toeing the parental line?" He took a swig from his IPA. "I always thought you'd turn out a hell-raiser. Like you were today." He smiled.

"My parents are kind people. I hate disappointing them." She'd more than made up for all those years of biting her tongue today. She rubbed the knuckle of her thumb over her breastbone. She'd let her parents down, and their disapproval must be monumental. How was she ever to face them? Face Chance? Hell, anyone in Serendipity?

They sipped their drinks in silence, and Hank finished his tacos. She stood, picking up their plates to clear their spots. He grabbed her wrist, and she looked down at him.

"If you were mine, I'd knock out any man's teeth who looked wrong at you. Any boyfriend worth his salt would do the same."

Her pulse leapt beneath his fingers. He must have felt it. "Chance is a good man." Just not good for her. Tears burned her eyes at the thought of the two years she'd wasted. The people she'd hurt. All because she hadn't realized that sooner. Hadn't developed a spine and broken things off with Chance a year and a half ago when she'd known he'd never get her heart racing.

She tugged at her wrist. "I'll be right back." Hank let her go, and she threw away their trash. She went back to Sanchez's and ordered another plate to go and a water. Grabbing the bag, she took a deep breath and turned to face Hank. "Ready to go?"

"Still hungry?" With a hand on her lower back, he guided her back to the parking lot.

"This one's not for me." She found the man curled up in his tent, a thick blanket pulled up to his hips. Savannah knelt by the half-zipped tent door. "Hi. I thought you might be hungry." She held up the bag. "The tacos here are really amazing."

The man pushed himself up and blinked. Savannah couldn't see much of him in the growing dark, but she saw when he smiled.

"I love Sanchez's tacos. Thanks." Stretching his hand through the flap, he grabbed the bag.

"And some water to wash it down." She gave him the bottle. "Take care of yourself," she said, and stood.

Hank was right beside her, his eyes soft. Dropping his arm over her shoulders, he raised a hand in farewell to the man in the tent, and guided her to his Jeep. "That was sweet."

She shrugged. "Someone buys me dinner, seems the least I can do is pay it forward."

At the passenger door, he turned her and cupped the back of her neck. "I know you're tired of being reserved, and you sure busted out of your mold today. But that doesn't mean you have to pretend you aren't sweet. A person can be both caring and crazy." One side of his mouth hitched up.

Maybe. She didn't know who she was anymore. But she liked whomever it was Hank saw. "Thanks," she whispered.

He opened the door. "Let's get you back to the condo. You've had quite the day and must be tired."

She got in and waited for him to walk around to the driver's seat. "Can we stop by a store? I want to get some cleaning supplies. Paper towels, bleach wipes." She bit her lower lip. "And maybe some stain remover. I might have ruined your comforter."

He grunted. "Not mine. Everything in there belongs to Kat."

Turning on her seat, she watched Hank as he pulled out into traffic. "Who's Kat?"

"My real estate agent. And an old friend." He tapped his fingers on the steering wheel. "We were stationed in Heidelberg at the same time."

"Your real estate agent was in the Army?"

He nodded, like it was no big thing.

Savannah settled back in her seat. It probably wasn't. Everyone needed a job coming out of the military. Real estate was as good as any. Better than a lot. But that experience was so far removed from her own, she had a hard time imagining it. If she'd served in the military, it would have been an even bigger shock to her parents than her escape on the back of a motorcycle. She bit back a giggle at the thought of the princess in a camo uniform.

Hank slid his gaze to her, then flicked on his blinker and turned into a grocery store's parking lot.

"You can wait here if you want." Savannah hopped out of the Jeep. "I know guys don't like to shop."

"I'm good." He padded after her and grabbed a cart at the front door, spinning it to wheel in front of him.

They shopped quickly, and before long they were pulling back into his condo's parking lot.

He cut the engine, and they sat there in silence for a beat.

"Well, I'll carry the bags in. Then I should get going." Hank rubbed the heel of his hand into his eye socket.

"It's late. You should stay. It's your place." Savannah rested her hand on his forearm. The muscles flexed beneath her touch, and she swallowed. "I can find a hotel."

"Which would defeat the purpose of my giving you a safe place to crash." He shook his head. "At this time of night, the drive back to Serendipity shouldn't be too bad."

"And have me worrying all night that you fell asleep behind the wheel? I don't think so." She pursed her lips. "We're two adults. There's no reason we both can't stay here. Right?" She wanted to sound light, unconcerned, like spending the night with a man was no big deal. But something about Hank made it a big deal. She trusted him not to make a move if she didn't want him to. But did she want him to?

"I have my sleeping bag in the back. I can take the couch," he said. "If you're sure it's all right?"

"Perfectly sure." She climbed out and grabbed two bags. Hank grabbed the others and retrieved his sleeping bag.

They climbed up the stairs. "I'm shorter than you," she said. "I can take the couch."

"Not when you're a guest in my home," Hank said, his voice final.

In the end she got the bed and the sleeping bag, since the comforter was still damp from her cleaning attempts.

And that was just the kind of guy Hank Evans was. She curled up on the bed, squeezing her pillow tight to her chest, and tried to forget that a kind, sexy man who appreciated her crazy lay not twenty feet away.

Chapter Four

"Hank?" Savannah called out softly from the bedroom.

His watch told him it was 2:38 a.m. Catching z's had been an exercise in futility. Seemed Savannah wasn't having any better luck. Or maybe he'd woken her when he'd gone to the john.

Hank tried to get comfortable on the couch. "Yeah?"

"Are you sleeping?"

Hank smiled. Only a woman would ask such an obvious question. "Yep. Having this conversation in my sleep."

"Oh." The nylon of his sleeping bag rustled, and he could just imagine her tossing and turning. Had she taken off her clothes to go to sleep? Her underwear? "I can't sleep," she said. "It's hot in here."

"Unzip the sleeping bag."

"That won't help. I'm already sleeping on top of it."

Good Christ Almighty. Was she sleeping naked on top of his bed just twenty feet away? His own temperature skyrocketed. "I'll turn up the A/C." They could both use it.

"Thanks." She sighed. "Why can't you sleep?"

After adjusting the thermostat, he plodded back to the sofa. "Because someone keeps talking to me."

"The gruff act isn't working for you," she said. "I can hear you smiling."

That didn't seem possible.

"I bet none of the bad guys are scared of Deputy Evans," she teased. "You may look all big and tough, but you're soft as taffy on the inside, aren't you?"

"Only you would think so." Or dare say it. But that reminded him. "Did you call your folks and let them know you're okay? I don't want any missing-person reports coming into the station."

"I texted them. Then I turned off my phone," she admitted, her voice soft. "I don't think I'm up to a conversation with them."

"Yeah, I get that."

"Hank? Do you . . . do you think I'm a coward, running away like I did? Because I'm starting to feel really bad about it." The defeat in her voice tore at him. Guilt was the real reason she couldn't sleep, and that was something he was all too familiar with.

Rolling to his feet, he walked to the bedroom and stopped in the doorway. "Are you dressed?"

She turned her head to look in his direction, her outline faint in the darkened room. "Of course I'm dressed. Why wouldn't I be dressed?"

He ignored that and headed for the bed. He crawled in beside her, nudging her over a couple of inches. When he got settled, he wrapped one arm around her back and rolled her into his side so her stomach was pressed into his hip. "You're not a coward. I don't want you thinking that. It took guts to get away before you made a mistake."

"Was it a mistake?" Curling her hand into his shirt, she wiggled around until she settled into him, her head on his shoulder. "Because it feels like I've been making mistakes all day. Who knows which one was the mistake and which one was right."

"Marrying someone you don't love is the mistake." She remained quiet, and he jostled her. "Right?"

"Right."

But she didn't sound sure. Was she regretting not being Mrs. Chance Worthington? "Guilt is a useless emotion. Don't waste your time on it," he said gruffly. "Now go to sleep."

"What do you feel guilty about?" Ignoring his requests seemed to be her favorite pastime.

He didn't answer her. Not at first. It wasn't something he talked about, not even with his brother. But lying there in the dark, knowing Savannah wouldn't be passing any judgment, loosened his lips.

"I got in a fight with my dad when I was eighteen. Called him on his pill use. How he was letting the family down. Told him to get his crap together." He could remember that fight like it was yesterday. He'd been in a couple of skirmishes in the Army, and those had faded to a blur of dust and gunfire. But not that day with his old man. "Punches were thrown. He kicked me out, but I would have walked even if he hadn't. We talked a little bit after that on the phone, but I didn't go home again until his funeral."

He swallowed past the thickness in his throat. Shame still ate at him. "I was angry, but I was also embarrassed by what I did. And because of that, I lost a lot of time with my family. Guilt kept me away, and I lost those last couple of years with my dad."

"But you're home now." Pressing her hand to his chest, she snuggled closer. "Maybe we should both take your advice. Stop feeling guilty."

He covered her hand with his own, holding her palm over his heart. "Maybe." It was easily said. Much harder to do. He cleared his throat. "Now go to sleep."

For once, she did what he said. With a breathy little sigh, she pressed the length of her body against his side and drifted into sleep. Her breathing evened out, and her muscles relaxed into the bed.

Hank stared at the ceiling. He was in bed with another man's fiancée. She still wore Worthington's big-ass diamond on her finger, something that hadn't escaped his notice. He was making another mistake. Something else he should feel guilt over.

But he didn't.

Instead, he held her close and fell into a deep sleep.

Something sweet-smelling wafted under her nose. Savannah sniffed, the soft cocoon of sleep being dragged from her. She sniffed again, and something shot up her nose. She woke on a sneeze.

Hank laughed. He sat on the edge of the bed, a white box in one hand and a jelly donut in the other. "You inhaled some powdered sugar. Sorry about that," he said, not sounding sorry at all.

"If one of those is for me, all is forgiven." She rubbed her eyes and looked at the pastry box. From its size, there should be at least six donuts in there. Give or take one. What a wonderful start to the day.

"You can have as many as you want. I didn't know which kind you'd like, so I got a variety." He showed her the assortment, a beautiful mosaic of pink and white icing and chocolate ganache.

She started with the jelly donut. "Thanks," she said around the bite in her mouth.

"Time to get up, sleepyhead." Hank stood and walked out of the bedroom.

She trailed behind him to the kitchen, already deciding which pastry would be next on the menu. The chocolate old-fashioned. Definitely.

"My shift starts in a couple of hours, so I have to get

going soon." Pulling two small bottles of orange juice from a bag, he handed her one and twisted the top off of his own. "I didn't want to walk out while you were asleep."

"Considerate of you. Your girlfriends must appreciate it." The fluffy dough clogged in her throat. Crap. She hadn't considered the idea of him having a girlfriend. But why wouldn't he? There weren't that many men with thick, pettable hair and deep, soulful eyes, who had muscles like a wide receiver, and who were wandering around single. Women were smart. They snapped men like Hank up quickly.

She tried to sound casual. "Are you dating someone?" She pulled the chocolate old-fashioned into four sections, concentrating on making them evenly sized.

"Not at the moment." He took a large sip of OJ, his throat rippling as he swallowed. Wiping his mouth with the back of his hand, he gave her a heated look. "I haven't been back in Serendipity that long, and the options are limited."

"The joy of living in a small town." Although the number of single women had just increased by one as of yesterday. She nibbled on her donut. Probably best not to mention that. Or throw herself at him. It wouldn't be smart. Besides, her attraction to him could all come down to the fact that he'd plied her with amazing food. She couldn't underestimate the power of grease and sugar on her hormones.

Stepping around her, Hank strode to the sofa in the living room. He picked up a pillow that had fallen to the floor and tossed it back on the cushions.

Savannah wiped her hands on her leggings. Plucking up the pillow, she fluffed it before arranging it neatly in the corner of the sofa.

"What are you doing?" he asked when she picked up the other pillow, gave it the same treatment before replacing it in the opposite corner.

"Trying to make things look nice. Appealing to a buyer." She cocked her head. The whole couch looked a little flatter after Hank had spent half the night on it. She knelt on the central cushion, bounced up and down. "The staging is important."

He groaned, and Savannah looked over her shoulder. His gaze was planted on her butt, his lips drawn into a tight line.

Her bouncing wound down. "I'm trying to fluff the cushions." Her cheeks heated.

"Don't stop on my account."

"I don't think it's working." She gripped the back of the couch, her fingers wanting nothing more than to grab the waistband of his jeans and tug him into her. Stupid fingers. "Maybe if you got down here, too?" And there went her stupid mouth. She'd just left one man. She shouldn't be trying to get close to another.

But when he set one knee on the sofa next to her, her heart leapt into her throat, and she didn't care if it was stupid. She wanted Hank Evans.

The soft cotton of his T-shirt brushed against her bare arm. Her head went fuzzy.

He covered one of her hands with his own, a callous on his palm scraping across her skin.

Her mouth went bone-dry.

She licked her lips, trying to bring moisture back.

Hank dropped his glance to her mouth. Cupping her face, he dragged his thumb across her bottom lip, then raised his thumb to his own mouth. He stuck the tip of his thumb between his lips and sucked. "You had a bit of sugar there."

"Is it all gone?" Her voice was breathy. Husky. "Or do you need to clean me up some more?"

He dropped his head. "I have a feeling cleaning you up could become my favorite part of the day." He brushed his lips over the corner of her mouth, the contact fleeting. She released a juddering breath. With the tip of his tongue, he licked the powdered sugar from her bottom lip, and that was it. The end of her hesitation.

Twisting, she threw herself at him, wrapping her arms around his neck. He crashed back on the couch with a muffled *oomph*, with Savannah lying on top of him. She turned his tease into a real kiss, devouring his mouth with all the pent-up frustration two years of pecks on the cheek would bring a girl.

Digging his hand in her hair, Hank cupped her head, angled her face the way he wanted. His other hand drifted, skimming up and down her spine, each pass heading lower. When he reached her butt, he cupped her cheek and squeezed.

She melted over him. Good Lord, what had she been missing out on? She had been going to resign herself to fifty years in a loveless marriage when men like Hank were out there in the world? Men like Hank who could do incredible things with his mouth?

He nibbled along her bottom lip, tugged gently, and she felt it in her core.

Do incredible things with his teeth?

She'd been stark out of her mind.

Tugging her head back, Hank caught his breath. He examined her expression. "Babe. You sure you want to do this?"

The rise of his chest lifted her and drew her back down. It was like they were one body. Nodding, she chased his mouth with her own, but his grip in her hair held her back.

She tried to explain. How of course she wanted to keep kissing him. Exploring the heat between them. After years of settling for tepid dates and a comfortable, respectable relationship, she was eager to throw herself into something that sent a thrill through her blood. Made her tingle and ache. "You bought me donuts," was what came out of her mouth.

His lips twitched. Yes, so her explanation hadn't been very eloquent. And hadn't made sense anywhere other than in her own mind. But she didn't care if he thought she was weird. Just as long as he put those lips on her.

"Babe, if this is the thanks I get for a donut, I can't wait to see what happens when I buy you a coffee cake." He tugged her hips down against his and captured her mouth. Neither one of them heard the door swing open.

A startled gasp, a giggle, and someone sternly clearing her throat.

Savannah turned her head, saw three people standing in the doorway, and yelped. She pressed up and tried to scuttle off of Hank. Her knee pushed between Hank's thighs, caught something delicate, and his eyes bulged.

"Sorry!" Her elbow caught him below the rib cage, and he wheezed. "Damn it!" she swore. The sofa was soft and kept sucking her back down. Giving up all pretense of grace, she rolled, landing on her back on the floor. She stared at the ceiling and prayed the intruders had been an illusion.

A pair of three-inch heels stalked into her peripheral vision beneath the coffee table. Nope. No illusion.

"Did you forget about the showing today?" A cool, professional, feminine voice asked. As if walking in on a couple making out on the sofa was an everyday occurrence. "Mr. and Mrs. Young were hoping to take a PG-rated tour of your condo."

Hank swung his legs off the couch. "Hi, Kat." He cleared his throat and tugged at the leg of his jeans. "Sorry, I did forget." Grabbing Savannah's hand, he stood, pulling her up to her feet as well. He straightened the strap to her tank top and brushed some lint off her hip.

Savannah stepped back, her face as hot as a ghost pepper. "This is your real estate agent?"

The woman stuck out her hand, and Savannah took the solid grip. "Katerina Gonzalez with Mission Realty. How do you do?"

Savannah took in the woman's slim pencil skirt and fitted jacket. The neat chignon of dark hair. The pleasant smile on her nude-painted lips. And realized she hadn't yet brushed her own hair. Or changed her clothes since yesterday morning.

She forced a smile. "Savannah Loving with Embarrassed to Death, Inc. And I've been better."

"I don't know," the woman by the door said. Mrs. Young, Savannah presumed. "That looked like the start to a good day to me."

The real estate agent turned to her clients. "I apologize for the confusion. The condo was supposed to be vacant. But I think even with the floorshow you should still be able to see the potential of the space." She held out a hand. "Shall we start with the bedroom?"

The trio drifted down the hall, Kat pointing out features as they went.

Hank rubbed the back of his neck. "I'm sorry about that. I'd forgotten she was showing the place this weekend."

"Don't worry about it." Stalking to the kitchen, Savannah cleaned up their breakfast mess and started gathering all the supplies she'd bought into bags. "I should get out of here anyway."

"You heading back home?" Hank poked into the donut box, came out with a pink-iced one covered in nuts.

Savannah considered. She needed to face the music sometime. Get her apologies out of the way. The idea filled her stomach with knots. After the yelling, after the looks of disappointment, she knew her parents would try to convince her she'd only suffered from cold feet. That the wedding should go on. That was an argument she wasn't prepared to have.

"I think I'll stick around Dallas for another couple of days. Maybe go to some museums and the botanical garden." It had been ages since she'd played the tourist. If she pretended she was on vacation, she could put off the unpleasant realities a little bit longer. "Do you know of any hotels around here that don't cost an arm and a leg?"

"Why not stay here?"

"Because your friend is showing the place." She shook her head. "I can't stick around."

He shrugged. "So go out for a couple of hours. See a movie.

Kat will be done by this evening and won't be showing the place again until next weekend."

"I do have some shopping I need to do." New clothes to wear. A towel to take a shower. She chewed on her lip, until Hank's gaze dropped to her mouth and he took a step toward her.

Settling his hands on her hips, he pulled her close. The button fly of his jeans rubbed against her belly, and heat settled low. "When you go shopping, buy something nice for tonight. I want to take you out."

She gripped his biceps. "You do? Don't you have to work?"

"After my shift. I can get here around eight." Tucking a lock of hair behind her ear, he dipped his head. "It seems like you've been locked up in everyone's expectations for too long. It's time you had some good, old-fashioned fun. And I want to be the man to show it to you. Does eight work?"

The logistics worked fine. Gave her plenty of time to get ready after the real estate agent left. But did the date itself work for her? Her body said hell yes. Her heart gave the idea a thumbs up. Her brain told her she was a dumb ass.

"That sounds great." One of these days her brain would have to win an argument. Apparently, it wasn't today.

Brushing his lips against hers, he dug his fingers into her skin, as if he were afraid she'd disappear. With a deep breath, he stepped back and grabbed a second donut. "See you later." Striding from the kitchen, he shouted, "Leaving now, Kat. Lock up when you're done."

The front door shut behind him as Kat and the Youngs strolled out of the back rooms.

Savannah shifted from one bare foot to another. "I'm just going to head out now, too." Darting to the bedroom, she found her flip-flops and slid them on. She grabbed Hank's sweatshirt and wrapped it around her waist. The group was in the kitchen as she sidled out.

Remembering her manners, she popped her head in. "It

was nice meeting you. Sorry about the mess and, well, just sorry."

"No worries." Kat jotted down a note on her clipboard, then looked up with a bright smile. "It was Hank who forgot, not you. Besides, it gave the Youngs some free entertainment." She winked at the couple.

Kat had to be reasonable, too. Poised, professional, sensible, all qualities that Savannah felt herself lacking at the moment.

With a nod good-bye, Savannah hightailed it out of there. The morning was still cool, the air holding just a hint of moisture. It was going to be another beautiful day. And she could spend it however she wanted.

Bouncing down the steps, she headed for the Ducati with a spring in her step. A whole day in which she could be herself, do whatever she wanted.

And a night with Hank to get ready for.

Revving the engine, she put the bike into gear and shot out of her spot.

Yes, today was promising to be one fine day.

Chapter Five

Hank stepped out of his Jeep and smoothed his hand down the front of his white button-down shirt. His palms were damp, and he shook his head in disgust. It was an absurd reaction for a thirty-year-old man picking up a woman for their first date. Reaching into the Jeep, he pulled out the bouquet of bluebonnets he'd picked along the highway. Thirty-year-olds typically didn't stop along the road to pick wildflowers, either, but something about Savannah brought out the fool in him.

He trotted up to his condo and opened the door. Pausing, he knocked on the open door and called in. "Savannah? If you have any more Chinese food in there, stand down. It's only me."

"Very funny," she called from the back. She darted past the open bedroom door, and Hank caught the swish of a red skirt and a wild mess of wavy blond hair. "I'll be ready in a second."

Hank settled into the couch, prepared for a long wait. Stretching his arm along the back, he remembered the action the couch had seen that morning and smiled. Maybe tonight it would see even more.

A minute later the soft clicking of heels tapping against the hardwood floor had him jumping to his feet. He turned and felt his jaw drop. He forced it shut. "Wow. You look . . . Wow."

Savannah Loving twirled before him. The hem of her skirt fluttered around her thighs. The black top she wore seemed to be made of nothing but straps, and clung to her body like a second skin. Flashes of bronzed skin peeked out of the top as she turned. Red heels completed her look, with little cutouts at the front that showcased her painted toenails.

She was like a shot of adrenalin to his veins. Absolutely amazing.

"Will I do?" she asked. She ran a hand over her hair. "I forgot to buy a hair dryer, so you're stuck with curls."

Hank didn't understand the connection between the two, and he didn't care. "You're beautiful, curly-haired or straight." He cleared his throat. "But you already knew that."

"A girl still likes to be complimented." Smoothing her palms down her skirt, she shot him an uneven smile. "Besides, I haven't worn something like this since college. Wasn't sure I could still pull it off."

She didn't have to worry about that. He would be sure to take over the job of pulling it off if she couldn't. He held the flowers out. "I made reservations at Five Sixty. Are you ready to go?" The sooner they left, the sooner they'd be back. He should have ordered dinner in.

Taking the bluebonnets, she buried her nose in the blooms and inhaled deeply, doing all sorts of interesting things to her top. "You picked flowers for me?" Her eyes were wide, disbelieving, and the look was a hook to his gut.

He shoved his hands in his pockets. "This can't be the first time you've gotten flowers." Even that putz Worthington wouldn't have been that stupid.

"Not hand-picked." She tapped the plastic band holding the stems together. "That's a creative use of your zip-ties."

He shrugged and thanked all that was holy that no other cop had seen him use the restraint on a bouquet. "Are you ready to go?" he repeated.

"Yeah. Let me go put these in water." She disappeared into the kitchen for a minute and came back with the flowers in an eight-ounce orange juice bottle she must have pulled from the garbage. She placed the makeshift vase on the coffee table and picked up a thin cardigan from the back of the couch. She shrugged it on. "Let's hit it."

He kept his hand on the small of her back as they walked to the Jeep. His fingers twitched as their connection broke after he'd handed her in. He trotted to the driver's side and slid in. Finding her hand on the armrest, he joined their fingers as he drove out of the lot and headed downtown.

She ran her thumb over his, seeming to want the connection as much as he did. The soft scent of vanilla filled the interior, and he wondered if it was perfume or body wash. There was so much to learn about a woman at the start of a relationship, and Hank was eager to find out everything there was to know about Savannah Loving.

"What did you do today?" he asked. "Aside from go shopping for that sexy outfit."

"Bought a novel and read in the park by your condo." She shifted, and her skirt rose up her thighs an inch. "I can't remember the last time I just did nothing. For the past year, every day has been either filled with work or wedding planning."

That cooled his jets fast. "Did you talk to your parents at all?" His stomach tensed. "Or Worthington?"

She shook her head. "I'll text my parents again tomorrow. And Chance . . . I need to speak to him. Soon." She sighed. "He deserves better."

Hank didn't know the man, but he figured Worthington had gotten exactly what he deserved. A man who didn't take care of all his woman's needs didn't deserve to hold on to her. And why a man would want the quiet, obedient Savannah instead of the spitfire beside him, he didn't know.

Flipping on his blinker, he turned into the parking garage under Reunion Tower. Hank didn't much care for the esteem in Savannah's voice when she spoke of her former fiancé. Did she still have feelings for him? Hank didn't know what was going on between him and Savannah, but he sure as hell didn't want to be her last fling before she settled down with the respectable doctor.

"Have you thought about what you're going to say to him?" he asked as he pulled into an empty spot.

Shaking her head, she climbed out of the Jeep. Hank followed. "What do you say to the man you treated horribly?" she asked. She stared at her toes as Hank walked around the car to join her. "How do you apologize for something like that?"

"Maybe you're not the only one who needs to be apologizing," Hank growled. Yes, she was feeling much too friendly toward her former flame. "You don't need to explain anything. Just tell him it's over and move on."

Savannah snorted and fell into step beside him as they headed for the elevator. "I take back what I said about your being a good boyfriend. If that's how you ended things with your girlfriends, you deserve a trophy for being a jackass."

"Talking something to death never helps a situation." The doors opened, and they stepped from the elevator into the center of the restaurant. Stunning three-hundred-and-sixty-degree views of the Dallas skyline greeted them.

A maître d' took Hank's name and showed them to their table. Hank pulled out Savannah's chair and settled himself across from her at the intimate two-top next to the floor-to-ceiling window. The restaurant revolved so slowly Hank barely felt the movement.

Savannah opened her napkin and draped it over her lap. "Let's not talk about home. Tell me about life as a cop. Do you enjoy the work?"

And so they ignored all their problems and enjoyed dinner as the skyline gradually spun around them. When Savannah laughed, she threw her head back. When she told him about the prank she'd been arrested for in college (but not charged), her eyes sparkled. And when she told him about her first-graders, her smile was bright enough to melt ice in December.

She ordered tiramisu, and Hank watched as she relished every last bite. "Are you done?" he asked when she finally dropped her spoon. "Don't want to lick the plate?"

"Don't tempt me." Leaning back, she rested her hands on her stomach and groaned. "It was all delicious. Thank you." She tucked her chin down and gazed at him with liquid eyes. "Thanks for everything. You came into my life at just the right moment, and I don't know how to repay you."

Hank had some ideas. He tossed cash on the table and stood. Tucking her hand in his arm, he led her to the elevator. "Do you want to go for a walk to work off our meal?" He prayed she said no. But he'd been raised to be a gentleman, and gentlemen didn't rush their women to bed.

"In these heels?" She stepped onto the elevator, and pointed the toe of her red pump.

Hank had to agree. Those heels were sexy. Much more suited to other activities. Ones where Savannah would be off her feet.

"But there is something I'd love to do with you." She leaned into him. "Take me home and I'll show you?"

He sped back to the condo, keeping an eye out for blue lights, anxious to get her home. His whole body felt tight, itchy, as though he wanted to burst out of his skin. He never could have imagined the annoying girl with pigtails would turn into this woman. Hot, sweet, and full of sass.

When she returned home to Serendipity, she'd better not fall back into her submissive behavior. Hank would have to make sure she didn't lose her nerve.

She hopped out of the Jeep and rested her hands on the roof. "Do you trust me?" she asked as he stood across the vehicle from her.

A smile stretched his face. "That depends on what you want to do with me."

"Stay here." Without waiting for a response, she spun and raced up the stairs on those heels.

Hank's excitement turned to confusion. He looked around the parking lot. Empty except for him. What was Savannah up to?

The sound of flip-flops slapping on the stairs drew his attention. She'd changed her footwear and put on the sweatshirt he'd given her. Her hands were behind her back.

He'd rather hoped that clothes would be coming off, not being added on.

She held up her keys and helmet. "Let's go for a ride."

"What? Now?" He looked at the Ducati parked two spots away.

She sauntered over to it and flicked her hair over her shoulder. "Scared?"

Oh, hell no. "I taught you how to ride, remember? I know my way around a bike."

Slinging a leg over the driver's seat, she bit her lip and looked up at him. "But I'm going to be driving. Scared yet?"

Hank's skin tingled. Striding to her, he plucked the helmet from her hand and plopped it on her head. He climbed on the Ducati behind her and wrapped his arms around her waist. "Hit it."

Savannah revved the engine and, with a howl at the moon, took off.

His hands clenched her waist. He couldn't say it was a comfortable feeling riding behind Savannah, not having control of the bike, but it was exhilarating. Her skirt flapped back over his pants, exposing her long legs. Her butt, nestled between his thighs, was round in all the right places. If she didn't run them off the road, this would be one hell of a ride.

She took the Northwest Highway and pulled over in a park with a view of the skyline. Cutting the engine, she lifted off her helmet, her hair swinging loose, and leaned back against his chest.

Hank wrapped her close. "This seems to be the night for amazing views of Dallas."

They watched the bright lights below with the stars faint above them.

"This is weird," she said softly.

"What is?" He tucked a lock of hair behind her ear and kissed the soft skin of her neck. Nothing about this felt weird to him. Everything felt right.

"This. You. I've known you as an adult for two days, and I feel more comfortable with you than I ever did with . . ."

"Worthington?"

"And everyone else in Serendipity." Cupping his hand at her waist, she rubbed her thumb over the top. "With you, I feel free to be myself."

"You are free." He tucked his chin on her shoulder. "And don't ever stop living the way you want."

Twisting, she looked him in the eye. "I know why I'm here, Hank. But why are you? I'm a wimp who almost married someone because her parents wanted her to."

He kissed her nose and each of her eyes. "I could tell you, but I'm not much of a talker. I'd rather show you." He climbed off the bike and nudged her hip. "Scoot back. I'm driving this time." She pressed her lips together and rolled her eyes, but wiggled onto the back seat. She secured her helmet as he slid in front of her. "Now, hold on tight. I don't want you flying off the back." He started the bike.

"Sure," she said dryly. "Safety first." Tucking herself up tight against his back, she wrapped her arms around his middle and squeezed.

And with the sweet woman pressed tight, Hank took off, eager to get her home.

They hurried to the front door. Savannah waited as he unlocked it, her pulse pounding in her throat, mouth gone dry. Her body wanted Hank as much as he seemed to want her, but a small part of her brain warned her this was a mistake.

A mistake on Hank's part.

She told her brain to shut up.

He pushed open the door and dragged Savannah inside, pulling her against his chest. She linked her hands behind his neck, and their mouths clashed together.

Hank kicked the door shut with his boot. Grabbing her around the waist, he lifted, and she wrapped her legs around his hips with a soft moan.

He felt so good under her hands. Strong. Solid. And so very, very hot, as if he were burning up from the inside.

He stumbled to the couch, his mouth crushing hers, their tongues tangling. She tasted the bite of tiramisu he'd stolen from her bowl, smelled the sage and moss of his cologne. He was like one giant buffet for her senses. She shrugged out of her sweatshirt, kicked off her flip-flops. Hank skimmed his palm down her bare arm, and goose bumps followed in his wake.

Without raising his head, he found the sofa and gently lowered their bodies. He covered her curves with his hard planes. He nestled between her thighs, and her mind short-circuited. Grazing his palm up her side, he cupped her breast, and she just about melted.

She suckled on the tip of his tongue, dug her hands into his hair, and loved the way he groaned. "Hank," she whispered. She tugged on his shirt, pulling it from his slacks, and skimmed her hands underneath and up his back. "You feel so good."

That was an understatement. He felt fantastic, but she didn't need to inflate his ego to epic proportions just quite yet. He scraped his teeth down her jaw and nuzzled the soft skin of her neck. Damn. Get her an air pump, and she'd inflate away. No man had ever made her ache so sweetly. Her pulse pounded. Her body heated, and she wanted to tear off her clothes. And then Hank's. Or maybe both at the same time. He sucked the lobe of her ear into his mouth and bit down.

She whimpered and rocked her hips into him.

He cursed.

"Babe," he said, trailing his lips down her neck to her collarbone. "You taste so damn good." He pulled one of the straps of her top off her shoulder and kissed the exposed skin.

Feeling for the hem of her skirt, he slid his hand underneath. She reached for the button to his slacks, and her engagement ring hit his abs and turned on her finger. She froze.

Why was she still wearing Chance's ring? Her heart twisted painfully in her chest, and her eyes burned. How could she let Hank touch her when she was wearing another man's ring? What kind of person did that? Hank thought he saw something good in her, someone worthy of his affection.

He must have been wearing blinders.

He stroked higher, inching toward her core. She grabbed his wrist, stopping his exploration.

"Something wrong? Did I hurt you?" He pushed his weight off of her, eyes narrowing with concern.

"No. Nothing's wrong." She dropped her head back on the cushion. Nothing, except she was a horrible person. "Just, this is moving fast. And I"—she swallowed—"I'm still wearing another man's ring."

"Then take it the hell off."

"The ring is just symbolic." She scooted backwards until her shoulders hit the armrest. "It's what it stands for that's the problem."

Hank sat back. "Do you still have feelings for him?"

"Yes, but not the way you think." Chance was a wonderful man. He'd listened as she complained about the administration at her school. Held her hand when she'd needed seven stitches in the ER after she'd fallen over a broken-off post on her father's ranch. She couldn't help but care about a man as decent as Chance Worthington.

But even though she cared for him, Chance had never made her feel like Hank did.

She sighed. "I'm just not ready." Pulling up the strap to her top, she tucked her feet under her. "This is moving really fast, and I need some time to think. I hope you can understand."

"I can be a patient man. I'm happy with waiting, especially for a woman like you." He tugged at the collar to his shirt. "But will you ever be ready for a man like me?"

"What do you mean?"

"I'm not a doctor. I'm not a Worthington. Not Serendipity royalty." He turned on the couch and looked her in the eye. "I'm just a cop who was born on the other side of the tracks from you."

She stood and paced to the wall. Her stomach churned. "First of all, we don't have railroad tracks through Serendipity. Second, is that the kind of woman you think I am? One who would reject a man with a blue-collar job?"

Pushing to his feet, Hank crossed his arms over his chest. "Well, you did turn down my brother when he asked you to prom. The Evans name wasn't good enough for you back then."

Any guilt she felt was swept away in a tide of anger. "Did it ever occur to you that I just didn't like your brother? He always struck me as a bit of a jackass. I'm coming to realize it's a family trait."

Padding past him, she stalked into the kitchen.

He followed and stood in the doorway. His gaze tracked her as she stomped to the refrigerator and pulled out a bottle of water.

"You're right," he said, rubbing the back of his neck. "My brother can be a jackass. And I can't believe I'm still worried about my family's reputation."

Her anger fizzled away. She stepped up to him and rubbed his arm. "Your father had a disease. It's nothing to be ashamed about. Everyone in town loves your mom and brother. And when they get to know you better, they'll love you, too."

"I'm sorry for being a jackass." He cupped her cheek. "It's weird. I haven't seen you for years, and now you're in my condo in Dallas. I don't quite know where I stand. If we had started dating in town, it would have been easier."

She licked her lips. "When I go back, are you going to want to see me? Or is this a fun fling while we're both away from our regular lives?"

"I don't care what town we're in; I want to see you." He lightly kissed her lips, and the last of her tension slipped away.

Everything felt right when Hank was kissing her.

"Will you see me? When I call you"—he brushed one of her curls off her cheek—"because I will be calling. Will you let me take you out? Hold your hand in public?" His Adam's apple bounced up and down. "If I'm your rebound, tell me now, before we get any more involved."

"Why wait to call me for a date? Ask me now." On this score, she could reassure him. She might be a hot mess who didn't deserve a man like Hank, but if he asked her out, she wasn't stupid enough to say no.

A smile tugged at his lips. "Savannah, will you go out with me this Friday night? You will be back by then, right?"

"With a date with you as an incentive, you bet your ass I will." Rolling up onto her toes, she kissed the corner of his mouth. "And you can hold anything of mine you want in public. Within reason," she amended.

He grinned. "Savannah Loving, you have made my return to Serendipity much more interesting. I should have pulled you over months ago."

"Yes." If she'd run into Hank months ago, felt the incredible chemistry between them, it might have changed things. "That might have stopped me from becoming Serendipity's runaway bride."

"No. No more regret." He squeezed her hips. "Not tonight."

She nodded. He was right. Regret and guilt didn't solve anything. Except maybe give her a kick in the pants to do the right thing. "Are you going to stay here tonight or do you have to get back home?"

"I can stay. My shift doesn't start till ten tomorrow morning. I'll take the couch."

"The bed's big enough for two." She stepped out of his arms. Walking around him, she tossed over her shoulder, "We proved last night we could both sleep in it without using it to its full potential. I think we can control ourselves again tonight."

She got ready for bed, washing her face clean of makeup and changing into the sleep cami and short set she'd bought. Stepping out, she peeked around the door to the bedroom. "The bathroom's free."

He looked her up and down, his gaze lingering on her legs. "Thanks. I got some sweats from my Jeep to sleep in."

She snuggled on the bed as he took a shower. When he stepped out of the bathroom, billows of steam followed him.

"I forgot to buy sheets," she told him. "So we're using the comforter as the base, and I unzipped your sleeping bag for our blanket." She lifted one edge of the sleeping bag. "Climb on in."

He did and stared at the ceiling as she snapped off the light. His body was tense, edgy, and Savannah knew it was going to be a long night for both of them.

Tossing his hand behind his head, he blew out a breath.

"Hank?"

"Yeah, babe?"

"Can you not take this the wrong way?" She didn't wait for him to answer, but flipped over onto her side, rested her head on his shoulder, and flung an arm over his chest.

"Uh . . . ?"

"I'm not changing my mind about sleeping with you tonight, but I don't want there to be inches of space between us." She lifted her head, scooted a little closer, and settled back down. "Is this okay?"

He brought his arm down and rested his hand on the small of her back. "I wouldn't want it any other way," he told her. Burying his nose in her hair, he inhaled deeply and pulled her closer.

She yawned. "Good." Even to her own ears, her voice sounded drowsy. "I can't remember ever sleeping as well as I did last night in your arms."

Cupping her elbow at his stomach, he ran his thumb up and down her skin. "Go to sleep," he said, his voice gruff.

Savannah smiled. No, Hank wasn't big on talking. But by holding her like this, not pushing her on having sex, he was showing her everything she needed to know.

Chapter Six

Savannah zipped up the sleeping bag and brushed the wrinkles out of the bed's comforter. It was Monday, but she didn't have to hurry to her job. She'd taken the next two weeks off, expecting to be on her honeymoon. But that didn't mean she could laze about. She'd stuck her head in the sand for two days, and it was time to face up to the firing squad back home.

Padding to the kitchen, she spotted another white box. She lifted the lid and saw the pastry choices for the day were bear claws and cherry Danish. Hank was a god among men. Danish in mouth, she pulled the piece of paper out from under the box and read Hank's note.

A smile tugged at her lips. Who would have thought the boy who'd rolled his eyes at her and yanked on her pigtail could be so sweet? And why couldn't he have moved back to Serendipity two years ago? This whole mess might never have happened.

She picked up a bear claw and pulled off one of the little toes. It was a good thing she'd run away in leggings. The way she was eating, she'd need the elastic waistband.

Trudging into the living room, she flopped back on the sofa. If she'd connected with Hank sooner, the mess with Chance might not have happened, but she was kidding herself if she thought it would have been smooth sailing. Hank was right about her parents—they wouldn't approve of her relationship with an Evans.

She shoved a bite of pastry into her mouth. And would she have gone along to get along with her parents? Turned Hank down if he'd asked her out two years ago?

The bear claw turned to dust in her mouth. She'd been such a coward. Following the path her parents chose instead of forging her own. And because of her weakness, she'd hurt a lot of people.

The key turned in the lock, and Savannah's gaze darted to the door, her heart leaping at the thought that Hank had forgotten something.

Kat Gonzalez stepped through the door. She jerked to a stop when she caught sight of Savannah. "Oh, I'm sorry. I should have knocked."

Rolling to her feet, Savannah shook her head. "No, it's fine." She started to run her hand through the rat's nest she called hair, remembered she was holding a bear claw, and lowered her arm. "I wasn't expecting you to come back until next weekend. Do you have another showing today?"

Closing the door, the woman dropped her purse on the narrow counter. "I was in the neighborhood and decided to swing by to see if anything needed to be straightened up."

Savannah curled her toes into the wood floor. "Because of me?" She cupped her other hand under her pastry to catch any errant crumbs. "I bought some supplies. I'll make sure to clean everything today."

"Thanks, I appreciate it." Kat tipped her head, and her sleek ponytail slipped off her shoulder.

"So, you were in the Army?" Savannah asked. She looked at the woman's skirt suit and immaculate makeup. Except for the acres of toned leg that you only got from jogging every day, it was hard to believe the beautiful woman had been in the military. "Hank told me about you."

Kat smiled. "I know my persona now is deceptive, but I

loved the Army. I would have re-upped if my parents hadn't thrown a fit. They wanted their baby girl back home popping out grandbabies."

Laughter burbled up Savannah's throat. "I get that. I almost married a really decent man to please my folks."

"A decent man?" Kat mock shuddered. "The horror."

"You have no idea." Savannah turned toward the kitchen. "Hey, you want a pastry?"

The real estate agent followed her in, and peered into the box. "I'll have to add another two miles to my run tonight." Picking up a Danish, she took a big bite. "Worth it," she said around her mouthful.

Savannah smiled. She had a feeling she and Kat could be kindred spirits.

"I remember when Hank brought me food in the morning when we were dating." Kat swirled her finger in the cherry jelly and licked it off. "Talk about a decent guy."

Savannah's stomach plummeted to her toes. "You and Hank used to date?"

Kat stopped chewing. Eyes wide, she swallowed her bite down. "I thought you knew. You said Hank told you about me."

"No. Yes. Of course." Savannah dropped her half-eaten claw in the box. "He said you were friends. I just didn't realize how close." She tugged on the hem of her tank top. So this was Hank's type? Professional, strong, and sensible? She looked down at her bare feet. The red nail polish seemed frivolous. Her escape had been a train wreck. Hank had met her on one of her worst days. She'd been one red-hot mess. How would that image measure up to the image of his tough-as-nails former flame?

"It wasn't a big thing." Kat wiped sugar off her hands. "It was just for a couple of months when we got out of the Army."

"No need to explain." And no need to prolong the embarrassment. "I'm going to get started on the cleaning." Savannah took a step toward the door and paused. "Oh, but I should tell you that there's a small stain on the comforter. I spilled some nail polish remover on it." She grimaced. "I'm sorry. I'll replace it."

"No worries. I can get a new one before this weekend."

"At least let me give you some money—"

Kat waved a hand. "I'll charge Hank for it," she said with a wink. "Well, I should get going. I have a new listing I need to work on. It was nice talking to you, Savannah. I hope you enjoy your stay in Dallas."

Friendly and professional to the end. It was hard not to like Kat, even though Savannah really wanted to try. Kat and Hank should have worked as a couple. Savannah wondered why they hadn't lasted.

"Thanks." She followed the woman to the door and waved good-bye before closing it. She leaned against the frame and let her head fall back against the wood. Her stomach churned. She felt adrift. Like she was being tossed about by a tornado with no way to control her landing.

And it was time she got her life together.

Pushing off the door, she got to work cleaning all traces of her visit from Hank's condo. She packed up her things and dropped her bag by the door. She picked up her bluebonnets and wandered to the kitchen. Dumping the water and throwing out the OJ bottle, she wrapped the flowers in a paper towel, but didn't have much hope that they'd survive the trip. But she'd try. The pastries, however, she'd have to leave behind. They wouldn't fit on the Ducati. And maybe it was time she got control of her eating, just as she planned on taking control of her life.

She flipped over the piece of paper Hank had written his note on and penned one of her own. He hadn't said anything, but she suspected he would come back to the condo tonight. And stupidly, she'd never gotten his phone number.

With one last look at what had been her haven, she scooped up her keys and left Hank's home. It was time to face the music.

* * *

Hank pointed his speed gun at the red pickup barreling down the highway. Fifty-three. Not high enough to pull it over. He dropped his arm outside the open window of his patrol truck and sighed. He enjoyed the slower pace of being a country cop. The lack of stress.

But when he was itching to get back to Dallas, to Savannah, the hours with little to do seemed to stretch into eternity. He drummed his fingers on the steering wheel and glanced at the dashboard clock. Again. And still an hour left on his shift.

Picking up the receiver to the radio, he called in to dispatch. "Hey, Janine. Anything going on I can get involved in? A robbery? Drunk and disorderly?" He dropped his head against the seat rest. "Hell, I'll even take a shoplifting case right about now."

The radio crackled. "Sorry, sweetie. All's quiet on the home front."

Perfect. Why did his hometown have to be so damn law-abiding? He glanced at the clock again. Not even a minute had passed. He hung up the receiver in disgust.

A trail of dust signaled a vehicle approaching. Hank waited, and waited, and didn't even bother raising the speed gun as the aged Corolla limped past.

He needed another Savannah tearing out of town on a Ducati to liven things up. His lips twitched. God, she'd been cute. And sexy. Long hair blowing back with the wind. Bare feet on the pedals. Not much was hotter than a woman on a fast bike. A woman like her would be hell on wheels to handle, and Hank looked forward to the opportunity.

His cell phone vibrated in his pocket, and he slid it out, looking at the screen. He answered. "Hey, Kat. What's up?"

"You're not with Savannah right now, are you?"

He sat up taller in his seat. "No. Why are you asking?"

"Well, I had a little conversation with her this morning,"

she said. "I went to buy a new comforter for your bed, and when I got back she was gone."

"Okaaay. So?" Tossing the speed gun on the seat beside him, Hank rubbed his neck. "She's probably out sightseeing."

"Well, in our conversation, I might have mentioned that you and I used to date. I don't think she was too happy to hear it."

"Why would you tell her that?"

She sniffed. "I thought she knew. It's not like I'm a dirty secret."

"No. Of course not." He dug his knuckle into his breast-bone. "I'm sure it will be okay. I'll talk to her." Why hadn't he told Savannah that he and Kat used to date? It shouldn't have been a big deal. He and Savannah both had pasts, and Hank hadn't thought it worth mentioning. If he'd told Savannah when he'd said he and Kat were friends, it wouldn't have been a thing.

"Yeah, well, like I said, I'm back in your condo. And she left you a note."

Hank waited. "Well," he said, beating a tattoo on the steering wheel. "What's it say?"

"Maybe you should come read it yourself."

"Kat." His tone showed he was out of patience.

She cleared her throat. "'Hank. I'm going to find Chance. I know you think he's partly responsible for my mess, but he's a good man, and I treated him horribly. It's time I grew up and did the responsible thing. The adult thing. I hope you understand. P.S. Thank you for the bear claws.'"

Hank's knuckles went white around the steering wheel. "'Thank you for the bear claws'?" Savannah was going back to her pansy fiancé, and all Hank got was a thank-you for the pastries?

"She did seem very polite," Kat said. "I liked her. I hope you two can make it work."

"Thanks, Kat," he bit out. "Gotta go." Hanging up, he tossed his phone next to him in disgust. Make it work? How could any man make it work with a woman who was a constant flight risk?

Was she with Worthington now? Had Worthington forgiven her for ditching him at the altar? Everyone in town thought the man was a great guy. Nice. *Decent.* Why wouldn't he take Savannah back?

So that was that. For a couple of nights Hank got to hold an amazing, impulsive woman, and now her wild and spontaneous time was over. She was going to grow up, whatever the hell that meant, and marry the man her parents approved of.

His heart burned, and he dug the heel of his palm into his chest. It was as it should be. Savannah would be well taken care of. And Worthington was the luckiest bastard alive. Right now, he was probably holding her, tasting her, burying his nose in her sweet mop of hair. . . .

Hank turned the key in the ignition. To hell with that. The damn fool woman might think she was doing the right thing, but she would die a little bit inside each day if she married that wuss. That flame inside of her would darken each day until it was snuffed out.

Hank wouldn't allow it.

He flipped on his sirens and hit the gas. The F-150's wheels spun, then the truck fishtailed in the dirt before he straightened it out and rolled onto the highway. He lifted the radio receiver again. "Janine, I need you."

The radio crackled. "Well, that didn't take as long as I'd thought. I had a five-year plan to slowly seduce you, and you caved in three months. I'm better than I knew."

He didn't have time for her jokes today. "I need you to get on the local grapevine and give me a location on Savannah Loving. It's urgent."

"Police business urgent? Is she in trouble?"

"She's only in trouble with me." Hank blared past Serendipity's *welcome* sign, the early evening sunlight slanting across it, and eased his foot off the accelerator.

"On it," Janine said. "Give me five."

It was three minutes before she came back on the radio. "Savannah's back at the scene of the crime. At the Bluebird Inn."

Hanging a U-turn, Hank looked at the nearly empty road and gunned it toward the inn. "Thanks, Janine."

"So, why are you looking for our runaway bride? Did she—"

Hank turned off the radio. The gossip mill was an amazing tool, and he had no doubt he would be a part of it tonight. But he didn't need to make it easy for people like Janine.

The grand Victorian came into view, its elegant roofline standing out against the blue sky. The yard was empty, and there was only one vehicle, the Ducati, in the parking lot—a far cry from the hive of activity it had been on Saturday. Pulling off the road, Hank cut the engine and jumped out of the truck. He pushed through the inn's front door and strode past the unmanned reception desk, to the parlor. Empty.

Pulse pounding, Hank turned in a slow circle. She couldn't be upstairs in a room with the yahoo. There was no way they'd wait two years only to give in to hot, steamy make-up sex. Grinding his teeth together, he ran for the stairs. If that son of a bitch was touching his woman—

He froze, hand on the railing, and peered out the window alongside the staircase. Savannah sat cross-legged in the backyard, head tipped back to take in the sun's dwindling rays. And luckily for Worthington's face, she was alone.

Hank turned and made for the garden. He hadn't been invited to the wedding, but he recognized the spot where she sat. It was where the temporary altar had been set up under an ivy-draped pergola. Where she was to have spoken her vows.

Pushing through the garden gate, he stalked toward her. The grass was flattened in a long line stretching from the gate to Savannah, where a carpet runner must have smashed it down. "Where is he?" Hank asked as he got close. He dropped to a squat before her and frowned. "Are you okay?"

She lowered her head and gave him a brilliant smile. "I'm perfect."

"You're a damn fool, is what you are." Plucking up a stem of grass, he chucked it down again. "You won't be happy with him. You ran away for a reason. Can't you see that?"

She leaned back on one hand and brought the other up to shield her eyes from the sun. "Won't be happy with who? What are you talking about?"

"You and Worthington." Hank swallowed down bile at that name. "Just because you got angry with me is no reason to go crawling back to that man. If he didn't make you happy in the two years you were together, he's not going to make you happy for the rest of your life."

She pursed her lips. "I'm not mad at you. Why?" She narrowed her eyes. "What did you do?"

He scratched his jaw. This conversation wasn't going as he had expected. "You were mad because you found out I used to date Kat. It wasn't serious, Savannah."

"I wasn't mad about that." Rolling her eyes, she got to her feet. Hank stood as well and helped her up.

She brushed grass from her butt. "I wasn't mad, but it did give me the kick in the pants I needed to do the right thing."

"Go back to your fiancé?" His stomach tensed, and he waited for her to say the words that would strike him like a blow.

"Are you insane? Of course I'm not going back to Chance." She flattened her lips and exhaled heavily from her nose. If he hadn't been almost giddy with relief at what she'd just said, he would have found her exasperation amusing.

Grabbing the front of his utility belt, she tugged him close. "I came back to explain to Chance why I couldn't marry him. And to apologize for running off." She tipped her head back. "I saw how strong and mature Kat is, how you guys are still friends, and it made me feel about two inches tall. Next to her, I saw that I had been acting like a spoiled brat."

Hank gripped her shoulders and took his first full breath

since he'd received Kat's phone call. "You're not a brat. You were in a bad situation. You've been in a pressure cooker of the town's and your parents' expectations for years. You had to blow sometime."

"Just my luck I lost it in front of all of Serendipity." She rested her forehead against his chest. "It's going to be embarrassing facing everyone. But at least I've made it right with the people who matter. I went to see my parents and Chance. My parents first. I think they still don't know quite what to make of my behavior, but I've convinced them a marriage to Chance would have been a mistake. And they want me to be happy."

"And Worthington?" Hank dipped his head, inhaled the sweet scent of her shampoo. She was warm and soft in his arms, and she fit against him like a puzzle piece snapping into place.

"That was even harder. He forgave me."

"Big of him." Hank couldn't keep the irritation out of his voice.

Savannah slapped his arm and curled her body closer. Her left ring finger was beautifully bare. "It was big of him. Although I don't think he was too broken up about my defection. But I didn't want him to think badly of me."

"You care too much about what people think of you," Hank said gruffly.

She wrapped her arms around his waist. "I care more about what you think of me. I don't want to be the type of woman who runs away from problems. I want to be someone you can be proud of. Who I can be proud of."

His body shook with his laughter. "Babe, you don't have to worry about that. I like you when you're wild and go tearing out of town. And I like you when you're sweet and cuddling up next to me. Just as long as you give all your crazy sides to me, as long as you're honest with yourself and go after what you want, not what anyone else expects, then I'll be proud to stand next to you."

She sighed and sagged into his body. He liked that most of all, when she let down all her walls and gave him her weight.

"Any more stops on this apology tour?" he asked. "Or can I take you home?"

"I'm just leaving the Ducati here for my uncle, so actually I do need a ride." She grinned. "I like the idea of showing you my condo. I even have sheets on my bed."

"Fancy." Wrapping his hand in her hair, he tugged her head back. Her mouth was right there. He couldn't not take it. Her lips were soft, yielding. He nibbled her bottom lip and swept his tongue along the seam.

She opened to him. Hot. Sweet. Enthusiastic. Their tongues tangled, sparred, and desire arrowed down his spine.

He pulled back, breathing heavily. "You're still going out with me Friday?"

She nodded and chased after his mouth.

"And tonight, tomorrow, and the next night?"

She rocked back on her heels, but kept her hands laced around his waist. "Hank Evans—are you asking me to go steady with you?"

"I am." He kissed one corner of her mouth, and the other. "And will you?"

"I will."

"Good." Clutching her shirt at the small of her back, he dragged her against his chest. "I'm going to hold you to that." He brushed his lips over the soft skin of her neck. "Babe, fair warning. If you run, I'll track you down. I've got resources."

She arched her back. "It's nice to know I'm worth fighting for. But Hank"—she stared him straight in the eye—"I'm done running. I'm going to start living the life I want. Being with the people who like me for me. Savannah Loving is finally her own damn person."

"Hmm. I kind of liked pulling you over. If you don't run, how will I chase you?"

She smiled. "I don't think you'll have to worry about

that." Taking his hand, she walked across the lawn toward the inn. "I didn't like handing back the keys to my uncle's bike, so I decided I'm going to buy my own. It will probably be a used jalopy since that's all I can afford on my salary, but I'll make sure it has enough horsepower to light up your speed gun. You can chase me to your heart's content."

And he would. Tugging her around the Bluebird toward his truck, he felt his feet were barely touching the ground. He'd come home to Serendipity to reunite with his family. His community. Thought he'd need time to adjust to the slower pace of life in small-town Texas.

He needn't have worried. Savannah brought all the speed, the heat that he could ever want. He didn't know what lay ahead. But he knew it was going to be a hell of a lot of fun keeping her in his sights.

Savannah was a headstrong, stubborn woman. And life was sweeter with her by his side.

Loving Hailey

Stacey Keith

Chapter One

When Hailey Deacon parked her ten-speed next to the Bluebird Inn, her heart was pounding, but it wasn't from the ride over. She sat in the shadow of the old Victorian, trying to catch her breath, and still her pulse wouldn't stop bumping.

Just admit it, you coward.

After almost four years of *maybes* and *what ifs* and *I hope he's happy at med school,* she was going to see Joshua Loving again. Four years of wondering what might have been if things were different. If she hadn't been plain Hailey Deacon of Serendipity, Texas, and he hadn't been Joshua Loving of the Mayflower Lovings, the closest thing to royalty they had in these parts.

But that was as far as it went, of course. Hailey leaned her paint-flaked ten-speed on its rusty kickstand and started toward the back entrance marked *Staff.* Her old feelings for him were as gone and buried as . . . well, a lot of things in her life. You went on because you had to. Joshua might have broken her heart, but they'd been eighteen then. Just kids. At twenty-two, they were both past all that.

Hailey pressed one hand against her fluttery chest. It was weird, working his sister's wedding, knowing he would be there. Maybe with a date. *Probably* with a date. Beneath the crisp white shirt of her catering uniform, Hailey felt her heart give another double thump. Oh, for crying out loud, *why?* She needed to be focused right now, not this jumbling mess of nerves.

You're the strongest girl I know, Josh had told her once. *Not just strong—a warrior.*

Okay, so she'd be a warrior. But when she glanced at her reflection in a window, her fledgling confidence did a face-plant. Even for a tomboy who preferred cargo pants, sleeveless tees, and dog tags, she saw at once that the thick black slacks were boxy and the pink bow tie made her look like a circus clown. She passed one hand over her ponytail to smooth the flyaways, cringing when she saw her bitten nails.

Get a grip, she told herself. *You don't care now, remember? Stop being such a . . . girl.*

She opened the garden gate that led to the back entrance and darted a look around. None of the Lovings were there yet—not Joshua, not his sister Savannah, not even their parents Marion and Joseph. They were probably inside the house getting ready.

Good.

She knew what Joshua's family thought of her. The Deacons—what were left of them, anyway—were "poor folk." Nowhere near good enough for the son and heir of the Loving family fortune. Unlike Savannah, Hailey didn't attend debutante balls or pledge sororities or go to spring cotillion with men like Dr. Chance Worthington.

No, Hailey worked. She had three jobs right now. Catering, which wasn't steady enough to do full-time. Dog walking. And being a pump jockey down at Wilbur Garrison's corner gas station. Serendipity was small—hardly the kind of Texas town that was cranking out high-paying jobs.

"Hailey!" Sam Besher waved to her from the pergola, which had ivy and yards of white tulle wrapped around it. Chatty, gossipy Sam fit in perfectly, as though she'd been decorated for the wedding, too—a self-described "candy box blonde" with her dyed platinum hair, pink push-up bras, and false eyelashes that could clear a bookshelf. She had a twelve-year-old boy whose dad had left them in Memphis and a kind of lazy cynicism about men that Hailey found exciting, probably because she herself didn't know the first thing about them.

But the backyard was beautiful. Metal folding chairs, sectioned into rows, had elaborate aqua bows and aqua seat cushions—more color in a garden that was full of the bright pink clusters of redbud, creamy yellow butterfly magnolia, juicy cones of purple grape hyacinth, and a trail of sunny trillium. Ten other catering people Hailey didn't recognize zipped around with stemware, cut flowers, and wedding programs. Even from a distance, Hailey saw the words *Savannah Loving* and *Dr. Chance Worthington* on those programs in gold curlicue letters.

That was what beautiful pampered princesses like Savannah got on their wedding day. What girls like Hailey got was carpal tunnel syndrome from carrying the trays.

She heard Harper, the wedding planner, squawking at some hapless male behind her. Grabbing a bunch of long-stemmed pink roses off a nearby cart, Hailey hurried to join Sam at the pergola. The only problem with the pergola was that if Joshua came outside, Hailey knew she'd have nowhere to hide. And she wasn't ready to see him yet. Or ever. She never wanted to feel the way she had the night he said good-bye.

"Harper's on the warpath, so you'd better watch it," Sam told her. "This shindig must be a bigger deal than I thought."

"The biggest." Hailey tried to focus on stuffing flowers into the puffy tulle bows that were tied to the four supports of the pergola, but neither her fingers nor her thoughts would cooperate. Sam was new to Serendipity. She didn't know who was important here. She didn't know that Joshua Loving had dimples that were deep enough to hold a magnum of champagne. She didn't know that he had the gentleness of the big and strong. At six foot three, he was over a foot taller than Hailey's five foot one. And Sam didn't know that Joshua had been Hailey's first and only love, probably because Hailey tended not to talk about it.

Hey, no one had ever accused her of being an open book.

Hailey pretended to fuss with the bows. Unlike Sam, she sucked at decorating. She was much better at changing the oil in a car, shingling a roof, mowing a lawn.

"I shouldn't have agreed to work this event," Hailey said.

"What's wrong, sweetie? You're not worried about Harper, are you? You know how type A she is. All bark and no bite."

"I'm more worried about paying my light bill." Hailey looked out over the sun-drenched garden. The yellow daffodils nodding gracefully in the breeze. The terra-cotta planters crowded with pink petunias. Sparrows splashing in a marble birdbath. Funny how it seemed as though nothing bad could ever happen here.

Yet a shiver of apprehension raised the hair on her arms. It might have had something to do with Joshua, but was probably something else. What, was she receiving psychic premonitions now? She was getting as bad as Grams.

Clipboard clutched to her chest, heels making little divots in the grass behind her, Harper came barreling toward the pergola. "The guests are arriving," she said crisply. "Hailey, you and Sam start prepping in the kitchen. I want those trays ready for the reception in thirty minutes with new waves every ten." Pointing to one of the ushers, she added, "You there. Straighten the aisle runner. This is a wedding, not a livestock show."

Hailey trudged toward the kitchen. Inside, the Bluebird Inn was cooler than the garden. The hallway gleamed with dark wood and cut-glass chandeliers. She could hear commotion upstairs—footsteps, some clearly male; voices, most clearly female. Every room was an obstacle course of chests and shoulders, which were pretty much all you saw when you were Hailey's height.

"This is a nightmare," Sam said behind her. "When I win

the lottery, the first thing I'm going to do is tell Harper to kiss my—"

"Joshua." Hailey halted at the entrance to the kitchen. She clutched the doorjamb for support. Sam collided into her. Joshua Loving was standing by the appetizers, clearly trying to shovel in as many as he could before the wedding.

The minute he locked eyes with her—that dark, intelligent gaze she felt in places that hadn't felt anything in so long— Hailey knew the last four years meant nothing at all. The dates with other guys when she had congratulated herself for "being mature" and "moving on." The curiosity she painstakingly concealed when asking mutual friends how Joshua was doing. The million times she told herself it wasn't love she was feeling, just a persistent case of nostalgia.

All of that was a lie.

Seeing Joshua was an arrow through her heart.

Joshua set down the appetizers and swallowed hard.

Hailey.

Next to him, his college roommate, Trip Driscoll, pointed to the empanada Joshua had dropped and said, "Dude, you gonna eat that?"

But Joshua had lost all awareness of his surroundings. The noisy kitchen. The jostling workers. The fact that he was standing here in a stupid tux. The only things he saw were Hailey's wide blue eyes. It was like staring at the sky too long, that kind of which-side-is-up dizziness that made him feel as though he were six years old again doing cartwheels. She was so beautiful. And it had been a long time since he'd seen her face-to-face instead of from the shadows.

It all came rushing back. The memories, good and bad. The guilt over what he'd done to her. The regrets that were *right there*, ready to punch him in the face.

"Oh, hey there, Hailey," he said, trying to play it off and act cool. Failing. "Good to see you."

She lurched into the kitchen—or was pushed maybe by a blond woman in an identical pink bow tie. "Wait a minute," he said. "Are you working my sister's wedding?"

Hailey gave him a half-hearted smile. "It's my job. I sort of go where they tell me."

"If you ask me, which you didn't, you invited way too many people." The blond woman stuck her hand out. "Samantha Besher. Sam, actually. Nice to meet you."

Trip elbowed him in the ribs, but Joshua had already guessed his college roommate was into her. Trip liked slightly older blondes. Joshua shook Sam's hand and waited for Trip to wipe the drool off his chin so he could introduce himself, too.

Sam could probably eat Trip for breakfast and spit out the bones. All Joshua wanted was a chance to talk to Hailey.

"Are you supposed to be in here?" Hailey asked. She found a pop-up box full of plastic gloves and tugged a pair over her hands. "I thought the kitchen was just for staff."

Joshua seemed to have lost ground, but that wasn't going to stop him. Just being in the same room with Hailey made him feel . . . well, like he might have found something he'd been missing for a long time. "I was hungry," he said. "Didn't get much to eat this morning. If they expect me to stand out there in the hot sun wearing this monkey suit, they're going to have to feed me."

There, that did it. Hailey cracked a smile, and Joshua felt as though he'd won a medal for pole-vaulting.

She passed him a tray of mini-sliders. For a second, her warm hand touched his, and the shock of contact raced through his veins.

"Still grazing, I see," she said dryly. "Here, have some real food."

Trip dove into the tray while Hailey and Sam went to another prep station to spear vegetables onto bamboo skewers. Joshua's legendary appetite deserted him. He could feel himself sweating in the hot kitchen. He wasn't sure what to say or how to approach her. All he knew was the urge to be near her reminded him of old times. Did she hate him? Most girls would.

Hailey still wore her deceased mother's opal-and-pearl ring. She still bit her nails. Somehow the sight brought back a rush of tenderness. He knew better than anyone what that one nervous habit said about her life. Who she was. What she'd been through.

"Dude," Trip muttered to him. "That's her, isn't it?"

"What?"

"That chick. You know the one. With the thing? And then you bailed?"

Joshua glared at him.

"She's so your type." Trip chewed lustily, clearly pleased with his discovery. "A little bit country, a little bit jock, and a whole lotta sexy."

"Could you please not say words?"

"Good thing I'm totally into her friend. Hook us up."

"You're on your own." Joshua watched Hailey and made a real effort to keep his gaze respectful and topside. Boy, it wasn't easy. He wished the kitchen weren't packed with people. There were even two little girls playing in one corner. He wished Trip were a million miles away. But what he really wished was for him and Hailey to be able to go off somewhere quiet and talk. Catch up a bit.

Liar. You know you want more than that.

When he'd come back to Serendipity for his sister's wedding, Joshua hadn't expected to run into Hailey. He figured he might see her here and there—while he kept a safe distance. But now that Hailey was right in front of him, he felt as though keeping his distance this time would be damn near impossible.

His mother, Marion Loving, stuck her head in the kitchen. She wore a tiny hat with a veil and a bluebird on it. "Joshua, why aren't you in the garden? The wedding starts in five minutes."

Marion's eyes slid over Hailey, but Marion didn't say anything. It wasn't as though she didn't recognize her or know it was Hailey standing there. Hot anger crept up the sides of Joshua's neck. He loved his mom, but it was no secret that Marion was a snob. She wore her wealth and breeding like a membership badge. Dad was no better. One time out on the golf course Joe had bogeyed a shot. He'd gotten so mad about it, he threw an entire set of signature golf clubs into the lake and then marched up to the clubhouse to buy a new one.

"So listen," Joshua said, worried that he wouldn't get another chance to talk to Hailey. In full view of his mother, the catering staff, Trip, Sam, and everybody, he said to her, "I'm here for two weeks on spring break. Let's go to lunch."

Hailey's heart-shaped face turned bright pink like a sunburn that had started on the inside. She opened her mouth and then closed it.

"For heaven's sake, Joshua, it's your sister's wedding," Marion said. "Can't this wait?"

But Joshua wasn't going anywhere till he got an answer. He gazed down at Hailey, blood pounding, wondering if he was certifiably insane. He had a sinking feeling that the answer was yes—but that her answer wouldn't be.

"I'm, uh, super busy," she said, flicking her gaze away. "Wedding season, you know."

Joshua sucked in a breath and turned to leave. *Ouch. That hurt.*

Trip slapped one hand on his shoulder and herded him out of the kitchen. "Ya blew it," he muttered. "You bombed so hard, she's going to be picking pieces of you out of her teeth for weeks."

"Wow, thanks."

"You were like a Scud missile of lameness," Trip said. "My grandma's got more game than that. Really, dude, I can't believe I hang out with you."

Chapter Two

"Who was *that?*" Sam wanted to know, giving Hailey a load of side-eye. "He looks like a young Matthew McConaughey. If Matthew McConaughey were a linebacker. Which he's not. And why on earth did you say no when he asked you out?"

Hailey arranged the spiced beef empanadas around a ramekin of lime sour cream. Her hands sweated inside the plastic gloves, and her thoughts kept revolving like Fourth of July pinwheels.

What bothered her wasn't that Joshua had asked her out. No, that would have been easy. It was the fact that seeing him made her heart combust. But how was that possible after he'd taken her heart and stomped it flat in the first place? After he'd promised to love her forever, to marry her, and then had abandoned her at the lowest point in her life—all because his parents decided that he and Hailey were too young to get married? You didn't just get over something like that.

What if she was one of those people who loved once and never loved again? Like Juliet from that play. Or even her own father, who'd never really bounced back after the death of his wife. Skyrocketing blood pressure had killed Hailey's mother shortly after labor. She was buried in the local cemetery. All Hailey knew about her was what she saw in the mirror every day. It was the same face that peered at her from her mother's photo in the hallway. And when her father had looked at her, she could sometimes see the grief in his eyes.

And then, just when she'd lost everything else, she had lost Joshua, too.

"Hello?" Sam said. "Do you speak English? I said if I had a guy like that who was hot for me, I'd take him home and ride him like a rented mule."

"Oh my God, Sam. *Really?*"

"Too much information? Sorry. It's just been me and a carton of ice cream for the last couple of months."

Harper rushed into the kitchen looking a little frazzled. "The ceremony's started. Are those trays ready?"

"Everything except the rest of the veggie platter," Hailey told her. She went to the kitchen sink to finish rinsing the cherry tomatoes. There was a window above the sink flanked by two open shutters and a sun catcher in the shape of a bluebird. Through the window Hailey saw Savannah Loving in her floofy wedding dress go rushing toward the carport. Had she forgotten something? Why didn't she just send somebody to get it?

Then Savannah turned around, and Hailey saw the expression of sheer panic and desperation on her face.

Uh oh.

Hailey turned off the water and stood watching with a growing sense of alarm.

"Something's going on out there," she told the others. "And whatever it is, I don't think it's good."

Sam, Harper, and a half dozen other caterers crowded around the window while Savannah thrashed her way out of the wedding dress. Underneath the dress, she wore a tank tee and leggings.

Harper let her clipboard go clattering onto the counter. "You have got to be kidding me."

Standing at the sink with a dripping handful of cherry tomatoes, Hailey watched Savannah straddle a badass Ducati motorcycle and take off just as her bewildered bridegroom came running out, yelling after her. He retrieved the wedding gown from the lawn and stood gazing at it with a curious expression of sadness and . . . Hailey looked closer. Good Lord, was that relief?

"Wow," Sam muttered. "I thought things like this only happened on bad late-night cable television."

"Poor Dr. Worthington," one of the younger caterers said with a dreamy sigh.

Harper dropped onto a nearby chair and then buried her head in her hands. "I'm hyperventilating. I think I have a rash. What if they decide this is my fault? They could stop payment on the check. My business could be ruined."

Sam grabbed a beer out of the fridge, popped the cap, and then wrapped Harper's limp fingers around the bottle. "I think the best we can do right now is get crazy drunk and pretend we didn't see it happen."

Hailey let the tomatoes roll into the sink, peeled off the gloves, and then deposited them in the recycle bin. She wasn't terribly worried about Chance Worthington. No one with hair that perfect would stay single for long. But she did worry about Joshua. He and Savannah had always been close. Hailey might have thought of her as a princess, but, to be fair, Savannah had her good points. Maybe at the last minute she'd decided not to become a Junior Leaguer like her mom. Maybe she was less spoiled and elitist than Hailey had given her credit for.

"I'll be right back," she mumbled.

The garden looked the same as it had before—a big Texas cake topper complete with fluffy bows and flowers—only now there was an air of stunned disbelief hanging over the place. That nice Felicity Patterson, owner of the Bluebird Inn, was in deep conversation with a tall stranger. Over by the appetizers, Marion had ten people fluttering around her while she did her "bring me the smelling salts" routine, only instead of smelling salts it was a vodka tonic. Hailey actually felt sorry for her. Marion had been publicly humiliated, and her daughter was a runaway bride. If that didn't get you a vodka tonic, what did?

Hailey searched for Joshua. No matter what might have happened between them, she couldn't bear the thought of him suffering. Maybe there was something she could say that might help. *Sure.* A tiny voice in her head accused her of having ulterior motives. But if there was ever a time to circle the wagons, it was now. Hard feelings had to be put aside.

Rounding the walkway that led to the carport, she heard voices and stopped. It was Joshua and his father. Neither one of them sounded calm. Or friendly.

"Let her run off then if her life is so damn awful," Joseph was saying. "Sixty thousand dollars I shelled out for this wedding. And she doesn't have the decency to *tell* me there's something wrong and she doesn't want to get married?"

"Dad, just calm down," Joshua said. "Savannah's devastated. I know she is. And I don't think she should be alone right now."

"Alone? What do I care if she's alone? What she did was inexcusable!"

"She's still your daughter," Joshua said. "What if something happens to her out there?"

"I swear to God, if you try to go after her, I will never forgive you. She made her bed. Let her lie in it."

Hailey hung back, wondering what she should do. Then Joseph relieved her of having to decide by storming past on his way to the garden. She'd never seen his face so red, not even when Joshua had told his father he wanted to marry her. On that day, Joseph had simply been curt and condescending. On this day, he just gave her a fierce look of annoyance and kept marching.

She peeked around the corner and saw Joshua disappear up the front porch steps. Was she right to talk to him? Hailey scraped one hand through her hair and considered her options. What if he was mad at her for blowing him off like that? What if he treated her like his father just had?

But this is Joshua.

She found him on the porch swing, leaning forward dejectedly, elbows on knees. He glanced up when he heard her feet on the wooden porch, and, for just a split second, his face was open. Naked. Not one trace of a young man's swagger. He looked as though he'd lost something and didn't know how to get it back again.

Seeing him like this, unguarded and alone . . . she felt the pull of attraction right down to her bones. Suddenly, she was eighteen again, and it was the summer after senior year. She was out looking for one of Grams's cats, and there was Joshua with his bashful smile and his sun-streaked hair, staring like he'd never really seen her before. Hailey had idolized him throughout high school, but they'd traveled in different circles. She was athletic, but not a jock. Smart, but not a brain. Not unpopular, really. Just not on the radar.

Joshua, on the other hand, had been worshiped by everyone. He had dated a cheerleader and driven a black Ford F-250.

Until that day when Hailey had heard Cooper mewing from the bushes and had watched Joshua's big, gentle hands retrieve the annoying cat, she'd never said more than hello to him.

She felt just like that now, felt the same speechless yearning. Wasn't time supposed to change all that? Deaden your feelings somehow so you could go on with the business of living? But when Joshua looked at her, a whole net of captive butterflies was released inside her stomach.

"Hey," she said softly. "Some day, huh?" She sat beside Joshua on the swing, which was hung a little high. He was so tall, his knees poked up, but her toes barely scraped the porch.

He leaned back and gave her an apologetic smile. "Well, now. Aren't you brave?"

"Brave?"

"For coming out here. You're not afraid I'm going to make an ass of myself again?"

"You're not an ass." She found a brown sparrow feather

caught in the chain of the swing and twirled it between her fingers. "It's good to see you again, Joshua. Really, it is. It's just that . . ." Hailey lapsed into a pained silence. She'd always struggled to express herself, especially when it came to emotionally complicated stuff.

"Yeah," he said heavily. "I know."

She couldn't wrap her head around the fact that he was in Serendipity and they were talking together on the porch. A porch that was a lot like the one she had at home, only this one wasn't lopsided and falling apart. On a white wicker table next to her, a watering can with a bluebird painted on it sat next to a pair of gardening gloves. Squirrels raced around the sycamore branches. In the distance, a train whistle reminded her of the hot summer nights when she and Joshua had wandered the tracks looking for lightning bugs and talking about their future together. Kissing him had made her head spin.

Hailey knew she wasn't good with words, but she was alive to beauty in nature and to animal sensation. The way her taste buds curdled when she ate lemons. The green glow of a leaf when the sun shone through it. The breathtaking sensitivity of Joshua's hands, their quiet strength and tenderness.

How he'd used them to help her discover what her body was capable of.

"I should have gone after her, Hailey," he said sadly. "I never should've let her go like that."

"Savannah can take care of herself." *She survived being a Loving, didn't she?*

Joshua absently rocked the porch swing, brow furrowed, hands clasped over his flat stomach. "Yeah, but she never told me. I had no idea she was unhappy. Why didn't she say anything? Savannah knows I have her back, no matter what."

Hailey hunted for the right words, but she was too powerfully aware of his presence beside her, of the shape of his strong thighs beneath the tux pants. "Maybe Savannah didn't know she was unhappy until today," Hailey said after a long pause. "She probably just needs a little time to sort things out."

Joshua rested his head on the back of the swing. "I feel completely useless. I came here to tell my parents the truth about my future plans. Now Savannah's run off, it's the worst time for them, and I don't think they could handle any more stress."

"What do you mean 'the truth'?" She felt uneasy suddenly, as though the sacrifices she'd made—that they'd both made—had been for nothing. It was one thing to think he'd given her up to save lives . . .

He turned his head to look at her, close enough that she could see his bristly boy lashes and the pallor of sadness beneath his tanned skin. There was knowing in his dark eyes, and the kind of mute hunger that burned through her own body like a cascade of fiery stars.

He had no business looking at her like that. Making her want things.

Joshua must have read her thoughts. He swung his gaze back up to the ceiling. "I don't want to be a heart surgeon. You know that. I never did. The Lovings have been cattle ranchers going back for generations now. Animal husbandry is in my blood."

"You wanted to be a veterinarian," she said. "We used to talk about it, remember?"

"Of course I remember," he said softly, and she knew he was thinking the same thing she was. Yearning moved through her again—for him, for the past. If only you could rewind time like one of Grams's old cassette tapes, back to the good years before her dad and her brother went on that hunting trip and never came back. Why couldn't a person stop these things from happening? The next morning when Hailey had answered the door, two police officers had been standing there, hats off, the bad news etched on their faces. Tanner and her dad had lost control of the truck. After the gas tank exploded, there wasn't enough left of either one of them to bury.

Joshua had been there with her when she went to the morgue. She'd just fallen to pieces. Without his strength and steadiness, she never would have survived. But a month later, he had been gone, off to university. And now, not only was she all alone in the world, but she and Joshua were worlds apart. She was still the girl his parents didn't want him to marry, and he was still the young man who lacked the courage of his convictions. If only he had loved her enough to follow his heart.

"I have to go," she said, rising suddenly.

"Please don't."

She turned to look at him. This wasn't the smiling, easy-going Joshua she remembered. Instead, his manner was self-reproachful in a way that made her wonder if people actually could change. She had to get away before it was too late and she started believing such nonsense.

"Take care of yourself," she said. "Try not to worry about Savannah. She's brave. And tougher than she looks."

His massive shoulders sagged. "You take care, too, Hailey. Thanks for the talk."

She forced herself to walk away, one foot in front of the other until she got to the end of the porch. Tears gathered behind her eyelids, shameful amounts of heat that she blinked sharply away.

Before going down the steps, Hailey stopped. She didn't dare turn around. In a voice she barely recognized, she said, "I hope you tell your folks the truth. It's easy to go with the flow, Joshua. What takes courage is standing up for the things you believe in."

Chapter Three

Hailey pedaled up the dusty street to the tumbling-down Victorian that had housed four generations of Deacons. Serendipity seemed so boring—Mr. Garibaldi's portable sprinkler bravely chugging water across the crabgrass. Screen doors clattering over the shrill voices of children. A rust-bucket pickup truck wheezing by. Serendipity's very sameness made her restless because Joshua was here.

What point was there in starting something now? It was hard to admit that she wanted to. But he was just going to leave again. That was what happened to the people she loved. They left her here to fend for herself.

She rested her bicycle against the overgrown rose trellis and went inside, wondering which version of her Grandma Adelia she was going to get today. There was the Grams who collected cats and read the poetry of Tennyson and Walt Whitman out loud after supper. Then there was the Grams who made spookily accurate predictions about things she couldn't possibly know. And finally the Grams who wore elaborate church lady "chapeaux," drank tea, and talked to people who weren't actually there. When Hailey heard the Victrola going, she knew Grams was in the parlor amidst all the clutter, tea poured for an invisible audience, her face half-hidden beneath a wide-brim hat burdened with decorative fruit.

"I'm home!" Hailey called to her. "We're having appetizers for dinner tonight." She'd taken a grocery sack of them home with her. Why not? There had been plenty left over.

Grams's ten cats came running into the kitchen. They mewed pitifully and rubbed their soft, warm bodies against Hailey's legs. Every day she had to count them just to make sure Grams hadn't snuck in another furry mouth to feed.

After pouring a few bowls of kibble and packing the appetizers inside the fridge, Hailey went into the parlor. Grams was playing four-handed bridge, sipping Chinese oolong, and scolding her imaginary bridge partners for their inattentiveness. Her blue eyes looked especially vague today, which was discouraging. Hailey always worried that Grams would retreat so far into her fantasy world she would never come back again.

Beneath the brim of a pink straw hat strewn with cherries, Adelia's face was sweet and surprisingly girlish. Grams might be crazy, but she was all Hailey had left now, and Hailey would do anything to protect her.

"Lord Byron was hiding an ace," Grams confided when Hailey pulled up a chair. "If I've said it once, I've said it a thousand times, he's not a man to be trusted."

All of Grams's "friends" were poets. She had her favorites. Lord Byron was never one of them. *Too sneaky,* Grams would say. *A man who cheats at cards will cheat at love.*

"You have news," Adelia said. "I guess the Queen of Hearts ran off with the jester after all."

"If you mean Savannah Loving, then yes. She took off on her uncle's motorcycle. Her mother was in hysterics."

Adelia nodded sagely. "Lady Marion." Then her eyes lit on Hailey, and this time they looked less vague. "The prince was there, too, I see. Such a fine lad, and no cardsharp either. He will make you very happy, my dear."

Hailey's heart galloped in alarm. She didn't want anyone

making her "happy." Grams might know things, but she didn't know *everything*. She still got it wrong sometimes.

Determined not to let the conversation go any further, Hailey jumped up. "I'm thirsty. Is Lord Byron going to drink his tea?"

"Of course, silly girl. He pours port brandy in his cup and thinks I don't notice."

Hailey went back into the kitchen, made herself a glass of cold sweet tea, and then went outside to the porch. Unlike the porch at the Bluebird Inn, hers was peeling, creaky, and crowded with succulents. The last of the season's fragrant Chinese wisteria hung from the house's shabby gingerbread trim. An enormous water oak spread its shady branches too close to the roof, which leaked anyway. Even when her father was alive, the roof had been Swiss cheese. Hailey had to put out a dozen buckets to catch the drips.

At least there *was* a roof. Sort of.

Joshua, on the other hand . . . Hailey took a long sip of tea and let an ice cube slide over her tongue. She'd never envied his wealth, but she did feel the differences between them. He used to sneak her into the boathouse, which sat on the edge of Loving Lake. An entire lake named after his family. They'd laughed about it as they lay entwined on the mattress he'd rigged up for them.

Everything had been so bright and beautiful then. They were so sure of what they wanted: a future together. A small veterinary practice here in town. Children. And all those rolling acres on which to raise them.

Sometimes she still lay awake at night thinking about it. Her life would have been so different if Joseph and Marion hadn't persuaded Joshua that eighteen was too young to get married. That if their love was real, it would survive four years of college. After Dad and Tanner's accident, Joshua had tried to convince Hailey to go to Austin with him. He wanted them to get married there, find an apartment, be happy. But Hailey couldn't run off and leave her grandmother alone in a drafty old house. Instead of waiting a semester before running off to university, Joshua had let his parents talk him into going right away, which proved, she guessed, just how unprepared he was to handle the sacrifices of marriage.

That was what she told herself at least.

Hailey rolled the sweating glass against her forehead, trying to get cool. Every time she thought about Joshua, her body heat went haywire.

Grams pushed open the screen door, clucking at her cats. Half of them followed her outside, milling around her legs. She sat on a rocker across from Hailey—the porch swing couldn't be trusted at this point—and cocked her head brightly to one side, like a bird.

"The truth can be a bitter pill to swallow, my darling girl, but it doesn't have to be," Grams said. "I know you were disappointed by him. The handsome young prince failed to slay your dragons."

Hailey pulled up one knee, folded the other beneath her, and thoughtfully examined her glass. "What's that mean, Grams?"

"It means the bluebirds will come back to Serendipity, if you let them."

"What?"

"You have to make a nest for them, my dear. The bluebirds of happiness just work like that. You need to make room for them in your heart."

Bingo.

Idling at one of Serendipity's few stoplights, Joshua spotted Hailey up ahead at Wilbur Garrison's gas station. In a town the size of this one, where everybody knew your business, it hadn't taken him long to figure out which job she was working today. And there she was in her mechanic's jumpsuit, with her shiny black hair scraped back in a sleek ponytail, clattering a gas dispenser back into a pump.

Hailey knew everything about cars because her dad had

raised her to be a son. Whatever a man could do, Hailey could do better. Richard Deacon hadn't been a bad father. Just broken. But he hadn't had one clue about raising a shy, sensitive, deep-feeling girl like Hailey. And Tanner, her brother, had just seen her as his annoying kid sister.

Still, Hailey's whole family had been close, which was more than Joshua could say about his own family. Unlike what his parents had done with their parents, Hailey would never put her Grams in a rest home.

After the light turned green, Joshua drove through the intersection and then pulled his Jeep off to the side and sat watching. Nobody understood Hailey the way he did. When she was hurt, she got quiet. When she was angry, she got quiet. You had to pay attention and listen to what she wasn't saying. Otherwise, you missed out on knowing her true strength and her inner beauty. Joshua had done a fair amount of dating in the past four years. No one came close to Hailey.

With nothing but the Jeep's roll cage to protect him from the blazing sun, Joshua inched the car forward, positioning it underneath a cottonwood tree. A sluggish wind cascaded through its leaves, making it sound as though they were whispering to him, rightly calling him a coward. *It's easy to go with the flow,* Hailey had said on the porch. *What takes courage is standing up for the things you believe in.*

Guilt gave him a queasy feeling in the pit of his stomach. He knew exactly what she meant.

His phone rang, and he glanced down to see who it was. Trip was at the Ice House skulling beers. Joshua swiped to answer. "What's up?"

"Did you talk to her yet?"

Damn. So Trip had guessed where he was going. "Don't you have women to annoy?"

"Doesn't mean I can't annoy you too, bro," Trip said. Joshua could hear the Ice House's old-timey jukebox in the background and the sound of people talking. "So you decided to go all in, eh? All three strikes?"

Joshua saw Hailey wave good-bye to her customer and then return to the service bay where a car waited on a hydraulic lift. Just watching her distracted him and made it difficult to follow the thread of the conversation. "What are you talking about?"

"You're selling, but she ain't buying. Ever think maybe it's time to put your cards on the table?"

Joshua thought about that. Maybe Trip was right.

"You know, for once you may not be all wrong," Joshua said. "Catch you later." He clicked off, put the Jeep in gear, and then drove to the gas station. The service bell sounded before he pulled up to the pump and then killed the engine. His heart was beating faster than the drums in the Nine Inch Nails song on the radio.

Hailey came out of the service bay, wiping her hands on a shop rag. Her blue eyes looked fearful when she saw him, which wasn't encouraging. But he couldn't lose this time. There was too much at stake.

Four years was a long time to test the sincerity of your feelings. Consider them tested.

"Unleaded?" she asked, flicking her gaze past him to the Jeep.

"Please. Let me do it." He got out of the car and then reached for the dispenser. Maybe he was old-fashioned, but letting Hailey pump his gas while he just stood there was more than he could handle.

Joshua glanced around. Was Hailey the only one working? Serendipity had no crime to speak of, but Joshua wasn't wild about her being alone all day. He grabbed the dispenser, unscrewed his gas cap, and then jammed in the nozzle. "Can we talk?"

"Isn't that what we're doing?"

She wasn't going to make this easy for him. Why should she? He deserved every awkward silence. *You can't mess this up. You can't.* He kept trying to think of the right thing to say. Maybe he should just speak from the heart.

"Savannah doing okay?" she asked. "I heard she was holed up somewhere north of here."

It was true. They'd gotten a text from her last night. Joshua might have been worried for his sister, and even a little pissed, but he was starting to soften up a bit. At least Savannah had followed her heart, which was more than he had done.

"I need to explain a few things," he said. "About what happened. About us."

Her clear, expressive eyes flickered. They were like church windows and had always burned bright. Now they just looked shuttered.

"What's past is past," she replied curtly. "Let's just leave it alone."

The point-of-sale display on the gas pump kept churning, just like Joshua's thoughts. He felt sick.

What takes courage is standing up for the things you believe in.

When the pressure trigger popped, it seemed as though something popped inside him, too. "I'm still crazy about you, Hailey. Not a day goes by that I don't think about you or wish you were with me. Every time I come back to Serendipity, I check on you to make sure you're okay. I know how badly I disappointed you. But don't ever think I forgot you, because it isn't true."

His heart was doing the two-minute mile. All he'd ever wanted was her. He'd tried to analyze it, weigh it, understand why. Some things just were. And the criticisms of their relationship—they were too young, too impulsive, too crazy—none of that had anything to do with his feelings for her. He knew that now.

Might as well tell her the whole truth. Joshua passed one hand over his forehead, which was slick with the sweat of a man whose back was against a very hot wall. "I've never stopped loving you, Hailey. I never will."

* * *

Hailey took the gas dispenser from Joshua, hung it up, and then leaned on the pump, breathing heavily. Was he still behind her? She kind of hoped not.

She could sense his confusion and yes, maybe his heartache, too. But she had a hard time believing his loss was anything like hers had been. Every inch of Serendipity had reminded her of him, all the walks they had taken, the talks they had, the night she knew that she was ready to . . . No, she couldn't think about that. If she thought about that, she'd go crazy.

Now here he was saying all kinds of sweet things, and it even seemed like he meant them, but how were you supposed to trust someone again after he'd broken your heart?

"I have work to do." She pivoted and went back to the service bay where Mrs. Elden's 1998 Oldsmobile Intrigue awaited an oil change. Hailey could hear him following her.

"What do I have to do to get you to believe me?" Joshua said. "Hailey, I'm just asking for a chance, one chance, to make it up to you."

She grabbed a socket wrench, loosened the drain plug, and let the old oil pour into an oil pan. "There's nothing to make up. I don't want your pity, Joshua."

"And I'm not giving it," he said. "That's not how I feel about you."

"Then how do you feel about me? Does your conscience hurt? Is that it?"

He dashed one hand through his hair and gazed down at her with that penetrating look she knew so well, the one that saw past all her fear and her defensiveness and honed in on the real her.

It was terrifying.

She wiped a trickle of engine coolant that spilled onto the crankcase. On a car this old, it was probably a good idea to inspect the head gasket. She started undoing screws. If she thought about cars, maybe she wouldn't have to think about him.

"Are you listening?" he asked.

"I hear the words you're saying."

"I'm confessing—"

"Oh, is this a *confession?*"

Hailey gave the screw a particularly vicious yank. So she was the worst kind of sin, was she, the kind of sin you had to confess? Not rich, not college educated, not Mayflower material. She even had a crazy grandmother. Who was less suitable than that?

"Do you think this is easy for me?" Joshua said. "I'm a guy, remember? I'm here with my heart on my sleeve, putting it all on the line for you."

Hailey felt her own reckless anger rising up. She wanted him to hold her and hated the wanting. "Putting it on the line for me? Like you did after Tanner and my dad died? Or when you decided to let your parents start telling you how to live your life?"

Joshua grabbed the screwdriver out of her hand and set it down on the tool case. He took both her greasy, nail-bitten hands in his bigger, stronger ones. Joshua had the hands of a surgeon, a pianist, a gentleman farmer. Hers betrayed the fact that she knew far more about tire tubes than tubes of lipstick.

Was that why she was so angry? Her skin prickled with dread. But she was prickling for other reasons, too. A familiar drugging heat was claiming her, inch by inch. She had every reason to fear it, especially since she knew it would win in the end. With him, it always won.

"I wish we weren't talking about this in a gas station," Joshua said. "But you didn't leave me any choice."

She couldn't wrench her hands away. She wanted to go back to pretending she was busy, didn't care, was over it. But the truth was she'd never been over it.

"I love you, Hailey," he murmured. "I know I screwed up. I know that I don't deserve a woman like you. But I want to deserve you. Please, just give me a chance to do that."

Chapter Four

5:09 p.m. Hailey tore her eyes away from the old grandfather clock in the living room and stared at herself in the mirror. A girl in a blue gingham sundress stared back. She didn't know this girl. Who was dressed up for a date with Joshua Loving. In about twenty minutes.

This girl she didn't know most certainly didn't belong in a blue gingham sundress.

She went back upstairs. Trying to make yourself more "acceptable" by dressing like a girl was the second sign that you were making a big mistake. The first was agreeing to go on a date with Joshua Loving. What had she been thinking?

5:16 p.m. Hailey was so keyed up, she had to look at her nightstand clock twice to be sure what time it was. She patted herself down to make sure everything was accounted for. Tank tee? Yes. Cargo pants? Yes. Heart beating a million miles an hour? *Yes.*

5:23 p.m. That was what the clock said when she went back downstairs. Grams came out of the first-floor bedroom wearing a pith helmet.

"Your dashing young Pegasus this way flies," Grams said. "His wings are made of hope."

"Are you sure you're going to be okay without me here to make dinner?" Hailey asked. "It's only for a few hours, but—"

"Better three hours too soon than one minute too late." Grams tramped into the kitchen. "Never fear, my sweet girl, there's plenty of ice cream."

The doorbell rang, which surprised Hailey since she rarely heard it and hadn't been sure it even worked anymore. Just one of a million things that needed to be looked into around here. And there went her pulse again, off to the races. She had a wonderful feeling about tonight—more butterflies, less moth-in-a-jar. When she opened the front door, the bottom dropped out of her stomach because Joshua was so handsome, he took her breath away.

He wore a blue shirt, sleeves rolled to the elbows, which did nothing to hide his wide shoulders and muscular chest. He'd always kept his hair a little long, usually to the collar, but being outdoors all the time had given it even brighter blond streaks. She caught the fragrance of his pine-scented soap and fresh, lemony aftershave, a combination that made her toes curl. The sheer maleness of Joshua had always hit her dead center. Now that punch radiated out to her fingers and toes. It set fire to every good intention she had of keeping her distance.

Okay, maybe she should have worn the dress.

His teeth flashed white in his tanned face. "I brought something for Adelia," he said, showing Hailey a box of opera cream chocolates. "May I give it to her?"

Hailey let him inside. She was touched that he'd remembered. Opera creams were Grams's favorite.

Grams appeared in the foyer with a pair of ancient binoculars dangling from her neck. "Chocolates? Oh, you are good. Lord Byron never brings me a thing."

Hailey cleared her throat. Joshua knew her grandmother's peculiarities, but to see them again so starkly would have made any man nervous.

He didn't bat an eye. "I'm happy to give them to you, Miss Adelia."

Grams accepted the box of candy and beamed at him approvingly. Then she strode back into the kitchen.

Joshua smiled down at Hailey. "You ever get the feeling she's the sane one and all the rest of us are nuts?"

"All the time." Hailey sighed. "Are you ready?"

They went down the porch steps and then out to his Jeep, which took some getting used to. The nice thing about a regular car was that you were hidden behind sturdy doors. In a Jeep, you were always on display. Hailey glanced over at him. Joshua looked almost *too* cool and in control. He said something about taking her to dinner.

It was just like old times, this feeling of happy togetherness. In a way, nothing had changed. She and Joshua had always been like interlocking puzzle pieces. But, in other ways, everything had changed. They were older, for starters. She was fully resigned to her fate here in Serendipity, to putting her life on hold so she could take care of Grams, her house, her responsibilities. Had Joshua changed, too? She sensed that something was different. But it still hurt that he hadn't fought for her. Not hard enough anyway. She would have fought to the death for him—for anyone she loved.

"This is freaking amazing," Joshua said, shifting into fifth gear as they took to the open road. "Being here with you. Even being in Serendipity."

"You forgot what a gossip mill it is."

"Hey, if they're talking about you, why not talk about them back?" He flashed her a boyish smile, complete with dimples, that only someone as manly as Joshua could get away with. He had always been the sun to her moon, the bright to her shadow. Maybe they balanced each other out.

"I never knew you liked Serendipity," she said. "You were all, 'This place is killing me—how fast can I get out of here?'"

He shrugged. "If you don't leave home, you never get a chance to appreciate it."

Hailey had a feeling he meant more than just home. *Time to change the subject.* She still wasn't sure this going-out business was a good idea. But when he'd forced her to look at him at the gas station, she'd seen such love and devotion blazing in his eyes. What else could she do except say yes?

But now, sitting beside him, she was drowning in a sea of memories. The power of his hard, muscular body on hers. The silkiness of his hair in her fingers. The lazy caress of his voice when he said her name. She remembered the passion and the tenderness and even the moments when they said nothing at all, when all they'd done was bask in the quiet joy of being together.

Them against the world.

Why couldn't the world have left them alone?

"Are you hungry?" he asked. "Because I know just the spot."

She racked her brain trying to think where. Serendipity had just two restaurants, Bubba Red's, a barbeque place on the square, and a new waffle joint. There was nothing romantic about either.

"It's going to be epic," he said, the corners of his lips twitching.

"Maybe," she replied. "The jury's still out yet."

He drove her to the middle of nowhere—only nowhere was a grassy hill seeded with wildflowers and a lone oak tree that spread its branches out in a cool, green embrace. The hill overlooked a valley where the shadows of clouds drifted by. It was all warm earth and sunshine and the slightly mossy chlorophyll smell of the oak leaves.

Hailey's senses stirred. "Restaurant, eh?"

He cut the engine and grinned at her. "I never said anything about a restaurant. Just that I knew a spot."

They found a perfect picnic place beneath the tree. Joshua

smoothed out a checkered tablecloth and then unpacked an ice chest full of sandwiches, cold sodas, and half a watermelon. "You don't belong indoors," he told her. "You belong here in nature."

It made her bashful the way he knew her. But there was a tingling warmth in her limbs that she could scarcely remember feeling before. As she helped set out the forks and napkins, dragonflies zoomed and birds burst out of the grass in a flurry of wings. It seemed as though her heart might burst, too.

How could she resist this? How could she resist *him?* How did you even protect yourself against someone who knew you better than you knew yourself?

They ate and laughed and took pleasure in all the same things—tiny daisies poking up through the grass. The limestone outcroppings and the glitter of a stream in the distance. Food was so much more delicious when you ate it outside. After dinner, they took turns digging into the sun-warmed watermelon bursting with juice. Joshua leaned against the tree with her and watched the rich, golden stillness of late afternoon turn into the kaleidoscope of sunset.

He gave a contented sigh. "This is perfect. It's about as different from my life in Austin as you can get."

"In what way?" she asked, watching him in the soft glow of sunset.

"There, it's all beer keggers and cramming for finals. Here, I finally feel at peace."

"Austin doesn't sound so bad," she said. "At least you're not stuck."

"Is that how you feel here? Stuck?"

She pressed her sticky-sweet lips together, worrying that she'd been disloyal to Grams. A good person wouldn't feel stuck. A good person would be happy to have even half as much as she did.

"Hailey . . ." Joshua's eyes were on her again, making her

wonder if he truly did see inside her. There was no getting away from his restless gaze. "I let you down, and I'm sorry."

Whoosh went the air from her lungs. Was it too soon to pick at this scab? Maybe it wasn't soon enough. Hailey didn't want to talk about the past. They were having such a good time now. Why spoil it?

"I didn't trust myself then," he said. "I didn't trust that what I felt for you was real."

"What makes you think it's real now?" she asked, surprised by how tense her voice sounded.

"Now I have something to compare it to. I know it's real."

She snuck a look at him from beneath her lashes. Words were cheap. *Do you know what's real? Sacrifice. Commitment.* "You're going back to Austin in a week and a half. There's no point in starting something now, Joshua."

"I'm not going back. I've accepted a year's internship near here. After that, I plan on taking the VCATs and applying to vet school over at TCU. I'm not leaving again, Hailey. Like it or not, you're stuck with me."

Joshua said it so casually, so matter-of-factly. He wouldn't meet her eye, but she sensed his hesitance came from nervousness, not avoidance. Her heart started thumping. "I don't understand. When did you decide to do all that?"

"I'd been thinking about it. But when I saw you again . . ." His voice was so soft, it felt like silk being dragged across her skin. "I know what I want, Hailey. And I know who I want it with."

Her lips went suddenly dry. She licked them, studying the patch of weeds in front of her. "What do you want?"

He leaned back, arms folded behind his head, and gazed up at the canopy of the tree. A hot breeze blew the leaves around and dropped a few dried twigs on his broad chest. "I want this, what we have right here. I want to become a large animal vet and work with the local ranchers. City life isn't for me, Hailey. I want a family. I want us to be happy."

Her head swam. Every dream she'd ever had, he held in his hand right now and was offering to her. Her heart felt like one of those old stone tablets with all the crazy writing on it, but Joshua knew the magic words because he was the only one who could read them. But what words could warm stone? She wanted so badly to believe him.

"But you haven't told your parents any of this yet," she said softly.

He lapsed into silence. Maybe she'd offended him by pointing out the truth, but the Hailey who let things slide, who didn't insist on being completely up-front, was long gone. The Lovings were going to lose their minds when they found out Joshua had no intention of becoming a heart surgeon. And they were *really* going to flip when they discovered that she was back in the picture. She would be blamed for all of it, and Joshua might even be disinherited. He had a cousin who'd joined the Peace Corps. The whole family—except Joshua—had turned its back on him. Didn't he see that he'd be next?

"My dad's still a mess over the whole Savannah thing," Joshua said. "Now he thinks I knew all along and didn't tell him."

He sounded so sad. Before she could stop herself, Hailey reached over and touched his hand. She meant it as comfort, but there was nothing comforting about the jolt of contact with him. The world melted away, and suddenly there was just her hand and his hand and this *feeling*—my God, it moved through her with the consuming heat of a fever. She couldn't stop touching him. She didn't care what happened if she continued.

His eyes held hers. There was no striving in them, no boyish eagerness. This was the way a man looked at the woman he loved. Joshua had so little cynicism about life, not like her. He wasn't afraid to be open, to be vulnerable. To need her.

Could she be that brave?

With a kind of mute, wondering hunger, he traced his fingers across her cheek. Her breath caught. She was floating high above her body, yet rooted to it by these white-hot filaments of desire. Was this really happening? Was she really here with Joshua or was she still alone in her bed, dreaming about him?

All those nights she'd spent trying to remember his scent or the feeling of him inside her. When he whispered her name, she didn't hear it with her ears, she responded to it with her heart. And when they kissed, her tears didn't appear to surprise him at all. Instead of dousing the flames of his passion for her, they seemed to fan them higher.

Joshua understood her so perfectly. He accepted her without question. She gave a shaky, joyful sob. No wonder her endless yearning for him had nearly eaten her alive.

"I love you, Hailey," he murmured. "Baby, I love you."

Her warm hair slid over her shoulders. He must have released it like he was releasing her, one binding thing at a time. He pulled her down toward him and grazed her lips with his, teasing and sipping. His lips were soft, unlike the rest of him. The rest of him was all muscle. When he hovered over her, supporting his weight on his elbows, she remembered how huge he was compared to her. It was a difference she always found arousing.

The world was a better place when Joshua was with her. He was the only one big enough and strong enough to show it to her.

Everything between her thighs softened for him. When he cupped her breasts with his gentle, knowing hands, she arched against him in unspoken invitation. The future, the past—none of it mattered now.

"Are you sure?" he said. "I would never want to rush you. And I didn't bring protection."

She couldn't form words. Instead, she rolled on top of him, straddling him the way he liked it. The way *she* liked it. Except that they had too many clothes on. Grabbing the hem of her T-shirt, she pulled it over her head and tossed it aside. She felt the rush of air on her naked flesh.

There was no point in fighting this, even if love *was* a velvet paw hiding the claws that shredded you. Joshua was touching her with such reverence. The sound of his zipper was the hottest thing she'd ever heard. She let herself tumble down into the dark deliciousness of his scent, his texture, his skin.

Joshua might have come back to Serendipity, but it was Hailey who felt as though she were coming home.

Chapter Five

She was everything he'd been waiting for. The clean healthy taste of her, the old-fashioned rose scent of her shampoo. Hailey had always reminded him of roses. She was a rose that had mysteriously grown in a garden full of weeds.

And now she was soft and warm in his arms. She was his. After years of dating women who never quite measured up to her—almost-perfect women who lacked her courage and her character—Joshua knew exactly what Hailey was worth. She heated his blood like no one else. She made him a better man. She'd burrowed her way into his heart without even trying.

But when he kissed her, he tasted the salt of her tears. And he knew where those tears had come from.

"It's okay, it's okay," he said against her lips. "I'm right here." He watched her dash the tears away with her hand. The last rays of sunlight turned her skin to fire, but it was his own skin that was burning up. He was so hard, he ached.

I will never let you go, he thought. *I'll never let you slip away again.*

She was so much smaller than he was. He'd forgotten how small. He had to exercise special care not to hurt her. He wanted to bury himself in the tight, hot center of her and empty himself, body and soul. But this was Hailey, not some girl at a frat party. When you loved somebody, everything was different.

He slanted her hot eager mouth over his, throbbing with need for her. Clasping her face in his hands, he intensified the kiss, letting his tongue dance with hers, the intimacy of it taking him right to the edge.

His fingers slid into the silky smoothness of her hair before wandering down the taut muscles of her backside, which he pressed firmly against him. She sucked in a breath.

My beautiful Hailey. Did you think I forgot?

Sex was a lie. Hailey knew that.

It made you weak. It made you drunk. It tore down walls and put up gauze instead, so that everything looked deceptively soft and fuzzy.

She'd done something she would hate herself for later.

So why did she feel so happy?

Hailey glanced over at Joshua as he drove her home, one hand slung casually over the steering wheel, the other lightly gripping the stick shift. The soft night air made her feel as though she were floating. The roar of the wind whipping through the Jeep made it hard to talk, but they didn't need to talk. The space between them was electric.

Without even taking off her clothes, he'd taken her to the moon and hadn't even asked her to return the "favor." She'd been too spent to offer.

What man didn't insist on getting what he felt was coming to him? What man put a woman's needs first?

And what am I going to do when he breaks my heart again?

"So would you say that was your best picnic ever?" he asked teasingly.

She didn't want to give him the satisfaction of seeing her smile, but she couldn't help it. "Maybe."

"Just maybe?" He raised his eyebrows at her, clearly expecting the truth.

Men were shameless. It was probably a big part of their charm.

"If I tell you it was great," she said, "you'll have this crazy big opinion of yourself."

"Oh, I don't want to hear that it was great. I want to hear it was the *best*."

She cut her eyes at him. "Well, the watermelon was pretty good."

He laughed and tenderly brushed a few strands of hair out of her face, letting the wind take them streaming behind her. Every time he touched her, her breathing quickened and goose bumps raced over her skin.

She looked at the night sky with the moon high overhead and thought, *I will always remember this. No matter what happens, I will have this night to look back on.*

"We should probably stop for gas," he said, checking his dashboard gauge. "I was all over hell's half-acre this morning and burned through a lot of fuel. But don't even think about getting out to pump it."

"Oh, for heaven's sake. It's what I do for a living."

"Yeah, but that's exactly why I don't want you doing it now. Can I just handle it myself? Please? Without your making a fuss?"

She heaved a sigh, pretending to be annoyed with him. Secretly, being treated "like a girl" made her feel . . . well, kind of special. Same thing when Joshua opened doors for her or pulled out her chair. They were such sweet, old-fashioned gestures. Hailey wouldn't admit to him in a million years that she liked them, but maybe she did.

The first gas station they found on the way home was Bucky Peterson's place on Decatur. The service windows were dark, and Bucky was long gone for the day, but he kept two pumps open. Hailey remembered because Tanner and her dad used to fuel up there before they went hunting.

"Okay, just stay here," Joshua told her. "I got this."

She stayed. It was harder than she thought it would be. While the tank was filling, Joshua found a squeegee and flung off the excess water. He made faces and flirted with her while dragging the squeegee across the bug-splattered windshield. She watched the muscles rippling in his forearms and found herself losing her train of thought. Why did something like forearms make you go all sweaty? His lips tugged up at the corners because he knew how annoyed she was sitting back and doing nothing.

"Am I doing it wrong?" he said. "Was I supposed to lift the wipers up first? Is it one long pass or do I go back and forth?"

She rolled her eyes. "You're just loving this, aren't you?"

A car pulled up on the other side of the service island. Hailey couldn't help but admire the lines. A blue Ford Mustang V6 convertible, 307 horsepower, with a rear drive that could hit sixty in just over five seconds. But when Hailey saw who was driving it, her confidence took a nosedive.

It was Mandy Adams and two other girls who were obviously home for spring break. Mandy had been Joshua's girlfriend in high school—head cheerleader, member of the student council, yearbook editor. *Rich*.

While Hailey had struggled to stay awake during algebra, Mandy had been on the school's PA system making perky, up-with-people announcements about pep rallies and bake sales. Their worlds were so different, they never collided.

Instead, Hailey had been forced to watch Joshua and Mandy holding hands in the quad and slow dancing at fall formal while she suffered through Bryan Lebronski's bad breath, sweaty palms, and clodhopper feet.

And now that awful feeling of inadequacy came bubbling

up, full force, from whatever dark place people kept their high school trauma. Mandy looked so tanned and wholesome and pretty, Hailey felt like a consolation prize.

"Hey, Joshua." Mandy smiled up at him from behind the wheel of her car. He'd been in the process of hanging up the gas nozzle, so he was halfway between his Jeep and Mandy's Mustang.

Joshua flushed. Hailey couldn't tell why, but she could guess. He was probably embarrassed to be caught out in public with her.

You know that's not true. How could you even think it? Joshua might have disappointed her, but he'd never acted as though he were ashamed to be seen with her.

What was wrong with her?

"Oh, hey, Mandy," Joshua said. He nodded to the two other girls in the car, both of whom gazed up at him with curious, feline interest in their eyes.

"We're headed over to the Ice House," Mandy said, irresistibly cuddly in her pink, fluffy summer sweater. "Wanna come with us?"

Hailey's stomach felt like there was something alive inside it, scrabbling to get out. She glanced down at her hands, which showed white at the knuckles from clenching. Boy, nothing like having lovey-dovey feelings to bring out all your deepest insecurities. Part of her wanted to jump out of the car and let Mandy and those man-eating friends of hers know that she was here. Another part of her wanted to melt onto the floorboards where nobody could see her.

Joshua said, "Hailey and I are pretty tired. I think we're just going to turn in."

Hailey froze. Three pairs of predatory eyeballs swung in her direction. They took in her hair and clothes and found fault with all of it.

"Hailey *Deacon?*" Mandy said.

Hailey waved. She didn't trust herself to actually speak.

After she and Joshua left the station, Mandy and her friends were going to tear her to pieces anyway, so it didn't really matter.

Mandy seemed determined to keep that smile in place, even though it had slipped a little. Word around Serendipity was that she still had a thing for Joshua. All Hailey knew was that he and Mandy had broken up only a month before he'd gotten together with her.

"What are you still doing in town?' Mandy asked. "I thought everyone from high school left already."

Hailey darted a glance at Joshua. *Help.* He dropped the squeegee in the bucket and then came around the driver's side. "Oh, well, you know," she said lamely. "No place like home."

"Aren't you even going to pump my gas for me?" Mandy called to Joshua. Her eyes were busy taking in his muscular arms and flat stomach. "You're not going to make *me* do it, are you? I don't even know how."

There was an awkward silence. Hailey started to get out of the Jeep. "Don't you do it, Hailey Jane," Joshua muttered. "Don't you dare do it."

"But they're helpless," she said, sitting back. "At least let me explain how it works."

He threw his hands in the air.

"It's really easy," she told Mandy. "Pop your gas cap first. The lever's on your left side down by your feet. Then slide your card in the machine, put the nozzle in your tank, and squeeze the handle."

Hailey heard Joshua's low chuckle. As they pulled out of the station, he tapped the horn and waved to Mandy and her friends.

"That was epic," he said. "Did you see the look on her face?"

"I don't know," Hailey said, gazing back at them wistfully. "Mandy's the kind of girl I always wanted to be in high school. She's beautiful. She dresses well. She knows how to be a girl."

"Don't even think that," Joshua said. "First of all, she's a girl, and you're a woman. Second, there's a big difference between being beautiful, like you, and having the money to dress well, like she has."

"Yeah, but—"

When Joshua looked at Hailey his dark eyes were somber, but they had a twinkle in their depths. "If you were Mandy, I wouldn't be this in love with you."

Chapter Six

After dropping Hailey off, Joshua took the back roads home. He wanted to relive the entire evening again. Fireflies flickered inside the culverts and against the dark screen of the trees along the way. Above him, the sky was awash with a thousand stars.

When he came home to visit, he liked to stay in the converted carriage house on Loving Ranch. He enjoyed the privacy away from his parents and the fact that there was plenty of room for his buddies. Trip was probably there right now, waiting for him, if he hadn't already crashed at some girl's apartment. Maybe they could grab a few beers, and Joshua could talk to him about Hailey.

Life was going great right now. He felt so happy, so sure he was on the right path. As far as he was concerned, running into Mandy again only confirmed it. Mandy was a reminder of whom he might have been if he had chosen a different path. One of the reasons he and Mandy had broken up was because she refused point-blank to go out with someone who had no intention of joining the country club. *Forget it,* she'd told him. *If I wanted to waste my time socializing with poor people, I'd go out with Tanner Deacon.*

Now Tanner was dead, and no amount of wishing would bring him back again. He'd only been a few years older than

Joshua, but they'd hung out and knocked back a couple of beers. Joshua liked to think Tanner would have approved of his dating Hailey again, but he still wished Tanner were here. It would have saved her a lot of heartache.

To enter Loving Ranch from the back meant having to get out and open the gates, which was a pain in the ass. With the bug-filled high beams of his Jeep lighting the way, Joshua dragged the iron gate to one side, drove in, and then dragged the gate closed again. The road here was dark and rutted. His headlights rocked drunkenly across dirt and trees, sometimes picking up the glinting eyes of animals.

But when he pulled in front of the carriage house and saw who was waiting for him outside, his happiness deserted him. It was his mom, his dad, and Trip—who looked as though he were secretly and urgently trying to wave him away.

Joshua parked the Jeep. He sat for a minute, thinking.

They must have found out he was dating Hailey again. And although he'd made no attempt to hide that fact, he hadn't exactly been advertising it either. His plan had been to wait till the right time, when his dad wasn't popping blood pressure medication and his mom wasn't nursing a vodka tonic. Well, so much for that.

Joshua got down from the Jeep. Whatever happened, he told himself firmly, he could handle it.

"Dude . . ." Trip's expression clearly said he'd been ambushed in the driveway and forced to cough up the truth.

"Trip, why don't you wait for me inside?" Joshua said.

Trip wasted no time retreating to the carriage house, his feet crunching loudly over the gravel. He shut the door.

Joshua stuck his hands in his pockets and gazed over at his parents, who were clearly furious. "Well, let's hear it."

"Not here." His dad jerked his chin toward the main house. "Inside."

Joshua followed his parents up the back steps into the kitchen. Longhorn skulls festooned the far wall, a tribute to their family's cattle-ranching history. If Joshua had fallen in line the way his parents wanted him to—hell, the way Mandy wanted him to—he'd be hanging on that wall right now, same as all the rest of those lifeless things.

"I'm sure you want to talk about Hailey," Joshua said, grabbing a stool by the kitchen island and pulling it under him. "And we can talk all you want. I'm okay with that. But I just want you to know it's not going to make any difference. I never stopped loving Hailey. If she'll have me, I plan to marry her."

His mom wrapped her fingers around a half-empty highball glass she must have left on the counter. She took a big swallow and studied the floor. Joe paced behind her. Two tiny veins as familiar to Joshua as they were to all members of the family throbbed in his dad's temples. "You're twenty-two years old," Joe said. "You've got your whole life ahead of you. Why do you want to tie yourself down now?"

"Because I love her. You and Mom were even younger when you got married."

"Times were different then," his dad insisted. "Men got drafted and went to war. You had to get married, especially if you wanted to . . ." His face turned bright red.

"Have sex?" Joshua said the word gently because he knew his parents were so uncomfortable with it. "Times *are* different. But that's why you should be happy for me. I don't want to marry Hailey for the sex. I want to marry her because she's the one."

His mom clacked down the glass harder than she probably meant to. "But the *Deacons*, Joshua? Seriously? Do you even care that her brother worked as a janitor at the high school? Or that she's a gas station attendant?"

Oh, here we go. His mom would never let go of her pretensions. That Mayflower thing was a stench that never went away. "I don't care," Joshua replied. "And I have something else to tell you that you won't like."

His parents looked up at him. Tense. Angry. Waiting.

"I'm not going into medicine," he said. "I've decided to become a veterinarian."

His mom buried her face in her hands, but his dad pounded a fist on the table. "I absolutely forbid it! I've got to draw the line somewhere with you two. First Savannah and now—no, I won't let you. Not happening, buddy. We talked about this already, and you agreed!"

The heaviness of those words weighed on Joshua. It felt as though he had no future, that he'd be stuck forever doing work he didn't love, marrying a woman who wasn't Hailey, and having kids he'd do the same damn things to as his parents were doing to him. Another generation of rich, damaged Lovings. He wanted so badly to ask his father for help with these problems, but his father *was* the problem. Joshua tried hard to swallow over the lump in his throat. In a way, their roles had reversed. He was the calm adult, and his dad was the irrational toddler.

Four years ago, he'd done what his dad had told him to do. Now, he was free for the first time—free to follow his heart, fall on his ass, whatever life threw at him. "I did things your way, Dad. Remember? With Hailey, you said to wait, and I waited. With school, you said to go into pre-med, and I went into pre-med. But I won't pretend anymore. And if you can't accept that, I'm afraid you and Mom are destined to be very unhappy."

His mother was noisily weeping. Savannah would have rolled her eyes at the drama. She'd been smart to take off. He was the idiot who tried doing things the "right" way, and now he was getting the full Martyr Marion treatment.

"I blame your Uncle Tom," she sobbed, casting blame on the black sheep Loving whose Ducati Savannah had used for her getaway. "The minute he showed up, everything went to pieces."

"It's not Uncle Tom's fault. He had nothing to do with this. Savannah and I . . ." Joshua dragged one hand behind his neck, hunting for the right words. "I guess we're both just as strong-minded as you two. And when it comes to love, we're going to follow our hearts."

"See how far that gets you," his mom said with a bitterness that surprised him.

"I look at Hailey, and I see the rest of my life," he said simply. Kissing her every morning before he drove off to work. Hearing her laugh at his dumb jokes. Chuckling at her heartfelt but adorably tone-deaf warbling in the shower. "Maybe someday you'll be able to see it. But if not, that's your choice. I've already made mine."

"Well, I'm not letting you throw your whole damn life away!" his dad bellowed.

"You don't even know Hailey," Joshua said heatedly. "You couldn't be bothered to get to know her."

His dad marched to the door, yanked it open, and then stood stiffly beside it. His eyes glittered with a self-righteous indignation that Joshua had seen before, but never directed at him. Yet instead of bullying him into submission, his father's anger left Joshua heartbroken.

What kind of man turned his back on his only son?

"If you can't be reasoned with, Joshua, then you aren't welcome here," his dad said. "Maybe when you don't have your family to turn to, you'll begin to appreciate what we've given you."

Joshua had sensed where this was going, but nothing had prepared him for the shock of actually seeing it unfold. His mother wouldn't meet his eye. Was she really going to let this happen? There was a hollow of cold, aching loss in the pit of his stomach as he got to his feet. "Dad . . . ?"

His dad held the door open more emphatically.

With a heavy heart, Joshua glanced at the wall with all the longhorn skulls on it. He took in the huge country kitchen, all the gleaming chrome and black-veined marble, where his family had spent so many happy mornings. He saw his mother staring blindly at her empty glass.

"Good-bye," he said.

The door closed behind him. His dad flipped the lock. A terrible finality hung in the silence.

Joshua had known being booted out by his family was a price he might have to pay for taking his life back.

Now he would pay it.

Crickets chirped sleepily in the bushes as Joshua took one last look around Loving Ranch. How many hours had he ridden Blackie, his big quarter horse, over these lush, rolling acres? How many long summer days of his childhood had he spent rambling through the woods and looking for frogs?

Now, there was no telling when he'd see his home again.

His eyes burned with tears he didn't want anyone to see, especially Trip, who of course came bounding out of the carriage house, a duffel bag in his hand. Joshua's own duffel bag. At least now, Joshua thought dully, he wouldn't have to go through the whole sad process of packing it.

"Dude, I had no idea they were going to go all royal family on you," Trip said, loyally pretending not to see that Joshua was falling apart, but doing a crappy job of concealing the anxious concern on his face. "I mean, I knew they had it out for your girl, but damn . . . They're making you *leave?*"

Joshua shouldered his duffel bag and blinked back the tears. You could always count on Trip to listen to stuff that was none of his business. He'd probably been lurking beneath the breakfast room window for the whole wonderful show. "Guess so," Joshua said.

"Where will you go?" Trip asked him.

"Hailey's, I suppose. Look, I'm really sorry about this. You're welcome to stay, if you want to. My folks aren't kicking *you* out."

Trip plunged one hand through his shaggy hair. "Nah. I got me a sweet deal with Hailey's friend Sam. You remember.

The blonde? She was coming to get me anyway, so I'll just wait till she shows up."

Joshua walked to the Jeep and threw his duffel in the back. "I'd tell you to have fun, but I already know you will."

Frowning, Trip stood in front of the Jeep with his hands in his pockets. "So this is it for you then? No more babes and brews? No more picking up chicks in the quad?"

"That was always more your thing than mine." Remembering Trip's failed attempts to lure coeds back to the dorm, Joshua could almost smile. But it felt as though that part of his life was a hundred years ago. Now things weren't so easy anymore. And Trip probably sensed, just as Joshua did, that there would be no returning to those freewheeling single days.

You have to grow up at some point, Joshua reflected. Being single wasn't for him. If he had to be honest, it never had been. And how much of a wuss did admitting that turn him into? He didn't care. He just felt so damn relieved.

He gave one last look around. All he'd ever wanted was a family, a real family, the kind that had your back. What life had given him instead was money, more money, status, and the kind of deal where someone else got to change his channel.

"See you back in Austin," Joshua said. "Call me if you get in trouble. I mean, *when* you get in trouble."

Chapter Seven

Hailey refluffed her pillow and then buried her head in it again, unable to sleep. The sheers at her bedroom window shone ghostly pale in the moonlight. A half dozen cats lay purring by her feet.

She couldn't stop thinking about Joshua. That she was still wildly in love with him was obvious, even to her. But it all seemed too much, too soon, especially for two people who tended to lose their minds around each other.

You've been living rent-free, Sam had told her earlier on the phone.

What's that mean? Hailey had asked her.

It's when you're always dreaming about someone, but you don't have to put up with the irritating reality of having him or her around on a daily basis.

But she already knew all about Joshua's "reality," Hailey thought. And Lord help him, he knew hers. She'd never shown her soft, naked underbelly to anyone the way she had the summer they started dating—her darkness, her loneliness. But Joshua had confided in her about his own loneliness, what it was like growing up Loving. The way she had it figured, they both had the same issues, just different childhoods.

Still, she didn't want to rush anything. Joshua was so

openhearted and sure of what he wanted; he rarely felt her same need for caution.

You can have a heart or a fortress, Grams told her once. *But you can't have both.*

Hailey punched her pillow again. Why didn't brains come with an off switch? No wonder she couldn't sleep.

She heard a noise outside and sat up. It sounded like someone calling to her. She stopped fighting her pillow to listen. Her heart pounded as she went to her balcony. Joshua stood in the moon-drenched garden below, a duffel slung over his shoulder. He looked like something out of a dream.

"What are you doing here?" she called down to him. Had he come back to finish what they'd started? Her pulse heated up at the thought. Her *everything* heated up at the thought. She was stupidly happy to see him.

"I didn't want to knock on the door and wake your Grams," he said. "Is it okay if I come up?"

"Meet me around front." Hailey raced downstairs, careful not to wake Grams, but knowing how pointless it was to try to be quiet because Grams was going to raise one eyebrow at her over breakfast anyway.

By the time Hailey opened the door, Joshua was already standing there. He came inside and swept her up in his arms. As always, she had to stand on her tiptoes to meet his lips. His were warm and passionate, which brought her to an instant boil. All her worries about moving too fast and "living rent-free" were drowned in a surge of liquid heat. The feel of his stubble against the softness of her lips, her fingertips, her cheeks, sent jolts of need spiraling through her bloodstream.

Now all she could think about was getting him upstairs.

"Did I wake you?" he asked. "I know it's late. But . . . wait. What are you *not* wearing?" He held her away from him, giving her a leisurely once-over that sent a shiver of pleasure through her.

"It's just a T-shirt and panties," she answered shyly.

"I'm about to show you how much I like you in a T-shirt

and panties." Joshua lifted her up, and she wrapped her legs around his waist. With his big hands supporting her from the bottom, he carried her through the dark house, up the stairs, and to her room. The bedroom door closed with a soft click, and suddenly an entire world of possibilities opened before them.

He dropped the duffel bag and then fell with her on the bed, bracing his weight on his elbows. With her legs locked around him, she could feel his excitement. It left her in no doubt of what he wanted.

With agonizing slowness, he skimmed a hand up the side of one breast. It lingered there, tracing her from the outside of her T-shirt. The slower he circled, the harder she bit her lip to keep from moaning out loud. He pushed against her, and she clung to him, panting.

She couldn't get enough of him. Of this. How had she gone without him at all? She was greedy for him. She had to drain this cup before life snatched it away from her again.

But one thing she knew for sure. There was no use fighting it anymore.

I love you, she thought as he pressed his lips against her tingling flesh. Joshua wasn't afraid like she was, shy like she was. He wore his heart on his sleeve.

Actually, in a lot of places.

He groaned and pulled her closer, hungrier now, obviously determined to have his way. She would have given him anything he asked for; it didn't matter. She knew it was stupid, but didn't care. Nothing mattered except feeling him inside her.

She was hardly even conscious of relief when he reached into his duffel for protection. His fingers visibly trembled as he tore it open. Impatiently, she watched him roll it on while she wriggled out of her panties.

After it was on, he found her. What had been empty was about to be exquisitely full. Gently, insistently, he worked his way in, making her feet pedal weakly on the cover. She wasn't used to sex. But then it all came back to her, along with the sense of urgent need. The white-hot friction that was half sin and half magic. And then the mounting waves of pleasure that came radiating out from some place deep inside her, some place only Joshua could reach.

The muscles between her thighs ached from being stretched, but need overrode it. She dug her fingers into the hard, smooth skin of his shoulders and let those waves bring her higher. There was a pounding in her ears that she might have remembered from before, from those endless summer nights when they lay entwined in each other's arms. The restless pounding told her what was coming next, what was coming *now*.

And then all at once the truth of everything rushed toward her in a burst of blistering fire. Her back arched. She cried out, shuddering. Joshua gave a hoarse shout as he, too, drowned in that sea of flames. She felt it through her fingers, the way his body churned above her, thrusting wildly, before he finally went still.

Minutes later, Hailey was still circling the earth somewhere, trying to catch her breath. She'd only ever been with Joshua, and knew she had no one to compare him to, but . . . if her love for him had been any less absolute, she never would have been able to give herself to him this freely.

Joshua brushed the hair away from her face. She knew his heart was thumping as hard as hers because she could feel it pressed against her. But she also sensed, without having to say the words, that he was feeling the same dizzying rush of love and happiness that she was. When he kissed her, she could taste it. She snuggled closer. Joshua's sheer size made him a world-class snuggler.

"You're the only thing that got me through this awful day," he said softly.

"Awful how?"

"My folks found out about . . . well, about everything. What they didn't know, I filled them in on."

Hailey's glow suddenly deserted her. She had a strange premonition of doom. "What did they say?"

"They kicked me out and told me not to come home again. I'm no longer welcome there. And I've got to tell you . . ." He frowned, clearly puzzled by her pushing away from him and scrabbling out of bed. "Baby, what's wrong?"

Along with having a sickening sense of déjà vu, Hailey knew then that *this* was what she'd feared all along. She kept gulping air because she couldn't get any. Grabbing her panties, she pulled them on and then sat at the edge of the bed with one hand bracing her stomach.

A crushing weight of sadness bore down on her. Life was so unfair.

"You sacrificed your family . . . for me?" she whispered.

"Sacrificed?" He sat up, clearly worried. "I told them the truth. They reacted about as well as I thought they would."

She went to the window that overlooked the garden. Joshua used to meet her down there next to the trellis of climbing roses. The roses were dusted silver by moonlight now. All she'd ever wanted was for the dream to go on forever. No parents, no college, nothing that might take him away from her. Deep down, she'd known his family would never accept her. She might have yearned for two parents to fill in the hole left by the loss of hers, but it would never be the Lovings. She had been crazy to even think it was possible.

Joshua's family could never love her. And she could never let Joshua give up something so important.

"You'd better go," she said over the lump in her throat.

"What are you talking about?" Joshua said in a tense voice. He looked stunned.

"I can't be the reason your family disowns you," she said. "Loving you means putting your needs ahead of my own. And what you need, whether you know it or not, is your family."

"No, I need you." Joshua got off the bed and came over to her. Not even his comforting nearness took the edges off her despair. Good things like him didn't happen to girls like her. Just more of the same in a long, dark tunnel that never ended. Tears slid down her cheeks, her throat, her chest. She tried to make them stop, but they kept falling.

"Look, I'm not going to make myself miserable trying to live the life my parents tell me to," Joshua told her. "I love my folks. I do. But this is *my* life. And I need you to be in it."

"You say that, but you're not even out of school yet. Who's going to support you during your internship? During vet school?"

"I'll take out student loans," Joshua said, shrugging.

Of course. He's never had to worry about money. He's never had to skip paying the gas bill in order to keep the lights on. It's all so easy for him.

"It doesn't matter," he said. "The only thing that does matter is that we're together."

"That's not true." She shook free of him and put on her clothes. "You don't know what you're saying."

"Hailey—"

"No." She couldn't make out his expression in the dim light, but he seemed as baffled and angry as she was sad. The truth was, even if you wanted to, you could never turn your back on your family. Not for long anyway. The world was too harsh a place.

Hailey didn't know a lot of things, but she knew this: in the end, all you had was family. After they were gone, you had nothing.

"You have to fix this," she told him. "We can't be together until you do. Families are a pain in the ass, but that's not important. You still need yours. Everybody does. That kind of love is the only love that will bring you home."

Dawn broke pink over the horizon as Joshua sat in his Jeep and stared at the Serendipity city limits sign. How many times had he driven right past that sign without giving it a second thought? *Come on back now, ya hear?* it said in red italic script.

Now that his life was falling apart, it seemed horribly ironic, even sinister.

He pulled onto the shoulder of the road and cut the engine. He had nowhere to go except back to Austin. His eyes were raw from lack of sleep, but that was nothing compared to the ache inside his chest. He'd had all these wonderful plans for his future. Now the only thing he felt sure of was endless amounts of misery.

He was a lover, not a loner. Worse, he was one of those pathetic saps who only loved one woman forever. And that woman was Hailey.

There were few cars this early in the morning. Joshua sat in the soft hush of dawn and listened to the birds awakening. The sky was pale blue and cloudless, which meant another scorcher of a day—a day without Hailey in it. He raked one hand through his hair and tried not to feel so lost and alone.

A part of him willfully refused to understand how she could tell him to stand up for what he believed in, but then reject him when he did it. Of all people, why would she insist he reconcile with his family? *Women.* What on earth did they want? Sometimes he wished he could be more like Trip—get in, get out, and get gone.

But if Joshua had to be fair, which he didn't want to be, Hailey had a point. In the end, all you had was family. Sure, they made you crazy. Maybe all relationships made you crazy. And yet . . .

He gripped the steering wheel with both hands and squeezed as hard as he could, every cell in his body blistering with rage and love and frustration. His friends always teased him about being the "chill" one, the gentle giant. Now he wanted to rip the steering wheel off its column and use it to smash things. He wanted to run over that city limits sign again and again until it lay crushed and mangled beneath his tires. Then he wanted to set fire to the country club that gave his mother all those crazy ideas about being too good to have Hailey Deacon as a daughter-in-law.

To hell with that.

Joshua jumped out of his Jeep and found a big branch lying by the side of the road. He grabbed it and snapped it with his bare hands. *Yes. Better.* He found another and then another after that, breaking and demolishing, feeling like a jackass, but unable to stop himself.

When he was done, the roadside was littered with broken branches, yet his mind felt clearer. The whole world would be a better place if people had somewhere to go where they could destroy stuff. It was very therapeutic.

Panting, he surveyed the damage and thought: *What are you doing, you idiot? You're supposed to fight for what matters. You're supposed to fight for Hailey.*

He knew what he would do. First, he needed to find a motel and sleep for a few hours. He couldn't do anything on no sleep. Then he'd take a shower and head over to the ranch.

No way was he giving up. Not now. He climbed back into the Jeep and started the engine. His dad did a lot of stupid, hardheaded stuff, but he always felt bad about it afterward.

Joshua shook his head. Why hadn't he remembered that?

His sister would be up in a few hours. High time they talked. Who better than Savannah to hash things through with? He'd call her and get some advice. For the first time in a while, he felt absolutely sure of himself. Only an overgrown child would let himself be driven away by anger and resentment. A man—a real man—put his foot down and did the right thing, not the easy one.

Joshua put the Jeep in gear and roared away.

Chapter Eight

When Hailey was sad about something, she found lots of other sad things to think about. An orgy of sadness. She figured it was more efficient to get it all out of her system at once. And there was one sad thought in particular that always wound up for the one-two punch when she was down: the night Tanner and her father had died.

She was at her other *other* job today, walking Mrs. Shapiro's husky mix, Bob. The problem with walking Bob was that it gave Hailey too much time alone with her thoughts. There was a dull pain where her heart used to be and a bucket of tears she refused to shed. Telling herself to stop obsessing over Joshua meant that Joshua was all she thought about. She had to really knuckle down and focus on something else.

When Tanner and her dad had lost control of the truck—what had that moment been like for them? The tree, caught in their headlights, rushing toward them. The sickening crunch of metal and plastic, the shattering of glass, the acrid smell of gasoline and smoke.

And then nothing.

After saying good-bye to Joshua, Hailey had felt as though she'd been in a car wreck of her own making. But the nothing she kept waiting for never came. Instead, there was this numb despair and the bleakness of her future. It didn't give her anything to hope for. She would stay right here in Serendipity, rattling around inside that broken-down ghost house until it disappeared into a pile of dust.

Bob dragged her along the street, straining the leash so he could stop and pee every few feet. She loved Bob, but not even his silliness could drag her out of her pit of despair. Funny how he was exactly the kind of dog she'd always imagined having with Joshua. They could have been one of those couples who insisted on the dog's staying off the bed, but who woke up every morning with it sandwiched between them. They were supposed to have ridden horses together and gone to the Ice House to drink beer and listen to live music. They were supposed to be making love, not arguing about what was owed to family.

But she couldn't be the wedge between Joshua and his parents. Maybe he wouldn't hate her for it right away, but he'd hate her for it eventually. There was too much at stake for him: His career. His family. His thousand-acre inheritance. She just couldn't let him sacrifice all that.

Not for a misfit like her.

Hailey took Bob back to Mrs. Shapiro's. He panted up at her, pink tongue lolling, as she shook kibble into his bowl and poured him some water. Then Hailey locked up and headed home.

There were a thousand things that needed fixing here— the bathroom sink was clogged, and it was high time she got around to repairing the porch swing—but Hailey felt as though she were moving through water. It was the heartache of four years ago, only worse. This time she already *knew* what life without Joshua would be like because she'd been through it.

She bit down hard on the tears, poured herself some tea out of the fridge, and sat on the porch. A bluebird flashed by and then disappeared into the trees. The air smelled of lawn clippings and the loamy richness of earth.

The screen door clattered, and Grams came outside wearing a wide-brimmed straw-colored hat.

"'When we two parted in silence and tears,'" she said. "Lord Byron, of course. A dreadful man, but such an astonishing poet." Instead of sitting across from her, Grams dropped beside her on the wicker sofa. "I'm sorry that you are sad."

Hailey nearly dropped her tea, she was so surprised. Grams seldom made direct, personal observations about her. It was all snippets of poetry and the occasional *Beowulf* reference. Before becoming an eccentric Southern lady, Grams had been a high school English teacher. Old age and misfortune might have lessened her grip on reality, but not her love of the classics. Now she seemed to be having one of her rare normal spells, and Hailey wasn't quite sure what to make of it.

"I'll be okay," Hailey lied. She knew every cell in her body yearned for Joshua and would never stop. She knew her one chance at happiness was gone.

"What nonsense," Grams said. "You won't be okay until you work up the courage to beard the lion in its den."

More riddles. Hailey's heart sank. Maybe Grams wasn't having a moment of clarity after all. "I don't know what you're talking about."

Grams touched the brim of her hat with both hands as though to check that it was still there. "You and your young man, of course. You asked him to fight for you, and he did. So why aren't you fighting for him?"

"Fight for him?" Hailey glanced at her in alarm. For a woman who didn't have a clue about the world around her, Grams had a strange way sometimes of getting at a hidden truth.

"'The heart that has truly loved never forgets,'" Grams said. "Go to his parents. Make them understand that you aren't a scared little girl anymore, but a woman to be reckoned with."

The suggestion stunned her. Hailey felt the hair lift on the backs of her arms. She'd never considered going to Loving Ranch and talking to Joshua's parents—probably because deep down she knew what a fool's errand it would be. They had nothing but contempt for her. There was no fixing that.

Plus . . . Hailey gulped down more tea and tried to push the thought away . . . maybe on some level she'd wanted Joshua to prove himself by choosing her over his parents. But he'd done that. And now she realized it wasn't what she wanted.

Had she made a big mistake? A mistake that would cost her that one chance at happiness?

No, this was stupid. It couldn't be done. She was an idiot to think Joshua's parents would listen to her.

Grams put one arm around her and drew her close the way she had when Hailey was little. "Life isn't going to roll out the red carpet for you," Grams said. "You have to fight for what you want, for what you believe in. I stopped fighting a long time ago and look what a crazy old lady I turned out to be."

"I can't do it, Grams. I can't go over there."

Grams's sweet face was next to hers, her expression gentle but firm. "If you think you can't, Hailey Jane, then that's exactly why you have to."

Hailey let her ten-speed coast to a stop in front of the wrought-iron gates of Loving Ranch and tried to catch her breath. A sick case of nerves had all but ambushed her, making her hands sweat, her muscles quiver, her heart pound like a mallet. This wasn't just a fool's errand. It was suicide.

They're going to destroy me.

Once Joshua's parents were done with her, she'd be an oil slick on the floor. They were going to see her as the worst kind of scheming opportunist, one with the audacity to come riding up here on her hand-me-down bike in her secondhand clothes—saying *what* exactly? That she loved Joshua? That without him she'd been in a slow process of dying for four long years?

She stared through the gate at the grand old house with its turrets and chimneys and its green slate roof gleaming in the sun. The house reminded her that she was nothing and came from nothing. It put her as firmly in her place as an imperious hand.

If she failed, she would go back to living the rest of her life eaten up with heartache and regret. She would go back to pretending that everything was okay, she was fine, nothing to see here, folks. Meanwhile, every corner of this town would be full of ghosts, full of memories of what she'd lost, memories she alone would be forced to live with day after day until she died.

Panic rose in her throat. *No, I can't do this.*

Yet even as she thought the words, her eyes roamed for an opening in the boxwoods that fronted the property. She wanted desperately to change her mind. She wanted to go home and hide. Yet Hailey knew she wouldn't even if it killed her because she loved Joshua and wanted what was best for them both.

After leaving her bike at the gate, she found an opening in the hedge and headed toward the house. At noon, the air was hot and still. It shimmered over the emerald lawn and made a gazebo ripple in the distance like a mirage. By the time Hailey rang the doorbell, she had to straighten her knees to keep them from buckling. *Please don't answer. If you don't answer, I can go away and never come back.*

Joseph opened the door and stood scowling at her. "What do *you* want?"

Hailey clutched the wall to steady herself. When her mouth opened, no sound came out.

Joshua. She needed to think about Joshua.

"Well?" Joseph snapped. "What is it?"

"I have to talk to you," she said faintly. "You and Mrs. Loving. I promise not to take up too much of your time."

"I know why you're here, and we have nothing to discuss."

"You think I'm trying to break up your family, but it's not true," Hailey said in a rush. "I'm here to save it."

The scowl deepened. In the foyer behind him, Marion Loving appeared. Hailey's heart sank when she realized Marion clutched a highball glass and had clearly been hitting the liquor cabinet. *Oh God, I'm so screwed.*

"Oh, for heaven's sake, Joe, you're not going to win this," Marion said. "Let the girl in."

He glanced at Marion with obvious suspicion and then peered at Hailey again. "Five minutes. That's all you get."

Hailey waited for him to let her inside. He gave an exasperated sigh and opened the door a little wider. With a cowed sense of her own insignificance, she entered a world of vaulted ceilings, chandeliers the size of boats, and expensive-looking Persian carpets. She'd been so worried about trying to get a foot in the door; she had no idea what to say now that she was inside. No idea at all.

Joseph crossed his arms and frowned down at her. Marion stood behind him with the precarious dignity of a woman who'd dedicated herself to drinking her troubles away. She didn't look as angry as her husband, but she didn't look welcoming either.

Hailey cleared her throat. She was covered in sweat. Okay, so they weren't going to invite her to sit down. Here was her one and only chance to make things right for her and Joshua. To secure their future together.

If you think you can't, Grams had told her, *that's exactly why you have to.*

Hailey looked at Joseph's flushed face. Underneath all that gruffness there had to be something human.

"I love your son," she began. "I love Joshua." Her courage faltered, but she grabbed at it. Forced it to stay. "You are Joshua's parents, and he loves you more than he can say."

Joseph seemed startled by that news, as though what had recently transpired made him doubt it. How did you doubt a son's devotion, especially a son like Joshua? But Hailey knew by the way they stared at her that her presence in their foyer made them uncomfortable. She had no time to waste.

"You can't go around telling people who they can or can't love," she said. "I don't think we get a choice in that, do you? As for me and Joshua . . . what our hearts want is each other."

"Oh, come on," Joseph scoffed. "You're nothing but children! You don't know *what* you want."

"Your son is old enough to drink, to vote, to fight for his country. Isn't he old enough to know what his life should be?"

Hailey didn't know what she had said to put that puzzled look on Joseph's face, but at least he wasn't staring daggers at her now. "I know you think I'm not good enough for him," she said, dying a little, hating that she had to be so honest. "Maybe you're right. Maybe I'm not good enough. Heaven knows, I'm poor; my people were poor. And we sure aren't talented at staying alive." She swallowed over a lump in her throat before going on. "But I do know what it means to love someone. I know what it means to put their needs first. It's why I'm here. Joshua loves you, and I love Joshua. He won't be happy, not really, without you."

She felt light-headed. All these words. She'd never said so many words. Especially to people who hated her.

Suddenly, there was a sound like a stifled sob, and Marion walked unsteadily into the living room and sank into a chair. She covered her face in her hands. Hailey didn't know what to do or what was going on, but it dawned on her that maybe, just maybe, they finally understood what their actions had cost them.

Hailey waited to see what might happen, too nervous to take a decent breath.

"Do you mind waiting in the kitchen?" Joseph asked heavily. "I need a moment alone with my wife."

Hailey didn't know where the kitchen was, but she took a walk anyway. Had she actually gotten through to him? She rounded the corner, found a stool next to a kitchen counter, and climbed on top of it. Her legs shook. Hope kept poking at her, but she was too much of a realist for hope. Joseph Loving was going to say "Thanks, but no thanks." He'd be polite about it this time, but people didn't really change, did they?

She heard a car door slam outside and then the sound of someone coming up the steps. A key scratched at the lock. The door opened. Her heart nearly exploded out of her chest when she saw it was Joshua. He was her rumple-haired, flannel-wearing salvation.

"Hailey?" he asked, clearly dumbfounded. "Baby, you are the last person I expected to see here."

In his heart, Joshua knew. He *knew*.

Hailey was here to fight for him.

It must have gone against every instinct she had to knock on that door. He had no idea what she was doing alone in the kitchen, but seeing her filled him with so much indescribable joy, he didn't think to ask.

Joshua crushed her in his arms, and suddenly he could breathe again. Her hair smelled like roses, like sunshine, like *her*. He'd been so afraid he would never see her again, yet here she was—sitting in his parents' kitchen no less. Every minute without her had felt like an eternity. Now he had everything he wanted.

If Hailey never spoke to him again, he would still love her. His love had nothing to do with what she could do for *him*. It existed because of who she was.

"I came back," he said, kissing the top of her head, still holding her. "I had to make things right with my family so I could make things right with you."

"I know." She raised her face to his, and her wide blue eyes glittered with unshed tears. "I was wrong to put it all on you, Joshua. Here I was asking you to go to bat for me, but I needed to go to bat for you, too. I love you so much."

In all the time he'd known her, Joshua had never heard her utter those words. He'd never doubted her love, but he'd never had the pleasure of hearing her say it. Warmth radiated throughout his body. He could do anything now. He felt invincible.

His parents walked into the kitchen, clearly surprised to see him there. Joshua kept his arm around Hailey as he turned to face them.

"I'm your family," he said. "And Hailey is the love of my life. We're going to find a way to work this thing out because I'm not giving up on any of you."

Chapter Nine

"This is crazy," Sam said, peering out the upstairs window of the Bluebird Inn. "I thought fairy tales weren't real, but some fairy godmother went and turned you into a princess."

Hailey giggled as she adjusted her veil in the mirror. She'd been giggling a lot these last few months, but it wasn't because she was a princess. Princesses didn't have flakes of drywall under their nails and a blister from using the nail gun. It wasn't because of her gorgeous, cream-colored satin wedding dress or repairing the house with Joshua and Grams or even knowing that the Lovings had accepted her as one of their own.

It was love.

"I gotta tell you," Sam went on. "Weddings usually make me break out in hives. But this one . . . it's not bad. Plus I'm the maid of honor, so bonus points for coolness. Oh, and this dress doesn't suck." She smoothed one hand over her pink satin bridesmaid dress and gave Hailey an endearing smile. "And then there's the part where you two are going to be *really* happy."

"I *am* happy," Hailey said. She twirled in front of the mirror just to see her dress flare out. She joined Sam at the window, her heart brimming over with excitement. The guests were already seated on folding chairs in the garden. There were so many of them—not the society people of Savannah's wedding, but regular folk like Mr. Anders from the post office and Carolyn Birch of Phil's Mini-Mart. Most of the people Hailey had grown up with.

The same aqua tulle bows that had decorated Savannah's wedding that wasn't had been gladly repurposed for Hailey's. Again the pavilion looked just like a birthday cake. Nothing too fancy, but everything exactly right for two people starting out in life together.

"Did you ever in a million years think this would happen?" Sam asked her. "A few months ago, you were the help. Now you're the bride."

Hailey shook her head. "I'm marrying my best friend. How many people can say that? Sure, I might pass out before I get there, but it's still the greatest day of my life."

"It's going to be wonderful." Sam gave her a hug that was way sloppier and more emotional than Hailey had ever received from her before. Was Sam getting sentimental? "Lord, pretty soon you're going to make *me* a believer," Sam said. "*Me*. The most cynical woman on earth."

"Hailey!" Savannah called up to her from the bottom of the stairs. After all the time Hailey had spent worrying whether asking Savannah to be a bridesmaid was cruelty or kindness, she had been touched when Savannah had said yes. "Come on down. It's starting!"

Nervous excitement swept over Hailey in one big gust. It carried her floating down the stairs and through a chorus of *oohs* and *ahs* that she'd usually be all embarrassed about. Joshua's mother gave her a kiss and her bouquet of calla lilies. Grams met her in the hallway wearing a hat covered in bluebirds.

"They're watching, you know," Grams whispered. "Your mother and father and Tanner. They can feel your happiness, even from heaven. It's well deserved, my dear."

A violinist struck up the wedding march. Blinking back the tears, Hailey went out into the bright, flower-filled garden where Joshua waited for her in his elegant tux. She saw the look of pride and happiness on his face. And she saw something else there, too. Strength. Quiet confidence. Self-reliance. She felt it, too.

If life brought them challenges, they would face them together. If life brought them joy, they would share that as well. But as Hailey placed her hand on his and started down the aisle, she knew deep in her heart that loving him was the finest thing she had ever done.

Joshua was forever.

Bachelor Honeymoon

Janet Dailey

Chapter One

Dr. Chance Worthington stood in the driveway as his bride roared off on her uncle's Ducati. He shook his head in disbelief while she vanished around the corner.

Un-freaking believable! She'd really done it.

He didn't know whether to laugh or cry.

Bending, he gathered up the cloud of tulle, satin, and lace that had landed at his feet. He had to hand it to her. Savannah had planned this escape and carried it out with all the finesse and timing of a prison break.

He should have been surprised. But he wasn't. Not really. He'd already suspected that Savannah was getting cold feet—especially after last night's rehearsal dinner, when he'd overheard her telling a friend that she felt like she was marrying her older brother.

His one regret was that he hadn't called her aside and talked to her then, if not sooner. Maybe they could have avoided this last minute fiasco. But even though he and Savannah had known each other most of their lives, they were eight years apart in age. Aside from the friendship between their families, they'd never had much common ground. Even in the few months they'd dated before their engagement, they'd never really been confidantes, let alone lovers. When he'd proposed, in front of her excited family, and slipped that showy diamond ring on her finger, their kiss had felt awkward, like two actors faking it onstage.

He'd told himself that he loved her—and he did. Savannah was a wonderful woman. She would have made the perfect doctor's wife. Marrying her would have been the right thing to do, the next logical step in his well-ordered life. But Savannah had wanted more—and she'd had the good sense to listen to her heart. He could only wish her well.

The scene in the garden was sheer pandemonium— guests milling about in confusion; Joe Loving cursing at his brother; the organist still fumbling the last notes of the wedding march.

Chance was dimly aware of the women who'd swooped in to console him, patting and cooing. He knew he wouldn't have to worry about being lonely. But it was too soon for condolences or invitations to a home-cooked dinner. He was still in a mild state of shock.

The wedding planner, a striking brunette Chance had noticed earlier, was shouting into her headset. He assumed that she was urging everyone to calm down. But no one was paying her any attention.

Dropping the abandoned gown on an empty chair, Chance made his way to the luncheon pavilion and headed for the bar, which had opened early. Right now, he could use a drink.

Wedding Planner Harper McClain had started the day with a bitch of a migraine. From there, everything had gone downhill. At 7:22 a.m. on the morning of the year's biggest wedding, her babysitter had called in sick. With no other option, Harper had rousted her barely four-year-old twins out of bed, poured them some cereal, and sat them at the table in their booster seats while she finished her clothes and makeup.

By the time she'd made it back to the kitchen, Jessy had

spilled her milk and Jenny had upended her cereal bowl on the floor. With no time to clean up the mess, Harper had washed and brushed her whining children, stuffed them into clean play clothes and sandals, grabbed a handful of granola bars and juice boxes, and rushed them out to the car.

With the twins buckled into their safety seats, Harper had roared out of the driveway. She'd ordered her staff to be at the Bluebird Inn at 8 a.m., ready to begin setting up for the 11 a.m. wedding ceremony. It was up to her to make sure everything was perfect and timed to the split second. And she was already running late. The digits on the dashboard clock had read 8:05, and she had still been more than twenty minutes from Serendipity.

The migraine had progressed from its blurred visual aura to a throbbing pain in the side of her head. It hurt like blazes, but at least she could see to drive—or that's what she'd thought until she'd caught sight of the flashing lights behind her and realized she'd just run a stop sign.

The officer had been all business. Harper had drummed an impatient finger on the steering wheel while he checked her registration and wrote up the ticket. As soon as he'd handed it to her, she'd driven off without even checking the amount of the fine and headed for the freeway. She'd never been late on the day of a wedding, and she'd certainly never shown up at a venue with her children in tow.

Why did it have to be today? And why did it have to be this lavish society wedding that could make or break her career?

Harper asked herself that same question now, as the exquisitely choreographed wedding disintegrated around her. The bride had shed her gown and fled like a biker version of Cinderella. The guests were milling like cattle about to stampede. Joe Loving was shouting at his brother. The bride's mother looked ready to commit murder, and the owner of the Bluebird Inn was practically in tears.

Only the jilted bridegroom looked unruffled. Harper could see him through the archway that led from the patio to the open-sided pavilion. He was sitting at the bar, sipping what looked like a brandy—a tall, cynical-looking man she hadn't seen before today. She knew Chance Worthington was a pediatrician, and that he was from a wealthy Fort Worth family. She'd also noticed that he was smoking hot, in a James Bond kind of way. What sane woman would run away from a man like that?

As his gaze met Harper's across the distance, he raised his glass in a sarcastic toast, as if to show that he didn't give a damn about what had happened.

Maybe that was why his bride had run off and left him. Maybe he didn't care enough, and she knew it.

Here on the patio, some of the guests were trying to leave. One of the bridesmaids was crying hysterically. The situation was getting out of hand. Something had to be done—and since Harper was the one in charge, it was her job to do it. Trying to be heard through the mike on her headset hadn't worked. But suddenly she had a better idea.

In the pavilion, the quartet she'd hired was waiting on the dais for the ceremony to end, so they could start the music for the reception. Stepping into sight, she caught the wedding singer's eye and gave her a wave. The singer returned a puzzled look, but finally nodded her understanding. A moment later, the mellow strains of "At Last" flowed into the patio.

The buzz of conversation stilled for a moment. Heads swung. A few of the guests, then more and more of them, began migrating into the pavilion where, wedding or no wedding, there was food, drink, and entertainment to be had. At least they could enjoy a nice party.

Harper would have stayed to do crowd control, but she'd left her twins in the kitchen. One of the catering staff had promised to keep an eye on them during the ceremony, but right now, nothing was going as planned. She needed to make sure her girls were all right.

By now the patio was almost empty. The preacher and the organist had left. The mother of the bride had vanished with the gown, and most of the guests had either headed for home or decamped to the pavilion. Wilted, trampled flowers littered the ground. One of the bride's white satin pumps lay in the aisle. Harper picked it up and glanced around for the mate. It was nowhere to be seen.

What a disaster—for her own career, for the Loving family, for the charming Bluebird Inn, and maybe even for the groom. Dr. Chance Worthington didn't appear devastated. But then, he'd just been left, literally, at the altar. That had to hurt. Perhaps he was too proud to show his feelings. Or maybe her first impression of him had been right. She could see him now, still at the bar, getting cozy with a sexy-looking redhead.

Harper dropped the shoe where she'd found it and hurried on toward the kitchen. She'd told her twins to stay in the breakfast nook, off the kitchen, and eat their snacks. She'd checked on them just before the ceremony. They'd been fine then. But now that the luncheon was on, the catering staff might be too busy to watch them closely. She could only pray that the two little munchkins had stayed put.

A loaded dessert cart was rolling down the narrow walkway. Harper jumped aside to let it pass, then raced in through the open kitchen door. The kitchen was a scene of organized chaos, with the staff rushing to load trays and carts with last-minute hot and cold additions to the buffet. It was as she'd feared. No one here would have time to look after two curious little girls.

Her heart sank as she peered into the breakfast nook and spotted the empty table, still littered with granola crumbs and juice boxes. Her worst fear had come to pass.

The twins were gone.

Chapter Two

Chance sat at the end of the bar, watching the wedding guests load their plates at the buffet and carry them to the decorated tables. A few couples were dancing to the music of the jazz quartet. Most of them, including his own relatives, seemed to be pretending he was invisible—maybe because they didn't know what to say to him.

"Will you be all right, Chance? If you need to talk, honey, I'm here."

The sultry voice at Chance's elbow was all too familiar. He should have known that Mavis Clemson, Savannah's older cousin on her mother's side, would show up to console him. Years ago, when Savannah was still in high school, he and Mavis had enjoyed a brief but very hot fling. It had ended when Chance had discovered that Mavis had a fiancé in another town. Now divorced, she was on the prowl again—and something told him he'd just become fair game.

He turned on the bar stool to face her. Mavis had always been pretty. In the years since he'd last seen her, some very good—and no doubt expensive—plastic surgery had turned her into a flame-haired goddess.

"Mind if I join you?" She took the stool next to him,

crossing her legs to inch up the clinging teal-blue sheath that showed every curve of her spectacular body.

"Suit yourself." Chance was hardly in the mood for company, but at least, with Mavis at his side, nobody was going to feel sorry for him.

"Savannah didn't deserve you," she said. "She was always the spoiled baby of the family. All she had to do was stamp her little foot and everything she wanted, including you, would fall right into her lap."

"Uh-huh." Chance sipped his brandy. Actually, he'd never thought of Savannah that way. She was a smart, spirited girl with the courage to extricate herself from a situation that wasn't right for her. Mavis had it wrong. Savannah deserved a better match than he would have been.

"And she was too young for you." Mavis's hand, with its long, manicured nails, came to rest on his knee, gently stroking and massaging, creeping subtly upward. "You're old enough to appreciate a woman with some experience." She leaned closer, her breath warming his ear. "I've got a room upstairs," she whispered. "Nobody will miss us."

Chance felt a responding tingle—he was only human, after all. But this wasn't the time or place. Sneaking off to bed with an old girlfriend would be little more than cheap revenge. And even Mavis deserved better than that—especially since he could tell she'd had too much to drink.

Gently he lifted her hand off his knee. "Thanks for the offer, but you'd soon figure out that I was using you. I guarantee we wouldn't like ourselves—or each other—in the morning."

"You always did have an easy way of letting a girl down, honey." She stood, teetering on her high heels, her face flushed. "Listen, they're playing 'Misty.'" She hummed a few measures along with the band. "Dance with me, Chance, for old times' sake."

"Something tells me you might not make it around the

floor." He stood, guided her to an empty table, and pulled out a chair for her to sit down. "Can I bring you something from the buffet? A sandwich, or maybe some punch?"

She shook her head. "Food doesn't sound that good to me right now."

"You're not sick, are you?" He brushed the back of his hand across her forehead. "You don't feel feverish."

She laughed. "I'm fine, Doc. Nothing that a good shot of bourbon wouldn't cure—unless you want to take me upstairs and tuck me into bed." She gave him a wink.

Chance ignored the invitation. "You've already had too much to drink. How about some coffee? It'll perk you up and make you feel better. Okay?"

She sighed. "Okay. Maybe then we can dance."

"Stay here. I'll see what I can do."

Chance checked the buffet table on the way to the kitchen. As he'd expected, there was no coffee. But he did find a pitcher of ice water. He filled a glass and carried it to the table. "Try this," he said. "It'll keep you hydrated while I check the kitchen for some coffee."

"Thanks a lot." Her reply was tinged with sarcasm. Chance realized he'd just offered her the equivalent of a cold shower. Sensitivity had never been his strong point. Maybe that was one of the reasons Savannah had left him at the altar.

As Chance made his way across the floor, headed for the kitchen, he found himself glancing around for that gorgeous dark-haired wedding planner. He'd felt a distinct spark when their eyes had met across the distance earlier. If there was any chance of teasing that spark to a flame . . .

But what was he thinking? He'd just been deserted by one woman, been propositioned by another, and was looking around for a third. By rights, he should be ready to swear off women for the next six months.

Earlier, the four-tiered wedding cake, a spectacular work of art, had been sitting in the middle of the pavilion, on a small, covered table, waiting to be carved. Now the cake had been wheeled to a corner. Somebody with a twisted sense of humor had plucked the miniature bride figure off the top, leaving the groom to stand alone.

Chance paused as he passed the cake on the way out. His mouth twisted in a bitter smile. He hoped he wouldn't be expected to cut it and pass out slices to the guests. Since Savannah's family had paid for the cake, what to do with it was their problem.

He was about to move on when he glimpsed something odd—a few scattered crumbs and dabs of icing on the white tablecloth. Moving to one side for a better look, he saw that on the back of the cake, which faced the corner, the butter-cream icing had been raked off in tiny furrows. The bottom layers looked as if a horde of gremlins had been secretly feasting on them. The cake looked fine from the front, but the back had been destroyed.

What was going on here?

A white linen cloth covered the table and hid the legs and casters. Now Chance saw it move slightly. Had a stray breeze stirred the cloth, or was something hiding under the table? An animal, maybe. A stray dog or cat, or even a coyote. After the crazy day he'd had so far, nothing could surprise him.

Ready for anything, Chance dropped to a crouch and, mindful of his hands, lifted the hem of the tablecloth.

He heard giggles. Two small faces, smeared with icing, emerged from the shadows. Chance saw identical pairs of dark eyes and identical mops of dark curls—two little girls, as alike as peas in a pod.

"Hi," one of them said. "Who are you?"

"I'm Dr. Worthington." Chance felt as if he'd fallen through the rabbit hole. "What are you two doing here?"

Another giggle. "Hiding."

"And eating cake."

"Yes, I can see that," Chance said. "Isn't somebody supposed to be taking care of you? Where's your mother?"

"She's busy. Everybody's busy."

"Are you a real doctor? Where's your white coat?" Both children were talking, but since they looked exactly alike, Chance couldn't tell who was saying what.

"I don't wear my white coat to weddings," Chance said. "Right now, I need to find your mother. What's her name?"

"Mommy."

Chance sighed. He should have expected that. "I know that's what you call her," he said. "What do other people, like your daddy, call her?"

"We don't have a daddy. He went away."

"Well, what do your mom's friends call her?"

There was a brief, murmured consultation between the two. "They call her Harper."

"Harper. Got it," Chance said. "Now, can you two stay right here while I go and find her?"

The twins nodded.

"No more cake, all right?"

Nods again, this time with disappointed faces. Chance had weighed the option of taking them along, but he didn't relish the idea of trailing the grounds with two sticky little imps in tow. He'd already raised enough gossip today.

"You'll stay here and be quiet. Promise?"

"Uh-huh."

Chance lowered the cloth and rose to his feet. After glancing around to make sure no one was watching, he strode off toward the kitchen.

Harper. There couldn't be many women by that name. Maybe she was one of the catering staff. At least someone in the kitchen should know who she was and have some idea where to find her. Once he knew the twins were safe, he would get Mavis her coffee, then slip away and leave.

Outside of office hours, Chance tended to avoid children. As a pediatrician, his work was an endless parade of crying, whining kids. He'd been kicked, bitten, peed on, pooped on, upchucked on—and also hit on by some of the moms. At the end of most days, all he wanted was to go home to his clean, quiet townhouse and put his feet up, or maybe go out to dinner for some adult conversation.

And then there were the times when he'd had to tell parents their child had a life-threatening condition. After witnessing that kind of heartbreak, he couldn't imagine going through it with a child of his own—and he'd seen it happen far too many times to dismiss the odds.

He and Savannah hadn't discussed having children, but he knew she'd sensed his reluctance. He could handle being a husband. But being a father was something that would take a lot of getting used to.

He found the way to the kitchen—a paved walk, screened from the festivities by a tall hedge. He was approaching the door when it swung open, almost hitting him in the face. A dark-haired woman in a peach-colored pantsuit came rushing out and slammed right into him. The impact knocked them both off balance. He staggered back, caught himself, and reached out a hand to steady her.

"Sorry," she muttered in a husky voice that pushed all his fantasy buttons. "Are you all right?"

Chance tried not to ogle. The wedding planner was even more spectacular up close than she'd been at a distance. A halo of dark curls framed a sensual face with big, dark eyes, a pert nose, and soft, full Angelina Jolie lips. And he hadn't even started on her body—much as he would like to.

His first thought was how he might parlay this awkward beginning into a dinner invitation. But then he realized something was wrong. She looked flustered, even scared.

"I'm the one who should be asking," he said. "How about you? Are *you* all right?"

"Oh—" There was a tearful catch in her voice. "You didn't hurt me. But no, I'm not all right. I had to bring my daughters to work, and now I can't find them. If something's happened—" She'd begun to tremble. "I don't know if I should call the police or make an announcement, or—"

Chance stifled a curse as the truth sank home. The dark

hair and eyes—blast it, he should have guessed that those little rascals were hers.

"I take it your name is Harper," he said.

Her eyes widened. "Yes. What—?"

"Relax. I know where your daughters are. They're fine. Come on, I'll take you to them."

As he guided her with a light hand at her elbow, the subtle fragrance of her hair teased his nostrils. Maybe this was some kind of karmic joke, he thought. After being left at the altar, he'd met someone who fit the description of his dream woman and found out she had baggage—double baggage.

Over the years, he'd made a rule against dating women with children—too many complications. Assuming Harper would even go out with him, could he break that rule? Or would he be better off reuniting her with her children and walking away?

As they entered the pavilion, he glanced toward the table where he'd left Mavis. To his relief, she was gone. With luck, she'd found a more willing conquest than he'd turned out to be. Now he could focus on helping lovely Harper, and maybe talk her into having dinner somewhere.

Was he even thinking straight? He'd been ready to say "I do" to another woman. Now he was rebounding like a Ping-Pong ball. Maybe he should back off and give himself some solo time.

But what were the odds that a woman like Harper would ever walk into his life again?

Harper felt a tingle where Chance Worthington's hand touched her elbow. At close range, he was jaw-droppingly gorgeous. She could feel the sizzling current that flowed between them. When she glanced back and their eyes met, she could tell he felt it, too.

But she'd be crazy to follow his lead. The man had just been left at the altar. Was he in denial about his runaway bride? Was he in the grip of rebound fever? Was he out for revenge? Or had her first impression been right, when she'd dismissed him as cynical and unfeeling?

One thing was certain. When it came to handsome, charming men who couldn't resist chasing every pretty thing in a skirt, she'd been there and done that. Where Chance Worthington was concerned, she'd be a fool not to keep her distance.

Her migraine had faded, but she was worn out and worried sick. After this train wreck of a wedding, the reputation of the Bluebird Inn was bound to suffer, as was her own. And she had yet to send the Lovings her final bill. What if they refused to pay on the grounds that the wedding had never taken place? Right now, all she wanted to do was collect her girls, go home, and bury her head in a pillow.

"Over here. I told them to stay put." Chance was guiding her toward the wedding cake, which had been moved to a corner of the pavilion. It was a spectacular cake, festooned with swirls and rosettes of icing and adorned with miniature roses. "Take a close look at this cake," Chance said.

What was going on here? Where were her twins?

Then she saw the destruction on the back side of the four-tiered confection and heard the giggles. Two small, sticky faces peeked out from under the tablecloth.

She lifted the cloth, revealing her two little girls covered in crumbs and icing. This was a disaster. With nothing else to say, she fell back on formality. "Dr. Worthington, I'd like to present my daughters, Jenny and Jessy," she said. "I'll understand if you don't want to shake hands."

"Ladies." Chance gave them a courtly nod.

"Hi, Mom!" Jenny's face was a smear of white fondant and chocolate cake.

"You found us!" Jessy's hands left sticky fingerprints as the twins crawled out from under the table. A buttercream rose was stuck on the end of her nose.

Dizzy with relief, Harper sank to her knees. Her precious

girls were safe. But she had to make them understand what they'd done.

"Are you mad, Mommy?" Jenny asked. Behind her, Harper heard Chance chuckle.

"I'm glad you two are okay," she said. "But yes, I am mad. Look at that beautiful cake! It isn't pretty anymore. You've spoiled it. That's a terrible thing to do."

"We're sorry." Jenny looked up with her sad puppydog expression.

"We were hungry," said Jessy.

"And the cake looked so yummy, we just wanted a taste." Jenny finished her sister's sentence.

"But it wasn't your cake," Harper said. "It was made for the wedding. It cost a lot of money, and now it's ruined. I'll have to tell Mrs. Loving what happened and offer to pay for it."

"How much money? A dollar?"

"More dollars than that." Eight or nine hundred, at least, Harper calculated—more than the money she'd set aside for new tires on her sport wagon. But if the story got out that she'd brought her children to a wedding, they'd ruined the cake, and she hadn't made good on the damage, no one would ever hire her again.

Her headache was coming back.

Chance had disappeared. Now he was back, with several cloth napkins and a pitcher of water. "I thought these two could use some cleaning up," he said. "If you need another pair of hands, I'd be happy to help you."

Ordinarily Harper wouldn't have let a stranger near her children. But this man was a doctor—a pediatrician. Her girls seemed to trust him, and she really did have her hands full right now.

He sensed her brief hesitation. "If you'd rather I didn't—"

"No, I appreciate the help. Jessy, would you like the doctor to wash your hands and face?"

"Uh-huh." Jessy, the bolder of the two, scampered over to Chance and held out her sticky hands. Her icing-smeared face wore an impish grin. Evidently Dr. Chance Worthington had a way with females of all ages.

They used the wet napkins to wipe down the twins as best they could. Harper usually packed a change of clothes for them in her car, but this morning she'd been too rushed to take care of that small detail. Their sponged-off shorts and T-shirts were stained, but they would have to do until she could get them home.

Unfortunately, she still had a job to do. She couldn't leave until the pergola, the other wedding décor, the food and dishes, the chairs and tables, and the rented pavilion had been cleaned up and put away or removed from the premises of the Bluebird Inn.

But she'd have to keep a close eye on her daughters. She'd faced enough disasters today.

"I couldn't help overhearing something," Chance said, as they piled the wet napkins to be picked up with the laundry. "Were you telling your daughters that you planned to go to Mrs. Loving, tell her what happened to the cake, and offer to pay for it?"

"What else can I do?" Harper asked. "What happened is my fault. If I can't be honest and cover the damage, I don't belong in the wedding business."

"Look at it this way," he said. "If the wedding had gone as planned, the cake would've been cut and eaten by now. It would never have been moved to that corner."

"You're saying it's the bride's fault?"

"No, just that it's not yours."

"I don't agree. If I hadn't brought my daughters, they wouldn't have ruined the cake. It's my fault."

"Whatever you think, you shouldn't have to pay, and I'm going to make sure you don't." Chance rose, stepped behind the cake table, and began pushing it back toward the center of the pavilion.

"What are you doing?" Harper clutched her girls to keep them from scampering after him.

"You'll see." As he moved the cake forward, people were turning to look. "Hey, everybody," he said, loud enough to be clearly heard. "We mustn't let this cake go to waste."

The pavilion had been erected on grass, which would have been rough going for the casters under the table. Still, Harper had no way of knowing whether what happened next was an accident or a deliberate move on Chance's part.

The front casters seemed to sink into the grass. The table pitched forward far enough to let the cake slide off and topple to the ground in a glorious splatter of icing, cake, and flowers.

As the wedding guests gasped, Chance turned around and walked away.

Chapter Three

The expression on Harper's face was worth whatever he'd done, Chance thought as he strode away from the crumbling remains of the wedding cake. She was staring at him in wide-eyed astonishment. Had it sunk in that he'd just saved her from paying a thousand dollars for a silly cake—an amount that was pocket change to the Loving family?

Maybe not yet. But dumping that cake was as close as he could come to slaying a dragon for her. And it was just possibly the best thing he could have done for himself. After the ego-bruising he'd suffered at the altar, it had felt damned good, like throwing a rock through the schoolhouse window. There was a spring to his step as he walked back to where Harper stood with her twins and ushered them back to the garden, where the flowers had been swept up and the pergola was being taken down.

"I can't believe what I just saw," she said. "Either you're very clumsy or you're out of your mind."

He gave her a schoolboy grin. "Maybe both. You'll never know for sure. But at least you're off the hook for the cake."

She was trying not to laugh, but lost the battle. Her laughter was musical. Her dark mocha eyes sparkled. Her luscious lips were so tempting that Chance could almost taste them.

But this was crazy. He was feeling like a hormone-driven seventeen-year-old. He'd loved Savannah, admired and respected her, and had wanted to give her a happy life. But the heat had never been there for him. Clearly, it hadn't been there for Savannah either.

But now that heat was burning him alive. He was in all-out *lust* for a woman he'd barely met.

A woman who came in a package deal with two adorable little monsters.

Whoa! Slow down! Chance told himself. *Get her phone number—she's probably got a business card. Think it over for a couple of weeks. If you haven't come to your senses by then, give her a call.*

"I suppose I should thank you," she said.

"No need. Maybe everything worked out for the best."

"The best?" One delicate eyebrow shot up. "Your bride ran away; the wedding cost the family a fortune, all for nothing. My daughters ruined the cake, you finished it off, and if the Lovings aren't happy with my part in all this, I may never work in Texas again. And you say it's for the *best*?"

"Sorry. I'm just trying to put things in perspective. If Savannah was going to leave me, better now than after a messy divorce."

Harper shook her head, making it clear what she thought of his logic. "I need to get back to my job," she said. "The wedding may be over for you, but I can't go home until everything's in order. Thank you for finding my daughters. Come on, girls, let's go. I'll make you peanut butter sandwiches in the kitchen." She turned away, took a small hand in each of hers, and headed for the kitchen door. One of the twins strained to look back at him with her mother's heart-melting brown-eyed gaze.

Let her go, he told himself. Today was no time to stumble into a new relationship. And, even if it was, the last thing he'd ever wanted was a ready-made family—or even the challenge of juggling private time with a single mother's busy schedule. Several attractive moms of his young patients had made it clear that they were interested. He'd never taken the bait, not even once.

Every sober, sensible instinct he possessed told him this wasn't a good idea.

So why was he so determined to keep her from walking out of his life?

"Wait!" he called after her. At the sound of his voice, Harper glanced back. So did her daughters.

"You don't have to settle for peanut butter sandwiches," he said. "There's plenty of good food on the buffet table. I know you won't want to take the girls over there, but I can fill some plates for you. The three of you can have a picnic in the peach orchard. How does that sound?"

Harper would have made an excuse and kept walking away. The man was too charming to be trusted. That he seemed to be pursuing her on what would have been his wedding day was the ultimate red flag. Chance Worthington was heartbreak on a silver platter.

At least he hadn't included himself in the picnic invitation. Nice touch, but she wasn't fooled. She didn't want to owe him any more favors.

However, the word "picnic" hadn't been lost on her daughters. They were jumping up and down, tugging at the hem of her jacket. "Please, Mommy! It would be so much fun!"

How could she say no?

She turned back with a sigh. "Oh, all right. I know you two are hungry."

The twins let go of her and raced back to Chance. Heaven help her, the man was like the Pied Piper. Jessy and Jenny barely knew him, and they were already under his spell. But then, he was a pediatrician, Harper reminded herself. He'd had plenty of practice charming young children.

That didn't mean that she was taken in, too.

"So what would you like?" he asked them. "I think I saw some fried chicken on the buffet table. Does that sound good?"

Both twins nodded an enthusiastic yes.

"And you should probably have some vegetables. What's your favorite?"

"'Sparagus," said Jessy.

"Carrots," Jenny said.

"And you?" He looked at Harper. "I'll bet you haven't eaten all day."

"Just some salad, thanks," Harper said. "And you don't really have to do this."

"Nonsense. It's my pleasure. Find a nice, shady spot, and the food will be on its way."

Chance had already decided not to join the picnic. He knew enough to back off before his company became intrusive. Harper needed a break. So did he. And before he could move past what had happened today, there was something he had to do.

In the pavilion, the serving crew was already cleaning up the cake. The musicians were winding down. Many of the guests were leaving, or had already gone. But there was enough food left on the buffet table to fill the order that Chance gave to one of the servers. He slipped the young man a generous tip to load a tray, carry it to the orchard along with a picnic cloth for Harper and her girls, and clear away the meal when they were finished.

That done, Chance walked back toward the house.

Savannah's parents were still at the inn. He'd noticed their car in one of the guest parking slots a little earlier. Chance guessed that they'd probably retreated to the bridal suite.

As he crossed the lobby and mounted the stairs to the second-floor room, he wondered what to say to them. It had been Savannah's decision to run away and ruin the wedding. But some of the blame had to be his. Whatever she'd wanted from him, and from their marriage, he had failed to give it to her.

He walked down the hall to the suite door and rapped lightly.

"Who's there?" Joe Loving's low voice rasped with annoyance. "If that's you, Tom, you can go to hell. I don't have a damn thing to say to you."

"It's Chance, Joe. I just want to talk."

The door opened a few inches. "Keep it down. My wife's asleep in the next room."

"We could go down to the bar," Chance suggested.

"No. I don't want to run into my brother. I might be tempted to punch him for giving Savannah the keys to that damned Ducati." Joe opened the door wider. "Come on in, if you don't mind whispering. Marion cried her eyes out over this mess. Said she'd never be able to face her friends again. It was a blessing when she finally wore herself out and went to sleep. She needs some rest before we head back home."

Chance stepped into the small sitting room. The place was in mild disarray, an open suitcase on the floor and Savannah's rumpled gown flung over a chair. A half-emptied bottle of bourbon stood on a side table. Joe poured two fingers into a glass and handed it to Chance. He was a big man, his powerful presence filling the room. "Sit down. I'm guessing you might need this."

"Thanks." Chance took it and lowered himself into a chair. "Have you heard from Savannah?"

"Not a word. And she's not answering her phone—if she's even got it on her. I'm damned sorry about this, Chance. We were looking forward to having you in the family."

"It wasn't your fault. I'm just wondering if it could've been mine. Did she say anything to you before the ceremony?"

"Just that she wasn't ready to get married. Nothing about you. Why, did you have a fight?"

"We never fought. We never even argued." Maybe that was part of the problem, Chance thought. No fire. No emotion.

Everything between them had been polite—and superficial, he realized. They'd known each other for years; yet they hardly knew each other at all.

"I thought you'd be the perfect husband for her," Joe said. "Not only because of your family connections, but because you're older and wiser. You could control her and settle her down, help her grow up. Give her some kids to take care of."

Chance had swallowed his bourbon too fast. He stifled a cough as it burned down his throat. "I'm sorry things had to happen this way, Joe," he said. "Believe me, the one thing I care about is Savannah's happiness. I would never have forced her to marry me if she was having second thoughts."

"Neither would I. But the fool girl doesn't know her own mind. Tomorrow, after throwing away a sixty thousand dollar wedding, she could decide she wants you after all. If she were to do that, would you forgive her and take her back?"

It was a sobering question. A vision of Harper's lovely, vulnerable face flashed in Chance's mind—a face he would have to choose never to see again. "That would depend on a lot of things," he said. "But I can't imagine Savannah's changing her mind about marrying me. Not after what she did today."

"You could phone her. Maybe she'd answer if it was you. And if you really opened up about your feelings, maybe she'd listen to you and come back."

"Sorry, that's her call, not mine." Chance had heard and said all he needed to. He stood, leaving the half-emptied glass on the side table. "I won't keep you any longer. I just wanted you to know there are no hard feelings on my part."

He offered his hand; the two shook, and it was done. Chance strode back down the hall, his step lightened by relief. He wasn't the one who'd made Savannah run, he told himself. It was the pressure from her family. It was the expectations that would be thrust upon her as Mrs. Chance Worthington.

Or maybe he was wrong. Maybe it really was *him*—his

age, his superior attitude, his staid manner, and his bachelor lifestyle.

He couldn't blame Savannah for shedding her gown and jumping on that motorcycle. Given her choices, he would have run away himself.

Walking back outside, he found himself wondering whether he was a fit life partner for any woman. At thirty-three, he liked a steady routine and an orderly life. His townhouse was kept spotless by weekly visits from a cleaning service. He had his favorite foods, his favorite TV programs, his favorite vacation spots. And when he wanted an occasional bed partner, with no strings attached, he knew some sharp women who were open for a little fun—not that he'd contacted any of them since his engagement.

But Harper wasn't a candidate for the occasional bed partner slot. She had two messy, noisy, adorable little complications who couldn't be ignored. And he could tell she was a good mother. Whatever happened, whatever plans *he* might like to make for the two of them, her children would always come first.

If he had any sense, he'd go out to his car, drive away from the Bluebird Inn, and never look back. He had first-class airline tickets and beach house reservations for a planned honeymoon in Maui. With his practice closed for two weeks, he could go solo and still have a relaxing time.

Or he could forget the trip, walk back to the hillside, and take a chance on pursuing Harper.

Chance shook his head. He'd be crazy to throw away a five-star Hawaiian vacation he'd already paid for. He could get a tan, walk on the beach, polish his rusty surfing skills, and take some time to get his head on straight. Maybe then he'd be ready to come home and phone the beautiful wedding planner. Or not.

The flight to Hawaii was scheduled for early tomorrow. He and Savannah had planned to spend their wedding night in the luxury suite of a nearby hotel and take a limo to the airport the next morning. The trip wouldn't be quite like the one he'd planned, but after this crazy day, he could use some R & R.

The decision to go was a no-brainer. But only a jerk would walk away and leave Harper wondering where he'd gone and why he'd disappeared. The least he could do was find her and tell her good-bye.

Now, through the blossoming trees in the orchard, he could see Harper and her twins. Harper was sitting up with a headset on. The little girls were curled next to her on the picnic cloth. They appeared to be fast asleep.

As he came up the hill, she gave him a look of weary relief. "Thank goodness you're here," she said. "I need one more favor, if you wouldn't mind. I've been trying to manage things from here, but I need to go back to the garden and make sure everything is shipshape. The girls are exhausted. They'll be cranky if I have to wake them. Would you mind staying here for about fifteen minutes to keep an eye on them? I promise I won't be long."

"Sure. Go ahead." Sparing a few minutes to help her wouldn't be a problem. He had plenty of time to make it to the hotel and check in for his morning flight. He would tell her about his plans when she came back.

"Thanks. I've already imposed on you too much. This will be the last time, I promise."

"No problem. We'll be fine. Now get going." He sat down on the picnic cloth next to the sleeping twins, enjoying the view of her sexy, high-heeled stride as she hurried off.

Jessy and Jenny—he had no idea which was which—were slumbering like little angels. But all children looked angelic in their sleep, he reminded himself. These two, as he'd already learned, could be a handful. He could only hope they wouldn't wake up until their mother returned.

Even on the shady side of the hill, the afternoon sun was warm. Bees buzzed among the blossoms. Birds called from the trees. From beyond the orchard, Chance could hear the sound of workers taking down the pavilion. The pergola and chairs were already gone from the garden. Soon this place would look as if nothing had happened here today.

But lives had been changed forever.

One of the twins stirred, opened her chocolate-drop eyes, and saw him. She smiled and sat up. "Hi," she said.

Her sister sat up, too, yawning and looking a little less friendly. "What are you doing here? Where's our mommy?"

"She had to work," Chance said. "But she'll be back in a few minutes. She asked me to stay with you."

"Are you our babysitter?" the sleepy twin asked.

"He's the doctor. Remember? The one who dropped the cake?"

"Oh." The sleepy twin brightened. They sat gazing up at him like two alert puppies. "Why did you drop the cake?"

"So you and your sister wouldn't get blamed for ruining it," Chance said. "And so your mom wouldn't have to pay for it. All right?

"Now, I've got a question for you two. I know your names are Jenny and Jessy, but you look just alike. How does your mother tell you apart?"

"It's easy for Mom. She knows us, even in the dark."

"But how can *I* tell you apart?"

"Easy. Look at our teeth when we smile."

Chance studied the two little grinning mouths. One of the twins had perfectly straight baby teeth. The other twin had a tiny gap between her two incisors.

"Jenny doesn't have a space. I do," said the twin with the gap.

"So you're Jessy. Jessy with *s*'s for 'space.' And Jenny with *n*'s for 'no space.'"

The girls giggled. Chance hadn't been sure his logic would make sense to them, but they must've learned the alphabet and how to write their names, because they clearly thought it was funny.

"You're really smart," said Jenny.

"Doctors have to be smart," said Jessy. "They have to know the names of all the bones."

"So how can I tell you apart if you aren't smiling?" Chance asked.

The girls giggled again. "You have to tell us a joke," said Jenny. "If we laugh, you can see our teeth."

Chance had to smile. Harper's children were bright, charming little imps. But he knew better than to be taken in by them. All children had their dark sides—their messy, noisy, cranky, demanding sides. And his "doctor's office" manner was just that. In real life, he was just a man who wanted peace and quiet.

"Look!" Jessy pointed. "Here comes Mommy!"

Chance breathed a quiet sigh of relief. Harper was hurrying toward them, her high heels digging into the grass. Jessy jumped up and raced to meet her. Partway, the little girl stopped and crumpled forward with a heartbreaking wail.

"What is it?" Heart lurching, Harper rushed toward her daughter. Chance jumped to his feet and came pounding down the path. They reached her at the same time.

"What is it, honey?" Harper looked her daughter over. She could see no blood or any sign of broken bones, but something serious had just happened.

"My foot! Owee!" Still wailing, Jessy held up her leg. Cradling her foot, Chance pulled off her open sandal. An angry red lump was rising on the side of her foot.

Chance bent closer. "It looks like a wasp or a bee sting. She isn't allergic, is she?"

"Not that I know of." Harper remembered horror stories of allergic children going into anaphylactic shock from stings. "How would we know? She's never been stung before."

"You'd know it right away if she was. But she looks okay," Chance said. "Right now, we've got to get that stinger out. Hold her still."

Jessy was still whimpering. Jenny had come to crouch close to her sister, her dark eyes huge in her small, pale face. "Don't be scared, Jenny." Harper reached out to pat her shoulder. "Jessy got stung, that's all. She's going to be fine."

Looking closely, Harper could see the yellow stinger, like a tiny dart in Jessy's tender, pink flesh. She held her daughter close as Chance took a credit card from his wallet and used the edge to scrape the stinger away. It was gone, but Jessy was still in pain. Tears were running down her face, and the red lump was swelling.

"Have you got any Benadryl?" Chance asked. "That'll calm her down and help with the pain and swelling."

"At home. Nothing here." She glanced at her shoulder bag, thinking, too late, what a good idea it would've been to pack some emergency supplies. *Bad mother.* "If only I'd thought to bring—"

"Don't worry about it. We'll find something inside." He scooped Jessy up in his arms and set off toward the kitchen. She clung to him, blubbering into his expensive white tuxedo shirt. Harper followed him with Jenny hanging onto one hand and Jessy's sandal in the other.

They burst into the kitchen. A pleasant-looking, older woman, standing at the sink, looked up with an expression of concern. Harper remembered hearing the inn's owner call her Aunt Molly.

"What have you got for a sting?" Chance asked. "We'll take anything that helps."

"Oh, dear! Poor little thing! There's ice in the fridge. And I believe we have a tube of cortisone ointment in the medicine cabinet. Or we can put baking soda on it like my grandma used to do."

"The cortisone would be fine," Chance said. "And thanks."

"I'll be right back." She hurried out of the room and returned with the ointment. Setting Jessy on the counter, Chance rubbed a small smear on the swollen bite.

"It still hurts," Jessy whimpered.

"It'll feel better in a little while," Chance said. "You're a very brave young lady."

The compliment coaxed a tear-streaked smile from Jessy. The doctor definitely had a way with children. It was surprising he'd waited so long to have a family of his own.

And now he'd be waiting even longer.

Harper had spoken with her assistant, Brad, who'd agreed to stay for the final check-over so she could take her girls home. Thank heaven for capable help.

"We can go now," she said. "I've got some Benadryl at home. How much should I give her?"

"The directions are on the bottle. They should be about right." Chance gathered Jessy into his arms. "I'll help you to your car," he said.

"Thanks—for everything. You've been a lifesaver." Would she ever see the handsome doctor again? Not likely, Harper told herself. If Savannah Loving was an example of the young society women he liked to date, Chance Worthington was way out of her league.

"I hope you won't mind giving me your card," he said. "Who knows? I might want you to plan my next wedding."

Harper gave him a startled look, then realized he was joking. After stashing Jessy's shoe in her purse, she reached into her jacket and gave him one of the cards she kept handy for anyone who asked about her business. "Here's wishing you better luck next time," she said.

He was still holding Jessy. When he nodded toward his pants pocket, she slipped the card inside. "Thanks," he said. "I can't say my luck's been all bad today," he said. "After all, I did meet you."

Heat warmed Harper's face. She steeled herself against the too-pleasant feeling. *Stop it!* she told herself. *This man thinks that because he's rich and handsome, every woman he meets will fall all over him. He's flirting with you because he can, and because it costs him nothing. But it doesn't mean a thing.*

"My car's out here, at the back of the parking lot." She turned away from him, holding on to Jenny with one hand and fumbling for her keys with the other. She usually kept them in the zip pocket on her purse. But the pocket was empty.

"Hang on." Stopping, she let go of Jenny's hand and rummaged through her purse. There was no sign of her keys.

"Is everything okay?" Chance asked.

She shook her head. "I can't believe this. I must've left my keys in my car when I got here this morning. I only hope I didn't lock them inside."

"Don't worry," Chance said as they walked out to the parking lot. "Every teenage boy learns how to break into a locked car. It's like a rite of passage. I've never forgotten how."

"Well, I hope you won't need to—" The words died in Harper's throat as she spotted the space where she'd left her blue Toyota sport wagon.

Her car was gone.

Chapter Four

"You're sure this is where you parked it?"

Chance's question, meant to be helpful, was met with grim silence. By now the parking lot was three-quarters empty. Even if Harper's car had been left in a different space, she would've had no trouble spotting it.

Jessy had started to cry again. Now Jenny joined her in a whining, sniffling duet that grated like sandpaper on Chance's nerves.

Harper looked as if she were about to cry, too. She shook her head in disbelief. "Why would anybody take my car? It's nothing special. It's even got a dented bumper. And it had the booster seats in the back. Now they're gone, too."

"Thieves will take anything with keys in it," Chance said. "Maybe it was kids taking it for a joyride. If that's the case, they'll probably just leave it somewhere. But if it went to a chop shop . . ." Chance let the words trail off as he realized he was only making her feel worse. "I can call the police for you," he said.

"I can call them," Harper said. "At least I've got my phone."

Chance waited, soothing the twins, while Harper gave the dispatcher the description and license number of her sport wagon, along with her contact information. She sighed as she ended the call. "Well, I guess there's nothing to do but call a cab and wait for it to show up."

"How far is your place from here?" Chance asked, though he should have known better. He was already getting in too deep.

"Half an hour if the traffic's not too bad."

"No problem. I can drive you. My car's by the side entrance to the inn." Chance had parked it there for a fast getaway with his bride.

"You're sure? You don't have other plans?"

He raised an eyebrow. "Think about that question."

"Oh." She gave him a half-hearted laugh. "In that case, if it's not too much trouble, we'd be happy to accept."

Actually Chance did have other plans. But he still had plenty of time to get to the hotel tonight and make it to the airport tomorrow morning for the flight to Hawaii. "Follow me," he said.

Jenny had stopped crying. But Jessy was still sniffling against his damp shirt. That sting on her foot would still be hurting. The sooner they could get some antihistamines in her, the sooner she could rest and feel better. They could pick some up at a drugstore, or stop by his townhouse here in Serendipity, where he kept a few samples in his bag.

As they took the brick path to the back of the inn, a new thought struck him. "Your keys were stolen with your car," he said to Harper. "Do you have a way to get into your house?"

She groaned. "Oh, no! I didn't think of that! Our condo is on the third floor. The door is deadbolted. There's no way to get in without a key. I don't suppose your boyhood skills extend to lock-picking."

"Not with a deadbolt. Unless you can find a spare key, you're going to need a locksmith."

Harper was silent. Chance could guess what she was thinking. She'd be stuck outside her door with two tired, hungry, whining children, one of them in pain, and probably both of them needing a bathroom, while she waited for a locksmith to show up.

"We could go to my townhouse," he said. "I've got Benadryl for Jessy and a place for your girls to relax and watch TV while you make an appointment with the locksmith. Once he's on his way, I can take you to meet him."

"Oh . . ." She hesitated, but only for an instant. "I know it's an imposition, but thank you. We'll try not to be a bother."

"No problem." Chance would still have plenty of time to make it to the hotel and catch his early morning flight. He could tell Harper about his planned trip, but that would only add to her stress. She already had enough on her plate.

"My car's right around here." He rounded the corner of the inn and stopped as if he'd run into a wall. The twins began to cheer. Jenny was jumping up and down. Jessy, still in his arms, was laughing and clapping her hands.

His silver Mercedes-Benz sedan had been decorated from bumper to bumper with crepe paper streamers and balloons, and tin cans had been strung behind. Painted across the rear windshield were the words *JUST MARRIED*.

Stifling a string of curses, Chance glowered at his car. He'd made it clear to everyone in the wedding party that he didn't want the car decorated. But somebody—most likely Savannah's brother Joshua, who'd been his best man—had gone with tradition and done it anyway.

Annoyed, Chance grabbed a fistful of colored streamers and yanked them off the car. A cry of protest went up from the twins.

"No-ooo—oo!" wailed Jessy.

"Don't! It's pretty!" Running ahead, Jenny plastered herself against the car as if trying to protect it. Chance glanced at Harper. She wasn't saying a word.

With a sigh of surrender, he fished out his keys and clicked the remote to unlock the car.

"Since you don't have any safety seats, I'll sit in back with the girls and hang onto them," Harper said.

"Good idea." He opened the rear door, helped her and Jenny inside, and passed Jessy into her arms. Then he went around the car and climbed into the driver's seat, but not before pausing to untie the string of tin cans from the rear bumper. He'd be attracting enough attention without rattling down the street. At least his townhouse was only about fifteen minutes from the Bluebird Inn.

Everything was under control, Chance told himself as he pulled away from the curb. He would do a good turn for Harper and her twins, get to know the beautiful wedding planner a little better, and have them home in time to start his trip. After his vacation, he'd give her a call and suggest dinner—*without* the children. From there, with luck, one thing would lead to another.

So far, his plan was looking good. So why did he feel as if an invisible storm were about to blow in, leaving that plan in tatters?

Wedged in the back seat between her daughters, Harper took a moment to breathe and think about her day. She'd planned and implemented every detail of the perfect wedding, a wedding that could have meant everything to her career. But it was as if the day had been cursed by an evil spell. The sick babysitter, the traffic ticket, the runaway bride, the missing twins, the ruined cake, the bee sting, and finally the stolen car.

And the day wasn't over. Here she was, riding through the streets of Serendipity in the decorated getaway car with the jilted bridegroom at the wheel. If she were watching this as a scene in a Hollywood comedy, she'd be laughing her head off.

Sadly, it was all too real.

Chance was hunched low in the seat as if he didn't want to be recognized. But the twins were having the time of their young lives. Strangers, seeing the decorated wedding car, were driving past, honking and waving. Pressed against the side windows, the little girls were smiling and waving back. Even Jessy was having too much fun to whine about her foot.

It was a blessed relief when Chance pulled up to his townhouse in an upscale, landscaped community. After driving the car into the garage, he helped Harper carry the twins inside. The interior of his home was tasteful and immaculate, with modern furnishings and a neutral color scheme. Black-and-white art photos hung on the walls, all in matching ivory mats and black frames. Harper kept a firm grip on her daughters, imagining their sticky little handprints on the walls and furniture. With luck, they wouldn't be here long. Meanwhile, she would need to keep her curious little imps from running amuck.

She took the girls into the spotless downstairs bathroom and washed their hands and faces. When they came out, Chance had turned on the TV and found a popular children's show. He also had a sample bottle of Benadryl with a dropper.

"Open up," he told Jessy. "This will make your foot feel better."

Jessy took the medicine without hesitation. She'd had it before and knew it was sweet. "Now you two can watch TV on the couch. I don't have many snacks here, but do you like string cheese?"

The twins nodded. Soon they were settled on the leather loveseat, covered with a fleece throw, nibbling on cheese as they watched an animal cartoon.

"You're amazing with children," Harper told Chance.

"I get lots of practice."

"You should have a few of your own."

A pained look flickered across his chiseled face. "I suppose that was the idea," he said. "Now what can we do about finding a locksmith?"

* * *

Chance kept an eye on the twins while Harper, who'd declined his help, sat at the kitchen counter with her phone and a pad of paper, making one call after another and shaking her head. Evidently this wasn't a good weekend to find a locksmith.

Finally, with a sigh, she put down her phone. "I can't believe this. They're all backed up. The soonest I can get somebody to come and open the door is first thing tomorrow morning."

Chance weighed the news. On the upside, he'd be spending more time with lovely Harper. On the downside, if Harper and her twins had to spend the night here—and he had little choice except to invite them—there was no way he could make his morning flight to Hawaii.

But never mind that. He could book a later flight and still have his vacation. For now, he could enjoy the company of the most desirable woman he'd ever met—even though she came with two little chaperones.

"I've got a guest room upstairs," he said. "It just has a double bed, but if you don't mind bunking with your girls . . ."

The other arrangement he had in mind would likely have gotten his face slapped.

"Thank you," she said. "And I'm sorry. I never meant to impose on you like this."

"Don't worry about it," he said. "Hey, we can make it a party. I'll order pizza and root beer, and we can stream a movie on TV—something the kids would like."

Her smile told him he'd made the right suggestion. "That would be great. But the girls are so tired and dirty. Would you mind terribly if I gave them a bath while we're waiting for the pizza to arrive?"

"That's fine. The tub's upstairs. I'll round up some old T-shirts they can use for nightgowns—you too if you want. That way we can put their clothes in the wash and have them clean for tomorrow morning."

"Thank you again." She rose from her place at the counter, looking exhausted. She'd had a long day. They both had. "The locksmith will be at my door by 8:30. You can let us off and get on with your plans."

"Whatever they might be." Chance was glad he hadn't told her about missing his flight. "Bathroom's down the upstairs hallway on your right. Toss the clothes out the door, and I'll put them in the wash."

While Harper hustled her twins upstairs, Chance called a good pizza parlor and ordered a large pepperoni with extra cheese and a half gallon of root beer. Then, with the sound of water running in the bathroom overhead, he called the hotel and the airline and canceled his reservations. The Hawaiian beach house was non-refundable. It would be waiting for the next two weeks, whenever he could arrange for another flight.

In the back of his bedroom closet, he'd stashed away a box of souvenir T-shirts from classic rock concerts. Most of them were worn and faded, but he'd kept them for the memories. The twins would enjoy the colorful designs. Why not let them choose their own shirts to sleep in?

After changing out of his tux and into comfortable sweats, he lifted the box out of the closet and carried it down the hall to the bathroom. Through the door, he could hear the faint whir and splash of the jetted tub. The girls' dirty play clothes had been piled just outside.

"Come on in," Harper's voice replied to his light knock.

He opened the door to find the twins in the tub, giggling and splashing in the swirling water. Harper was kneeling next to the tub. She'd taken off her jacket. Underneath she was wearing a lacy tank top that showed off her creamy skin and luscious figure. She was laughing with her girls, her face flushed from the steamy warmth, her hair curling in damp tendrils.

The sight of her roused an ache in the depths of Chance's body. He imagined that dark hair spread on a pillow, that soft, lovely face smiling up at him the way she was smiling now. *Damn it*, he wanted her in the worst way. But there were two adorable little reasons why it wasn't going to happen. Not tonight, at least.

"I dug these out of my closet." He held up the box of concert shirts. "The pizza's ordered. It should be here soon. While we're waiting, I'll toss your laundry in the wash."

"Oh—thanks. Just leave the shirts here. We'll be downstairs in time for pizza—if I can talk the girls out of their bath. They love it."

"Take your time." Whistling to himself, he closed the door, gathered up the small pile of laundry, and took it downstairs to the washer. He hadn't been crazy about the idea of inviting Harper's little family here and missing his flight. But when he weighed curling up on the couch with pizza and a beautiful woman against the prospect of spending what would've been his wedding night alone in a hotel, even with the twins in the mix, he wasn't sorry.

The pizza and root beer arrived. Chance was setting everything up on the coffee table when his three guests came downstairs. Jessy was wearing the Journey shirt, which hung almost to her ankles. Jenny had chosen the Rolling Stones shirt, and Harper—he caught his breath at the sight of her—had shed her pantsuit and was clad in his favorite tee, the Grateful Dead. The hem skimmed her legs at mid-thigh, still showing enough to scorch his fantasies.

"I hope you don't mind my borrowing this," she said. "My clothes got wet when I was bathing the girls."

"Nobody ever wore it better," he said, trying not to imagine what she was—or wasn't—wearing underneath. "Sit down. The party's about to begin."

They sat at opposite ends of the sofa with the girls between them. It was a safe arrangement, Chance told himself.

If he'd been sitting next to Harper, he wouldn't have been able to keep his hands off her.

While Harper poured the root beer, Chance passed out pizza slices on paper plates and brought up a TV menu of children's movies. The twins chose *Despicable Me*, which they said they'd seen, but liked enough to see again.

With the fleece throw across their laps, they settled down to munch pizza and watch the movie. After the train wreck of a day, Chance felt his nerves begin to unwind. He hoped Harper was relaxing, too. In its own way, her day had been as stressful as his.

Chance hadn't seen the movie. But as the tale of a curmudgeonly man forced to take in three little orphans progressed, he couldn't help wondering if the twins had chosen it with an agenda in mind. By the time the man had become a happy, loving father and even found a girlfriend, Chance was sure the little schemers had known exactly what they were doing. By the end of the movie, the girls had both fallen asleep—Jessy with her head in her mother's lap and Jenny snuggled against Chance's shoulder.

He used the remote to switch off the TV. Harper gave him a tired smile from the far end of the sofa. "I think they're done for the day," she said. "Would you mind helping me get them upstairs?"

"Won't they wake up?"

"Not when they're this tired. Trust me, they'll be like little rag dolls." Harper eased to her feet, worked her arms under Jessy, and lifted the little girl to her shoulder. Following her example, Chance picked up Jenny and cradled her in his arms. Harper glanced toward the stairs. "Lead the way," she said.

Chance walked ahead of her with his precious burden. Harper followed him up the stairs and down the hall to the darkened guest room. The double bed was already turned down. Going to opposite sides, they lowered the little sleepyheads to the pillows and gently tucked them in.

Chance fought back a surge of tenderness. Something was getting to him. Maybe it was the sappy movie. Maybe it was the gorgeous woman standing on the opposite side of the bed, making his old Grateful Dead shirt look sexier than a black lace teddy. Whatever it was, he was fending off an un-accustomed attack of the warm fuzzies. He could get used to this, he thought.

Almost.

"There won't be much room for you in that bed," he said in a low voice.

"I'll manage." She gave him a smile, ignoring what his words might've implied. "Don't worry, I've done this before. I'll just sleep around them, like a mother cat."

"You're not going to bed now, are you?"

"I thought I might." She walked him to the open bedroom door. "I know it's early, but it's been a long day, and I've got the locksmith coming to my place in the morning. So thank you in advance for everything. I hope we haven't put you out too much."

"Not at all." Chance forced himself to turn toward the hall, but couldn't take another step away from her. He wasn't ready to say good night.

If he let her go now, he would spend the rest of his life wondering what he could have done differently.

His fingertips brushed her cheek, feeling her softness. "Come back downstairs with me, Harper," he said. "Please. I think we need some grown-up time."

Chapter Five

This wasn't a good idea, Harper told herself. Chance Worthington was temptation wrapped in velvet. Every time he touched her, or even looked at her, she felt the danger to her heart. He was everything she'd ever wanted in a man—handsome, gentle, accomplished, great with her kids, and meltingly sexy. But falling for Chance would be like sky-diving without a parachute. The ride would be thrilling. But the pain at the bottom would be swift and certain.

She'd be a fool not to keep him at a distance.

"Come on," he said. "We've both had a hell of a day. We deserve some downtime—and I've got a good bottle of pinot noir downstairs, just begging to be opened."

Harper surrendered with a sigh. He was right. She needed a break. And she was a big girl. She could handle a glass of wine and a civilized conversation without getting in over her head. Before going back downstairs, she adjusted the bedroom door, leaving it open a few inches in case the girls woke up. Not that it was likely to happen. Jessy and Jenny were sound sleepers, and tonight they were wiped out.

While Chance opened the wine, Harper busied herself cleaning up the pizza mess and wiping off the glass coffee table. She'd enjoyed watching the movie with her twins. Too often, at home, she had to plant them in front of the TV while she worked on her computer, calculating bids or updating her website. She needed to provide for her little family, even if her work cut into her mothering time. But she knew her girls were missing out. Sometimes the guilt was overwhelming.

Chance dimmed the lamps and set a lighted candle on the table. The subtle, masculine scent of sage, blended with lavender, wafted into the room. "Sit down," he said. "That's an order."

Harper brushed an imaginary pizza crumb off the couch and took a seat. Chance set two crystal glasses on the table and poured three fingers of dark red wine into each. After handing one to Harper, he raised his glass in a toast.

"Here's to the wedding that didn't happen. Cheers!"

"Cheers!" Harper clinked glasses with him and took a sip of wine, letting the rich flavor warm her throat. "If your bride hadn't run out, this would have been your wedding night," she said. "Are you all right with that?"

"Sometimes things work out for the best. Let's hope this is one of those times." He set the glass on the table. "Slide back and give me your feet. You've earned this."

Intrigued, Harper moved back against the corner of the couch and allowed him to lift her bare feet into his lap. He gave her a knowing smile. "After watching you run around in those high heels all day—and believe me, I was watching you—I know you've got to be feeling some pain. Just lean back and relax."

Harper sighed as his strong fingers began to massage the arches of her feet. "How does that feel?" he asked.

"It feels positively wicked! Don't you know it's every woman's fantasy to find a man who'll give her foot rubs?"

"So that's the secret. Maybe I'll keep it to myself."

Harper's only reply was a little moan of pleasure. But as the exquisite sensations rippled up her legs, she couldn't help imagining him rubbing Savannah's pretty little feet. She'd gotten to know Chance's fiancée when they'd planned the wedding together. Savannah was as smart and spirited as she was beautiful. But she hadn't seemed all that excited about getting married. Her mother had made most of the decisions about the décor, the guest list, and the reception; it had been almost as if Savannah couldn't be bothered.

Was Chance missing his bride now, thinking about the wedding night that wasn't going to happen, while he consoled himself with another woman? Harper was tempted to ask him. But that would be prying into his private thoughts—and it would spoil the pleasant coziness that had settled around them.

"So tell me about yourself, Harper," he said. "I'd like to know more about the woman sitting on my couch dressed in my Grateful Dead shirt."

Harper shrugged. "You'd only be bored. Nothing about me is very interesting."

"Let me be the judge of that."

"All right, if you're sure. How much do you want to hear?"

"Everything from the first moment you opened your eyes, if you feel like telling me."

"Keep rubbing my feet, and I'll tell you anything you want to know."

His laughter was warm and reassuring. "For starters, you can tell me a little about your history. Are you a Texas girl?"

"Almost. I was born in Omaha. But after my dad left, when I was about the age of my daughters, my mom moved home to Abilene to be with her widowed mother. I grew up there. By the time I was twenty, both my mother and grandmother had passed on."

"And your father?"

"We never heard from him again."

"I'm sorry. That must've been hard."

"It was. I had to grow up fast. But I learned to fend for myself—not a bad skill."

Chance's fingers found a sensitive spot where her arch met the ball of her foot. She stifled a moan of pleasure.

"What made you decide to become a wedding planner?" he asked.

She took a sip of wine, savoring it before she spoke. "It was necessity. I was newly divorced, pregnant with twins, and needed a job. My friend had started a wedding planning business, and she was kind enough to hire me as a behind-the-scenes assistant. I did phone calls, billing, setting appointments, things I could manage mostly from home with the babies. The girls were two when my friend got married, moved out of town, and left me to take over the business. She's still a financial partner, but I do the work and manage a team of five people, four of them part-time. Business has been good, but after today—" She shook her head. "We could be in for a rough patch. I worry—" She broke off. "See, I told you it would be boring."

"You were divorced and pregnant?"

"Nigel, my husband, was a free spirit who'd never wanted children. When he found out I was pregnant, he demanded that I get an abortion. I refused, and he left—ran off with his massage therapist. How's that for a soap opera ending?"

"Unbelievable. He sounds like a real piece of work." Chance's thumbs stroked the base of her toes, soothing away the aches and pains from a day in high heels—which she wore to weddings for the sake of her professional image. She should ask him to stop this now, Harper thought. It felt too good. She could already imagine his hands moving upward, his touch igniting sparks of need.

"Do you get any support from the jerk, or is that question too personal?" he asked.

"It isn't, and I don't. When the divorce became final, he agreed to sign away his parental rights. He doesn't deserve those girls, and they don't need a person like him in their lives. I'd work my hands bloody before I'd ask him for a cent."

"And you haven't found anybody else?"

Harper shook her head. "Between my daughters and my work, I don't have time for much of a social life. And I'm not in a hurry to make another mistake like the first one. If the magic ever happens again, it'll be with a man who cares as much for my girls as he does for me. Meanwhile, I've got plenty on my plate to keep me busy . . . and that reminds me." She sat upright and swung her feet to the floor. "My assistant said he'd text me when he got everything wrapped up at the Bluebird Inn." She rose and turned away to get her purse, which she'd left on the kitchen counter. "I can't believe I forgot to check my phone until now."

"Don't." He caught her hand, tugging her back toward him. "Sit down. You're off the clock now."

"But I'm the one responsible." She resisted slightly, but not enough to pull away.

"Is your assistant a capable person? Do you trust her to handle things when you aren't there?"

"My assistant is a young man named Brad. He's worked with me for two years and, yes, he's very responsible."

"Then let him do his job. You don't have to micromanage everything, Harper. You'll just burn yourself out that way. Sit down and let yourself breathe."

He tugged a little more insistently, pulling her down beside him. This time, Harper let him. She sank back into the cushions with a weary sigh, still worrying about the wedding, the car, the locksmith, and her children.

"That's more like it." Resting his hands on her shoulders, he turned her to face away from him. She felt the tension as his fingers began massaging her knotted muscles. "Relax. You're as tight as a bowstring."

Harper closed her eyes. Little by little she felt her taut nerves begin to unclench. "You've missed your calling," she murmured. "You could do this for a living."

"If I did it for a living, it wouldn't be any fun, would it?" he teased.

She stifled a moan as his fingers worked their way lower,

skimming the back of her bra through the oversized T-shirt. Had he done this for Savannah when she was tired after a long day—given her foot massages and back rubs that ended in lovemaking? If she let Chance make love to her now—and something told her it could happen if she let it—would he be thinking of his lost bride? She'd tried to convince herself that the question was none of her business. Now, she realized, she needed to know.

"Do you still love Savannah?" she asked.

His hands paused. He was quiet for a moment before he answered. "I do. But not in the way you might think. I cared enough to want the best for her. And the best, as it turned out, wasn't me. When she ran back up that aisle, kicking off her shoes and tearing off her veil, it was like watching a little wild bird fly out of a cage and take to the sky. I was shocked. But part of me wanted to cheer her on. Does that answer your question?"

"I think so—not that I had any right to ask."

He turned her to face him again. It was as if his knowing gaze could see through all her barriers, all the fears, betrayals, and loneliness she never wanted to feel again. "You're here," he said. "That gives you the right."

His fingers cupped her chin. As his lips brushed hers, Harper's pulse broke into a gallop. Heat blazed in the depths of her body, burning away all common sense. She wanted him. She needed him with a yearning hunger she was powerless to resist.

She went molten against him. Her arms wrapped his neck, pulling him closer to deepen the kiss. Her tongue teased his—hesitantly at first, then in a sensual invitation that could mean only one thing.

With a growl of arousal, he caught her close. As the kiss heated and caught fire, his hands found their way beneath the loose-fitting shirt. Ripples of pleasure flooded her body. She whimpered, wanting more, wanting his touch—wanting to feel him everywhere.

Her pulse leaped as he unhooked the back of her bra and cradled her breast in his palm. A sweet ache radiated down through her body. She felt the throbbing need, the wetness that soaked her panties. "Yes . . ." she whispered, dizzy with wanting him. Later she might be sorry. But right now, she didn't care. Nothing mattered but what this man was doing to her—and what she wanted him to do.

"Upstairs." His voice rasped the word. He lifted her to her feet and guided her up the dimly lit staircase to the landing and down the hallway. By the time they reached the bed, they were tearing off each other's clothes. Chance yanked the covers down and paused to add protection. Then he was beside her in the bed, holding her, taking her body. She gave herself to the feel of him, the smell and taste of him as he carried her on a rocket ride to the stars.

Satisfied to the tips of her toes, Harper curled next to Chance, feeling his warmth and listening to the soft rumble of his breathing. Heaven.

It would be all too easy to close her eyes and drift off beside him until morning. But her girls were sleeping in the guest room down the hall. She couldn't risk having them wake in the night, afraid and unable to find their mother.

Easing away from him, she slid to the edge of the bed and felt for the floor with her feet. Chance slumbered on, his eyes closed, his dark hair tumbling over his forehead. Tenderness surging, Harper checked the urge to reach out and stroke a fingertip down one stubbled cheek. His lovemaking had thrilled her beyond her wildest dreams. But it was over now, she told herself. It was time to wake up and face reality.

The Grateful Dead shirt lay on the rug where she'd dropped it. She slipped it over her head, gathered up her bra and panties, and, with a last, lingering look at Chance, tip-toed out of the room and down the hall.

The twins were sound asleep, their little bodies sprawled

across the bed. Harper shifted them far enough to make a space along one side of the mattress. There was just enough room for her to lie on her side, with a protective arm over her little ones. She slid into place and tugged the edge of the blanket over her hips. She wouldn't be comfortable enough to sleep, but that didn't matter. She had too much on her mind to rest.

Lying in the dark with her eyes open, she forced her thoughts back to the real world. Her interlude with Chance had been wonderful—and needed. But it was time to walk away. She had a demanding job and two daughters to look after. And Chance was recovering from a shattered relationship. Whatever he might have told her, he had loved Savannah enough to propose to her. And if Savannah changed her mind and came back to him, Harper had little doubt that he would still want her as his wife.

He would want her back, even though he'd just cheated on her with another woman—a silly, romantic fool who'd meant nothing to him.

Heaven help her, what had she done?

Chance opened his eyes. It was morning, and he was alone in the bed. No surprise there. Harper would have long since gone back to her children. Too bad. He would have enjoyed picking up where they'd left off last night.

For a few moments, he lay still, remembering her luscious body in his arms and her sweet little cries as he brought her to climax again and again. Whatever their differences, he and Harper certainly had no problem in bed. For him, at least, the next time couldn't happen soon enough. The thought of more time with her, getting acquainted both in and out of bed, had him looking forward to the days and weeks ahead.

Maybe, if he could talk her into it, he could even buy extra plane tickets and take her and the twins to Hawaii. It was a crazy idea, but worth some thought.

Rolling over, he glanced at the bedside clock. It was twenty minutes to eight. He sat up, mouthing a curse. Harper needed to be at her condo by eight-thirty to meet the locksmith. Why hadn't she awakened him sooner?

He swung out of bed, splashed down in the shower, and, without bothering to shave, yanked on his jeans and a shirt, grabbed his sneakers, and hurried downstairs.

Harper and her twins were in the kitchen. Jenny and Jessy, wearing clean play clothes, were at the table eating cereal. Harper was dressed in her peach-colored pantsuit, slightly rumpled but complete down to her high-heeled shoes. He started to give her a smile. Then he saw the cold expression on her face. Chance's spirits sank. He should have known it would happen. She was already having regrets.

The girls were glancing from him to their mother, as if sensing the tension between them.

"Good morning, ladies," Chance said, breaking the silence. "Are you ready to go home?"

"Actually, there's been a change of plans," Harper said. "The police called me early this morning. They found my car. It was abandoned at a strip mall a few miles from here. They said the keys were inside, so I've already canceled the locksmith."

"Is the car all right?" Chance sat down to put on his shoes.

"As far as I know. The officer left the keys under the floor mat, so there shouldn't be a problem. All you'll need to do is drive us to the car. Then you'll be rid of us for good."

For good.

Harper's meaning was clear. As far as she was concerned, last night had never happened. Once he let her off at her car and made sure the engine would start, she planned to thank him, drive away with her girls, and never look back.

Chance masked dejection as his plans went up in smoke. Harper had been on fire last night. What had happened to change her mind? Did it have something to do with Savannah?

Whatever it was, he couldn't let her leave without knowing

where they stood. If there was a way to keep this wonderful woman from walking out of his life, he had to find it fast.

"As long as the car's not going anywhere, how about letting me take you to breakfast?" he said. "There's a good waffle house in the neighborhood. They have great fresh strawberry waffles with whipped cream." Chance glanced at the twins, hoping for some support.

"Thanks, but I'm anxious to get my car back," Harper said. "Besides, the girls are already having cereal."

"This cereal is *yucky!*" Jessy spoke up. "It's *brown*, and it doesn't have any taste."

"We have *colored* cereal at home," Jenny said, frowning at Chance. "It tastes a lot better. You should get some for the next time we come."

Chance saw Harper flinch. He could guess what she was thinking. If she had her way, they wouldn't be coming back here at all.

"We want waffles!" Jenny said. "Please, Mommy!"

"Please!" Jessy echoed.

Chance met Harper's gaze across the kitchen. "It's up to you," he said.

Harper rolled her eyes. "All right. But you two have to clear the table now and clean your room when we get home. Deal?"

"Deal!" The twins high-fived each other and jumped up to carry their unfinished cereal bowls to the sink.

"If you've got some spare sheets, I'll change the guest bed before we go." Harper was all cool politeness. *Damn it*, when would he get a chance to talk to her alone?

"Don't bother, thanks. I've got people to do that. But I'd like to check Jessy's foot before we go. We need to make sure that sting is healing all right. Sit down, Jessy."

"It feels lots better." Jessy sat on a chair and held up her foot. Only then did Chance realize that he could already tell the twins apart, even without seeing their teeth.

He unbuckled Jessy's sandal. The swelling around the

sting had gone down, leaving a flat, red dot. "Does it hurt?" he asked her.

"It just itches a little."

"That means it's getting better. You'll be fine."

"Do we have to call you Dr. Worthington? Don't you have a name?"

"My name is Chance. If your mother doesn't mind, you can call me Dr. Chance. Does that sound all right?" He glanced at Harper. She gave a slight nod. Ice-cold. What had he done to the woman?

"Let's go get waffles," Jenny said. "Come on, everybody."

They trooped out to Chance's car. Harper sat between the twins as Chance drove the five blocks to the restaurant, a new place in Serendipity with a covered patio and an open kiddie play area with swings and a slide. The Sunday morning traffic was light, the sun already too bright for Chance's mood.

The hour was early, and the patio tables were empty. After the server seated them, brought coffee for the grown-ups, and took their order, the girls ran to play on the swings. That gave Chance a few precious minutes alone with Harper.

"Should we talk about this?" he asked her.

"Why talk about it?" She stirred creamer into her coffee. "I should never have gone to bed with a man who'd just been dumped by his bride—a beautiful, intelligent woman who could still change her mind and come back. Last night was a mistake—one I don't plan to make again."

"It wasn't a mistake for me, Harper." He reached across the table and covered her hand with his. "I never expected you to walk into my life on my wedding day, but it happened, and I have no regrets. I know it's too soon to talk about love, but if there's any chance it's out there for us, I don't want to lose it—or you."

Her hand was rigid under his palm. "Then answer this question for me. What if Savannah changes her mind and comes back to you? Will you tell her the truth—that you had a meaningless one-night stand with the wedding planner?"

"Blast it, Harper, it wasn't—"

"Come push me, Dr. Chance!" Jenny called. She was sitting on the swing, trying to pump, but not having much success.

"Me too!" Jessy climbed onto the empty swing beside her.

Chance rose with a sigh. He'd hoped to get somewhere with Harper, but so far the conversation was headed down the wrong path. Maybe they both needed a break.

Stepping behind Jenny, he put his hands on her shoulders. "Hang on tight," he said. "Away we go."

Sipping her coffee, Harper watched Chance push her daughters in the swings, using a juggler's skill to keep both little girls flying at a safe distance above the ground. Jenny and Jessy were squealing with delight, begging him not to stop.

They had wanted *him* to push them, not their mother. It was as if, in their innocent way, they'd already given him their affection and complete trust.

Why couldn't it be that simple for her?

Chance was everything she'd ever wanted. But how could she trust a man who'd walked away from his failed wedding with scarcely a sigh of regret—a man who'd made tender, passionate love to her on what would have been his wedding night?

If life had taught her one thing, it was that men left. They left because they were bored, because they were sick of responsibility, because they'd found somebody else, or maybe just because they could. And Chance Worthington was no different from the others.

Chance had already won her daughters' hearts. Harper could see that they adored him. But sooner or later—perhaps because of Savannah—Chance was bound to walk away. When that happened, her precious girls would be crushed.

She needed to protect them. She needed to stop what was happening before it was too late.

Chapter Six

From where he stood, Chance could see the waiter coming outside with their breakfasts on a cart. He slowed the swings, anticipating what could happen next.

"I see our waffles!" Jenny leaped out of the swing, saved herself from a stumble, and raced back toward the patio.

"Come on, Dr. Chance." Jessy climbed out of her swing, took Chance's hand in complete trust, and walked back to the patio with him.

Now that he was getting to know the two little girls, Chance was amazed at how different from each other they could be. He'd discovered something else as well. In his years as a pediatrician he had dealt with hundreds of children, giving them checkups, shots, and stitches, treating fevers and injuries, reviewing tests—all the things that were part of his job. But in all that time, until Harper's twins came along, he had never actually *played* with a child. It was surprising how much he enjoyed it.

"Hurry, Dr. Chance!" Jessy tugged at his hand. "Our waffles will get cold!"

Harper, still looking strained, was waiting for them at the table. She took a packet of wipes out of her purse and cleaned her daughters' hands before they were allowed to eat. The plates of waffles, piled high with fresh strawberries and whipped cream, looked delicious, but she'd ordered coffee and wheat toast for herself. Not a good sign, Chance thought. She seemed determined not to enjoy herself.

Picking up a knife and fork, she began cutting Jenny's waffle into bite-sized pieces. When Jessy looked up at Chance, he realized she wanted him to do the same for her. Following Harper's example, he sliced up Jessy's waffle before starting on his own.

"Thank you." She gave him an angelic smile.

"You're welcome." Chance could tell that Harper had raised her girls to be polite. She was a good mother, and very protective.

What kind of father would he be? Chance found himself wondering. Would he have the patience to put up with children full-time, especially if they weren't his own offspring?

But why was he asking himself that question now?

The twins were hungry. They wolfed down their waffles and hot cocoa and raced off to play again while the grownups finished breakfast. Chance had eaten slowly, hoping the girls would do exactly that, giving him more time with their mother.

"You have great kids," he said, watching them climb the slide and zip to the bottom, squealing with laughter all the way. "You've raised them well."

"Thanks, but I can't claim much credit," she said. "They've taught me more than I've taught them."

"I know what you mean. Look how much fun they're having. No hesitation, just going for it."

An unexpected image flashed through Chance's mind: *two little girls racing along the Hawaiian sand, laughing as the foamy surf tickled their feet . . . their mother lying on a towel, the sun warming her beautiful skin . . . tropic nights with the children dreaming in their beds . . .*

He willed the picture away. The idea was a crazy one. And given the way their mother felt about him, the odds against its happening weren't worth the bet.

"That's what worries me," Harper said. "My girls only know what they feel. They're already becoming attached to you. And they haven't been schooled by hard knocks like I have. My heart's been broken before. I know what to expect, and I can handle it. But Jessy and Jenny don't understand about loss and rejection, Chance. That's why I have to end this now, before—"

"Before somebody gets hurt? Is that what you're afraid of?" Her silence answered his question.

"Is that the plan, Harper? Never let anybody into your lives, because they might leave? Protect your daughters from heartbreak and disappointment so they won't ever learn how to heal and move on? All this because you were hurt by a selfish jerk who didn't know a good thing when he had it?"

When her jaw tightened, Chance knew he'd said too much. But he'd meant every word of it.

"Please don't tell me how to raise my daughters," she said. "In your practice, you deal with children day in and day out. But you've never been a parent. You don't have a clue how it feels to lie awake at night, wondering how to give them what they need and how to keep them safe. Until you do, you have no right to judge me!" She crumpled her napkin, dropped it beside her plate, and rose from her chair. "I think it's time to go and get my car. I can call a cab if you like."

"Don't be silly." He rose with her, leaving cash on the table as she crossed the patio to fetch her twins. Minutes later they were in his car, heading for the address the police had given her.

Driving alone in the front seat, while Harper kept her children secure in the back, Chance forced himself to ask a painful question.

Why this woman?

After Savannah's escape from their wedding, he'd been mobbed by attractive, eligible, and willing females. He could've chosen any one of them—or, more wisely, played the field for a while, enjoying the variety.

Why was he fixed, like a heat-seeking missile, on this driven, contrary, untrusting—though lovely—woman? A woman who came with two little pixies who, charming as they were, demanded constant attention?

Was it the challenge? Was this ready-made family something he needed in his life? No answer he could come up with made sense.

Any man who valued his sanity and self-respect would drop Harper off at her car, drive home, and phone another woman, preferably one with no complications. But for some reason, that option didn't hold much appeal.

What he needed was a break, and his unused Hawaiian getaway might be just the ticket. He would tell Harper his plans, reschedule his flight, and be gone first thing tomorrow, or even sooner. When he got back, he could call her—or maybe not, if he'd come to his senses by then.

The strip mall where Harper's car had been found was no more than a few minutes away. As they pulled into the parking lot, she spotted her blue Toyota sport wagon, parked at the curb outside a closed electronics store.

"There it is!" she told Chance. "It looks all right. Drive me over there, and I'll check."

Chance drove up and parked several spaces away. "You and the girls stay here," he said. "I'll check the car for you."

Before she could argue, he climbed out of his car and walked over to her Toyota. Instead of opening the door, he walked around the vehicle, crouching to peer underneath the chassis and ducking his head to look into the wheel wells. His actions puzzled Harper at first. Then she remembered a news story she'd seen on the Internet—an item about explosive devices being used to booby-trap stolen and abandoned vehicles. It had happened in Texas—twice.

The hair on the back of her neck prickled. Her arms tightened around her twins as she realized what was happening. Chance was checking her car to make sure it was safe.

She held her breath as he opened the driver's side door— something the police would have already done, she reminded herself. All the same, she could hear her heart beating as he freed the hood latch and walked around to raise the hood. For a long moment he peered into the maze of blocks, wires, and hoses. He was risking possible danger to protect her and her children, Harper realized. True, the chance of a bomb's being in her car was remote. But he cared enough about their safety to put himself at risk. That meant something to her.

Now that she thought of it, Chance had found her missing children, destroyed the cake they'd damaged, doctored Jessy's foot, taken her and her children in overnight, treated them to pizza and a movie and, with her full consent, given her a memory that would make a French courtesan blush.

In turn, she'd been a defensive, judgmental, standoffish pain in the rear.

It was probably too late to salvage their relationship. But she owed him an apology, at least. And maybe, for the future, it was time to think about some of the things he'd told her. She'd spent a long time building walls to protect herself and her daughters. If she wanted to move beyond her past and find happiness, she would need to break those walls down.

The problem was, she had no idea how to start.

With the hood still up, Chance slid into the driver's seat and put the key in the ignition. Harper forgot to breathe as he turned it. The engine sputtered and died. On the second try, it coughed, caught, and started.

With the engine running, he climbed out and opened the back door of his car so Harper could climb out with her children. "Your car seems okay," he said, "but it's almost out of gas. There's a station around the corner and down the block. Why don't you follow me there? That way, you won't miss it, and if you run out, I'll be there to help."

She lifted the girls into their booster seats and made sure they fastened their own buckles. "You've done far too much for me, Chance. I want you to know I'm grateful."

His mouth twitched slightly, the only sign that he'd heard her. "Let's get you some gas," he said. "Follow me."

By the time Harper had buckled herself into her seat, he had started his car and pulled ahead of her. She drove close behind him. As they turned into the station, the engine started to sputter. The car stopped dead a few yards short of the first pump. Chance and a helpful stranger pushed it the rest of the way.

Harper used her credit card to start the pump. While the tank was filling, she turned to Chance, who was waiting by his own car. Summoning her courage, she took a deep breath and spoke.

"I want to apologize, Chance. For the past twenty-four hours, you've dropped everything to be there for us. We've inconvenienced you in so many ways, and you haven't complained once."

She caught the hint of a twinkle in his eye. "Well, it's not as if I had other plans," he said. "Besides, it's been a very entertaining twenty-four hours. Especially . . ." He let the words trail off, his meaning clear.

Harper's cheeks warmed. "A woman who's been on her own as long as I have learns to keep her guard up. You didn't deserve the awful things I said to you this morning."

"Then why did you say them?"

She hesitated, her heart pounding. "I was scared, I guess. Scared of what I felt last night. Scared of being let down again—and knowing it could still happen. If you want to walk away and never see me again, I'll understand. But if you're willing to forgive me, I'd like to make it up to you. I'm a pretty fair cook. Would you like to come to dinner at our place tomorrow night?"

He hesitated, frowning. Her heart sank.

"No?" she asked.

"I'd be happy to come. I mean, I want to. But it would have to be tonight. Tomorrow, if I can get a flight, I may be on my way to Hawaii."

"Hawaii?" *With Savannah?* She almost asked before biting back the question.

"Before the wedding, I closed my office for two weeks and reserved a beach house in Maui for the honeymoon. Since the reservation is nonrefundable, I figured I might as well use it myself, just for a break." He laughed uneasily. "Sort of a bachelor honeymoon."

"Why not? A bachelor honeymoon sounds like a great idea—or maybe a great fifties movie title," Harper joked. "If you still want to come, I can make dinner tonight. It might not be as fancy as I'd like, but you'd be welcome."

"Sure. Let me know where and what time. I'll bring some wine."

"Is eight too late? I know you have to pack."

"I'm already packed. My bags are in the trunk."

"Oh—of course." She glanced at the gaudily decorated car, which was still attracting honks and waves from people who drove past the service station. "Here, I'll give you my address." She pulled a business card and a pen out of her purse and scribbled on the back. "The phone number's already on the card. Give me a call if you can't make it."

He gave her a serious look. "Of course I can make it, Harper. Trust me. I'll be there at eight."

Chance waited long enough to make sure Harper's car would start. The twins waved at him as she drove away. Chance waved back. As the car vanished from sight, he felt strangely alone. Harper and her children had been with him since the wedding disaster. He'd been so busy taking care of them that he'd scarcely had time to think about Savannah and how this change of plans would affect their lives.

Sooner or later they would have to deal with the arrangements they'd made: the prenuptial agreement and addendum to his will, as well as his life insurance policy, which would need to be legally voided; the spacious condo they'd bought together, which would have to be sold unless Savannah wanted to buy out his share; the wedding gifts that would need to be returned, and so much more. Knowing Savannah, there wouldn't be a problem with any of it. She was a genuinely nice person. But just thinking about the process made his head ache. Hawaii was just what he needed right now.

He'd told himself that getting married was the right thing to do at this stage of his life, and that Savannah would be the perfect wife for him. But as it turned out, it wasn't what Savannah had wanted. Looking back on the whole idea, maybe it wasn't what he'd wanted either.

From the service station, he drove to a car wash and had his Mercedes washed and waxed. With the gaudy wedding paint gone, it was time to go home, put the wedding behind him, rearrange his life.

From the nook that served as his home office, he called the airline. "We can get you on a red-eye flight at ten tonight if that will work," the reservation agent told him. "But the Monday flights are sold out. Unless there's a cancellation, we can't get you on another flight until Tuesday."

Chance weighed his options. The ten o'clock flight sounded tempting, but it would mean canceling dinner with Harper. The last thing he'd said to her today was that he'd be there. Let her down, and she'd never trust him again. Neither would her little girls, who'd heard his promise. Somehow that mattered almost as much.

"We'll have to make it Tuesday," he said.

"We can get you on at two in the afternoon. That flight still has a few seats left."

"That'll have to do." Chance booked the flight and went

online to arrange for a rental car. That done, he emailed his attorney and financial manager about the canceled marriage. At least, with the flight delayed until Tuesday, he'd have time to take care of the legal loose ends.

He could also call Harper and put off their dinner until Monday night. He was reaching for the phone when he decided against it. She was expecting him tonight. Why upset her plans—especially when he was already eager to see her again?

In spite of everything that had happened, he still found himself wondering about Savannah. What had been in her pretty head when she'd roared off on that motorcycle? She must've had some kind of plan? Was she hiding out with a friend? Had she gone to a new love somewhere? Chance was curious. But as long as she was happy, it didn't matter.

What would he do if she came back and still wanted to get married? But Savannah wasn't like that. She would have been absolutely sure she was doing the right thing, and there would be no changing her mind.

Sooner or later, maybe when he got back from Hawaii, they could talk and come to some kind of understanding. But he would leave that up to her. He was already moving on, and it felt good.

Harper had spent the afternoon cleaning her condo and making lasagna. At seven, with dinner in the oven, she'd fed her twins the mac and cheese they loved, bathed them, read them a story, and set them in front of the TV while she changed, fixed her hair and makeup, and put the finishing touches on the meal. The girls had promised to go to bed right after they said good night to Dr. Chance.

She was just lighting the candles on the table when the phone rang. Her heart dropped. She should have known Chance would cancel at the last minute, she told herself. Maybe Savannah had put in a surprise appearance.

Braced for disappointment, she blew out the candles and picked up the phone.

"Hi." It was Chance's voice. "I'm right out front—I think. I just wanted to make sure I was in the right place before I rang the wrong doorbell."

Her heart took wing again. "Let me check out the front window. I should be able to look down and see you." She lowered the phone and flitted to the window. In a moment she was back. "I see your car. And I see you had it washed. You can park in the visitor row and come on up. The elevator's just inside the front door."

As she waited, Harper struggled to control her fluttering pulse. It was only dinner, she told herself. And even though she'd slept with the man, there was no reason to expect anything but a polite—and permanent—good-bye at the end of it. Chance was out of her league—the playboy doctor who'd been mobbed by beautiful women the minute his bride roared out of sight. He could do better than a harried single mom whose life revolved around her children and her work.

Still, when the doorbell rang, her pounding heart told her the truth. She had fallen hard for Chance Worthington. But she'd be a fool to dream of a happy ending. A children's fairy tale would be more likely to come true.

Chance rang the doorbell and waited. His pulse skipped at the sound of Harper's footsteps coming closer from the other side of the door. They'd only been apart for a few hours, but the anticipation of seeing her again created a pleasant buzz. He felt like a seventeen-year-old picking up his first prom date.

She opened the door, looking flushed and slightly breathless. Her sleeveless black dress, which clung at the waist and flared at the hem, was cut low enough at the bodice to show a hint of cleavage. She'd added silver earrings and strappy red sandals to the ensemble.

"You clean up nicely," he joked, taking her in. She looked sexy enough to devour on the spot.

"Thanks," she murmured, accepting the bouquet of spring blossoms he'd brought. "You haven't exactly seen me at my best."

Yes, I have, he thought, remembering her in his bed with her lush breasts bare beneath him and her hair spread in dark waves on his pillow.

He took a moment to glance around the apartment. The small place was tasteful and cozy, with green plants, books on the shelves, an upright piano in one corner, and a colorful hand-knit throw flung over the back of the sofa. It was just what he might have expected of Harper.

"These flowers are lovely," she said. "I'll put them in a vase while you say good night to the girls. They begged me to let them stay up until you came."

Chance had brought a bottle of good merlot from his own collection. He set it on the counter and walked into the living room, where the twins were watching a children's show on TV. They were freshly bathed and dressed for bed—Jenny in a nightgown and Jessy in pajamas. When they saw him, their faces lit. They jumped off the sofa and ran to him, bouncing around his legs.

"Turn off the TV, girls. It's bedtime," Harper called from the kitchen. Chance spotted the remote on the coffee table. He picked it up and clicked the switch.

Jenny tugged at his hand. "Will you tuck us in, Dr. Chance?"

Chance caught Harper's eye. "Is it all right?"

"It's fine. They've had their bedtime story. So don't let them con you into another one. Dinner will be on the table in a few minutes."

"You heard your mom. Show me to your room. Let's go."

Skipping and giggling, they seized his hands on either side and led him down the hall. Their bedroom, lit by a mermaid night-light, was exactly what Chance would have imagined for little girls—lots of pink, matching twin beds with ruffled coverlets, a shelf of books, and a dollhouse in one corner.

Chance turned down the covers on both beds, guessing that was expected. But he'd never tucked a child into bed. He hadn't even been tucked in himself. "Now what?" he asked. "Do you just climb into bed?"

"Now we say our prayers," Jessy prompted. "You kneel down with us right here and listen."

Chance had been raised in a home without religion. He'd never been a praying man. But to please the girls, he knelt down next to one of the beds with a twin on each side and folded his arms, as they did.

Jenny went first, with a murmured prayer Chance could barely hear except for the "amen" at the end, followed by a silent pause. Jessy nudged him. "You're supposed to say 'amen,'" she whispered.

"Oh." Chance complied. When Jessy's turn to pray came, he was ready. With prayers done, the twins climbed into their beds and let Chance pull the covers up to their chins. It was a sweet moment, making him wonder what he'd missed growing up with two workaholics for parents.

"Good night, Dr. Chance." Jessy yawned as she spoke.

"Good night, Dr. Chance," Jenny added.

"Sleep tight." Chance walked out of the room and down the hall, leaving the door slightly open.

Lasagna, salad, and garlic bread waited on the elegantly set kitchen table. Harper stood at the counter, struggling to open the wine. Chance had resolved to play it cool tonight and let her take the lead. But she looked so deliciously helpless that he couldn't resist. Stepping behind her, he circled her with his arms and brushed a kiss on the back of her neck. "Need any help?" he asked.

She stiffened slightly, and he sensed that he'd overstepped. Releasing her, he took the bottle and used the corkscrew to pop it open. "Have a seat. I'll pour." He pulled out her chair before filling the wineglasses. "This looks wonderful. You've outdone yourself."

"Not really. I just used what I had on hand." She dished a square of lasagna onto his plate. "So, are you set to fly off on your bachelor honeymoon tomorrow?"

"Not quite." Chance helped himself to salad and garlic bread. "As it turns out, I couldn't get a flight until Tuesday. I'd have called you and rescheduled our dinner, but by then it would've been a bother for you to change your plans. Besides"—he gave her what he hoped was a winning smile— "I couldn't wait to see you again."

She cast him a skeptical look. Chance had never had any trouble charming women. So why was he finding Harper such a challenge? Why did he find himself wanting to get up, sweep her into his arms, hold her against him, and tell her that, whatever happened, he would never do anything to hurt her or her girls?

Heaven help him, was he falling in love with her?

Chapter Seven

Chance watched Harper from across the table as she sipped her wine. Candlelight sculpted her expressive face. Reflected flames danced in the velvety depths of her eyes.

What was happening to him?

It was as if the crazy, scattered pieces of his life had come together in a way that had never made sense until now.

He loved her. Simple as that.

But it wasn't really simple at all. A day ago, when they'd first set eyes on each other, he'd been about to marry someone else. From there, things had happened too fast to be believed. Harper wasn't ready to trust him, and he couldn't blame her. He'd only just begun to trust himself.

They needed more time—time alone and time with the children—to put their relationship on a solid footing.

"Are you free tomorrow?" he asked. "We could make a day of it, maybe take the girls to the zoo, where they'd have a good time. Then, if you can get a sitter, you and I could end the day at a nice restaurant somewhere."

Her expression remained the same, except for her eyes. Chance saw the protective barrier slip into place. "I thought this was supposed to be a farewell dinner," she said.

"Is that what you want it to be, Harper?"

An eternity seemed to pass before she answered. "Not

really. But if this is going to end, I'd rather end it now, before it can leave any more wreckage behind."

"And if we don't want it to end?"

"What are the odds of that?"

"We'll never know unless we give it a try, will we?"

She put down her glass. "Chance, I don't know about this. It's all so sudden—"

He cut her off before she could turn him down flat. "Let's give ourselves tomorrow, at least. Then we'll both have time to think it over while I'm gone."

She shook her head. "Tomorrow is out. I've got a new client coming into the office at ten—a big society wedding that could get me some good press. If she likes my ideas, I'll be busy with her all day, and for weeks after that. I can't afford to put her off."

Chance sighed, deflated but not ready to give up. "You'll need to eat. I hope we can manage dinner, at least."

Before Harper could answer, her cell phone, which she'd left on the kitchen counter, began to jangle. She rose with an apologetic look. "Sorry, this could be important," she said.

Let it ring! Chance wanted to tell her. But he bit back the urge to speak up.

She glanced at the caller ID before answering. Stress tightened her features. "This is Harper McLain," she said in a crisp tone. "What?" There was a pause. Her face fell. "Well, if you're sure, I understand. Please let me know if you change your mind."

Ending the call, she sank onto the chair like a marionette with broken strings. The phone lay beside her plate. "That was my client," she said. "I guess I'll be free tomorrow after all."

"I'm sorry," he said. "Not that you'll be free, but that you've lost an important customer. I'm guessing that weddings are a cutthroat business. Lots of competition."

"You can't imagine." She shook her head. "I should've

known, after your wedding fell apart, that word would get around."

"But it wasn't your fault. Not at all."

"That doesn't make any difference. There's a lot of superstition involved in weddings. What happened at the Bluebird Inn is like a curse that nobody wants to repeat. I'm sure Felicity Patterson is getting her share of cancellations, too. Too bad. It's a lovely place."

The phone rang again. Harper hesitated, then picked it up. Chance could tell from the conversation and her downcast expression that it was one more client calling to cancel. Ending the call, she slumped in her chair. She looked ready to cry. "This is awful," she said. "I've got people working for me who need to earn a living. What am I going to do?"

Chance reached across the table and laid his hand on hers. "Do you mind if I make a couple of suggestions?"

"You're the doctor."

"First, you're worn out. You're in no condition to handle anything tonight. Let's turn the phone off. If you get any more calls, they can go to voice mail. You can answer them in the morning after you've rested." Without waiting for her to do it, he took her phone and switched it off.

She gave the phone a nervous glance. "And second?"

"You mentioned you had a very capable assistant."

"Brad's a gem. He's wonderfully creative, and he handles the brides and their mothers better than I do. He's even good with estimates and billing. I don't know how I'd manage without him."

"Then my suggestion is that you call him first thing tomorrow, tell him what's happening with the clients, and that you need him to take over while you get some rest. If he's as good as you say he is, he'll jump at the chance to prove himself."

"Any more suggestions, Dr. Worthington?" Chance sensed

an edge in her voice. She'd been through the weekend from hell. Maybe he'd pushed her too far.

"Just one more," he said. "I suggest that we finish this great meal you cooked, and then, while I clear it away, you stretch out on the couch and wait for me to come and give you a nice back rub."

She hesitated, then smiled. "Now that's something I could really use."

"Eat up, then. This lasagna is too good to waste."

They made it through the rest of the meal on small talk. Harper told him more about her work and her children. She listened while Chance told her about growing up in a prominent, wealthy family, and how his father had almost disowned him when he'd made up his mind to become a doctor instead of managing the family real estate empire.

Hearing about his life, Harper couldn't help thinking how different her own had been. She'd never known a time without worry and struggle. Would there be enough money for food and rent? How could she save her failing marriage? How could she, as a single mother, provide for her twins? How could she manage a business and still find time to be a mother?

Chance appeared to have sailed through life, choosing the right friends and schools, the right profession, even the right woman to marry. He and Savannah had shared the same roots, the same values, the same social status. What could a man like Dr. Chance Worthington see in a woman with two young children, a woman constantly fighting to keep her head above water?

When they'd finished eating, he escorted her to the couch, invited her to lie down, slipped off her sandals, and covered her with the knitted throw.

Eyes closed, Harper lay listening to the sounds of Chance

clearing the table and loading the dishwasher. She couldn't remember the last time anyone—let alone a man—had helped her in the kitchen. Chance clearly knew the way to a woman's heart. He'd already found his way to hers. The only question was, when was he going to break it?

Was she strong enough to hold on to this giddy ride until it was over, or would she be better off ending it now?

Still mulling the question, she began to drift.

"Wake up, sleepyhead."

Harper stirred and blinked. She was looking up into Chance's laughing eyes.

"Hello," she murmured, still muzzy. "How long was I asleep?"

He feathered a kiss on her mouth. "Half an hour, at least. It's almost ten. You were sleeping so soundly, I didn't have the heart to wake you."

"But for so much time . . . what have you been doing?"

"Sitting in the rocker, watching you. You're beautiful when you sleep."

He kissed her again. His lips, lingering on hers, ignited whorls of heat inside her. Sleep had left her feeling relaxed and highly sensual. His slightest touch on her skin was enough to set off shimmers of shameless desire.

Her fingertip stroked a path down the side of his face and along his jaw. "How about that back rub you promised me?"

He slid an arm under her back. "I don't think we've got time for a back rub," he said. "But we might have time for something better."

He stood, lifting her off the couch. She clung to him as he carried her down the hall toward her bedroom. "The girls—" she whispered.

"I checked on them just before I woke you. They're fast asleep. They'll be fine."

By the time he stood her next to the bed, she was aching with need. He reached for the zipper at the back of her dress. Pulling his hand away, she lay back on the coverlet and raised her skirt. "*Now!*" she whispered.

Understanding what she wanted, he chuckled, pushed down his jeans and briefs, and added protection before he stripped off her lace panties. Their lovemaking was swift, urgent, and explosive, with a climax that left them both shaken.

They lay still for a long moment. Then he kissed her. "I'd better go," he said. "Your girls might not be ready to wake up and find me in your bed."

"That's probably a good idea." She sat up as he rearranged his clothes. *Maybe later on that will be all right,* she wanted to say. But that might be assuming too much. "Later on" might never happen.

"I'll see you and the girls tomorrow around ten. Will that give you enough time to be ready?"

"It should be fine." She walked with him across the darkened living room to the door. He paused long enough to give her a lingering kiss. Then he was gone.

As Harper stood at the front window, watching the tail lights of his car vanish into the night, a dark weight seemed to settle over her. It puzzled her at first. After all, the dinner had gone well, their lovemaking had been glorious, and he'd promised to spend the day with her and the twins tomorrow. So why was she feeling this premonition that things wouldn't turn out as she'd hoped?

It meant nothing, she told herself. It was just her usual way of protecting herself from disappointment. Expect the worst—that way you'll either be prepared when it happens or pleasantly surprised when it doesn't. That had always been her way of dealing with life's twists and turns. But Chance had told her he would come tomorrow. Hadn't he always kept his word?

* * *

The next morning, the black foreboding was still there, looming like a rain cloud over the sunny Texas morning. Harper had already resolved not to tell the girls about the planned outing. If they were expecting it, and it didn't happen, they would be crushed.

First she called the sitter, gave her the day off, and arranged for her to come that evening. Then she called Brad, gave him the news about the cancellations, and asked him to cover for her. He was upbeat, as always. "Don't worry," he said. "I've got a couple of leads I'm chasing down. Something will work out. Anyway, you deserve a break, Harper. You've been running yourself ragged. I've got things under control here, for as long as you need me."

Harper thanked her young assistant and ended the call. Brad was a jewel. She needed to follow through with the idea of making him a partner in the business. Otherwise, sooner or later, he could be lured away by the promise of more money elsewhere.

By 9:45, she had the apartment tidied and the girls ready to go. Chance would be on the road by now. Soon she'd see his car pulling into the parking lot and hear his footsteps coming down the hall toward her door.

She was about to dismiss her gloomy premonition when her phone rang. The caller was Chance.

"Are you all right?" she asked.

"Yes, but I'm going to have to call off our outing. I hope the girls won't be too disappointed."

Her heart sank. "The girls don't know yet. I was going to let you surprise them. What's happened?"

He sighed. "I was on my way to your place when I got a call from Savannah. She wants to meet me for lunch today at Bubba Red's."

The dark cloud closed around Harper.

"All right. Well, I guess that's that." Her voice was flat with disappointment. She should have known how this relationship would end. All Savannah had to do was pick up the phone, and he was rushing back to her. Harper tried to tell herself it didn't hurt, but it did. It hurt a lot.

"I know how this sounds, Harper, but believe me, it's mostly business. Before the wedding, Savannah and I made some arrangements that will need to be canceled. There are papers that need to be signed, other things that have to be resolved. I'm on my way to my lawyer's now to make sure everything's in order. And of course Savannah and I need closure. We need to talk about what happened and hopefully part as friends. This might be my only chance to do that. I don't know how long it will take, but I should at least be free to take you to dinner tonight."

"Don't bother." Harper knew she sounded like a jealous bitch, but she couldn't help it. She'd given him her trust, and her children's trust. And he'd let her down in the worst way— for Savannah.

"Since you'll be going to Hawaii tomorrow, I guess all I can say is good-bye, and have a nice trip. Maybe you won't be going alone after all."

"Listen to me, it's not like that. I have to do this, and— damn it—I love you, Harper!"

"Good-bye, Chance." She ended the call, sank onto a kitchen chair, and buried her face in her hands.

"Why are you crying, Mommy?"

"Are you sad?"

Harper felt a touch on her shoulder. Her daughters were standing next to her chair, looking up at her with worried faces. She gave them a tearful smile. "Just a little sad. But I'll be all right."

What could she say when she'd just made the worst mistake of her life? Chance had asked for her understanding, and she'd refused to give it to him. He'd even told her he loved her. And she'd behaved like an insecure, jealous fool.

"But *why* are you sad?" It was Jenny who asked.

"I'm sad because I just said mean, stupid things to someone I care about," Harper replied.

"But you always tell us not to say mean things," Jessy said.

"I know. And I'm very, very sorry."

Not that it would make any difference. Chance had attractive women throwing themselves at him. Why should he waste time and effort on a woman who'd pushed him away?

She'd been a fool. But that was no reason to punish her daughters.

Harper forced herself to smile. "I'll tell you what would make me feel better," she said. "How would you like to go to the park today? We can play on the playground and ride the train, visit the petting zoo, and take a pony ride—anything you want."

"Can we have corn dogs for lunch?"

"And ice cream?"

"And cotton candy?"

"You bet!" Harper turned off her phone and reached for her keys. "Bathroom first. Then we'll be on our way!"

Chance walked out of Bubba Red's feeling as if a heavy weight had been lifted off his shoulders.

The meeting with Savannah couldn't have gone better. The moment they'd walked into the restaurant and caught sight of each other, they'd both known that she'd done the right thing.

Looking more relaxed and radiant than he'd ever seen her, she'd greeted him with a hug. Over ribs and cornbread, they'd said what needed to be said—that neither of them had really been in love. They'd only been doing what they felt was expected of them. She'd gladly signed the legal documents he'd brought, both of them joking about how this, at least, was easier than a divorce. Then they'd wished each other well and parted friends.

But she'd left him with one piece of advice. He remembered it now, as he pulled out of the parking lot and headed for the freeway—and Harper's place.

"You need to hear this, Chance. All my life I've tried to do what was judged to be right and proper. I cared more about other people's approval than I did about my own happiness. When I ran out on our wedding, I set myself free. Now it's your turn. Ask yourself what you really want, and follow your heart. That's what I did, and I've never been happier."

Would Harper be waiting for him? Would she understand what he'd needed to do? Chance had tried calling her, but she'd turned off her phone, and he hadn't wanted to leave a message. He needed to talk with her, preferably face-to-face.

Ask yourself what you really want, and follow your heart.

What he really wanted was a crazy idea. But if Savannah could run away from her own wedding to follow her heart, he could follow her example.

As he drove into a visitor's spot at Harper's condo, he saw her car pull into its space. By the time he'd crossed the parking lot, she was helping her twins out of their booster seats. The girls had balloons and were wearing face paint. She'd taken them somewhere fun, a good sign. He could only hope she'd be receptive to what he had to say.

She turned and saw him. Her eyes widened. She didn't speak. Was this a bad time? Never mind, it was now or never.

Follow your heart . . .

Only as he came close did he see the tears in her eyes. Those tears told him it would be all right to take her in his arms and say what he'd come to say.

"Listen to me, Harper." He held her gently, the girls crowding around them. "I love you, and I have a wonderful idea. You're going to hear me out. Then you're going to say yes, because I won't take no for an answer."

* * *

Maui, Hawaii, one week later

The tide was coming in, each gentle wave lapping higher on the beach. The two little girls raced along the edge of the surf, laughing as the foam tickled their bare feet. Chance ran between them, holding their hands to keep them safe.

Harper watched them from her place on a beach towel. At first she'd thought Chance was out of his mind when he'd invited her and her children along on his so-called bachelor honeymoon. But it had been a perfect idea. The girls were having the time of their lives, and he was showing her, in every way, what a great dad he would make.

They'd made no decisions about the future—there would be plenty of time for that. But she and Chance were getting to know each other in every way, in and out of bed. For now, they were living moment by moment, day by day, and as long as they were together, that was enough.

Epilogue

One year later

Above the rooftop of the Bluebird Inn, a bluebird glided gracefully over the lush gardens, singing her flight song of happiness. It was good to be home.

Hailey saw the flash of bright wings and smiled. Except for the sweet addition of the nesting birds, standing in the garden of the Bluebird Inn gave her a feeling of déjà vu.

Six months ago, almost to the day, she and Joshua had said their vows here. Now Joshua's sister, Savannah, was marrying the man of *her* dreams. And Hailey, who'd never thought Joshua's family would accept her, had received so many visits from his mother, that even Joshua finally rolled his eyes when Marion came trundling up the walkway bearing homemade cinnamon buns.

As maid of honor, Hailey had not only organized Savannah's bachelorette party—a first—she'd helped decorate the garden.

Only an angel's handful of puffy clouds dotted the sky today. The air smelled of fresh-cut, sun-warmed grass and lemony-sweet roses. Larkspur nodded in the soft breeze.

The bluebird swooped down from the oak branches, watching them curiously with her head tilted to one side. A bumper crop of baby bluebirds now chirped from the birdhouses Tom and Felicity had built. Grams made frequent trips down to the peach orchard to talk to them.

At present, Grams was having a lovely chat with herself and beaming from the front row. She had on a new organdy hat and tea gloves, but if Hailey had to guess, there was probably a jar of earthworms in Grams's pocketbook. There was a good chance Grams would tiptoe down to the birdhouses at some point and shove those things inside, all pink and wriggly, and . . . Well, Hailey wasn't the girliest girl in the world, but even she put her foot down at worms.

The ceremony was about to begin, and she smiled at Harper, who was hurrying to join her new husband among the seated guests. As Joshua came strolling outside, the sight of him in his tux again made Hailey's heart go all fluttery. No one looked more debonair in a tux than Joshua. He was done with his residency. But what really made her smile was knowing that Joshua and his sister had reconnected. They'd found each other all over again this last year. And, he believed, as Hailey did, that his sister was making the right choice with Hank.

Life was funny like that. When you found the perfect person, you just knew.

"You take my breath away," Joshua said, giving her an exuberant kiss. "You make me wish we weren't in public right now."

Hailey glanced around and then whispered, "I have motor oil under my fingernails that I can't get out."

"That just makes you sexier," he teased. "I love knowing my wife is the only woman here who can rebuild a car engine and look this good in a bridesmaid dress."

She smiled up at him, her heart brimming with love. Sometimes the right things *did* happen and the right people *did* find each other. Maybe the human heart stood empty from time to time, just like those bluebird houses had. But when happiness came home to fill it? There was nothing more beautiful.

Joshua tucked her arm under his and gazed down at her with a happy smile. *We've found love,* Hailey thought. *All four of us. And when you have love, you've found the secret to everything.*

She was so busy looking into her husband's eyes, she didn't notice the bluebird had again taken flight and sailed over her head to land on the cement birdbath behind her.

The bluebird splashed water on her feathers near the garden gate, where an older man linked arms with a young woman dressed in a white wedding dress.

"Well, let's try this again, shall we?" Savannah's father gripped her hand, keeping it pinned to his arm.

He needn't have worried. Unlike the suffocating panic and dread she'd felt twelve months ago, today she could barely keep her feet from racing up the aisle after her brother and Hailey. To the man she loved.

She looked through the garden gate to the end of the aisle. Hank stood tall, his shoulders filling out the suit jacket he wore like nobody's business. His brother, Seth, stood next to him, tugging at his tie, looking uncomfortable in the semi-formal attire The yard of the Bluebird Inn was filled to capacity; people who hadn't even been invited to the wedding were standing on the sidelines, waiting to see if Savannah Loving would take off once more.

Savannah didn't care. She wanted the whole world to watch her speak her vows to Hank Evans.

Everything about this wedding was going to be different from her first, not least that it was actually going to happen. She and Hank wouldn't hear of her parents paying, not after Savannah had lost their money the first time around. This wedding was a simple affair. A celebration with their closest friends, and the rest of the town who wanted to come out for a peek. She'd picked her own bouquet of bluebonnets that morning, now bound with one of Hank's zip-ties, and three students from the local high school were playing string instruments.

She and her father stepped under the gate's arch, and waited for the orchestral music to turn to the wedding march. Savannah curled her bare toes into the grass. She lifted the hem of her long boho white gown and wiggled her red-painted toes.

Her father sighed. "Are you sure you don't want to wear the shoes your mother brought? We're not hippies, you know."

"I'm positive." She rubbed his arm. Her father had come a long way in the last year in accepting his children's surprising life choices, but the bare feet were still a step too far for him. Hank had been right that her family hadn't been thrilled with her new choice of boyfriend. It was a double blow that Joshua had also fallen in love with someone "from the wrong side of the tracks." Longtime prejudices weren't easy to let go of. But Hank and Hailey had finally won the Loving family over. After all, her parents just wanted their son and daughter to be happy, and no one made her happier than Hank. And when he'd gotten down on one knee at Five Sixty and proposed, she'd been the happiest woman in all of Texas.

The first strains of the wedding march sounded. Savannah leaned close to her dad. "Do you remember what you said to me a year ago while we were standing here? You said, 'Stop being silly. That's a good man standing up there. He'll make you happy.' Do you remember that?"

Her dad nodded, a slight flush reddening his cheeks.

She squeezed his arm. "Say it again. Without the silly part, please," she said, her lips curving up. "Say it again, because this time it will be true."

They were supposed to start walking down the aisle in time with the music, but her father turned and took both of her hands in his own. "Darling girl. That's a good man up there. He'll make you happy." Bending down, he kissed her cheek. "Now, everyone's going to start to talk if we don't get moving. They'll think you've changed your mind again."

Brushing her hand under her eye, she nodded. Her heart felt so full, it almost hurt. "I love you, Dad." She took a deep breath and turned toward her future. Hank's gaze darted between her and her father, a crease of worry marring his brow. He hadn't yet given up the idea that her parents would try to talk her out of marrying him. Silly man. She gave him a huge grin, and his shoulders relaxed.

With a slight hiccup, the student band started the wedding march again, and she and her father fell into step. The grass was soft and warm beneath her feet, and the sun heated her bare shoulders. She felt completely free. Free to love the man of her dreams. Free to be the person she truly was.

Her life had been in shambles last time she'd stood on this lawn. And she still couldn't believe she'd waited until the last darn moment to realize the mistake she'd been making. Was still ashamed of the hurt she'd caused. But maybe she'd needed to make those mistakes. Life was a series of events, and, if she'd behaved differently, who knew what other path she might have been on. Whether it would have led to Hank. Maybe only by making all those mistakes could she discover just who she truly was—and the man she truly wanted.

"Thanks, Dad," she whispered. She didn't know if he heard her above the music. But his words meant everything to her. He'd said them before twelve months ago.

But today, she believed them.

Her father handed her off to Hank. Slipping her hand into his large, calloused palm, she squeezed. It was just another beautiful day in Serendipity, Texas. A bluebird sang nearby, uncaring of the wedding that was happening beneath him. Yesterday the local high school team had won their baseball game. Tomorrow would be another lazy Sunday filled with visits on front porches and fried chicken and sweet tea.

But today was different. Today was hers. She looked into Hank's whiskey eyes, loved the way they crinkled around the edges, and she knew.

Today was the day her dreams came true.

The bluebird gave a satisfied little hop and took to the air again, circling over the small crowd sitting in folding chairs and landing unseen on the petal-strewn path beside the wedding party.

Chance sat beside Harper as Savannah spoke her vows to the man she loved. He felt the rightness of it, as if both their lives had come full circle. Savannah had followed her heart, and in the end, so had he.

Strangely enough, it was that earlier wedding, the one that didn't happen, that had led him to the love of his life. He and Harper had married last month, right here at the Bluebird Inn. Jessy and Jenny had walked their mother down the aisle, and Chance had said his vows not only to Harper but also to his new little daughters. Now he couldn't imagine life without them.

Harper's hand crept into his. He held it tight. *Thank you, Savannah,* he thought. *That mad escape from our wedding was the best thing you could have done.*

The bluebird found a delicious mealworm that the owners of the Bluebird Inn had put out for her. What lovely hosts they were. With the worm tucked into her mouth, she flew back to her four babies, growing big and strong in the nesting box.

"Since you shared your special day with us . . ." Tom Loving paused to slide his arm around Felicity's waist. The guests and the wedding party were seated under the reception pavilion, and the wedding toasts had just come to an end. "We have some special news to share with you."

Every gaze in the place momentarily swung from the new bride and groom to Tom and Felicity, who'd been married last July in these same gardens.

Overcome by the happy emotions of the moment, Felicity

rested her hand on her abdomen. They'd decided to wait until she was in her sixth month before announcing their impending bundle of joy. She'd done her best to camouflage her expanding belly, wearing loose-fitting clothes, but she was getting too big to keep up the charade.

"You're pregnant!" Savannah squealed and hopped from her chair to rush over and envelope Felicity in a warm hug.

And then everyone was hugging Felicity and slapping Tom on the back and giving them heartfelt congratulations, and flinging questions at them.

"When are you due?"

"July 4th." The same day she and Tom had married.

"Boy or girl?"

"A boy."

"What are you going to name him?"

"Tom Junior."

There were sighs of joy and another round of enthusiastic hugs, and Felicity's heart filled to the bursting point. She knew at last the curse had been broken. All the sorrow she'd suffered, all the loss she'd experienced, had led her to this breathtaking moment.

To this man.

And the baby they would soon welcome into the world.

Tom had come into her life and brought the bluebirds home. Brought her more bliss than she could possibly fathom, and she was grateful, so very grateful for the love brimming all around her.

The bluebird flitted through the pavilion to delighted laughter, and she whistled a soft *kew, kew*.

Yes, yes. There was great happiness here in her rich new home, with so much more to come.

Lori Wilde creates more magic in

HAPPY IS THE BRIDE

New York Times Bestselling Authors
LORI WILDE * JANET DAILEY * CAT JOHNSON *
KATE PEARCE

1 Wedding, 4 New York Times *Bestselling Authors,*
5 Happily Ever Afters!
**Stirring up all the romance and excitement a bride
could hope for—plus a healthy dose of unforeseen
shenanigans—four of today's most dazzling bestselling
authors deliver the wedding of the year, where there's
something—and someone—for everyone . . .**

Opposites attract when a wealthy cattleman and a penniless
artist decide to get hitched at a Texas dude ranch in tornado
country—and the whirlwind festivities are as filled with
surprises as their love . . . especially when the guest list
includes: one pretty party crasher on a mission, a sheriff
known as the One-Night Stand King, and a workaholic
event planner who definitely did not plan to fall for a
laid-back cowboy. Toss in a shocking behind-the-scenes
bet, a fateful power outage, and a man of honor and
a best woman determined to see the worst in each other
(between hot kisses), plus thrilling lessons in love
at first—and second—sight, and the celebrations
are going to go all night long!

Start a new series with Allyson Charles!

FOREVER HOME
Love Unleashed

Isabelle Lopez has never been a dog person.
Raising her daughter alone and building a real estate
career leaves no time for four-legged furballs.
When she finds an abandoned mutt and a litter of
pups in a foreclosed apartment, Izzy intends to drop
them off at a shelter and walk briskly away.
Instead, her "heroic" deed makes her a local celebrity.
Her boss is thrilled. Commissions are up.
And thanks to gorgeous shelter owner Bradley Cohen,
Izzy's disciplined life is suddenly much,
much more complicated.

He's got a sexy smile, a wicked sense of humor,
and a big, noble heart. Even as Izzy tries to get her
libido to *heel, boy,* Bradley sets out to convince her
there's more to life than padding her bank account.
But Izzy knows a trade secret that puts Brad's
beloved shelter at risk, and she can't warn him.

Their relationship was barely getting started;
suddenly it's in the doghouse. Now Izzy and Brad
need to figure out what matters most, and whether
this could be much more than animal attraction . . .

Dreams come true with Stacey Keith!

DREAM ON

Deep in the heart of Texas is a small town where secret wishes have a funny way of coming true . . .

With a nine-year-old daughter, an overdue light bill, and a job slinging burgers while zooming around on roller skates, Cassidy Roby is not living the glamorous life. But Cuervo, Texas, has its charms: quiet streets, loving family, and the down-home familiarity of knowing which of your neighbors are mean as snakes. With Cassidy's reputation, she knows what will happen if she steps a foot out of line. But how can she help it now that Mason Hannigan's back in town?

As Cuervo's high school quarterback ten years ago, Mason was all rock-hard abs and yes-ma'am manners. Now that he's living the glitz and glory of the NFL, he's all that plus a couple million bucks. The desire blazing between them is too hot to hide. Cassidy has some experience getting her heart broken by the hometown hero—and having the whole world watch her try to pick up the pieces. Will adding fame, fortune, and paparazzi be a playbook for disaster—or lead to the biggest adventure of her life?

Get to know the Tylers of Texas with Janet Dailey!

TEXAS FREE

***She's a woman with a burning need
to break free from her past . . .***

Rose Landro is on the run. Seeking refuge at the
Rimrock Ranch, she is finally ready to claim the land
her granddaddy left her and make a fresh start.
But her return is rife with controversy when cattle
begin disappearing—and a handsome menace named
Tanner McCade starts watching Rose a little too closely.
Could the new cowhand be connected to the men she's
hiding from? Or is there another reason the rugged
stranger is shadowing her every move?

He's a man ready to fight boldly for his future . . .

There's a secret in Rose Landro's eyes, a mystery that
Special Ranger Tanner McCade is determined to uncover.
Even if the beauty isn't behind the cattle rustling he's
investigating, she's way too skittish and all too exquisite
for Tanner to just let slide past his piercing gaze.
Then he discovers a vulnerability in Rose that has him
aching to protect her—and longing to possess her. . . .

Connect with Us

Visit us online at
KensingtonBooks.com
to read more from your favorite authors, see books
by series, view reading group guides, and more.

Join us on social media

for sneak peeks, chances to win books and prize packs,
and to share your thoughts with other readers.

facebook.com/kensingtonpublishing
twitter.com/kensingtonbooks

Tell us what you think!

To share your thoughts, submit a review,
or sign up for our eNewsletters, please visit:
KensingtonBooks.com/TellUs.